WITH
YOU
ALWAYS

Books by Jody Hedlund

The Preacher's Bride
The Doctor's Lady
Unending Devotion
A Noble Groom
Rebellious Heart
Captured by Love

BEACONS OF HOPE

Out of the Storm: A BEACONS OF HOPE Novella
Love Unexpected
Hearts Made Whole
Undaunted Hope

ORPHAN TRAIN

An Awakened Heart: An ORPHAN TRAIN Novella
With You Always

ORPHAN TRAIN
BOOK ONE

WITH YOU ALWAYS

JODY HEDLUND

BETHANYHOUSE

a division of Baker Publishing Group
Minneapolis, Minnesota

Published by Bethany House Publishers
11400 Hampshire Avenue South
Bloomington, Minnesota 55438
www.bethanyhouse.com

Bethany House Publishers is a division of
Baker Publishing Group, Grand Rapids, Michigan

Printed in the United States of America

Library of Congress Cataloging-in-Publication Data
Names: Hedlund, Jody, author.
Title: With you always / Jody Hedlund.
Description: Minneapolis, Minnesota : Bethany House, a division of Baker
    Publishing Group, [2017] | Series: Orphan train
Identifiers: LCCN 2016050050| ISBN 9780764230400 (cloth) | ISBN 9780764218040
    (trade paper)
Subjects: | GSAFD: Christian fiction. | Love stories.
Classification: LCC PS3608.E333 W58 2017 | DDC 813/.6—dc23
LC record available at https://lccn.loc.gov/2016050050

Scripture quotations are from the King James Version of the Bible.

Cover design by Jennifer Parker
Cover photography by Mike Habermann Photography, LLC

Author is represented by Natasha Kern Literary Agency.

17   18   19   20   21   22   23   7   6   5   4   3   2   1

For I the LORD thy God will hold thy right hand,
saying unto thee, Fear not; I will help thee.

Isaiah 41:13

CHAPTER 1

Elise Neumann stared out the cracked third-story window to the muddy street below, watching the omnibuses and carriages slog their way through the muck. Pedestrians dodged puddles as they hurried along. A lone newsboy stood on the street corner attempting to sell his papers, his cheeks and hands black with ink. Even at the early morning hour, the city was bustling.

To think that only a day ago these dangerous and dirty streets had been her home.

Behind her came Marianne's soft whisper. "How long have you been awake?"

Elise turned. "Not long." Her sister's face still shone from the hard scrubbing she'd given it yesterday when they arrived at the Seventh Street Mission. It wouldn't be quite as easy to wash away from their minds the trauma of being homeless orphans.

She was still pinching herself to make sure she wasn't dreaming, even though the rumbling of her stomach told her she was very much awake.

"I'm going to work today," she told Marianne quietly with a glance to where the other three children lay on pallets. She didn't want to wake them yet. She hoped they'd sleep all day.

Marianne brushed back her wavy brown hair that was still in need of a washing. "Miss Pendleton said we didn't have to start today, that we could take a few days to rest."

"We need the money." They had none. In fact, they had nothing but a small sack of clothes and belongings to remind them that they'd ever had parents or a home. With each passing day, it was becoming more difficult to remember a time when they'd been happy and safe together in Hamburg, when both Vater and Mutti had been alive, when Vater had his thriving bakery, when they had everything they needed and more.

At a faint scuttling, Marianne shuddered and hugged her thin arms across her chest. Elise had slept deeply last night—the first time since Mutti had died over a month and a half ago—and she hadn't heard the rats in the walls or the cockroaches on the ceiling. But in the quiet of the early morning, their cacophony of skitters and squeaks had been all too loud.

Miss Pendleton, the owner of the newly opened Seventh Street Mission, had explained she was still in the process of cleaning up the massive building that had once been a brewery. When the brewery had closed several years ago, gangs and thugs had taken over the unused building, leaving a trail of destruction in their wake.

Bullet holes dotted one wall, while another had a jagged gap that had been hastily patched. The ceiling was coated in black soot, evidence someone had burned a coal fire for warmth. The floor had been swept, but a residue of grime remained.

It was better than the streets, Elise reminded herself. Much better.

Even more important, Miss Pendleton had promised her and Marianne one of the coveted seamstress positions in her workshop. Elise planned to put the promise to the test that very morning. She was desperate for a job. She'd promised Mutti on her deathbed she'd take good care of her siblings, and so far she'd failed to do so.

Besides, she couldn't rely upon Miss Pendleton's or the Seventh Street Mission's charity. Already Miss Pendleton had provided them several meals yesterday. She'd given them dry blankets and pallets. And she'd sent for a doctor to care for poor little Nicholas. At one year of age, the elements and lack of food had quickly taken a toll on the infant. Thankfully, except for dehydration, the doctor hadn't found anything wrong with the boy. After a day of rest and plenty of fluids, color had begun to return to his cheeks.

"Stay with the children." Elise combed her hair back with her fingers and began to plait it. In the scant light coming through the window, her thick blond hair appeared gray. She didn't doubt that it was. The dust of the streets engrained every fiber.

Marianne didn't argue. Even though she was only a year younger than Elise's nineteen years, Marianne had always deferred to Elise. It made Elise's job of caring for her siblings easier. They listened to her without question. But the weight of responsibility could be unbearable at times, especially because she couldn't seem to take care of them the way they deserved.

Elise's fingers snagged in her hair. They were chapped and red from the exposure to the rain. And stiff. She just prayed she could make her fingers work to do the detailed stitches that would be required of her.

Marianne brushed her hands aside. "Let me do it."

Elise relinquished her hair into Marianne's deft but tender

fingers. In no time, Marianne had her hair braided, coiled, and pinned at the back of her head. Elise pressed a kiss against her sister's cheek in thanks and then tiptoed across the room.

She paused above Sophie, who was sandwiched between Nicholas and Olivia. Sophie had her bony arms draped protectively across each of the children. For the first time in weeks, Sophie's pretty face was smooth, devoid of worry lines. Elise almost thought she could see the girl's dimples in her cheeks. They rarely made an appearance anymore.

In sleep, Sophie looked so vulnerable, almost as helpless as Nicholas and Olivia. Sophie was petite and hadn't begun to change into a woman yet. She could easily pass for a child of ten instead of fifteen.

Elise sighed. Maybe now in a safe place, with steady meals, Sophie would begin to flourish. She desperately hoped today would be the start of a better future for them all.

She made her way down a rickety stairway until she reached the first floor. After returning from the privy in the back alley, she followed the sound of voices and low laughter. The hallway was narrow, illuminated only by the open doors of rooms near the front of the building. The scent of fresh paint was strong, along with the lingering odors of vinegar and lye, a sure sign Miss Pendleton had already labored hard to make the first floor of the building usable.

Before Elise reached the workroom, she stopped and took a steadying breath, then forced herself to step inside. She found herself in a workshop filled with women sitting at long tables, sewing shirts. Their chatter tapered to a halt, and soon all eyes focused upon her.

None of the faces looked familiar. Many of the women held raised needles, dangling with thread. Others had needles jabbed through linen. The tables were covered in the cut pieces of men's shirts in various stages of construction. Though Elise had sewn vests at her last job, she was familiar enough with seamstress work to recognize the different tasks the women had been assigned. Some were stitchers, others finishers, and still others embroiderers.

Rumors abounded about new machines that could do the sewing in place of hand-stitching. Like everyone else, Elise couldn't imagine how a contraption of metal could be as accurate or thorough as a human.

While she never thought she'd end up a seamstress, it was one job in New York City available to women. Most sweatshops were already full, but Miss Pendleton had guaranteed her work. And she was counting on it. Desperately.

She searched the room for the petite, dark-haired woman wearing black mourning garments. However, Miss Pendleton was not present.

"May I help you?" A woman spoke with an English accent, pushed away from one of the tables and stood. She was tall with pale skin, which made the dark circles under her eyes more visible. Her drab brown hair was parted severely down the middle and smoothed into a coiffure. Her plaid dress of silk and taffeta, which at one time had probably been stylish and elegant, was now faded and ragged.

"I'm looking for Miss Pendleton," Elise said. The moment she spoke, the curiosity in some of the faces changed to mistrust, even anger. Seven years after immigrating, Elise couldn't shed her German accent. And apparently these women weren't German, which meant they were probably Irish.

Unfortunately, the Irish and German immigrants couldn't ever seem to get along. Roving gangs from either side were

11

always fighting one another in the streets and alleys. Both ethnic groups had large populations here, and they were competing for the same limited jobs and homes.

"Miss Pendleton is not available." The tall woman's eyes weren't hostile, merely curious.

"Miss Pendleton told me I could find work here."

The women exchanged glances among themselves. Elise's stomach cinched. Was there no work after all? Had Miss Pendleton misled her?

"As you can see," the Englishwoman said, "we have no more room for additional workers."

Elise surveyed the spacious room once again and this time noted there were only four women at each table. Each had her own work surface with plenty of natural light from the windows, as well as oil lanterns positioned throughout the room.

The sweatshop she'd worked in previously had been a small tenement apartment. Up to twelve workers had squeezed into a room that was a fraction of the size of this one. They'd had little lighting and only their laps to work on. "I don't need much space."

The Englishwoman glanced over her shoulder at one of the tables to a curly redheaded woman, who pursed her lips and gave a curt shake of her head. Her eyes and her pretty freckled face were street-hardened, lacking any compassion in a world where the competition for survival was brutal.

"You will need to find work elsewhere," the woman said again, almost apologetically.

Elise was tempted to protest—or beg. She considered herself a woman of some pride. But after living on the streets once already, the thought of returning sent a rush of panic through her. She wasn't afraid for herself but didn't want to expose her family to the danger again. "If you give me a chance, you'll see I'm an excellent seamstress."

"I am truly sorry," the woman said.

"What will I do?" The desperate question slipped out before Elise could contain it.

"Yer young and pretty," said the redheaded woman. "The men'll like ye well enough."

The implication made Elise's scalp crawl. "I'd rather die than sell my body."

"My, aren't we a proud one," said another lady from a nearby table.

"Aye," said another, almost spitting the word through a scowl. "You'd do it if it meant you didn't have to watch your wee one starve before your very eyes."

Others began to speak up, and angry voices escalated around the room. If their gazes had been unfriendly before, they turned downright hostile now. Elise took a step back. She couldn't understand why her simple statement would make the women so angry. Prostitution was wrong. Why were they crucifying her for taking a stand against it?

Unless . . .

Elise clutched the doorframe. She'd been so tired yesterday that she had a hard time focusing on Miss Pendleton's explanation behind the Seventh Street Mission, but somewhere in Elise's mind she vaguely remembered Miss Pendleton mentioning that the women in the workshop had been rescued from a life of degradation. Had she meant prostitution?

All traces of hope flittered away, like flower petals falling to the floor waiting to be crushed. She may as well leave. There would be no work for her here, not as a German woman. Especially not now that she'd insulted them.

Elise turned from the workshop and started down the hallway back the way she'd come. She'd let the children sleep as long as possible, get one more meal, and then they'd be on their way. But where would they go? Would she be forced to return to Uncle's, even though the situation there was intolerable?

What about Reinhold? Her friend had offered to marry her in order to provide a place for her family, despite his barely being able to afford to care for his own mother and siblings, and his aunt and her children. He was probably worried sick about her by now. She'd had no way to contact him since they'd run away.

"Elise" came a voice from down the hall.

Elise pivoted to see Miss Pendleton entering the building. Behind her came the brawny Reverend Bedell. Although he had a kind face, he was big and broad-shouldered, a giant of a man who wasn't afraid to use his fists. Elise had seen him break up a fight once, and he was impressively strong. Miss Pendleton had told them yesterday with pretty pink cheeks that she and Reverend Bedell were engaged to be married, and the wedding would take place just as soon as her time of mourning for her mother was over.

Miss Pendleton rushed toward her with short, clipped footsteps. She was petite and thin, her face delicately angled and almost severe. But what she lacked in size she made up for in determination and purpose.

"I'm surprised to see you awake so early this morning." Miss Pendleton held herself with a poise and grace that reminded Elise all too keenly of their differences in social status. She knew better than to lump Miss Pendleton together with other rich aristocrats, and yet Elise struggled not to feel some resentment toward the woman.

If not for Count Eberhardt, her family would still be happily together in Hamburg. Vater would still have his bakery, and she would be working alongside him doing what she loved with the people she loved. All it had taken was one minor offense against the calloused count for him to decide to ruin Vater's reputation with a false rumor.

Elise could never forget the deep grooves in Vater's forehead and the despair in his eyes when he finally realized he would have no more customers to buy his breads and pastries.

"I hope you found something to eat in the kitchen." Miss Pendleton stopped close enough that the freshness of her clothes and hair, a flowery scent, made Elise self conscious of her own deplorable stench, the sourness of her unwashed body and clothes.

"I only need food for the children," Elise said.

"You must eat something too. I insist." Miss Pendleton nodded toward the stairway that would take her to a kitchen and dining room on the second floor. Although the rooms were still under construction and far from finished, Miss Pendleton had a simple fare available for the workers to buy for a small fee.

From down the dimly lit hallway, Elise caught a glimpse of the tall Englishwoman standing in the doorway of the workroom. When Miss Pendleton followed Elise's gaze, the woman retreated into the room.

"You mustn't consider working today." Miss Pendleton regarded her with keen gray-blue eyes. "I thought I made that clear to you last night."

"Yes, but—"

"You will be my guest here for a few days. Then when you've regained your strength, I'll introduce you to the supervisor, and she'll give you a position suited to your abilities."

"The women told me there's no more work to be had here."

"Nonsense." Miss Pendleton spun and began to retrace her steps down the hallway. "I'll introduce you right now."

Elise didn't move.

At the door to the workroom, Miss Pendleton stopped and motioned to her. "Come now. Don't be shy."

Elise wasn't shy. She was simply realistic. But even as she doubted Miss Pendleton, the questions surfaced as they had before. If she didn't work at the mission, where else would she work? Where would she find a place to live? Could she subject her family to living on the streets again?

Miss Pendleton smiled at her with a warmth and kindness that somehow reassured Elise everything would be all right. Surely after Miss Pendleton's introduction, the women would accept her and overlook her insult. Surely they could forget the initial misunderstanding.

When Miss Pendleton beckoned her again, Elise returned to the workroom.

"Ladies," Miss Pendleton said as she stepped into the room, "I'd like to introduce you to our newest worker, Elise Neumann."

Silence greeted Elise. And downcast eyes. In fact, no one looked at her except the tall Englishwoman.

Miss Pendleton's brows rose, the response clearly not what she'd expected. "Miss Neumann assures me she's quite skilled in many aspects of sewing. So I'm certain she'll be an asset to our business."

Still the room was silent. The noise from the busy street drifted in through the windows, which were already wide open on the June morning to allow the coolness of the early hour inside before the heat of the day became unbearable.

"Mrs. Watson?" Miss Pendleton smiled at the tall woman, who was standing a short distance away at the head of one of the tables. "I'm sure you'll be glad to have someone of Miss Neumann's experience join you. Oh, and her sister will be working with us too."

Mrs. Watson didn't return the smile. Instead she glanced at the redheaded woman again, who had focused her attention on the shirtsleeve in front of her, busily dipping her needle in and out of the linen.

Miss Pendleton's smile wavered, but she reached over and squeezed Elise's arm.

Mrs. Watson cleared her throat. "Miss Pendleton, I am afraid we do not have any room at present for more workers. Perhaps when the workshop across the hall is ready . . ."

"I'm sure we can squeeze in two more temporarily."

"There are other women already waiting to work here, women we have had to turn away." Mrs. Watson's voice dropped to almost a whisper.

Miss Pendleton gave Mrs. Watson a sharp look. "I'm well aware of our problem of having to turn away women. And it breaks my heart every day. I want to help everyone and eventually I hope to assist many more."

Mrs. Watson fixed her attention on the floor, which except for a few loose threads was surprisingly clean.

"In the meantime, Mrs. Watson, I pray for God to guide me to those He wishes me to help, which I believe includes you and all the women in this room. Hereafter it also includes Miss Neumann and her siblings." Miss Pendleton raised her chin as though daring anyone to defy her.

No one spoke.

"They are the first boarders here," she continued. "And soon I hope to open the doors to many more who need a safe place to live."

From the few rapid glances some of the women exchanged, Elise had the foreboding that they would see the news as favoritism and would like her even less.

"So, Mrs. Watson, can I count on you to welcome Miss Neumann and her sister into our workroom?"

Mrs. Watson nodded. "Yes, ma'am. We shall do our best."

"Good. I'm very glad to hear it. After all, we want to extend the same grace and love to others as has been extended to ourselves, don't we?"

"Yes, ma'am," Mrs. Watson said again.

Though Miss Pendleton seemed satisfied with her answer, Elise couldn't shake the feeling that her new job was doomed from the start. As much as she needed the help of the Seventh Street Mission, she suspected sooner or later she would have to find her hope and help elsewhere.

CHAPTER 2

"I've called you both home today to tell you I'm dying."

Thornton Quincy stared at his father's blue lips. Dying? No. He started to shake his head, but Bradford spoke first.

"You're only having another fit," Bradford said from the opposite side of the bed. "The pleurisy will pass like it did last time."

"It won't pass." Father's hoarse whisper ended in a fit of coughing that brought the doctor and his assistant scurrying from the corner.

Thornton stepped back to give them room to tend Father, but Bradford didn't budge. He grasped Father's hand tighter. His twin's lean face, the distinguished taper of his jaw and cheeks, his perfect nose—they were all a mirror image of Thornton's own features. They shared the same dark wavy hair and equally dark-brown eyes. They were both five-foot-seven, one hundred fifty-five pounds, and built with a wiry strength that had held them in good stead during plenty of scrapes growing up.

In their younger years, they'd easily been able to trick their nursemaids regarding their identities. During school they'd fooled more than one tutor. Even their friends had fallen prey to their tricks. But now, at twenty-four, they'd grown slightly more distinct from each other.

"You're not dying," Bradford said again with an authority to his voice so like their father's. "I predict you'll be out of bed and back to normal within the month."

The doctor and his assistant were hefting Father upward onto a mound of pillows. The taut lines in Father's face spoke for themselves. He was in an inordinate amount of pain. "Time for opium, Mr. Quincy," the doctor said.

At the center of the enormous bedroom, Thornton felt suffocated. Every inch of the room was wallpapered in a maroon fleur-de-lis pattern, including the ceiling. The thick tapestries were pulled tightly against the daylight, and several wall sconces provided flickering amber light that served to make Father's bluish skin look gray and waxy.

Sweat made a steady trickle down Thornton's backbone beneath his shirt and suit coat. He wanted to toss off his coat and roll up his shirtsleeves, but he forced himself to remain the refined gentleman his father expected him to be.

When Father was breathing easier and the opium had taken the edge off the pain, he motioned for Thornton to return to the bedside. He reached for Thornton's hand and clasped it just as he did Bradford's. For a man rarely given to displays of physical affection, the grasp, though frail and clammy, was unexpected. It was the desperate grasp of a man who saw the end of the race and wasn't ready to reach the finish line.

"Sons," Father started, "I'm convinced I need to prepare for my death." Bradford began to protest, but Father silenced him with a shake of his head. "I invited my most trusted advisor, Mr. Morgan, here today so he could help me explain my last wishes."

As if on cue, a short, rotund man in a tight-fitting black-and-white-striped suit entered the room, wearing a tall black hat that was likely intended to make him appear a much larger man but instead highlighted his diminutive size.

"There's no need to share any last wishes, Father," Bradford said. "Not when you'll be here for years to come."

"Let's stop pretending I'll live forever," Father retorted in a tone that retained some of his strength. "If the doctors are wrong in their prognosis, then we'll count ourselves blessed to have had more time. But since it appears I may not recover, I need to make some decisions regarding the future of my business."

Mr. Morgan slipped a paper from his inner coat pocket and began to unfold it.

"I've laid out my plans with Mr. Morgan," Father continued. "Now I'd like him to read my wishes."

With his belly protruding and serving as a podium, Mr. Morgan rested the paper there and began to read in his usual straightforward manner. "In order to determine which of my sons is worthiest to inherit sole control over all my investments and companies, I am issuing a six-month challenge. The two conditions are as follows. First, each son must build a sustainable town along the Illinois Central Railroad. And second, each son must get married to a woman he loves. Whoever succeeds in doing both by the end of the six months wins the challenge and becomes owner of Quincy Enterprises."

Mr. Morgan folded the paper and returned it to his pocket. All the while Thornton could only stare at the man in disbelief.

For a moment, the announcement left Bradford speechless too. Thornton met his brother's dark gaze across the bed. In the shadows of the room, he tried to figure out what Bradford was thinking. Did he like the challenge? Or was he disturbed by it? When they were younger, Thornton had always been able to read his brother's thoughts. But in recent years, a veil had dropped between them.

"This is quite a surprise," Bradford said slowly as though measuring each word.

Thornton wanted to blurt out that it was ludicrous, but instead he kept his voice as even as Bradford's. "Have you considered dividing the assets equally between us?"

His father gave a derisive snort. "Of course not. And weaken the business by having it parceled off? No, it stays together. The winner of the challenge owns it all, is president and sole proprietor of the enterprise. And the other of you will have to settle for vice-president."

"That makes sense." Thornton tried to infuse confidence into his response, yet inside he felt like the twin who could never say the smart thing, who was forever falling short of being able to please Father.

"I don't like the idea of competing against Thorn for something with such big stakes," Bradford said. "It's one thing to wager in a game of bluff or a yacht race. But this? This is our future."

"I don't like it either," Thornton admitted.

"If you don't want to compete, then abdicate." Father looked directly at him—not at Bradford—and his eyes contained an unspoken challenge. It was the challenge to prove himself.

But wasn't that what he'd been trying to do his whole life? Prove himself to his father? Prove himself as worthy as Bradford? And hadn't he always failed to measure up in his father's eyes no matter what he did or how hard he tried to be like Bradford? What would make this time any different?

Bradford quirked one of his brows, revealing a determined

gleam in his eyes. His brother loved challenges, thrived on competition. He wouldn't back down, and their father knew it. If anyone would abdicate for the sake of peace, for the sake of maintaining good relationships, Thornton would.

But what if this was his last chance to earn his father's respect and show him that he was the kind of man he could be proud of?

"Six months isn't enough time to build a town," Thornton finally said. It wasn't like land development was anything new to him or Bradford. They'd been in business with their father for several years and had already been working to sell off and develop land grants in Illinois along the new railroad. Once eastern farmers were convinced to buy the land and resettle in Illinois, the profit was used to pay for the cost of building the railroads. Then companies like Quincy Enterprises planned how to build towns along the railroad at strategic locations where the prospects for additional profit to the railroad were thought to be high.

"True," Father answered, still grasping both of their hands. "That's why you'll finish developing two areas that already have a substantial number of farms and can sustain a town. The work is already started, and now you need to make it succeed. If I die before the end of six months, then Mr. Morgan will be the ultimate judge of your towns."

"What are the stipulations that will quantify growth?" Thornton asked at the same time that Bradford posed a similar question.

Father started to answer, but then closed his eyes, weariness creasing his face—a face that had once been regally handsome and refined but now was aged beyond his years from the stress and demands of building his fortune. "Mr. Morgan, would you answer?"

The advisor pushed up his spectacles and glanced first at

Bradford and then at Thornton. "We'll be taking into consideration things like population, revenue, land sold, number of businesses, and the usual kinds of development—houses, churches, schools, mills, hotels, and all the other amenities necessary to attract and keep new settlers."

Bradford gave a curt nod, the matter settled.

But Thornton had a dozen other questions. "If we're busy developing our towns, how will we have time to fulfill the second requirement, to get married? Especially considering the fact that neither of us is currently in a relationship?"

His father's eyes remained closed, but he released an exasperated sigh. "I don't think it's too much to ask that my sons finally get serious about carrying on the Quincy name, is it?"

"It's not too much," Bradford quickly reassured their father. "We both know plenty of young ladies here in New York."

"You can't just marry any young lady," Mr. Morgan spoke up. "Your father's written wish is that it be someone you love."

"And how will you measure love?" Thornton asked before he thought to hold back the question.

"I loved your mother," Father said. "I think I'm qualified to know what love is and what it isn't."

Thornton swallowed his growing frustration, especially when Bradford's lips quirked into a confident smile. His twin had always liked one woman or another. And they liked him in return.

Of course, women liked Thornton too. He'd never lacked companionship or ladies vying for his attention. But falling in love wasn't something a person could make happen, was it? Not within such a short time span.

"The point of adding the stipulation of loving the woman," Mr. Morgan said, "is to prevent a hasty marriage of convenience simply for the sake of winning the challenge."

"In other words," Father said in a caustic tone, "I want you to learn to love someone besides yourselves."

The words stung Thornton. Couldn't his father see that he loved him, that he loved Bradford, that he'd adored their mother? Even though she'd been gone for over a decade, a day didn't pass without him thinking about her.

Didn't his father realize he'd had no time for romantic inclinations over the past years because he'd been dedicated to helping Quincy Enterprises thrive?

Before he could voice any further concerns or questions, Father dismissed them, and then the doctor ushered them from the room indicating that Mr. Quincy needed to rest if there was any hope of survival.

Once the door closed behind Thornton, he paused in the wide hallway and released a deep lungful of air. Bradford raked a hand through his wavy strands and blew out a breath too. They both stared at Mr. Morgan as he strode away on his short, squat legs. The plush carpet that formed a runner down the hardwood floor muted the man's choppy steps. When he disappeared around a corner, Bradford spoke first.

"That was delightful, wasn't it?"

"Thrilling," Thornton replied.

Bradford stepped toward the opposite wall and straightened one of the many paintings that lined the halls of the Quincy New York mansion—originals purchased by their father during his travels in Europe.

"You know I don't want to compete for the company any more than you do." Bradford eyed the painting and adjusted the gilded frame a fraction of an inch more before stepping back.

"Come now, Brad," Thornton said. "Let's be honest. There

isn't another person alive who relishes a challenge as much as you."

Bradford grinned, revealing his straight white teeth. It was a crooked smile that could so easily disarm, one that could work magic when needed. Thornton knew because he'd wielded that very same smile himself over the years to get what he wanted.

"You know me too well," Bradford said.

"What do you expect?" While they'd seen each other less in recent years and had both been busy traveling and doing business for their father, Thornton liked to think they still shared a camaraderie whenever they were together.

"I don't suppose you want to admit I'm the better man for taking over the company and prevent us both from having to live in Illinois out in the middle of nowhere for the next six months?" Even if Bradford spoke the words lightly in jest, something sharp in his eyes pricked at Thornton.

"Are you the better man?" Thornton tried to keep his tone equally light.

Bradford shrugged nonchalantly and glanced at one of the pictures, likely in an effort to keep Thornton from reading him. "We may be identical in many ways, but you can't deny I'm more business-minded. And Father knows it."

"If he knows it, then why is he issuing this challenge?"

"Because he doesn't want to hurt your feelings any more than I do."

Thornton wanted to deny Bradford's words, wanted to believe his father considered him a worthy opponent and competent enough to run the company. But old insecurities rattled inside him like loose pistons in a steam cylinder.

As though sensing the sting of his words, Bradford reached out and squeezed Thornton's shoulder. "You're a good man,

Thorn. And you have a bright mind. But I think we both know I've always been better at company affairs than you."

Thornton's mind jumped back to the time when he and Bradford had been ten years old, only months after their mother had died. Father had traveled more often that year, leaving them home for weeks at a time in the care of their nursemaids. But on one of his weeks at home, he'd given them each a bonus allowance to spend however they desired. Of course, Thornton had purchased the rare copy of Euclid's *Elements* that he'd wanted, along with a special edition of *Poor Richard's Almanac*.

"Books?" His father's brows had risen in surprise, revealing disappointment as he questioned him. "Don't we have enough of those already?"

"Not like these," Thornton had replied eagerly, attempting to explain to his father how special the books were.

His father cut him off. "Did you know your brother invested his allowance in the stock market?"

At the pride emanating from his father's eyes as he glanced at Bradford, Thornton's excitement over his new books had deflated until there was nothing left but a dusty layer of embarrassment. He'd wanted his father to look on him with pride too, to be pleased with him the same way he was with Bradford. From that moment on, Thornton tried to be just like his brother.

Although Thornton had spent years emulating Bradford so that his father would love them equally, he never quite felt as though he'd accomplished the feat. Thornton may have been able to fool everybody else into thinking they were identical, but somehow he'd never been able to fool his father.

"Listen," Bradford said, pulling Thornton out of his morbid thoughts. "We can go through with this challenge if you want. But it seems like a waste of time since I'm better at it. And I don't think you really want to run the company anyway. You'd be happier as vice-president."

Would he? Thornton pictured his father's stern eyes daring him to abdicate. His chest expanded with the need to prove that his father could be proud of him. He tossed Bradford a grin. "I can't deny you the chance to compete, now, can I?"

His brother was still for a moment before returning the grin. "I guess not. A little friendly competition never hurt anyone, did it?"

"Just think of the grand time we'll have going after the ladies," Thornton added.

"Very true, my good man. Then I claim Dorthea van Alstyne."

"If you want to have a poodle, be my guest."

Bradford shoved him good-naturedly. "She's a beautiful and wealthy poodle."

"I myself prefer someone like Rosalind Beaufort."

"If you want to have a great Dane, be my guest."

Thornton laughed at his brother's sparring. "If only we knew what they called us behind our backs."

"Peacocks?"

"More likely mules."

They shared another chuckle before Bradford held out his hand. "If you insist on going through with this, then may the best man for the job win."

Thornton grasped his brother's hand, feeling the firmness and surety that belonged to Bradford. "May the best man win."

CHAPTER 3

A bump against Elise's elbow sent her needle too deep into the fine white linen. In the wrong spot.

"Oops. I beg yer pardon" came a voice behind her.

From where Elise sat at the end of the worktable, she didn't need to look to see who had jostled her. She knew it was Fanny O'Leary, the redheaded Irishwoman.

Elise neatly folded the shirt and set it on the table next to a pair of new scissors, a nearly empty spool of thread, and a cushion that was stuck haphazardly with dozens of silver pins.

"No, Elise," whispered Marianne next to her. "Ignore her."

Elise pushed her chair back from the table. The scraping of the wooden legs against the cement floor issued Elise's declaration of frustration. She was done ignoring Fanny and everyone else who'd bullied her during her first week at the Seventh Street Mission. She'd sat meekly long enough.

She stood, her hands fisting at her sides. The rest of the women had grown silent and fixed their attention on her, reminding Elise of the first day she'd stepped into the workroom.

She pivoted to find Fanny slipping into her seat two tables

away. Elise glared at the young woman who, in spite of the freckles peppering her nose and forehead, had one of the prettiest faces among the workers, fuller and more vibrant than the pale hollowness of the others. She clearly did her best to tame her unruly red curls under a scarf. But even so, runaway curls wisped around her face.

The woman picked up her needle and began to thread it. The waver of a smile told Elise that she was well aware of the frustration she was causing and that she enjoyed it.

"I won't quit," Elise said into the silence that was framed by the clatter of wheels and horses on the street outside the open windows. "You can keep on with your rudeness and unkindness to me, but I'm here to stay."

"Elise." Mrs. Watson, the manager, rose to her feet, her lanky frame overshadowing Elise's. "I am truly sorry you feel we are rude to you, especially after we have made room for you and your sister at the table."

Elise knew Mrs. Watson wasn't in the least sorry. Perhaps she didn't encourage Fanny's behavior, but neither did she attempt to stop it or any of the other spitefulness. When Elise had returned from her lunch break yesterday, the front panel she'd been working on all morning hadn't been at her spot. From the exchanges of snide glances between the women, Elise guessed someone had purposefully hidden the garment. No amount of searching revealed it. And Mrs. Watson was of no help whatsoever in demanding its return.

"I've hoped to prove myself by my hard work, my quick, even stitches, and my attention to detail." Elise lifted her chin. "But I can see you've already judged me and are determined to make my time here miserable regardless of what I do."

"That is simply not true," Mrs. Watson said. She darted a

glance toward the open doorway, likely worrying Miss Pendleton would overhear them.

Elise hadn't spoken a word about the mistreatment to Miss Pendleton. She had too much pride to run to her benefactor, not after everything the kind woman had already done. Even if the other women made the job troublesome, the eleven-hour workday and pay were better than any she'd known before.

"I know you don't think we deserve to work here," Elise said, "but we have no parents, no place to live, and no one else we can turn to."

"Poor babe" came a sarcastic mutter from the direction of Fanny's table, although this time Elise suspected one of Fanny's friends spoke them.

Elise bristled. "I dare you stand up and repeat that to my face."

Marianne tugged Elise's sleeve, attempting to pull her down into her chair. But Elise straightened her shoulders and prepared for battle. If she had to defend herself with her fists, so be it.

"Go on, Dimna," Fanny said, prodding the woman sitting next to her. A straw-thin woman glowered at Fanny, revealing a missing upper tooth next to several other gray teeth. Fanny nodded at her curtly, her freckled face hard and commanding.

Elise wasn't sure what control Fanny had over the other women, but she was apparently their leader, and when she spoke they did her bidding. Dimna rose from her chair. Her mouth was set grimly, her eyes flashing with resentment. Her garments were too big for her shapeless, bony frame.

"We got no pity for ye," Dimna stated in a brittle voice. "Not when Miss Pendleton has made ye her pet."

"Pet?" Elise was surprised at the accusation.

"We can all see that she's giving ye special favors that none o' the rest of us get."

Elise couldn't deny Dimna's accusation. Miss Pendleton had extended help to her family in a special way. "Then you're jealous."

Fanny shoved Dimna, sending her several steps toward Elise. The young woman squared off and held up balled fists.

"Don't fight, Elise." Marianne's whisper was threaded with desperation. "They're goading you into this."

Dimna's knuckles were white from the tightness of her clenched fingers. Her eyes narrowed and taunted Elise. "Yer too scared to fight me."

Elise's fingers twitched with the need to show these women her strength. But her gut told her Marianne was right. These women were hoping she'd take the first swing. If she did, they could report her to Miss Pendleton.

She dropped her arms to her sides. "I don't want to involve Miss Pendleton in our dispute, but you may leave me no other option—"

"That will not be necessary," Mrs. Watson interrupted, once again glancing at the door. "A short break is in order. I shall send you on an errand to D. and J. Devlin for more thread since we're running so low."

Elise didn't argue. Within moments she was out on the street, a few coins from Mrs. Watson in her pocket for the purchase, along with directions on how to reach the clothing manufacturer. Elise had already learned from listening to the other women that Mr. Devlin was an associate of Miss Pendleton's deceased father. He'd agreed to Miss Pendleton's risky proposal of starting a sewing workshop in her mission, even though nothing like it had been done before.

Apparently, the venture had been mutually beneficial. D. and J. Devlin provided the precut shirts, and the women in the workshop sewed the pieces together into the finished product. It was the same kind of arrangement many of the tenement sweatshops had with the manufacturer. Trained cutters worked at the company building to cut the material into the various pieces needed for a garment, and then most of the sewing work was contracted out and supervised by the sweater, the middleman who was in charge of the stitching work done in his home.

Miss Pendleton was their sweater. She paid the contract fee for the unmade clothing and received payment for the completed garments. Out of that she paid everyone who worked in her shop.

Elise sighed, releasing the tension of the past week. The summer sunlight rarely made it past the tall buildings, strings of drying laundry, and storefront awnings to touch the sidewalks of the city. Nevertheless, she was grateful for the blue sky overhead.

She wove around a woman pushing a baby buggy and past an elderly man hobbling along with a crutch. For midmorning the street didn't seem as busy as usual, with scant children milling about, not as many omnibuses clattering past, and fewer peddlers attempting to sell their wares from carts.

She supposed much of the populace had been up late last night celebrating the Fourth of July. The riverfronts would have been crowded with people vying to watch the fireworks. She had no doubt many were still in their beds, sleeping off drunken stupors.

Elise and her family hadn't ever participated in the festivities. Although many in Kleindeutschland, their German immigrant community within New York City, were curious about the American holidays, Elise never had a desire to join in, especially for a holiday that rang so hollow. Independence Day. Her people weren't independent. In fact, they were stuck here in the bowels of the city, laboring all the time but never able to climb out of the pit of poverty and despair they'd fallen into.

Her family had moved to America, the land of no kings, to be free of oppression. They'd thought they could begin a new life without the same kind of distinction between classes, without the fear of injustice and unfairness. After all, didn't the American Declaration of Independence state that all men were created equal with certain inalienable rights, life, liberty, and the pursuit of happiness? It was hailed as the land of opportunity.

But after seven years in her new homeland, she was no closer to that elusive opportunity than when she'd first arrived. In fact, her family was in a worse state. Father's bakery had floundered from the beginning. With so much competition, he'd struggled to invest the small amount of capital he'd managed to retain from the sale of his bakeshop in Hamburg. He'd taken loans to purchase the equipment he needed. And when he died suddenly, the debts had been too numerous to repay. The bank foreclosed on the bakery and cast Mutti out without a cent to her name.

It felt as though they were reliving the nightmare with Count Eberhardt all over again. Elise had learned that even in America, the wealthy were calloused, cold, and merciless. They didn't care about what would happen to a mother and her children without a home or job. They only thought about their own interests, and it didn't matter whom they hurt in order to assure their own security.

"Penny for the poor?" A feeble call came from the street corner. A man in rags held a tarnished tin cup in his gnarled, blackened hand. He stared straight ahead, his glassy eyes not focused on anyone. Instead, he rotated his position to the sound of nearing footsteps.

"Can you spare a penny?" He jangled the cup in the direction of a young boy trotting past. The youth slapped the tin cup, and it clattered to the sidewalk several feet away, causing the coins inside to roll out in all directions.

The boy scooped up two of the coppers before scampering across the street without a backward glance.

How dare the boy steal from a blind beggar? Even if he was hungry and without a home, surely his situation was not as helpless as that of a blind man. "Stop!" Elise called out, racing after the boy. "Return those coins!"

The youth increased his pace until he was sprinting down the sidewalk, dodging vendors and pedestrians as if he made an everyday exercise of running through New York City's streets. Likely, the young thief *did* make an everyday occurrence of stealing and running. After all, there weren't many other ways for children here to earn money. Elise had learned that from personal experience.

Yet even when she and her siblings had lived on the streets, they'd never resorted to stealing. No matter how hungry and desperate they'd been.

As the boy turned the corner into an alley, Elise halted. It was futile to chase him. He probably knew every hiding spot in Lower Manhattan, and if he didn't outrun her, he'd disappear before she could catch him and demand he give the money back to the beggar.

Elise returned to the blind man, who was on his knees skimming his hands back and forth on the ground, frantically searching in spite of the soles that landed on his fingers. Elise surveyed the area and saw the cup wedged against the brick front of a millinery, likely kicked there carelessly by a passerby. She retrieved it and scanned the sidewalk, not expecting to see any of the beggar's coins. With no luck, she approached the man. "I found your cup."

He pushed to his knees and peered in her direction with unseeing eyes. "Thank you, miss."

She pressed the tin into his bruised fingers. He fumbled for it, his cracked fingernails scraping the metal. Beneath his hat, his hair was greasy and unwashed, and his cheeks were hollow. She guessed he was about the same age her father would have been if he were still alive.

Didn't he have anyone, family or friends, who cared what became of him? How did he survive on his own without anyone to help him? It was difficult enough to live on the streets with the ability to see. Elise couldn't imagine how hard it must be without sight.

The beggar sat back on his heels. He wasn't wearing shoes. Rather, his feet were wrapped in damp newspaper. The newsprint had blackened his big toes, which poked through the layers.

"I'd like to give you something," she said, "but I have nothing . . ." Her hand strayed to her pocket. If she gave this man a coin or two, would she still have enough left over to purchase the thread?

She shook her head. The money wasn't hers to give. It belonged to Miss Pendleton. Besides, if she dropped it in his cup, what if another thief came along?

"Don't worry, miss," the man said giving her a shadow of a smile. "Your kindness is enough for me today. And I thank you for it."

Elise straightened, determined to do something more. "Will you be here later?"

He hesitated, and a cloud of fear crossed his face. Did he think she would turn him in to the police? As a vagrant he could be put in prison or carted off to Blackwell's Island Asylum. With rumors of overcrowding, rotten food, and frequent outbreaks of disease, just the thought of the asylum was enough to make a person shudder.

"Don't worry," she quickly offered. "I'll bring you food and money."

"That's very kind of you, miss. Very kind." The trembling of his hand told her he wasn't convinced.

"I mean you no harm, I promise." She touched his hand, already deciding she would bring him her noon meal. She could go without today, just as she had plenty of days in the past.

She resumed her walk along Seventh Street, but her footsteps dragged. She had so much for which to be grateful—considering she had been begging for her food last week. Yet anger and lingering bitterness still warred within her. "It shouldn't be this way," she muttered to herself. "Blind men. Children. Young women. They should *not* have to live on the streets."

She caught the faint scent of pumpernickel and sesame seed, which brought back a rush of memories of her father, of his hands covered in coarse flour, his apron tight across his middle, his nose and cheeks red from the heat of the ovens. She passed a cabinetmaker's shop, the shoemaker, barber, and a locksmith.

Finally she was standing before the open door of a bakery. Inside, a woman was busy kneading dough at a worktable behind the counter. A few brown loaves remained in a basket on the counter, along with hard-crusted rolls. Elise guessed most of the freshly baked goods had already been delivered to patrons in the early hours of the morning.

She and Marianne had been in charge of delivering their father's breads to his customers. Though she'd done her part to help with the business, she always liked it best when Vater allowed her to work alongside him as he created some of his more delectable pastries: apple strudel, marzipan tart, and Berliner Pfannkuchen. She could almost smell their sweetness emanating from the bakery before her.

At a shout and the banging of a door somewhere inside, the woman behind the counter rested her hands on the dough and glanced at the stairs leading down to the cellar and the oven. She wiped a sleeve across her forehead to staunch the flow of perspiration, which was constant in the summers as a result of the sweltering heat that rose from the oven.

Vater had worked long hours in his tiny shop here in America, tromping down the rickety wooden cellar steps to his oven. In the poorly ventilated and cramped hovel, he'd tend his baked goods. He'd always come back up, his face dripping with sweat and blackened from the soot of the burning coal. Sometimes he worked around the clock, barely sleeping at all. While he earned enough to keep food on the table in their apartment home above the shop, he'd never been able to make their life as comfortable as it had been back in Hamburg.

"Can I help you?"

Elise realized the woman behind the counter had turned from her lump of dough and was looking directly at her.

"No," Elise started. "I was just—"

"Then get out of here." The woman's voice was angry, and she reached for the long handle of a nearby peel.

Elise backed out of the doorway and darted past the storefront window. She suspected the baker's wife had to threaten lingering urchins bent on stealing from her. But life in the city hadn't left the woman so hardened and skeptical that she would think the worst of everyone, had it?

Is that what bitterness did to people, drain them of all goodwill? Maybe it did with other people, but it wouldn't with Elise.

She walked several more blocks before turning onto Centre Street with its overflowing taverns and breweries. She'd traversed a short block when shouts filled the street. She watched as people—men, women, and children—ran in her direction. Their eyes were wild, their expressions frightened, their movements frantic. A young boy rushed toward Elise. Under the brim of his cap he kept tossing terrified glances over his shoulder so that he wasn't fully aware of where he was headed. Elise was too startled by the coming onslaught to move out of his way.

Even though he was small, perhaps five years old, his shoulder rammed against her stomach and rib cage, and the momentum made her stumble backward. She was surprised when strong arms caught her.

"I've got you," said a man behind her. Instead of landing painfully on her backside, she found herself being propelled by the man until she was standing straight again.

"Thornton Quincy at your service," he said with flair, holding one of her arms and steadying her. "Are you all right?"

Before she could answer, another man ran past and bumped into her shoulder. She would have floundered again if not for her rescuer's hold.

"We better get out of the way before we're trampled to death." He began tugging at her.

She was about to say her thanks and yank herself free of the stranger's grip, but she saw that the crowd had quickly swelled and was moving fast toward her, and she froze.

"Come on!" the man yelled.

This was no time to argue. He hadn't been jesting when he said they were about to be trampled. She allowed him to pull her along down Centre Street the way she'd come. Several children ran past them. Disheveled and screaming women stumbled behind. Carriages careened past, pulled by frantic horses.

At the sharp bang of gunshots, Elise tripped. Without breaking his stride, her rescuer clutched her arm harder and kept her on her feet. But even as her hurried steps evened out, her pulse stuttered forward. "Who's shooting?"

"It's the Bowery Boys and the Five Pointers," called a youth sprinting past. "They've been joined by the Roach Guards and Dead Rabbits."

Gangs fighting each other? That was nothing new. Rival gangs often fought on the streets. But apparently this fight had escalated and was now spreading. She certainly didn't want to be caught in the middle of it.

As if coming to the same conclusion, the man gripping her arm tossed a question at her over his shoulder. "Can you run?"

For the first time, she glimpsed his face—a strikingly handsome face with well-defined features. His eyes were dark brown, almost as dark as his hair. What had he said his name was? Something Quincy . . .

She nodded, bunched her skirt, and began to run. As Mr. Quincy dodged around people, she attempted to match her pace with his. She was afraid she might slow him down and that he'd grow frustrated with her and decide to leave her behind at the mercy of the panicking crowd.

The shattering of a glass storefront across the street startled her. Shards of glass flew into the air and onto the sidewalk, followed by screams. Bricks smashed against the window until the glass was obliterated, leaving a space wide enough for several raggedly dressed men to enter the store.

If the gang war wasn't enough, now looters were taking advantage of the disorder.

By the time Elise turned the corner, her chest was heaving. She needed to slow down to catch her breath. She was dismayed to see the turmoil had spread to the surrounding streets, and that a group of men was charging down the street armed with iron bars, paving stones, bats, axes, and bludgeons.

At the sight of the small army, Mr. Quincy jerked her in the opposite direction, dragging her along with him. She raced to keep up, stumbling and tripping in the confines of her skirt. Behind them, shouts and heavy footsteps echoed with increasing volume. All around, shopkeepers were slamming their doors shut.

"I think we should find a place to hide," Mr. Quincy called over his shoulder.

"I live close," she replied breathlessly, noting the stores she'd passed a short while ago. Even the blind beggar was still in his same spot, calling out questions to those racing past him. His tin cup dangled from the twine he used to hold up his trousers. His hands were outspread. Instead of begging for money, he was begging for information, but once again no one could be bothered to help the man.

"Wait!" She attempted to jerk free of Mr. Quincy.

He slowed his steps. "Where do you live?"

"We need to help him." She started toward the blind man, but her rescuer's hold on her arm prevented her.

"We need to get to safety." Mr. Quincy's handsome face was creased as he scanned the street filled with crowds of people running in various directions, attempting to find refuge before being caught up in a gang war.

"We can't leave him out here by himself," she insisted.

"Who?" Mr. Quincy didn't see the beggar on the street corner, even though he was almost directly in front of them.

"Over here." It was her turn to lead the way. In a few short steps she was next to the beggar on the corner. Mr. Quincy's eyes widened at the sight of the blind man. She half expected him to release her and move on his way. He'd clearly done his part to lend a hand to someone in need. Now he had no further obligation to do more for anyone.

But he nodded at the blind man and quirked one of his brows. "What are we doing?"

"We need to move him to safety."

At the sound of her voice, the blind man swiveled. "It's you, miss." His hands reached out for her.

"Yes, it's me," she answered, gently taking his hands into hers.

"Can you tell me what's happening?" he asked in a wobbly voice.

The crashing of more glass and angry shouts split the air. She slipped her arm through the beggar's. "The gangs are fighting. And now thieves are looting."

"Oh no, miss. Oh no . . ." He shuffled along next to her, and she was grateful when Mr. Quincy took the beggar's other arm.

"This way." She nodded in the direction of the mission, which was still half a block away. With his limping gait, the beggar slowed them down. By the time they'd gone half the distance, Mr. Quincy was practically carrying the man.

Bricks flew around them, one of them narrowly missing Elise before crashing into a window. "Hurry!" she gasped. "We're almost there."

Big block letters that read *Seventh Street Mission* had been painted in white across the front of the building just ahead.

She let go of the beggar and ran to the door. She jerked on it, expecting it to swing open, but it was locked.

Mr. Quincy with his heavy load came up behind her. She beat against the door with her fist. "Open up! It's Elise Neumann!"

A man's face appeared in one of the square windowpanes. A large man with blond hair and kind eyes.

"Reverend Bedell!" she shouted. "Please hurry!"

After a moment of rattling, the door swung wide. Big hands reached for her and pulled her inside. Mr. Quincy and the beggar stumbled in after her. Then the door slammed shut, and the lock clicked back into place.

CHAPTER 4

Thornton Quincy held a board over the window as Reverend Bedell hammered the last nail in place.

"There," the reverend said. "Hopefully that will keep out anyone who wishes to do us harm."

"I hope so too." Thornton wiped the beads of sweat off his brow. With all of the first-floor windows closed and boarded up, the building had grown stuffy and hot. He had no doubt that as the July day progressed, conditions would become unbearable.

The reverend stood back, hammer in hand, and surveyed what appeared to be a sewing workroom. Needles, thread, and half-finished shirts lay on the tables. Chairs were shoved aside as though rapidly abandoned.

"I appreciate your help," the reverend said. "I likely wouldn't have thought to secure the windows until too late."

Thornton nodded. "I've never seen the streets so volatile."

"Neither have I, and I've seen a great deal in my years living down here."

By *down here*, Thornton knew the reverend was referring

to Lower Manhattan, where the masses of immigrants resided. For Thornton it had always been a place he could go whenever he needed to find cheap labor. He didn't come often. He usually hired out the more aggressive recruitment to their land agent, Mr. Du Puy, who had been quite successful in getting hundreds of Irish and German immigrants to lay the rail for the Illinois Central.

But Thornton was too pressed for time to wait for Du Puy. He was already one week into his father's challenge and needed to find more construction workers immediately while the summer weather allowed for building. In addition, he had specific needs for various tradesmen. He didn't want just anyone. He wanted to handpick the most qualified.

Preliminary plans for the town and a few small structures had already been in place in both his and Bradford's towns. Thornton had finished platting it with his surveyor, Hewitt.

This wasn't the first railroad town Thornton had helped to develop. He'd had his hand in several along the New York and New Haven Railroads. He was familiar with the specifications of the standard railroad town. Each block was 3,000 square feet with lots 140 feet deep, backed by an alley. Main Street lots would be long and narrow, guaranteeing the first buildings would be uniform in size so as to attract smaller, independent merchants.

Exactly how to lay out the town in conjunction with the railroad had been a matter of intense debate with his surveyor. But Hewitt had finally agreed to try the more innovative parallel arrangement. They would build two halves of the town on separate but equal sides of the tracks. The two sides would have identically named streets. On one side would be First Avenue North, and in the same spot on the other side of the tracks would be First Avenue South, as was the usual pattern of naming north-south streets with numbers and east-west streets for trees.

Thornton had sent Hewitt ahead with the design for the town, as well as more construction crew to begin the train depot and a bunkhouse. The town was much farther down the Illinois Central than Thornton would have preferred, almost in the middle of the state—too far from Chicago and at least a four-day train ride from New York City. But most of the Illinois Central Railroad grant land to the north was already sold and developed.

At least Bradford's town was in the same isolated location, ten miles to the north. Since Bradford had named his town Wellington in honor of his father's forename, Thornton had decided on Quincy.

Quincy, Illinois. The town very well could decide the fate of his life. All week he'd done nothing but think about and plan for the town. Until today. Until now.

At a pounding on the front door of the mission, Thornton stiffened, reminded once again how dangerous the state of affairs on the streets had become in such a short time. One minute he'd been meeting with an immigrant contact and the next he'd been in the middle of a gang war.

The reverend pulled a knife from his boot and stepped out of the workroom. Thornton followed down a hallway to the same door he'd entered less than an hour ago. By the time they reached the door, no one was there.

"I think I better stay here and keep watch," the reverend said, glancing out one of the panes to the chaos on the street.

"I'll help."

"Good. I'd appreciate having another man here to help me defend the women just in case . . ." The reverend touched the small of his back, and Thornton guessed he had another weapon there, probably something small like a pistol.

Thornton didn't have any weapons on him. He wasn't accustomed to battling street thugs like the reverend apparently was.

"You can hang on to this." The reverend held out his knife as though guessing the direction of Thornton's thoughts. He unstrapped a sheath from his calf and handed that to Thornton too.

Over the past hour, while boarding up the windows, Thornton had learned that Reverend Bedell was engaged to the owner of the mission, a Miss Pendleton. In spite of the circumstances, his excitement about his upcoming nuptials had been obvious, as had his love for the petite woman who'd bustled about issuing orders and calming everyone.

Thornton had also learned that the Seventh Street Mission was new and had been started to provide alternative employment for women seeking to escape prostitution.

At the revelation, he'd been taken aback that the pretty woman he'd rescued and brought to safety had once been a prostitute. When he asked about it, the reverend laughed and assured him the Neumann girls were a result of Miss Pendleton's soft heart and not prostitution. Thornton was relieved to hear the news. The woman he'd rescued had seemed too young, too innocent to have lived such a lifestyle. But then what did he know of such things?

The reverend combed his fingers through his unruly hair and peered down the long hall toward the stairway at the opposite end. "Would you mind standing guard while I go up and see how the women are doing?"

"I'll do my best," Thornton said. "Although I'm warning you, I'm about as good at wielding a knife as I am a needle."

The reverend grinned. "Then you're an expert fighter and seamstress?"

Thornton chuckled. "I know nothing about doing either."

Bedell clamped him on the shoulder. "Don't worry. If someone tries to break in, all you need do is show them those five inches of steel and they'll turn and run."

"I can do that."

After the reverend left, Thornton leaned against the wall. The reality of the danger outside washed over him. Even with the door closed and windows boarded, the shouts and sounds of destruction reverberated down to his bones. He didn't consider himself a fighter. He hadn't been jesting when he informed the reverend he knew nothing about knives, except that the butter knife went on the right side of the plate next to the spoon.

He supposed that was why he'd hesitated in accepting the challenge against Bradford. He'd rather spend his days being the peacemaker than the aggressor. When he thought about the scrapes he and Bradford had gotten into as boys, usually Bradford had been the one to lead the charge into danger or mischief. He simply followed.

Even now, he second-guessed his decision to plunge into their father's challenge. Maybe Bradford was right. Maybe Father had developed the test in an attempt to be fair. But what if he expected Bradford to win anyway?

Thornton exhaled a tense breath. Whatever the case, he was in the challenge now. He couldn't quit or he'd disappoint his father even further.

"Mr. Quincy?" Striding down the hallway toward him was the young woman he'd rescued.

He pushed away from the wall and straightened. When they'd arrived, she was so concerned with situating and feeding the blind beggar that she'd gone on her way without another word to him. He'd admired her concern for someone less fortunate than herself. And he was impressed that even amidst the danger to herself, she'd gone to the beggar and helped him.

She drew nearer, and he was struck again now as he was earlier with how fair she was. Though the windows were boarded, sun streamed in through the cracks, allowing in enough light that he could see her clearly. Her face was much too serious for a woman of her young age, but her features were pretty in a natural way, without any of the guile and practiced poise of the women he knew. Her eyes were a pure blue made bluer by the light blond of her hair. From her slight accent, the plainness and simplicity of her dress, and the braided coil, he suspected she was German.

"Miss . . ." He realized that in the race for their lives he hadn't had the opportunity to discover her name.

She stopped several feet away. "Miss Neumann. Elise."

"Miss Neumann—"

"Please, call me Elise."

"Then I insist you call me Thornton."

She nodded. "Thornton." His name rolled off her tongue as though she didn't quite know what to make of it. In true German fashion, she'd blended the *h* to the *t* so that his name came out *Tornton*. "I didn't have the chance to thank you for helping me."

"I only did what any gentleman would have."

"No. You were much kinder."

He shrugged. "It was nothing."

She didn't respond but studied him with her large blue eyes. They were so innocent and yet so grave. He couldn't keep his gaze from dropping to her willowy yet beautifully curved figure.

She was perhaps a little too thin, but certainly attractive. Not that he should notice, not when he was focusing on Rosalind Beaufort and had spent every free moment over the past week with her.

"How is our blind friend doing?" he asked, trying to divert his attention to a safer topic. "Is he settled in?"

"He's upstairs with the others. He finally decided I'm trustworthy and told me his name is Isaiah."

"So you didn't know him before today?"

"No. Why should I? The city is full of beggars."

Thornton had assumed she'd had previous interactions with the man and was startled to realize he was a complete stranger. "That was thoughtful of you to rescue him."

"Do you not wonder what kind of world we live in that allows a blind beggar to fend for himself on the streets?"

The question took Thornton off guard. No, frankly he'd never wondered about such matters. In fact, he couldn't remember the last time he'd given a beggar a passing glance. He didn't come into Lower Manhattan often, but when he did, he had business on his mind. "I hadn't thought of it," he responded honestly. "But I can't help wondering how the gangs can wage war against each other and why nothing is being done to stop them."

"The police are afraid of them and leave them to their own devices most of the time."

At that moment, something banged against the door, causing Elise to jump. Thornton withdrew the reverend's knife and inched toward the door. They'd debated boarding up the small paned window, and now Thornton was glad they had. He peeked through a crack, only to find that whoever had been attempting to break in had already moved on, apparently deciding it wasn't worth the effort.

He watched the street a moment longer and then sheathed the knife before he accidentally hurt himself with it. When he turned, he caught the glint of a blade in Elise's hand. He held his hands up in mock surrender and grinned. "Don't hurt me."

"Don't worry," she said and tucked the knife away. "I only chop off fingers."

Her expression was so serious, that for a moment he couldn't tell if she was jesting or not. When she glanced up, he caught the faint glimmer of mirth in her eyes.

He held out his hands. "I beg you to spare my right hand. And perhaps two fingers on the left?"

"Only two?"

"Are you in a generous mood? Will you allow three?"

Her lips twitched with a smile, and she cocked her head as though considering his offer. "And what payment will you give me if I spare you this time?"

He dug a hand inside his pocket and came up empty. From a second pocket he pulled out two peppermints, three pennies, and a fabric flower that had fallen off Rosalind Beaufort's hat yesterday when they'd watched the regatta. She and her parents had been delightful company. They enjoyed watching the rowing and sailing races put on by the Regatta Club. Bradford had been there too with Dorothea.

Apparently, Bradford was as anxious to get started on finding a wife as he was. *Finding* was the easy part, Thornton realized yesterday when he watched Miss Beaufort smile and laugh at everything he'd said. There were plenty of nice girls like Rosalind Beaufort. He could woo her with his charm and money. He might even be able to make her fall in love with him, if he worked hard enough at it. But how could he make himself fall in love with her? He'd heard that love could grow over time, but could it develop in just six months?

Thornton rubbed his thumb over the soft flower. It was delicate and blue and he'd hoped to remember Rosalind every time he touched or saw it. But now, grazing his thumb across the soft petals, he could only think how the blue was the same shade as Elise's eyes.

"A token from the woman you love?" Elise asked, looking pointedly at the flower.

"No," he said too morosely. If only he could lay that claim. "Sadly I've never been in love."

One of her thin brows rose.

"Have you?" he asked.

"Have I been in love?"

The moment she repeated his words, he was embarrassed for having asked them. "I'm prying where I shouldn't." He jingled the items in his palm and then held them out to her, flower and all. "Here. My bargain and apology all in one payment."

She started to shake her head, but he dumped the contents into her hand before she could finish her protest. The peppermints had left a sticky residue on his palm that he wiped on his trousers.

"You're far too generous." She pocketed the items. "I don't know how to thank you."

The seriousness of her expression took him by surprise for only an instant before he interpreted the sarcastic lilt of her tone. He always appreciated wit, but Bradford was usually the only one who could match him spar for witty spar.

"Don't worry about feeling indebted to me," he replied with the same seriousness. "I'm sure you'll find some way to repay me for the sticky peppermints covered in lint. Eventually."

"I'll repay you now."

"I suppose you have a sticky gumdrop covered in lint that you'd like to share with me in return?"

Her lips inched into the beginning of a smile. "Sorry. I don't have anything so grand as that. But I will help you tend your wound."

"My wound?"

She lifted a hand to just above his ear. Her touch brought a sharp sting, making him wince. When she pulled back and showed him her fingers, they were slickened with blood. "Looks like maybe you were grazed with a piece of glass."

He skimmed the spot for himself, feeling the oozing blood and a thin but neat split in his skin. "I didn't realize I'd been cut. I wonder when it happened."

"With all the senseless violence, it could have been at anytime."

The stomping of footsteps coming their way signaled the reverend's return. "The women are all doing well." As the burly man made his way down the hallway, he glanced first in one workroom and then poked his head in the other across from it. "They're a little scared, and worried for their families, but they're safe."

"Good—" Thornton's words were cut off by slamming and cursing against the door. Elise had her knife out before he could even fumble for the handle of his.

The reverend brushed past them both with the kind of confidence that said he knew his size and strength could easily intimidate. He peered out a crack and yelled, "Go away before you find a bullet in your backside."

The rattling and banging of the door came to an abrupt halt. Thornton had no doubt the reverend's booming voice had scared the perpetrator away as much as the threat of a gunshot.

After a minute of silent vigilance, the reverend turned. "I think we're in for a long day."

Thornton nodded. He obviously couldn't go back out on the streets until the rioting and looting stopped. "I'll help in any way I can."

"You've already been a big help," the reverend said.

"Are there any other doors that need guarding?"

"Only two at the back of the building near a loading dock. But I've got them padlocked."

Elise glanced at his cut again. "Then you'll spare Thornton—Mr. Quincy—a moment so I can doctor his wound?"

"By all means," the reverend said. "I didn't know Mr. Quincy was hurt or I wouldn't have imposed on him."

"Don't feel bad, Reverend," Thornton reassured with a grin. "I didn't know I was hurt either. It's a good thing God made women so they can show us all the things right in front of our faces—or on our faces—that we miss."

The reverend gave a hearty laugh. Even though the man was older than him by at least a decade, if not more, Thornton found himself appreciating the man—his kindness, his ready smile, and his sense of humor.

Thornton followed Elise to the second floor. Immediately he was assaulted with the stench of mold, rotting wood, and dust. Floorboards were missing in some places, the ceiling crumbling in others. There were holes in the soot-covered walls, and cobwebs dangled from the beams.

Elise led him into a large room that had been converted into a dining room, complete with tables and chairs that were filled with women huddled together in groups, talking among themselves. At the sight of him, they grew silent and stared at him too boldly.

With untidy hair, pale faces, and faded garments, they were lusterless, like brass buttons that had been rubbed too hard, until they'd lost their shine. These were the kind of women he expected had lived loosely and immorally. Standing on the fringe of their midst, Elise looked like a dove among house wrens. He was struck again by how lovely and innocent she appeared by comparison.

She took him to the blind man first. Isaiah was seated at the end of one of the tables, eating a thick piece of bread slathered in butter. He paused in eating his meal and thanked Thornton profusely for leading him out of harm's way. When Thornton shook the man's blackened hand, Elise's comment came back to taunt him. *Do you not wonder what kind of world we live in that allows a blind beggar to fend for himself on the streets?*

After leaving Isaiah, Elise led him over to a group of children sitting in a corner by themselves. "Marianne," she said to a pretty brown-haired woman holding a little boy on her lap. "Allow Mr. Quincy to sit in your chair while I tend to his cut."

Thornton guessed Marianne to be a younger sister since her features so closely resembled Elise's. As she rose and hoisted the infant to her hip, Thornton offered her a grateful smile. Her brown eyes widened in return, but she didn't smile back.

"Sophie." Elise waved at a young girl sitting on the floor playing a string game with another much smaller girl. "Go find Miss Pendleton and ask her for the doctoring bag."

As the girl did so, Thornton could see the clear resemblance between Sophie and Elise. Both had the same blond hair and blue eyes, only Sophie had slightly more delicate features. "So you have four siblings?" he asked as he lowered himself to the chair.

"Marianne and Sophie are my sisters." Elise dipped a strip of cloth into a cup of water that was sitting on the table. "Olivia and Nicholas are orphans who we've been taking care of. Their mother was living with us. But one day she disappeared, supposedly to look for work. No matter how hard we tried to find her, we never could. The two have become a part of the family now."

He wanted to say that Elise and her sisters looked like orphans themselves, hardly old enough to be taking care of someone else's children. But she touched the cloth to his cut, and the painful pressure stopped all words and thoughts.

She held the linen firmly to his wound. He closed his eyes for a moment, squeezing back an unmanly desire to suck in his breath. When he opened his eyes, the frayed edge of her black sleeve filled his vision. It was only then that he noticed both Elise and Marianne wore all black, customary for someone in mourning.

"Who did you lose?" he asked softly.

She removed the pressure against his cut, returned the linen to the cup of water, and added more water. With her lips pressed together, she touched the linen to his wound again. He was afraid he'd offended her with his prying and that she would repay him by pushing against his cut roughly. So when she dabbed at the area more gently, he was surprised.

"I beg your pardon," he started. "I shouldn't have asked—"

"Our mother died in May. Over six weeks ago."

"And it seems like just yesterday?"

Her fingers stilled. He glanced at her face hovering above him and saw her swallow hard before nodding. "I'm sorry" was all he could think to say. He knew how it felt to lose a mother. Though it had been years since his mother's passing, there were times when he keenly missed having her encouragement, her spiritual guidance, and her unwavering belief. She'd always accepted him regardless of how he differed from Bradford.

He wanted to say something more to comfort Elise, to tell her that eventually the pain would become more bearable, even if it never truly went away. Before he could find the words to express himself, Sophie returned with not only the doctoring bag but also the petite Miss Pendleton.

From the moment he'd met the woman, he recognized her name. Her father, Ambrose Pendleton, had been one of the most ruthless businessmen in New York City. Very few men were sad to see him die. His own father had despised Ambrose for his cheating and underhanded ways.

Nevertheless, Thornton liked to give people a chance to prove themselves. He'd been lumped together with Bradford too often in the past, had been judged for Bradford's deeds—both good and bad—instead of being measured for his own. He decided he didn't want to do the same to others.

While Miss Pendleton and Elise applied salve and bandaged his wound, he discovered Miss Pendleton to be very forthright about her plans for the mission. She spoke of her desire not only to hire more seamstresses, but to provide a dormitory for them as well. She claimed she was modeling her mission after the place Charles Loring Brace, the founder of the Children's Aid Society, had started for homeless boys several years ago.

She said she'd gone over to The Newsboys' Lodging House and toured it to see how it was run. The *New York Sun* had contributed the space, a loft, at the top of their office building on the corner of Fulton and Nassau Streets. The facility had forty beds, a large washroom, and a dining area that could be converted into a schoolroom. The boys had to pay six cents for a bed and four cents for a meal, cheaper than even the most unsanitary and unsafe of hotels, which usually charged seven cents a night for a bed.

Miss Pendleton said her goal was to set up the mission in a similar fashion. She wanted to provide a safe place for her workers to board and for a low fee. Already she was offering simple meals to them during the workday and hoped to expand that to an evening meal.

"Such an endeavor must be very costly, Miss Pendleton," he said, standing and lightly touching the patch of gauze above his ear.

"It is," Miss Pendleton replied. Elise tucked the bandages back into a leather case. "God has provided for us every step of the way."

"The brewery itself must have cost a fortune." Even if it was a run-down piece of real estate, the property was in a prime location.

"I sold my home in order to purchase it."

For a moment, he was speechless. What would lead someone to make such a sacrifice for women who would never be able to repay her, those who had lived such vile lives? Why had she chosen to help them?

He wanted to voice his questions, but Elise and her sisters were watching him with wide, curious eyes. He was sure they were wondering about him by now, where he'd come from and what he was doing in this part of the city. Truthfully, he was a bit embarrassed to admit to who he really was, especially in light of how little they had.

"Although we are able to maintain all we've started at the mission," Miss Pendleton continued, "I regret I'm not able to move forward with repairs and improvements as quickly as I'd like."

"That is regrettable." His attention crept to the discolored stains on the floor where various brewery mechanisms had once stood. An opening in the floor, now covered by a grate, had probably contained a chute distributing malt into a mash tun and boil kettle somewhere on the first level of the building.

"However, the reverend and I are seeking donors," she said, "people who might be interested in contributing to the mission on a regular basis."

"That's a good idea."

She raised her brows at him. "I was hoping you'd think so, Mr. Quincy." She stressed his last name. When her gaze met his, it was clear she was well aware of who he was and just how much wealth he had.

At a whimpering, Elise reached for the little boy they called Nicholas. Thornton wasn't accustomed to being around children or babies. Even so, as Elise hugged the boy close, kissed his downy hair, and tucked his head under her chin, a strange, tender warmth spread through his chest.

Maybe his meeting with Elise hadn't been so accidental after all. Maybe God had brought him here today for a reason. After all, if Miss Pendleton could sell her home to help these women, certainly Quincy Enterprises could support their cause.

"I may know of a donor, Miss Pendleton," he finally said, cautiously, hoping Miss Pendleton read in his tone and expression his desire to keep the matter private.

"Excellent." She picked up the medical case and snapped it closed. "Then let's be sure to talk more later."

He nodded, and she gave a curt nod in return. As she made her way across the room with her short steps, his momentary satisfaction was interrupted by one glaring thought. He didn't have time for charitable efforts. And he didn't have time to sit around the Seventh Street Mission all day and help guard it.

He had a challenge to win and he couldn't waste a single minute if he hoped to come out on top. Yet another part of him demanded he stay and do the right thing, even if it cost him dearly.

CHAPTER 5

Elise balanced a plate and a cup of coffee in one hand and a lantern in the other. The hallway was dark with the coming of night, and she didn't know the mission building well enough to traverse its corridors without adequate light.

"Hello?" she called, lifting the lantern higher to illuminate the hall.

A shadowy figure moved away from the wall. "Elise?"

"You're still here?"

"No, I've left. What you're hearing and seeing is only a figment of your imagination."

She couldn't keep from smiling. "Then I suppose the imaginary person won't need the food and coffee I have."

"Oh no," he said. "Don't you know that even figments need sustenance too?"

She drew nearer until the light fell upon him, turning his dark hair to a blue-black, the color of a starling in the sunlight. His face was pale, his eyes exhausted, yet his jaw was set with determination.

He'd discarded his hat, tie and coat, and had unclasped the top button of his shirt. Earlier in the day, she'd decided he was a business owner of some kind or perhaps rented properties here in Lower Manhattan. From his finely tailored garments, clean hands and fingernails, and self-assured way of conducting himself, she could see he wasn't a common laborer or tradesman.

But now, with his shirtsleeves rolled up, his hair mussed, and his forehead lined with weariness, he seemed less lofty and more like an average man.

He took the coffee from her and tested the liquid with a sip before gulping several swallows.

"Sorry it's not hot anymore," she said.

"I'm not complaining." He tipped the cup up and drained it.

She exchanged the empty mug for the plate of food. "The meal isn't hot either."

He dug into the potato dumplings and chicken in gravy she'd prepared for dinner. The cook Miss Pendleton had hired to come once a day to prepare a meal for the workers hadn't shown up. Elise finally offered to make something out of the chicken delivered earlier that morning before any rioting started. Miss Pendleton eagerly agreed, admitting she'd never cooked a meal in her entire life.

Even if the coal-burning stove had been small, the workspace cumbersome, and the choice of ingredients sparse, Elise relished every moment of preparing the meal. She hadn't had the opportunity to cook anything since Christmas Day, back when they were still living with Uncle Hermann, when she helped Mutti and Aunt Gertie make a special dinner out of the few items they'd managed to purchase.

Elise enjoyed cooking meals and experimenting with new recipes, applying all she'd learned from Vater. Her opportunities to practice her culinary skills in recent years had dwindled to almost nothing. She'd worked such long hours in the sweatshop that she had so little energy after returning to Uncle's apartment each night. But even if she'd had the energy, they survived on the simplest of fare with little variety—fried fish, bread, and occasionally sauerkraut.

"This is really good," Thornton said between bites.

"Everything is good when you're hungry."

"Perhaps." His spoon scraped the plate as he scooped up the last remnants of gravy. "But this was especially tasty."

His praise warmed her heart.

"Give my regards to the cook," he said, handing the plate back to her.

"I will." Elise placed the empty cup on the plate that was practically licked clean. "She thanks you and wants to know if you'd like a second helping."

He studied her, his tired eyes crinkling at the corners with a smile of understanding. "Tell her I'd love to have more if she can spare it. And let her know it was one of the best meals I've eaten in a very long time."

"In light of such a compliment, she may be willing to bring you another cup of lukewarm coffee."

"More lukewarm coffee? I don't deserve such a treat. But tell her I humbly accept."

How was it this man could make her smile so easily when few people could elicit even the tiniest amount of joy from her? She supposed in some ways she convinced herself that she didn't deserve joy, not when she'd failed to protect and provide for her family. They deserved so much more than a life of poverty, and she hadn't been able to change their circumstances . . . except for the worse.

As her humor faded, his expression turned more serious. "How's Miss Pendleton doing?"

"She's worried about the reverend and rightly so."

Thornton peered out a crack between the boards covering the window nearby. "I expected him back by now."

After the long day of waiting and speculating about what was happening on the streets, some of the women had talked about leaving. They were worried about their children being home alone amidst the violence and wanted to be with them. Elise would have wanted to leave too were she in their situation. Reverend Bedell was sympathetic and agreed to accompany them for their protection.

"Do you think something happened to him?" Elise asked.

"I've been praying he's safe." Thornton rubbed a hand across his eyes. "The streets have been quiet for the past hour. Hopefully the worst is over."

"Would you like me to stand guard for a little while so you can take a break?"

He hesitated. "I'll be all right now that I've had that delicious meal." The delay was enough that Elise wondered if he was anxious to return to his home too. She guessed a man like him probably had more important things to do than watch over the women who worked at the mission.

She went back upstairs and filled his plate with more chicken and dumplings. Then, with another tepid cup of coffee and the full plate, she returned to the front hallway. He ate the second helping more slowly, seeming to savor every bite. Finally he finished the meal along with his coffee.

"Are you sure you don't want me to stand guard so you can rest for a bit?" she asked, taking the empty plate and cup from him again.

"No." His eyes were softer, the worry lines gone from his

forehead. "But I would appreciate the company. Otherwise I'm afraid I'll die of boredom."

"I may not be all that more exciting."

"Trust me, you're more exciting than I am."

She wasn't sure if Miss Pendleton would approve of her staying with Thornton unchaperoned. Nevertheless, she set the plate and cup on the floor next to the lantern and leaned against the wall across from him. She couldn't refuse his request for company, not after the way he'd helped all day and without a single complaint.

Besides, there was something intriguing about him. She could banter easily with him, and for a while he entertained her with stories of his escapades during his childhood with his twin brother.

"Bradford sounds like he was quite the instigator," she said after reining in her laugher in response to his story about how he and Bradford had climbed out of their bedroom windows and crawled across the roof of their house in order to switch rooms. Bradford had been the one to suggest the plot after their nursemaid locked them in their rooms and then bedded down in the hallway between their rooms to prevent them from switching places in the middle of the night as they'd done too many times in the past. But the nursemaid failed to take into account what lengths the brothers would go to in causing trouble.

"Bradford was the mastermind behind most of our adventures," Thornton admitted with a nostalgic smile. "And I willingly went along with him, so I wasn't without blame."

"It sounds like you really love your brother."

"We're still friends," Thornton said slowly as if choosing his words carefully. "But the downside to being a twin is that only one of us can come out on top." In the flickering lantern light, emotions played across his face. Regret, frustration, sadness?

"Does it matter if there's a 'top' or not? Can't you be equals?"

Thornton released a sigh that made his shoulders sag. "Unfortunately, no. Not with a father like ours."

Before she could find the words to respond, a rattle of the door handle made them both jump.

"Thornton." A raspy voice spoke from outside. "It's me, Guy. Reverend Bedell. Let me in."

Thornton quickly unlocked the door and swung it open, helping the reverend inside before closing and locking the door again.

Elise assessed the reverend at the same time as Thornton, noting he appeared disheveled but unharmed. "You're all right?" Thornton asked.

The reverend nodded. "Yes, I'm fine. And the women are home safely."

Elise let out a breath, relieved.

"Thank God," Thornton whispered.

"Yes, I thank God for another miracle. It was no easy feat delivering them to their apartments, considering some of their buildings were overrun with gangs, who were on the rooftops showering the police and any other militia with stones and bricks."

"Has the fighting stopped?" Elise asked.

Before he could answer, Miss Pendleton came running down the hallway toward them. Her normally tight hair was loose, and her usually composed face was taut with anxiety.

At the sight of her, the reverend broke away from the door and started toward her with long strides that spoke of his own relief. When he reached Miss Pendleton, she gave a small cry and threw herself into his arms at the same moment he swept her into an embrace. He held her for a long moment before pressing a kiss against her forehead.

Finally the reverend released Miss Pendleton, but held her hand as they ambled toward where she and Thornton stood near the door. Miss Pendleton's smile at the reverend could have lit an entire city block. From the tenderness with which he regarded her, Elise was reminded of the love her father had bestowed upon Mutti. He'd adored her. With each passing year of increasing poverty and debt, he blamed himself for the hardships his wife had to endure. Sometimes Elise couldn't help but think that all his guilt and despair had been the cause of his failed heart.

She reached up and fingered the outline of Mutti's wedding ring, which hung on a thin leather strip beneath her bodice. She traced the edges of the cross that formed the front of the silver band. Other than the cross, the ring was simple and without jewels, not the kind of heirloom she had to worry about anyone stealing. Even so, it was the most precious thing she owned. Mutti had given it to her just before she died.

Elise watched as Reverend Bedell kissed Miss Pendleton's temple. It was refreshing to see a couple who cared so deeply about each other, a couple who also worked well together. It was as if God had handpicked them for each other—if that sort of thing was really possible. She certainly didn't expect such an intimate relationship for herself. She was too busy to think about love and marriage.

"So when's the wedding?" Thornton winked at the reverend.

His grin widened. "Not soon enough."

"Guy," Miss Pendleton whispered with a reprimanding tug on his arm. Even in the dim light, it was easy to see her face had turned a bright shade of pink.

Elise tried not to fidget at the nature of the jesting, but she was suddenly aware of Thornton's arm near hers. When he smiled and winked down at her, her heart began to race. She pressed her hand against her chest, feeling Mutti's ring again. She'd never reacted this way to a man before. Of course, she hadn't had any real suitors, and even though Reinhold had asked her to marry him, he didn't count. He was her friend only, more like a brother than a beau.

She held herself absolutely motionless so Thornton wouldn't sense her strange reaction. Thankfully he didn't seem to notice and instead queried the reverend for more information about the condition on the streets.

The reverend informed them of the news he'd gleaned during his time away. The hostilities had escalated. By midday close to a thousand armed men from rival gangs were fighting in the area of Five Points. The police had attempted to stop the aggression and had begun arresting gangsters. But as soon as the police left the area, the fighting resumed in greater force. The Dead Rabbits and Bowery Boys each set up barricades of pushcarts and large stones, all while firing weapons, hurling bricks, and clubbing each other.

Thieves, thugs, and other criminals who weren't affiliated with the gangs used the opportunity to attack businesses, stealing whatever they could get their hands on and wreaking destruction in their wake. Several fires had been set to houses with the residents still inside.

When the police learned the fighting had grown in scale, they tried to return to the area but had been pushed back, many of them getting injured in the process. The police commissioner then called in the military, and around nine o'clock in the evening the New York State Militia, their bayonets affixed and ready for use, marched down White and Worth Streets. Two police regiments had accompanied the militia, going ahead and fighting back the gangsters and rioters.

"The show of force was enough to send the gangsters fleeing back to their hideouts," the reverend said.

Thornton shook his head, his expression one of disbelief at all the reverend had shared. "Do you think they're done now with their brawling or will it resume again?"

"Well, the police and national guardsmen are patrolling the streets and arresting anyone who looks suspicious."

"I guess that means I should wait to leave?" Thornton asked.

"Yes, since you look so suspicious, you probably shouldn't show yourself." The words were out before Elise could stop them, and once they were, she wished she could take them back, especially as Miss Pendleton's eyes narrowed at her in disapproval.

Thornton chuckled. "I think you're right. After all, I do look like quite the rogue, don't I?"

Another sardonic remark was on the tip of Elise's tongue, but she glanced at Miss Pendleton and held it back. Instead she forced herself to respond respectfully, as a young woman ought to. "I was only jesting. The truth is that no one would mistake you for anything other than a gentleman."

Thornton's brows rose. His brown eyes dared her to tease him again, as though he was waiting expectantly for more.

Rather than give him what he wanted, she said, "I should be going." She retrieved the empty plate and coffee cup and started down the hallway.

"Good-bye, Elise," he called after her. "It was nice meeting you."

She nodded at him in return. And as she shuffled down the hall, she suspected his good-bye would be the last time she'd hear from Thornton Quincy.

CHAPTER 6

Marianne Neumann peeked around the corner and saw him. She jerked back against the brick wall, her breath coming in sudden bursts. She hoped but hadn't expected him to be outside today with his family. He usually wasn't there. Or at least he hadn't been on the previous Sundays she'd returned to her old neighborhood to look for him from a distance.

Had she just dreamed him there? Did she miss him so much that she'd begun to imagine seeing him? She slid along the wall and looked toward the front of the tenement, where families were resting on their day off, attempting to escape the stifling heat that became trapped in the tiny two-room apartments.

Her gaze locked on him immediately. His build and broad shoulders were hard to miss. His brown hair was sun-streaked after the months of working outdoors doing the construction work that had given him thickly muscled arms. Her heart pattered faster at the sight of him, and she couldn't keep from soaking him in. When he reached for one of his little sisters and tossed her in the air, Marianne smiled at the girl's squeals of laughter.

At the moment Reinhold lowered his sister to the ground, he glanced in her direction and froze. Marianne quickly jumped out of sight and pressed herself against the building again. Had he seen her? Part of her hoped he had. But another part told her she shouldn't be there.

Every Sunday that she'd made the thirty-minute walk to Kleindeutschland, she found herself having to fight back guilt. If Elise knew where she was, she wouldn't be happy about it. Even if Uncle Hermann had been about to evict them, even if he'd found new tenants, there was no telling what he might do if he saw them again, especially because they'd stolen from him.

Marianne shook her head in frustration. No, they hadn't stolen. The money had been rightfully theirs—the wages they'd earned from their long hours of sewing in the sweatshop. Even when Mutti had been alive, Uncle had shown no compassion toward his sister. Instead he'd required Mutti to give him most of their earnings—to pay for room and board, he'd claimed.

Uncle had always demanded much, had belittled them, and had been dangerous when drunk, which was often. Then after spending all their earnings at the beer hall, there had been very little left for food and fuel. Even then he'd demanded more money from them. And when they'd had none left to give, he crammed more boarders into the tiny tenement so he'd have their earnings too.

Marianne swallowed the rising fear that came whenever she thought of her uncle and what he was capable of doing if he caught them. He'd likely turn them over to the police for being thieves. But the truth was, when they ran away, they'd only taken back what was theirs in the first place.

Of course, there was also the small matter of Friedric Kaiser, one of Uncle's new tenants. The dangerous young man had decided he wanted to have Elise as his girl. They couldn't risk his discovering their new home either.

But they'd been living at the Seventh Street Mission for over a month. Surely they were secure enough that talking with Reinhold wouldn't jeopardize them. The rioting last month left the city reeling for days, and repairs to businesses were ongoing. The mission, however, was unscathed compared with many other buildings of the area that were looted and destroyed.

Miss Pendleton had just opened the second workshop at the mission. Now there were over forty women employed, all doing seamstress work. The dear woman had given Elise the job of managing the new workers, which had brought a raise of ten cents an hour. Now Elise was earning $1.90 per week, thirty cents more than she'd made working in the tenement sweatshop with Uncle Hermann.

Marianne had hoped the switch to the new workshop would ease the tension that still existed with the Irish workers, but it hadn't gone away.

Jealousy. Marianne could see it in the eyes of the other women when they looked at her or Elise. They were jealous Miss Pendleton had given Elise the supervisor position even though most of them had worked at the mission longer. They were jealous Miss Pendleton allowed them to live there even though the dormitory was far from ready for occupancy. They were jealous because Sophie and Nicholas and Olivia were able to stay there too, while they had to leave their children home alone during the workdays.

Though the petty disagreements and underhanded bullying continued, at least they were safe, well-fed, and together. Now that they were finally situated, why shouldn't she tell Reinhold where they were living? Why shouldn't she resume their friendship? It wouldn't hurt anyone, would it?

She took a tiny step toward the corner. But as she moved, a hand clamped down on her arm. Panic pushed a scream up her throat. The hand shifted to her mouth and captured the scream before it could alert anyone nearby of her predicament.

"It *is* you" came Reinhold's surprised voice.

She swiveled to find Reinhold standing next to her, his ruddy face close, his green eyes alight with pleasure. He released his hold over her mouth, and a smile filled his handsome face.

At the sight of him, she gave a squeal of joy. She couldn't contain her excitement and threw her arms around him.

His low rumble of laughter accompanied his arms closing about her, enfolding her for a heavenly moment of pure bliss. He'd apparently caught her spying and had sneaked around through the alley behind her. When he pulled back, she wanted to cling to him. Yet he held her at arm's length and assessed her, his smile growing wider.

Marianne couldn't keep herself from drinking him in. He wasn't overly tall, but that only made him all the more perfect for looking directly into his mesmerizing eyes. Should she tell him right now that she loved him and wanted to marry him? Before she lost her courage? She'd been dreaming about marrying him since the day they'd first met. Now that she was eighteen, maybe he'd finally see her as a woman instead of a little girl.

"The one Sunday I decide to take a break in my search and I find you."

"You've been searching for us?" Her heart opened wide at the thought that he'd missed her. Maybe even as much as she'd missed him.

His smile faded, his expression turning almost angry. "Of

course I've been searching. I've been going nearly mad with worry. Why didn't you or Elise tell me you were running away? Why didn't you come back sooner and let me know you were okay?"

"I have been coming back," she admitted shyly. "Almost every Sunday. But you've always been gone."

"I've been using every spare minute of my day off scouring the streets trying to find any clues about where you'd gone. After having no luck, I decided you somehow found the means to leave the city."

"So you decided to give up?"

"I don't think I could have ever given up," he said, the anger tapering from his voice. "I just thought I should take a day off to be with my family."

She couldn't help herself. She threw herself into his arms again. He hugged her tightly as though to reassure himself she was real. She burrowed her face into his shirt and dragged in a deep breath of his musky scent. This time when he started to release her, she clung to him, not caring that she was acting slightly desperate and lovesick.

"Marianne," he said gently, prying her loose. "Tell me everything. I need to know you're all safe and well."

She gave him the quick version of their story, about how after leaving Uncle's they'd lived on the streets for over a week before Miss Pendleton had found them and brought them to her new mission where they'd been for the past month.

"You're living in the Seventh Street Mission?" he asked, his brows lifting and almost touching the brim of his hat.

She nodded. "We have jobs as seamstresses—"

"But isn't it a place to reform prostitutes?"

Marianne flushed and glanced down at the cracked pavement.

74

"Pardon my vulgarity," he was quick to add. "It's just that I never thought to inquire there. I never imagined you or Elise would do something like that—"

"Reinhold Weiss!" She stomped her foot and almost reached up to slap him. "How dare you think Elise or I would stoop to doing something so shameful?"

"I didn't think so—"

"You better *know* so." She huffed and crossed her arms over her chest to keep herself from doing him bodily damage.

He searched her face. Apparently he found the answer he was looking for, because his taut features relaxed. "Then you're truly safe and secure?"

"Truly."

"Sophie and Olivia and Nicholas?"

"They're all fine."

"I just wish Elise would have sent word to ease my mind." It was his turn to look down at the sidewalk. "Why didn't she?"

When he finally glanced up again, she was taken aback by the hurt in his eyes. "We've been really busy working. And she was afraid of Uncle or Friedric finding out where we were."

"But surely she knew I wouldn't tell them."

"I know." Marianne released a long sigh. "I told Elise we should send you a note."

"And what did she say to that?"

"She said we would once we were settled."

Reinhold mulled over her words and seemed to take comfort in them. Then he squeezed her arm. "I'm glad you're okay, Marianne."

She wanted to tell him she was okay now that she was with him, but at the sound of shouting around the corner, he propelled her backward behind him. "Maybe you should go."

He was right. She needed to get away before anyone else recognized her. And she needed to return to the mission before Elise grew suspicious and realized she was gone.

She was tempted to hug Reinhold again, except he'd already put another step between them. "When will I see you again?" she asked, not caring that her tone was laced with desperation.

"Now that I know where you're living, I'll try to visit soon." His words brought a smile to her heart. "I'll be waiting."

He gave her a fleeting wave. As she turned to go, she realized she would be counting the days until his arrival.

⸙

"I won't go," Sophie said. She sat in the only chair in their third-story room and held Nicholas on her lap. The little boy sucked the thumb of one hand and absently fingered the silky end of Sophie's braid with the other.

"You have to go," Elise insisted. Her frustration was mounting with each passing minute. At half past six in the morning, that didn't bode well for the day.

Sophie didn't budge from the chair. "I'm staying here to watch Nicholas and Olivia just like I have every other day this summer. I don't know why that needs to change."

Elise wanted to roll her eyes and say, *Because whether we like it or not, life changes.* Instead, she took a deep breath, counted to five, and tried to respond calmly. "I know you're not hard of hearing, Sophie. And I've already told you why at least a dozen times."

According to Miss Pendleton, the state of New York had passed its Truancy Law last year, the first state to make such a law. All children between the ages of five and fifteen had to go to school, unless they were gainfully employed. If they were caught by the police, they could face jail or indenture.

"But I have a job." She drew Olivia to her side and kissed the girl's head. Olivia gave a sleepy yawn but hugged Sophie back.

"You know as well as I do, watching Olivia and Nicholas isn't a job." Elise held Sophie's gaze, which was as stubborn as her own.

"Someone has to watch them," Sophie said. "They can't be alone all day."

"They won't be. Marianne and I will check on them." Elise didn't like the idea of Olivia entertaining Nicholas for hours on end, but at least she and Marianne were close by, and Olivia could come get them if she needed something—unlike most of the other workers who had no choice but to leave their young children home at the mercy of neighbors or nearby relatives.

In the early morning light cascading through the open window, Elise could see the battle raging across Sophie's delicate features. She'd been caring for the two children for months and had become like their mother. In fact, Sophie was a better mother to Olivia and Nicholas than their real one ever had been. They adored Sophie as much as she adored them.

Elise wondered if Sophie had grown too attached to the young orphans and they to her. She worried about the day when someone stepped in and decided the children needed a real home. What would Sophie do then? How would she ever be able to let them go?

As kind as Miss Pendleton had been in allowing them a room for a pittance, it wasn't a permanent solution. How could it be? Living at a mission among former prostitutes was not the kind of life she'd envisioned for herself or her sisters. No, it was only a short-term arrangement. Eventually she hoped to save enough money so they could find their own apartment and live independently.

In the meantime, she planned to make the most of their time here. That included sending Sophie to school. "Vater would have wanted you to go to school," Elise finally said, voicing her truest and deepest reason for wanting Sophie to attend school. "He'd be very disappointed if you don't get an education."

"Then it's a good thing he doesn't have to know."

"Sophie," Marianne chided from where she stood fixing her hair into a coiled braid. "Both Elise and I were lucky to get as much education as we did. Now you have the opportunity to go, and you should take it. Not everyone can."

"Stop treating me like a child. I'm educated enough."

When Vater died and they'd had to stop school to work as seamstresses, Sophie had already learned to read and write and do some arithmetic, but she hadn't been in school for long. Not long enough to please Vater. "You don't have many more months until you turn sixteen," Elise said, "until you are no longer required to attend school. So just go."

"No."

Elise released an exasperated sigh and threw up her hands in defeat. "Then you'll have to be the one to tell Miss Pendleton you're not following her wishes. I won't do it." Elise crossed the room that had become their home. It was still in need of repairs and crawling with rats and cockroaches and other vermin. But they'd worked hard in the evenings to scrub it as clean as they could and had even painted the walls white.

In addition to a bed, Miss Pendleton had found an old chest of drawers for the room. Sophie had displayed her brass candle holder, a kneeling angel holding up a lampstand. It was a gift from Mutti, as Elise's cross ring was. Next to the candle holder sat Marianne's music box with a figurine of a girl tending her geese, another deathbed gift from Mutti. Other than the clothes they wore, these items were all that remained of the life they'd once known, all they had to remind them of the happy family they'd been in the days before Count Eberhardt had ruined it all.

As Elise began to open the door, Sophie spoke firmly but with a hint of apology. "I promise I won't cause any trouble for us. In fact, I have a plan I've been meaning to talk to Miss Pendleton about."

Elise paused.

"You know how Miss Pendleton doesn't like that the women have to leave their children at home alone when they come to work? And you know how she's been trying to find a solution?" Sophie paused as though to ensure she had Elise's full attention. "Well, I'll offer to watch their children for them—for a small fee, of course."

Marianne's hands stilled with a pin only half in her coil. "Can they afford to pay you?"

"I won't charge much."

Elise regarded Sophie for a moment, struck once again by how girlish she looked. But how much of her girlhood had been lost to poverty and despair? At least she and Marianne had memories of happier times to keep them company on the darkest of days.

"We'll talk about it later," Elise finally said. Her workers would be arriving soon, and she liked to make sure all the supplies were ready by the time they sat down to sew.

Elise made her way down the hallway to the steep stairwell.

"Elise, wait," Marianne called after her.

Slowing a little, Elise allowed her sister to catch up.

"I saw Reinhold yesterday," Marianne said over the loud

clattering of their footsteps against the plank stairs. Her sister's words seemed more a guilty confession than a simple sharing of information.

"Where?" Elise came to a halt, and Marianne bumped into her.

"He said he's been searching for us all of these weeks."

At the thought of Reinhold worrying about them, remorse rushed in. She should have tried harder to get him word of their whereabouts. But she supposed that if she was completely honest with herself, she'd been afraid of telling him because she was sure he'd insist again that they get married. She didn't know if she'd be able to resist another proposal.

"I can't see him, Marianne."

"Why? He misses us."

Elise didn't know how to explain her feelings regarding Reinhold. He was a good man. He'd make a fine husband. But she didn't want to marry him because he felt obligated to take care of her. If she married him someday, she wanted it to be because they loved each other. She wanted a marriage like her parents had. Was that too much to ask for now? Could desperate people be so choosy?

Before she could formulate an answer to Marianne's question, loud voices came from the first floor. The commotion was unusual for such an early hour.

Elise hurried down the stairs and hallway toward the original workroom that was already lit. As she drew nearer, she recognized Mrs. Watson's English accent along with Reverend Bedell's. When she entered the room, Mrs. Watson and several other workers were speaking in urgent tones with the reverend. Their faces were pale and somber. If they noticed her, they didn't acknowledge it.

"All the outsiders working for Lewis and Hanford were told

they won't have any sewing this morning either," Mrs. Watson was saying.

"We have nothing to worry about," the reverend said. "Mr. Devlin runs a sound business. Even if some of the other garment manufacturers are having trouble and laying off workers, we'll be just fine."

"But we heard there's a panic at the banks too."

"It will pass." The reverend spoke the words with too much force, as though perhaps he was attempting to convince himself as much as the women.

Only then did Elise notice how wrinkled the reverend's shirt and trousers were, the same garments he'd worn yesterday. Had he slept in them? From the dark circles under his eyes and the way his hair was sticking up in places, Elise suspected he hadn't gotten much slumber, if any.

Something was definitely wrong, but it was clear the reverend was trying not to worry them.

"Then the women should still plan to come to work this morning?" Mrs. Watson asked.

"Yes, of course," Reverend Bedell responded.

Mrs. Watson hesitated, and the women with her wore guarded hope in their expressions.

The reverend waved a hand at the tables that were already filled with the precut shirt pieces they'd received yesterday. "As you can see, we have shirts to sew. You may let everyone know we'll begin work at the usual time."

As the women exited the building to deliver the news to the workers lined up at the door, Elise wavered a moment in the workroom, wishing the reverend would reassure her too. But he turned and fingered one of the cut pieces of cloth, evidently not realizing she was still there.

His shoulders dropped as did his head, as if without the women in the room he couldn't bear the weight of his troubles any longer.

For as much as he'd tried to instill hope into Mrs. Watson, he obviously didn't feel the optimism for himself. If Lewis and Hanford, the city's biggest manufacturer of clothing, had no work for seamstresses, then was it only a matter of time before the economic troubles spread to D. and J. Devlin too?

Elise could only pray it wouldn't be so, that the reverend was right in saying they had nothing to worry about. However, something told her trouble was on the horizon and it would be only a matter of time before it rumbled their way, bringing the worst storms yet.

CHAPTER 7

He was losing the challenge. No matter how hard he tried, he couldn't deny the facts.

Thornton stood at the train depot and surveyed the buildings along Quincy's Main Street. In two months, the construction crew of Irish immigrants he'd hired had built the train depot with its public dining room, a hotel, the livery stable, general store, and a crude tavern. Several other identical buildings stood side by side, waiting for their new business owners to take possession—the tailor, blacksmith, and butcher. Thornton had already connected with each of the men who'd purchased the lots and buildings from him. Any day now he expected the new families to arrive to set up shop.

A Methodist church was half constructed, as were several private residences on North First Avenue. He hoped to have the houses completed within the week so the new families could move right in.

Thornton was pleased he'd had no trouble selling off the platted lots in town. He tried not to feel guilty that he'd succumbed to using the Illinois Central pamphlets, which pictured Illinois as The Garden State of the West, with a snug farmhouse, trees shading it, and well-fed cattle grazing in the foreground next to an enormous fenced-in field of corn.

Although the picture was more of a fairy tale than a reality for the almost treeless stretch of prairie that surrounded Quincy, he'd used the advertisement anyway. After all, the 700-mile-long track that ran through the entire length of Illinois was now the longest single railroad in operation in the United States. The state was bound to prosper eventually.

Like other towns to the north that the railroad had already created, Quincy would serve as a service center for the surrounding farmers, who would benefit from the ease of transporting their crops and livestock to eastern markets. The railroad would profit as well once Thornton sold the town lots and the rest of the area's farmland. Even if Quincy Enterprises had to invest capital initially, in the long run such development would generate a greater demand for passenger and freight services and bring substantial profits.

The only problem was that he still couldn't keep up with Bradford's progress. No matter how many more workers Thornton hired, Bradford always seemed a step ahead.

"What can I do, Hewitt?" Thornton asked, lifting his hat and letting the hot breeze ripple through his hair. The clock was ticking. With August almost over, he had only four months to go.

His young assistant rubbed his hands together as though washing them in the warm air. Behind the rims of his spectacles, Hewitt surveyed each building before coming to rest on the ramshackle wooden structures with dirt floors that stood at the edge of the town and provided shelter to the construction workers, mostly single young men who caused a ruckus every night at the tavern. Even if they were loud and unruly, they were dependable workers. Thornton couldn't complain.

"You need to hire more workers, sir," Hewitt said. "Bradford has twice the number of construction workers you have." Though Hewitt was a year younger than Thornton, he'd done a stellar job surveying and platting the town, and he continued to be an invaluable help to Thornton.

Thornton watched as a group of men raised a beam for the second-story frame of one of the private residences. If he hired more workers, he'd have to find a way to house and feed them. He'd need more supervisors. And he'd have to increase the shipment of lumber coming down from the mills in Chicago.

"You should hire women, sir." Hewitt made a womanly gesture with his hands. "They can cook, clean, wash, and sew. And you don't have to pay them as much as the men."

True. He'd be able to cut some of his costs and perhaps invest the money into building a school. He had told the immigrant farmers he'd have a school for their children this fall, but in reality the school was low on his priority list. Yet if he hired more workers and minimized the amount he had to pay them, then he might just be able to fulfill his promise. Besides, a school would make his town look complete and would definitely impress his father.

A swirl of dust rolled down Main Street, bringing with it a distant train whistle. Far to the north on the horizon, a plume of black rose into the cloudless blue sky. The billowing smoke was a beautiful sight, almost as pretty as the New York skyline at dusk.

Hewitt patted his bowler hat, which already sat as low on his head as it could go. "News is that more businesses in the East are closing their doors every day. Lots of people are losing their jobs. The lucky ones who still have work are forced to take a cut in wages."

Thornton had been in New York two weeks ago, and Wall Street was bedlam. What started with the Ohio Life Insurance and Trust Company suddenly closing its doors had escalated into an all-out panic. Banks and businesses were in an uproar. Westervelt and Company had just defaulted. As one of the city's largest shipbuilders, thousands of workers were laid off as a result. *Putnam's Magazine* had gone under. Cyrus Field's paper business had been suspended.

New York City was a disaster, and most other East Coast cities were following suit. After spending as much time as possible with Rosalind, Thornton had wrapped up business as quickly as possible and then returned to Illinois to get away from all the problems. The recession wasn't impacting Quincy Enterprises too heavily. In fact, the financial crisis seemed to have given his father a boost of energy he hadn't had in months. The last Thornton had seen his father, he was out of bed and on his way to his office. His father thrived on the failures of others, especially by moving in and buying them up.

"Garment workers have been hit especially hard," Hewitt said, dipping his hand up then down as though he were sewing. "You know the women are always the first to be fired."

Thornton's thoughts jumped to the Seventh Street Mission and the twenty-four hours he'd been confined there. It had been almost two months since the Dead Rabbits Riots, which was what most were calling the riots that had started during the Fourth of July celebrations. He hadn't thought of the Seventh Street Mission since then, except with guilt that he hadn't contacted Miss Pendleton regarding her donation request. He'd been too busy.

If the garment manufacturers were going under, what would happen to her workshop? And what about the pretty young woman he'd met there? What would happen to her and her sisters if the workshop closed?

Thornton snipped off the concern for the mission before it could grow. Miss Pendleton was a wealthy woman. If the mission experienced any problems as a result of the recession, she'd figure out something. He couldn't worry about fixing every broken business endeavor in the city or he'd have time for little else.

No, he had to keep his focus on his new town if he had any hope of competing with Bradford. Maybe he wouldn't win the challenge, but at the very least he wanted to show his father he was capable and competent and worthy of his admiration and praise.

"I'll do it, Hewitt." Thornton brushed at the dust on his coat sleeves before spinning and opening the door of the train depot.

"What, sir?" Hewitt hurried to follow him.

"Next time I go east, I'll hire women workers."

"Very good, sir. Very good. I'll check into the newspaper advertisements."

"What kind of advertisements?"

"Placed by eastern aid associations working to relocate the unemployed women."

"Fine," Thornton said with a sweeping glance around the deserted depot. The benches were empty and would remain that way for months to come. Currently he was the only one coming and going from Quincy. Everyone else came to stay.

Even the dining room attached to the depot was empty. He and Hewitt and a couple of the construction crew supervisors were the only ones who ate in the sparsely furnished room. He'd hired his stationmaster, Mr. Gray, to do double duty, managing the depot as well as running the dining room. Mr. Gray's wife did most of the cooking.

Thornton crossed the waiting room to his office, which he'd located at the back of building behind the ticket counter. "Narrow down the best agency," he said over his shoulder to Hewitt. "Get references on the women. Then we'll bring them out and put them to work as soon as we can make the arrangements."

Hewitt saluted. "Will do, sir."

Miss Pendleton's face was paler than usual. Her lips were pressed together as she waited for the women to finish taking their seats at the worktables, which were empty of the usual precut shirt pieces. The women from the workroom across the hall were standing along the walls—Mrs. Watson, Fanny, Dimna, and the others. Their faces were somber, their eyes reflecting fear.

Elise felt Marianne's trembling fingers against her own. Over the past two weeks, they'd counted themselves fortunate to have work when so many others had lost their jobs. Even though they'd had to take a reduction in pay, they were happy to have something when others had nothing.

Only yesterday they'd heard of several riots over food. Without the means to pay for food, people grew hungry, tempers were easily ignited, and panic was only a spark away from combusting.

Elise squeezed Marianne's hand and tried to silently reassure her sister they would be fine. But the part of her that had seen the storm coming knew it was finally here, and there was no escaping the hail and thunder.

"Good morning, everyone," Miss Pendleton said after the

last woman had filed into the room. The September morning was still dark outside. Several lanterns hung from ceiling beams, providing light to the room. The slight coolness of air coming in through the open windows reminded Elise once again that winter would be here before long and with it the brutal cold and snow that would make living on the streets deadly.

"As you know, I've been doing everything I possibly can to negotiate for contracted work." Miss Pendleton's voice wobbled. From behind her, the reverend placed a hand on her shoulder. In the midst of the financial crisis, the couple had decided to postpone their wedding, which was to have taken place at the end of August. Miss Pendleton claimed she couldn't go forward with the joyous occasion when so many were struggling.

"It's with my utmost regret I must inform you this morning that D. and J. Devlin has closed its doors. After searching hard all week, I've failed to find any more manufacturers who are willing or able to contract with us. "

The women were silent. In the distance a church bell rang, signaling the top of the hour, the start of a workday that would not begin after all. Elise suspected that, like her, the others had known it was only a matter of time before they were out of work along with everyone else. No matter how kind Miss Pendleton was, no matter how much she advocated for them, and no matter how much she and the reverend prayed, there simply was no way to prevent the inevitable.

"I want you to know," Miss Pendleton continued in a strained voice, her eyes glassy with unshed tears, "I have loved having you here every day. You have been a joy to know. And during your absence I will miss you all dearly."

Several women around Elise sniffled, and she was surprised to find her eyes stinging with tears. Miss Pendleton had been a true blessing, and she'd never forget her as long as she lived. Elise suspected many of the others felt the same way.

"I also want you to know I will be doing everything possible to find contract work. I won't stop. When I'm able to locate work again, the reverend and I will notify you at once."

The women nodded, but hopelessness radiated from their eyes. They knew as well as Elise that women had a difficult time finding work during good times. But now . . . it would be impossible. For most of these women, returning to prostitution would be the only way to keep their children from starving. Would it be the only way for Elise to provide for her family now too?

She shuddered with such force that Marianne released her hand and wound her arm around Elise, drawing her into a side embrace. Elise leaned into Marianne gratefully but was unable to keep at bay her experience the first day of work at the mission, of the words she'd spoken to the women, of how proud she'd been, of how she'd looked down on them for the lives they'd once led.

Shame filled her. Maybe all these weeks the others had sensed her attitude of superiority. Maybe they'd been right to be offended by her.

"In the meantime, until we can reopen, I want you to come to me for anything you need," Miss Pendleton said, wiping at her eyes. "I will do everything I possibly can to help you survive the difficult days ahead."

Elise had overheard Miss Pendleton speaking with the reverend about the lack of donors to their mission. Although the reverend had visited numerous churches all summer and attempted to raise support, the response had been poor, and Elise suspected Miss Pendleton was providing much of the mission's maintenance out of her own funds. She hadn't been able to make any further improvements on the dormitory. Now it appeared she wouldn't be able to go forward with her plans at all.

The reverend leaned in and whispered in Miss Pendleton's ear. She nodded and then spoke again. "For those who might be able to relocate, please consider applying at the New York Children's Aid Society. They've just set up a special office to place out seamstresses and trade girls in the West."

"They won't accept the likes of us," said one of the women. "They only want women of good character."

"You are of good character," Miss Pendleton said. But whether Miss Pendleton believed in the women or not wouldn't matter to the person doing the hiring.

"They require references," another woman said.

"I'll give a good reference to any woman who needs one."

Elise shook her head along with the others around her. Even if Miss Pendleton was willing to give a reference, which of them could leave family behind to fend for themselves, especially now?

As the women left the room and the mission, some stopped to thank Miss Pendleton, while most left silently with heads bowed in dejection. When the others were gone, Elise rose and followed Marianne.

They stopped in front of Miss Pendleton and the reverend, who were leaning on each other. They'd had such high hopes for the mission. It wasn't fair that their good intentions should come to naught.

"Thank you for all you've done for us," Elise said past a tight throat. "I don't know how we would have survived these past weeks without your kindness."

Miss Pendleton straightened. "Why, Elise, you're not planning to leave the mission, are you?"

Elise glanced at Marianne, whose brown eyes radiated the

same anxiety that filled Elise's. She and Marianne hadn't yet talked about what they might do if the mission closed. Elise hadn't wanted to think about that possibility, as if by ignoring it she could pretend it might not happen.

"Won't you need to close the building?" Elise didn't understand much about the corporate world of loans and big businesses, but surely Miss Pendleton wouldn't be able sustain the building on her charity alone.

Reverend Bedell slipped his arm around Miss Pendleton. "We may not be able to keep the sewing workshops open, but we're determined to continue to have chapel and offer inexpensive meals to our parishioners when we can."

"But without work I can no longer pay the fees for the room and meals."

"You don't have to pay me right now," Miss Pendleton whispered with a glance over her shoulder to make sure the others had gone. "You can continue living here for as long as you need a place to stay."

"Thank you," Elise said. "You're very kind. But we can't live off your charity."

"Have you considered applying to the Children's Aid Society for their placing-out program?" Reverend Bedell spoke softly, his expression earnest with his usual compassion.

"I can't leave everyone behind." Elise didn't want to think about what would become of Marianne, Sophie, and the two young ones if she left.

"If you get a job in the West, then you can send some of your money home to them," the reverend said.

"And if they're living here," Miss Pendleton offered, "I'll be sure to keep watch over them."

Elise stared between the two, the tall burly man and the petite woman who had shepherded them as kindly as parents. Could she really consider leaving her family behind with these two people, even with their assurances?

"Perhaps this will be a chance for you to begin your life somewhere new," the reverend said.

Wasn't that what she'd been wanting? To find a more permanent solution to their situation? She'd known they couldn't stay at the mission forever, that eventually she'd need to find a different job and new home.

Even so, there were so many factors to consider, so many things that could go wrong. She swallowed the sudden lump of fear. "I don't have any money to go west."

"From what I understand, potential employers are expected to pay the traveling fees," the reverend said. "The cost is then taken out of your earnings once you begin working."

Marianne's trembling fingers once again sought hers. When she caught Marianne's eyes, she could see that her sister was as worried as she was. They'd never been away from each other. And the prospect of being separated was terrifying.

"Think about it, Elise," Miss Pendleton said gently, as though sensing her inner turmoil. "You of all the women who've worked at the mission have the greatest chance of gaining employment in the West."

Miss Pendleton didn't have to point out the fact that the placing agencies weren't interested in hiring former prostitutes. They would want the "worthy poor," women of good moral character, without the taint of alcoholism or loose living.

"I don't know." Elise sighed. It was a monumental decision, one she couldn't make without more thought.

Miss Pendleton patted her arm. "Well, whatever you decide, I want you to know you're always welcome here."

Elise thanked the couple again and exited the room with Marianne on her heels. "Are you seriously considering leaving us?" Marianne asked, her loud whisper echoing in the empty passageway.

"How can I not—?"

A tapping against the window in the door drew their attention. There in the growing light of the morning stood a stocky young man. His hat was pulled low over brown hair that curled along the edges. Even within the shadows of his hat, his ruddy complexion and rounded features were unmistakable.

"Reinhold!" Marianne's voice rose with excitement. She let go of Elise and scampered to the door.

Elise approached more slowly. Reinhold had visited several times to see them since Marianne had informed him of their whereabouts, usually in the evenings after he finished work. After his initial relief at seeing them had passed, he'd spent the first ten minutes of his visit scolding Elise for not telling him where she'd been. Elise knew she deserved every word of his reprimand. She should have told him instead of hoping he wouldn't find her and ask her to marry him again.

Even now, the guilt lingered.

"What are you doing here so early?" Marianne asked, pulling Reinhold inside and closing the door behind him.

Only then did Elise see the weariness in his eyes and the hard set of his jaw. She knew before he spoke what he would say.

"I lost my job yesterday."

Marianne's smile fell away just as quickly as it had come. "That can't be. You're so strong and such a hard worker. They need you."

"They don't need anyone," he said bitterly.

Reinhold had been the envy of everyone in their tenement

in Kleindeutschland for his construction job. To be sure, it was hard labor, helping to build the tall tenement buildings, but it was steady work and paid much better than sewing garments.

For several seconds, none of them spoke, the direness of his situation speaking loudly enough. He was the primary wage earner in his family, supporting his mother and five siblings, along with an aunt and two cousins. Without his earnings the family would face a crisis, especially since his mother and aunt had been some of the first to lose their seamstress work.

"I'm sorry, Reinhold," Elise said at last, knowing her words couldn't ease his frustration or make the situation better. Yet he lifted his gaze to hers and he seemed to take comfort from her anyway.

"Mother is talking about taking the two little ones to the orphan asylum."

"No." Marianne's whisper contained all the horror that flooded Elise's heart.

"And then sending the others to the juvenile asylum."

Elise had only briefly considered the orphanage that housed unsupervised and vagrant children. Everyone knew the children there were hardened, some even dangerous, and that it was no place for innocents. Not only that, but such institutions were understaffed, overcrowded, and hardly better than the streets. She shook her head. "Your mother can't do it. You can't let her."

"What choice do I have, Elise?"

"We'll think of something else."

"Already they are hungry. Without my wages, they'll starve. At least at the asylums they'll have something to eat."

"You can't find any other work?"

"No, there's nothing. And there are hundreds—no, thousands—of men just like me who are looking."

Elise's chest constricted. The masses of unemployed would be the same for women, if not worse. She would never be able to find a job in New York City or in the surrounding area. If she wanted to save her family and keep the younger ones from having to go to an asylum or orphanage like Reinhold's siblings, then she would have to get a job in the West. It was the only option she had left.

CHAPTER 8

The long burst of a steam whistle and the squeal of brakes grated on Elise's nerves, causing a shiver to creep up her backbone. She huddled deeper into her threadbare woolen coat, the cool morning temperature reminding her winter was coming and that she was doing the right thing, even though everything within her protested having to leave.

"I'll miss you." Marianne swiped the tears from her flushed cheeks, only to have them replaced with more.

Sophie was dry-eyed, her shoulders rigid and her chin jutting, signs she was trying to remain strong. Olivia and Nicholas clung to the young girl, their eyes haunted with the memory of one abandonment, and their faces etched with the fear of another.

"I promise I'll be back." Elise touched their sandy-brown heads. They didn't respond except to continue to stare up at her. She *was* coming back. They had to believe she wouldn't leave them indefinitely, that she wouldn't do this if there were any other way.

As it was, she was one of the fortunate the Children's Aid Society had added to their placing-out list. She'd gone to the office they'd temporarily established in a building at the corner of Broadway and Amity Streets. She was made to stand in line all day. When she finally had her turn for an interview, she was overheated, thirsty, and wilted. She'd perched on the edge of the chair on the opposite side of the desk from the austere aid worker.

At that moment, her desire for a position in the West was so keen her legs began trembling beneath her skirt. She was afraid the worker would hear her knees knocking together. The worker had read Miss Pendleton's letter, which praised her seamstress skills and attested to her good character. Without it, Elise doubted she would have been accepted.

Now, three days later, standing at the train depot and saying good-bye to her family, she was once again overcome with doubt. What had possessed her to think she wanted to move?

The *ding-ding* of a bell nearby and the laughter of children somewhere down the station platform were too cheerful for the occasion. Another loud whistle sounded, this one coming from the engine a short distance away. Black steam billowed from its chimney, filling the air with the smell of burning coal. A broad-boned woman wearing a severe-looking day suit appeared in a doorway of the passenger car closest to Elise. She didn't step down but instead surveyed the gathering on the platform, the other sniffling and sad-faced women and their families.

Was this woman a placing agent from the Children's Aid Society? The one assigned to accompany them to their new positions and make sure they were properly employed and housed?

Elise's mouth went dry again just thinking about all the changes that awaited her in the days to come. What if things didn't work out the way she hoped? What if she wasn't given seamstress work? What if she arrived and discovered there was no employment whatsoever? What if she ended up stuck in the West with no means to return to her family or tell them what had become of her?

Elise couldn't hold back another shiver, this one more of a shudder in its intensity. She closed her eyes and wished she could pray, wished she could draw confidence in God like Mutti always had. But a wall stood in the way. It had been there for a long time, and Elise wasn't sure how to scale it.

"Ladies, your attention, please!" the hefty woman on the train called in a singsong voice. "Ladies, please!"

The crowd gradually faded to silence as their sights shifted to the woman. She clapped her hands vigorously several times until finally everyone was looking at her.

She straightened her hat, which had tipped to an awkward angle during her clapping. "I am Miss Shaw of the Children's Aid Society. I'm pleased to let you know that I'll be accompanying you during your lovely journey to the wholesome towns and cities of the West where you will begin your desirable new employment and your wonderful new lives." Her tone was much too chirpy, like a little bird happy to see spring.

Did she not realize how difficult this was for all of them?

"Please finish your good-byes with all haste," Miss Shaw continued, "and then form a line to board the train."

A flutter of panic set to flight in Elise's stomach. This was it. She was really going.

Marianne clutched her arm, and her tears flowed unchecked. "Oh, Elise, are we doing the right thing?"

Elise drew Marianne into an embrace and squeezed her. "I hope so. I truly hope so."

Marianne wrapped her arms around Elise as though she wouldn't let go. Her muffled sobs tore at Elise's heart.

A painful ache throbbed in Elise's throat, but she forced it down and pried herself away from Marianne. "Promise you'll do everything you can to take care of the children."

Marianne bobbed her head.

"If I know you and Miss Pendleton are watching over everyone, then I'll be able to go without feeling so terrible about it."

"I promise," Marianne said through a half sob.

Before leaving the mission for the long walk to the train station, Elise had said her good-bye to Miss Pendleton and thanked her for all she'd done for them. The kind woman once again assured Elise she'd watch over the others, that they could stay at the mission for as long as they needed. When she'd said good-bye to Reinhold last night, he promised to watch over her family too.

Another burst from the steam whistle rose in the air like a sharp command, dictating Elise to go. She hugged Nicholas and Olivia before turning to Sophie. Unlike Marianne, Sophie didn't fall into her arms. Instead, the girl's thin body was stiff and her eyes empty. Had she cried one too many tears already in her short life so that she had none left?

"Be a good girl for Marianne," Elise said as she cupped Sophie's cheek. "Obey her in everything."

"She's not Mutti," Sophie said, her lip trembling.

"I know she's not. Neither of us can ever replace Mutti. But we promised Mutti we'd take care of you."

"I'm getting old enough to think for myself," Sophie replied.

Sophie's answers only tightened the knot of anxiety inside Elise. But she wasn't surprised by them since Sophie, already forced to grow up too early, was on the cusp of womanhood.

Elise pressed her cold fingers against Sophie's cheek in one last caress. "Please promise you'll be careful."

Sophie gave a brief nod before hugging Olivia and Nicholas closer.

"Ladies, ladies!" Miss Shaw called out again in her melodic voice. "You must board our train right away or risk being left behind."

Elise reached for the carpetbag near her feet. It was in almost new condition, with a bold blue-and-gold Oriental design. Elise felt entirely out of place carrying a bag so fine. But Miss Pendleton had insisted she have it, claiming she had no need of it herself anymore.

With a final kiss to Marianne's wet cheek, Elise spun away from her family and forced herself to join the line of women boarding the train. Once Miss Shaw confirmed her name was on the list, Elise looked back over her shoulder and caught a last glimpse of Marianne and Sophie. In the crowd, their forlorn faces were all she saw.

The pain in her throat swelled again. She hesitated in the doorway, unsure if she could go through with this and step inside. But the woman behind her released an irritated sigh that propelled Elise onto the train, away from what mattered most to her in the world. Somehow she managed to take halting steps into the passenger car full of women. On either side of the aisle, the benches faced each other so that women were clustered in groups of four. Elise searched for an open spot in one of the groups and swallowed her trepidation.

Most of the women were already settled in, their hats and coats hanging on pegs next to the windows, their bags stowed by their feet or under benches, their eager gazes studying the train's interior. Like her, this was probably the first time most of them had ever ridden on a locomotive.

"Are you going to stand for the duration of the trip?" the

woman behind her said in a testy voice, "or are you planning to take a seat?"

Elise made her way down the aisle, tripping over feet and bags that protruded in her way. As she stumbled toward the rear of the passenger car, one of the faces in the last seat caught her attention. It was a pretty, freckled face hemmed by stray red curls that had escaped the headscarf holding them captive.

Fanny O'Leary. The Irish seamstress who had made her life miserable these past weeks. What was she doing here? How had a woman of her loose living managed to convince the Children's Aid Society to allow her a place on the list?

Fanny happened to glance up at the same moment Elise was looking at her. Something like fear flashed in Fanny's eyes before she lowered her head and stared at her hands folded tightly in her lap. She shrank, as though she were trying to make herself invisible.

What if Fanny had lied to the Children's Aid Society about her past? What if they believed she had an unblemished reputation?

"Please, take your seats, ladies!" Miss Shaw's voice rang through the car. "There should be adequate space for everyone."

Though the spot next to Fanny was empty, Elise moved to the set of benches across the aisle and situated herself beside a young lady who was staring out the window with tears running down her cheeks. On the opposite bench, two hefty women who looked alike enough to be sisters sat chatting quietly to each other. They paused only briefly to nod at Elise as she sat down.

Miss Shaw started giving instructions, pointing to a closet behind Fanny's bench, indicating it was the toilet. Now that Elise was situated, she caught a whiff of the sourness of the closet and realized why the back seats had been the last to fill.

Water for drinking was located in an area behind Elise, and a coal-burning stove was positioned at the front to provide warmth if the night air became too chilly. With all the women packed closely together along with their belongings, Elise doubted they would be anything but overly warm, as she was now. The wooden slats that made up the walls of the train car seemed sturdy enough to keep out the wind and weather.

She shrugged out of her coat, trying not to bump the weeping woman next to her. Suddenly the train lurched, and Elise grabbed the bench to steady herself. Under her feet came a squeal, metal against metal, and a slow churning of wheels.

As the train strained forward, the landscape out the window began to change and Elise felt strangely dizzy. She knew from Reverend Bedell that eventually the train would work its way up to speeds that went faster than a horse. She could hardly imagine what that might be like when already the brick buildings outside were sliding past much too rapidly.

The noise from the engine whistle and the rattling and shaking of their passenger car made speaking to one another difficult—not that Elise wanted to carry on any conversations. Maybe she wasn't grieving as openly as the woman next to her, but she was mourning her losses just the same. The keenest loss of all echoed through her mind and kept rhythm with the churning wheels. She'd failed her sisters again. Failed again. Failed again. Failed again.

⁂

Thornton opened his eyes with a start. The train was no longer moving, and the slow hissing of the boiler and the silence of the pistons told him they'd stopped.

He sat up in his seat and peered out the window. At the sight

103

of the homey, two-story train depot, white with red shutters, he knew they were in Pine Grove.

"Why are we stopping?" he asked the attendant who'd been assigned to his private car.

"Taking on a few more passengers, sir." The young man was attired in a crisp navy suit, polished black leather shoes, and a black derby.

Thornton rubbed his hands across his tired eyes. "Do I have time to get a cup of coffee?"

"Aye, sir. Other passengers have disembarked too."

"Very well." Thornton allowed the attendant to help him back into his suit coat. He stifled a yawn as the man opened the door, allowing the bright noon sun into the train car. The lack of sleep over the past week in New York City had finally caught up with him. Not only had he been busy lining up new workers, but he'd tried to make the most of every opportunity to spend time with Rosalind Beaufort. The late-night parties, dances, and the opera had all taken their toll.

He descended the metal step onto the platform and took a deep breath of the fresh country air. Seeing the quiet and quaint town that surrounded the depot soothed his frayed nerves. As he started for the depot, he realized he was actually relieved to be leaving behind the whirlwind schedule. No, he wasn't relieved to say good-bye to Rosalind. Most definitely not. He would miss her. Or at least he wanted to miss her.

He was simply anxious to return to Quincy, he told himself. Before departing, he'd tasked Du Puy with hiring more construction workers and sending them out as soon as possible. In the meantime, Thornton had taken care of meeting with representatives of the Children's Aid Society's placing-out program. He gave them the specifics of exactly the kind of women he needed. Just yesterday they assured him that ten of the forty women leaving this week were his. In fact, the agent leading the group, Miss Shaw, had introduced herself to him that very morning before they'd left New York and had reassured him he was getting the best of the women.

Swallowing another yawn, he brushed past the other passengers lingering on the platform and entered the depot. The scent of freshly brewed coffee drew him to the scant tables and chairs that comprised the dining room, which was no more than an area of ten feet squared. Even if his town was smaller than Pine Grove, he'd had the foresight to plan for a much larger eating area in anticipation of the people who would one day disembark at his town—at least he hoped they would.

He took a seat at one of the tables and raised a hand to the proprietor. The elderly man came quickly with a coffeepot and cup. Once he had the murky sludge in hand, Thornton sat back, the spindles of the chair uncomfortable against his back. He took a sip of the liquid and almost spit it out. It had a distinctly burnt flavor.

He sighed and was about to raise his hand and call the proprietor over again when a woman entering the depot caught his attention. She had pale blond hair that was braided and coiled at the back of her head, exposing a long elegant neck. From the side, her profile was very pretty, her chin and cheeks and nose strong in a fresh, natural way. When he realized several other male patrons' heads had also turned her direction, a prick of guilt needled him. He shouldn't have eyes for other women, not when he was trying so hard to focus on Rosalind.

Against his will, his eyes returned to the lovely woman. He had the strange feeling he'd seen her before, though he couldn't place where. When she stepped away from door and turned to survey the depot, he had full view of her face and her eyes. Blue eyes, the color of the wide-open prairie sky.

He *had* seen her before. His mind scrambled to remember her name and where he'd met her. At the same moment, her gaze swept the room and came to a halt on his face. Her eyes widened with clear recognition.

Think, think, he admonished himself, even as he smiled at her, pushed back from the table and stood. What was her name?

She returned his smile, albeit tentatively.

He could feel the attention of the other men in the room shift to him, and before he could stop himself, he crossed the room to greet her. "Hi," he said, wondering why he felt so breathless.

"Hello," she said, tucking a wispy strand of her hair behind her ear and watching him, obviously waiting for him to be the first to speak.

"Do you remember me?" he asked stupidly. "I'm Thornton Quincy."

"Yes, I remember you." She cocked her head slightly and quirked one of her brows.

If only he could get her to say her name, then he might be able to place her. "How have you been?"

"Unemployed, but thankfully I have a new job." The word *thankfully* came out sounding like *tankfully*. Ah yes, the German accent.

"And what's your new job?" Was she part of the Children's Aid Society's group traveling on the train? He studied her face, grasping for any hint that might identify her.

"I'm going to California to pan for gold."

A woman? Pan for gold?

Again she waited for him to speak, and this time a glimmer of humor sparked in her eyes that told him she wasn't serious.

Suddenly he remembered when he'd met her. He'd rescued her the day of the Dead Rabbits Riot and had accompanied her back to the mission. During the time he'd been trapped there, she was good company.

But what was her name? Irene? Elaine? Eleanor?

"So have you figured out who I am yet?" she asked.

"I'm slowly piecing it together," he confessed.

"You've forgotten my name, haven't you?"

"I'm ashamed to admit that I have."

"Elise Neumann."

"Elise." Now it came back to him. "I knew it started with an *E*. Can you give me credit for that?"

The door of the depot opened behind them, bringing with it the burst of the train whistle, the signal they'd soon be departing. Around them, passengers began making their way outside.

"Do you need anything before we leave?" Thornton asked with a wave toward the dining room, the tables now littered with empty bowls, spoons, and mugs. "You'll have to get something quickly."

"Miss Shaw gave us an apple and wedge of cheese," she answered, "and now I'm completely satisfied." At the hint of sarcasm in her voice, the memory of his time at the mission came rushing back. He'd genuinely enjoyed spending time with Elise. How could he have forgotten her name?

"Then you *are* with the group of woman from the Children's Aid Society?"

"Yes." She followed the others to the door, and he accompanied her, holding the door wide as she exited into the September sunshine. "They've assured me I'll have a job waiting for me in Illinois."

His pulse gave a strange leap. Was she one of the ten women

headed for his town? "Illinois is not quite California. You won't find any gold to pan there."

Her lips twitched but didn't quite make it up into a smile. At the shadow that darkened her blue eyes, he could see she wasn't exactly thrilled about her new job prospect. She crossed to the passenger car behind his, and as she neared the step he realized he wasn't ready for their conversation to end—not when it had just started, not when he had a dozen questions to ask her. But he had no idea how to delay her so he could talk to her longer.

He did the only thing he could think of. He took hold of her arm.

She halted abruptly and looked down at his fingers encircling her upper arm.

"What happened to the mission?" he asked. Deep inside, he already knew the answer.

"Miss Pendleton did her best to keep it open. We had work longer than most other seamstresses."

He nodded and tried to ignore the remorse that reared up to remind him of how he'd neglected to contact Miss Pendleton about making a donation. "Your sisters and the two infants? How are they?"

Her eyes lost all mirth. "I had to leave them behind."

"I'm sorry." It was the only thing he could think to say, but once the words were out, he wished he hadn't spoken them. They were completely idiotic. *He* was idiotic.

"I guess that's life," she said in a tone edged with bitterness. "During hard times, those of us with the least always lose even more. And those with the most come out on top."

Once again he wasn't sure how to reply except to defend himself. "There are plenty of businesses that have been hit very hard and that have lost everything."

She searched his face, and after a moment her eyes filled with sympathy. "Now it's my turn to apologize."

Did she assume he'd lost everything? That Quincy Enterprises had been hit hard? He fumbled for an answer that wouldn't make him seem like an even bigger idiot. Because the truth was, after some initial instability, the company was doing better than ever.

"I'm doing all right," he mumbled, not really sure he wanted to admit he was doing much more than all right, that he was likely wealthy beyond her wildest imagination. He had a feeling that if she knew he was part owner of the railroad they were riding on along with many others, she probably would never speak to him again.

And he didn't want that to happen. The possibility of having her companionship over the next few days of journeying to Illinois was more than a little appealing.

"All aboard!" a trainman shouted from the engine cab. Behind him on the tender car, a fireman stood on top of a mountain of coal, shoveling it into the fire chamber so the fuel would heat the water inside the boiler. The steam from the boiling water would then press upon cylinders, propelling the locomotive forward. The whole idea that an entire train could run on steam power had always interested him.

Right now, however, his fascination with the locomotive engine paled in comparison with his desire to continue speaking with Elise.

"I need to go," she said, then glanced again at his fingers holding her captive, and then at her passenger car where a few of the other ladies were in the process of boarding.

"Promise you'll allow me to see you at the next stop? We'll go to dinner together." He wished he could ask her to ride with him in his private car, but not only would that be entirely inappropriate, it would also give away his wealthy status, which wasn't something he was ready to do at this point. Maybe if she got to know him better before he said anything, she might be more tolerant of the difference in their situations.

"If I promise," she said with humor lightening the blue of her eyes, "then you'll allow me to return to my seat?"

"Something like that."

"I guess you leave me no choice but to promise."

He smiled and released her. "I'm rather good at twisting arms."

"Perhaps you should consider it for a full-time occupation." She started walking away from him, and when she flashed him a smile over her shoulder, his chest swelled as though she'd handed him an award.

CHAPTER 9

Elise stared out the window at the passing landscape. After almost a full day of riding on the train, she'd finally grown accustomed to the amazing speed. The two sisters sitting across from her had told her the train could go as fast as thirty miles per hour, but usually ran less than that because of curves and inclines and frequent stops to pick up or drop off passengers.

The scenery had fascinated her and kept her occupied for hours. In fact, the view seemed to change every few miles. Rolling hills cultivated with golden harvests would transform into granite cliffs all around her, as though the hill had been blasted wide open to make room for the train track. After passing through the deep-cut rock, they would emerge into a lush river valley studded with trees that gleamed in the sun like jewels of emerald, burgundy, and gold.

Sometimes the train passed through thick forestland that looked untouched by humankind. They'd once crossed a river gorge on a bridge that was high above the rushing waters. She didn't stop gripping the wooden bench until they'd safely reached the other side and were back among the wooded hills. In recent miles, the land had become more level with gently rolling hills—still pretty, but not quite as majestic as earlier.

She shifted her attention to the train compartment, which was stuffy and sour, especially since the passenger next to her had been sick to her stomach on and off throughout the day. While the poor woman managed to empty her stomach in the toilet closet, the bitter odor lingered around her. The stench of the toilet had worsened as the day had progressed too.

The shifting of the sun and lengthening shadows of the trees told Elise that daylight would soon be fading. She was more than ready for another break, a longer one like they'd had at the noon hour. A chance to stretch her legs, to walk around, to breathe the fresh air that was so clean and different from New York City.

Her desire to get out of the train certainly didn't have anything to do with Thornton Quincy or the promise he'd extracted from her to let him see her again. Had he really said that or had she only imagined it?

He was the last person she'd expected to see today. In fact, she'd long forgotten him since their brief time together the night of the rioting. Or at least she'd tried to put him out of her mind. She couldn't deny that for days afterward, she'd saved the dainty blue silk flower he'd given her and hoped he would stop by and see how they were faring. She'd wanted to make sure he'd made it back to wherever he needed to be.

But as the weeks had passed and as the financial situation throughout New York steadily deteriorated, she'd had too many other worries to give Thornton Quincy another thought. Until today.

She'd been so despondent all morning, remembering Marianne's and Sophie's stricken faces and Olivia's and Nicholas's frightened ones. And she'd worried about the hundred and one horrible things that could happen to them while she was away. But then once she'd met Thornton, her wildly careening thoughts and worries had seemed to level out. She wasn't sure why, but she'd been able to regard her predicament more rationally again.

She wasn't leaving her siblings forever. They were safe at the mission, and eventually she'd save enough to send for them. If Illinois was anything like what she'd witnessed today, she couldn't imagine any better place to live.

The squeal of the brakes and screech of the wheels sent a charge through Elise. This was it; they were stopping. She'd get to see Thornton again. If he was still on the train and hadn't disembarked at one of the dozen little towns they'd stopped in. *And* if he'd really meant what he said earlier.

Once the train finally came to a complete stop and the churning and clanging and hissing had died away, leaving the car strangely silent, Miss Shaw clapped vigorously from the front of the car. "My dearest ladies, I know that some of you came prepared with your own food for our lovely trip. But for those of you who did not, you will have time to purchase a hot meal here. The fee will be added to your travel expenses and deducted like everything else from your first earnings."

Elise stifled a grumble at the injustice of her situation. Who knew how long she'd have to work to pay off the ticket and meal expenses accrued on the journey? But what could she do since she'd left the meager remainder of her money with Marianne? She'd wanted Marianne to have something just in case . . .

Standing and stretching, she slid a glance at Fanny, who was looking out the window at the train depot, a much larger building than the one they'd stopped at earlier. Fanny hadn't spoken to her all day, clearly avoiding her. And that was perfectly fine with Elise.

Elise waited behind the others to exit, and when she stepped outside, she tried not to scour the crowd too eagerly for Thornton. When she didn't see his tall frame or his sharp, handsome profile, she released a breath and told herself not to be disappointed. She didn't know the man. He wasn't beholden to her and surely had more important people to see than her. Perhaps he'd only suggested meeting with her to be kind.

Elise followed the stream of passengers toward the train station, an enormous two-story building made of solid brick with a white sign above an arched colonnade that read *Elmira*. Glancing beyond the station, she was surprised to see the train tracks ran directly through the middle of a busy downtown area. Carriages clattered along a street lined with shops and businesses. Pedestrians strolled along sidewalks, businessmen strode briskly, and a vendor on one corner appeared to be selling fresh farm produce.

"There you are" came a cultured voice next to her, followed by a distinctively masculine scent that reminded her of allspice and warm butter. She turned to find Thornton Quincy, wearing a crisp black suit and waistcoat, grinning down at her.

Her stomach did a flip. Before she acknowledged his presence, she quickly composed herself and asked, "Do you remember my name this time?"

"Of course. I've thought of little else all afternoon. Elise." His voice was rich and almost intimate. "I won't forget it ever again. Of that you can be certain."

"That's very noble of you to say," she countered calmly. "But I won't hold you to it."

Without asking permission, he reached for her hand, tucked

it into the crook of his arm, and began to lead her away from the train station. "I know of a restaurant down the street that serves excellent food," he said. "Let's go there."

She didn't protest; she didn't want to. As they rounded the depot, she allowed herself to study him more. She was struck again, as earlier, at the refined taper of his jaw and cheeks, now smooth, the rough stubble he'd worn earlier shaven away. A few strands of dark hair showed beneath his hat and fell haphazardly across his forehead.

As though sensing her perusal, he raised his brows. "Will I do? Am I presentable enough?"

"I'm still debating." Even as she quipped, she focused on a passing wagon pulled by a sturdy team of horses. He was more than presentable, but she certainly couldn't reveal that.

"I'll have you know I spent the past half hour at my grooming so I could impress you."

He needn't have spent any time on his appearance and he still would have impressed her, but she jested in return. "Then I'm afraid I won't impress you in the least since I'm wrinkled, dusty, and smell like soot." Or worse. Like the toilet at the back of the train car.

He laughed and tucked her hand closer as he guided her across the street. Once they were safely on the other side, he slowed his step and leaned toward her. "You could do nothing more to impress me since you have already won me over."

She was at a loss for how to respond. Fortunately, she was spared further embarrassment when he stopped in front of an establishment with an awning above the door with the words *Bennet House* across it.

As he opened the door and ushered her in, at the sight that met her she took a rapid step back. The dining room was much too elegant for a simple woman like her, with silk white cloths on the tables that contrasted with the dark mahogany wood, ornamentally carved and polished to a shine. Fancy white napkins folded into scallops decorated the tables, along with silverware and fresh-cut flowers. Several chandeliers cast a soft glow over the room, which was busy but surprisingly subdued even as servers moved around the tables.

She fumbled for the door handle behind her. "I can't eat here," she whispered to Thornton.

With a laugh, he pulled her away from the door. "Of course you can."

She tugged back. "No, I can't."

"What's wrong?"

"A meal here will cost me a week's wages, if not more," she whispered. When he'd spoken earlier in the day about many businesses losing all they had, she'd assumed he was speaking from personal experience, that perhaps he was like her, branching out to find employment somewhere new. Maybe she'd been mistaken.

His dark brown eyes regarded her for a moment before finally widening with understanding. "Actually, it won't cost you anything because I intend to pay for the meal."

She shook her head. "I can't accept charity."

"This isn't charity, Elise. Can't a man treat a pretty lady to dinner?"

He thought she was pretty? She lowered her gaze to the spotless wooden floor, suddenly unable to think clearly.

"Ah, Mr. Quincy." An older gentleman in an immaculate black suit and bow tie approached Thornton. "It's very nice to see you again."

"Thank you, Mr. Bennet. It's nice to see you too."

Mr. Bennet? The owner of the establishment? Elise tried not to stare at the man.

"Would you like your usual room for the night?" he asked, casting a quick glance at Elise that made her wish she had taken more time to groom. She could have at least restyled her hair.

Thornton shook his head. "No. Just a meal tonight. I only have an hour."

"Very good, sir. Then we shall serve you right away."

Thornton nodded his gratefulness and waved Elise ahead of him, indicating that she should follow Mr. Bennet. The proprietor took them to a more secluded table near the back of the room. Thornton pulled out her chair and waited for her to sit before rounding the table and taking the spot across from her.

She folded her hands in her lap, afraid to touch the tablecloth for fear she'd leave a smudge. She had the strange longing to pick up the silverware and admire the heavy feel of it, or to bury her face in the bouquet of asters at the center of the table. She hadn't seen anything so lovely in years.

But she was sure every eye in the room was upon her, wondering why she was there and accusing her of being an imposter. Before she could say anything to Thornton, a serving man approached him. Thornton spoke to the man in hushed tones before the man nodded and spun away.

"So," Thornton said, leaning back in his chair with an easy smile, "now that I have you all to myself for the next hour, I want to hear all about you." He folded his hands on the table and looked at her with such lusciously dark eyes that she felt for a moment as if he really did care.

"There isn't much more to tell." She wanted to pinch herself to see if she was only dreaming. Was she really in this elegant restaurant, having dinner with this suave and sophisticated man?

"Then start by telling me how you're doing."

"I'm alive."

"Well, that's good to know. I'm glad we have that settled."

She smiled at his wit. She'd never a met a man quite like Thornton, someone who could start a conversation about anything and who could make her smile in spite of the heaviness in her heart.

As they talked, she was surprised at the ease with which she could share with him all that had happened over the two months since she'd last seen him. She was even more surprised at how carefully he listened. By the time their meal arrived, she was finally beginning to feel comfortable, only to have her stomach tie in knots again at the sight of the veal cutlets with a champagne sauce, broiled oysters, and creamy mashed potatoes garnished with parsley.

All the while she ate, she couldn't keep from thinking about Marianne and Sophie and the two little ones and how she could feed her entire family with this one meal. It was too much for just her. But by the time their server placed crystal dishes of lemon custard in front of them, she was embarrassed to realize she'd eaten every morsel.

After they finished their custard, she sat back strangely satisfied in a way she hadn't been in a long time. The conversation with Thornton was actually just as fulfilling as the sumptuous meal, the kind of meal Vater would have made long ago, the kind of meal she'd love to make herself.

"Did dinner pass your high standards?" Thornton asked when he ushered her out into the evening. With the sun dipping behind the tree line on the horizon, a chill had settled over the western New York town.

Elise had neglected to bring her coat from the train, so she held in a shiver. "It was the best food I've eaten in a very long time."

"Me too," he said. "Ever since the chicken and dumplings I had at the mission prepared by the world's greatest cook."

She smiled as she walked next to him. "I see how you operate. With flattery."

"You have me all figured out."

Faint piano music spilled from a tavern down the street, along with the laughter and noises of a public eating room. Even though the street was still milling with people, for a moment Elise felt suspended in time and space with just him. Fiery orange, deep blue, and faint purple painted the sky overhead. A lone star shone amidst the breathtaking sight. She breathed in a deep, contented breath.

"So is it working?" he asked.

"Hmm?"

"The flattery? Is it working its magic on you?"

"What magic would you like it to work?" Once her words were out, she inwardly flushed at how brazen her question might come across.

"I was hoping it would convince you to let me see you again tomorrow." The statement was so soft, it beckoned her to meet his gaze. When she did, her breath caught at the sincerity in his eyes, and something else she couldn't define but that sent a warm shimmer through her.

Before she could formulate an answer, a loud train whistle rose into the air, reminding them they needed to hurry back to the depot.

"Come on." He captured her hand in his.

She didn't have the chance to protest his fingers wrapping around hers as he tugged her along, nor did she want to.

"If we're late, the conductor may decide to make me ride on top of the coal tender as punishment," he said over his shoulder with a wink.

The wink weakened her knees. As she stumbled along after him, she found herself breathless and laughing.

When they reached the platform, it was bustling with stragglers like them rushing to board. She withdrew her hand from his reluctantly, yet knowing she needed to be careful with her conduct. She couldn't give the Children's Aid Society any reason to let her go.

At the step of her passenger car, she found herself suspended slightly above him, looking down on his angular features that radiated self-confidence. She had no doubt he knew how appealing and handsome he was.

"Thank you for dinner," she said.

"Thank you for agreeing to go with me."

She wanted to thank him for helping to make the day slightly more bearable, but instead she turned to go.

"Elise," he called after her.

With one hand on the rail, she glanced behind.

"I'll see you tomorrow?" His expression contained so much hope that she couldn't deny him even if she'd wanted to—which she didn't. She gave him a quick nod before rushing into the car and putting him out of sight.

She hurried down the aisle, realizing she was one of the last to board. As she passed Miss Shaw, she tensed and half expected the woman to grab her arm and demand to know where she'd been. Thankfully, Miss Shaw didn't seem to be paying attention to her. No one was. And after Elise lowered herself onto the hard bench in her spot next to the window, she released a relieved breath. She eased her shoulders back and couldn't keep from smiling at the thought that Thornton wanted to spend time with her again tomorrow.

The train lurched forward, the movement sending her forward enough to see across the aisle, where Fanny O'Leary sat staring at her. For the first time that day, Fanny finally acknowledged Elise was there. Of course, the young Irishwoman was smirking.

Elise's smile fell away, along with all the pleasure from the past hour. No doubt Fanny had seen her with Thornton. From her seat by the window, Fanny had a perfect view of the train depot and a perfect view of her holding hands with Thornton.

Elise's muscles tightened. What would Fanny do with her newfound information? Elise wouldn't put it past the woman to figure out a way to stir up trouble. And trouble was the last thing Elise needed. She couldn't afford to lose her job, this last chance to make something of her pitiful life and finally provide for her sisters.

As much as she'd enjoyed spending time with Thornton today, she couldn't put her job at risk by spending time with him again. What was the point of it anyway? Even if he was kind, sweet, and enjoyable to be with, they had no future beyond a day or two of traveling on the same train.

No. Despite his very handsome face and winsome smile, she simply couldn't take the risk. Although she had promised Thornton she'd see him tomorrow, she realized now it was one promise she would have to break.

CHAPTER 10

Thornton stood near Elise's passenger car and waited for her to come out. The crispness in the early-morning air drove the remnants of sleep from his body and sent a surge of wakefulness through his blood.

He tried to maintain a casual pose. He didn't want to appear overeager, but the thrum of his pulse and the fact that he was attuned to every person descending from her car probably gave him away.

He'd slept even more poorly than usual on the train, not because of the starting and stopping and jostling, but because he couldn't cease thinking about Elise. Her pretty face was a part of his dreams. Her spunky, half-cocked smile. The wideness of her blue eyes. The delicateness of her mouth and nose.

She was unlike any woman he'd ever met, and he'd met quite a few over the years. She treated him like just an average man, like a friend, rather than someone to impress or win over, as so many other women did. Of course, part of that was because he hadn't exactly been forthright about who he was and how much power and wealth belonged to his family. But maybe that was just as well. That way he didn't have to worry about her harboring an ulterior motive for spending time with him.

Was that why he was having a hard time falling in love with Rosalind Beaufort? Because their relationship felt like a business deal, the merging of two wealthy families? His father couldn't fault him for his efforts at attempting to love her. Every time he traveled east, he did everything possible to conjure affection for her. She was a beautiful, poised, and sweet girl in every way, and he honestly did enjoy spending time with her.

But he'd never once felt this broad range of emotions for Rosalind that he did now while waiting for Elise—excitement, thrill, anticipation. The desire to be with her, to talk, to jest. With Rosalind, everything was more formal and polite. But with Elise, he supposed he liked this ability to set aside convention and simply be himself.

He straightened and frowned at the doorway of her car. The flow of women exiting had tapered. Where was she? He surveyed the crowd milling about on the platform. Had he somehow missed her? His muscles tightened at the thought. And he was slightly embarrassed at how much he wanted to be with her. He barely knew her. But what he did know he liked. A lot.

He stared at the compartment. Did he dare go up and peek inside? After only another moment's hesitation, he bounded up the steps, but stopped abruptly when she opened the door.

"Good morning," he said with a smile. "It's a good thing you made an appearance. Otherwise you would have forced me to come inside and drag you out."

She didn't smile. In fact, she was much too sober, almost as if she were disappointed to see him. Even though she was as lovely as usual, her face was pale and revealed dark circles under her eyes.

"Ready for coffee?" he asked, holding out his hand.

"Thornton," she whispered with a nervous glance over her shoulder into the car. "I can't spend time with you."

His smile dropped, and he let his hand fall away. What was she talking about? Had he read her wrong last night? She'd had a good time with him, hadn't she? "I don't understand," he managed to say.

Her gaze darted around the platform. "This new job means everything to me, and I can't jeopardize it." With that, she pushed past him and started down the steps.

He was too stunned to stop her. How would spending time with him jeopardize her job? Obviously she didn't realize he had the power to ensure her employment.

"Elise, wait." He started after her. "You don't have anything to worry about."

"That shows how little you know my situation." She kept walking toward the depot, and he matched his stride with hers.

"No one will take away your job because we have a cup of coffee together."

"I can't risk it."

"I promise. You're perfectly fine."

"No, Thornton, you don't understand." She strode ahead of him. "Now, please, I think it would be best if we didn't speak to each other again."

His heart began to race at the thought of never having another conversation with her. "It wouldn't be best." He grabbed her hand, which forced her to stop.

She glanced around, her eyes filling with panic, and attempted to tug her hand loose. "Please, Thornton."

At the distress in her voice, he released her.

She hurried away, tossing him a glance and a mouthed apology. Then she opened the depot door and slipped inside.

He stared at the place where she'd been and tried to comprehend her rejection. What had he done wrong? If she was worried about losing her employment, then he'd talk with the representative of the Children's Aid Society. Who was it? Miss Shaw? Yes, he'd ask her to check her lists. If Elise wasn't one of the women hired for employment in Quincy, he'd make sure Miss Shaw added her.

In the meantime, if Elise was afraid of being seen with him in public, then he'd have to figure out a way to make their meetings more clandestine. Because one thing was certain—he wasn't giving up seeing her.

ᥱᎧᕟᎧᎀ

"Miss Neumann?"

With a hand on the door of the depot they'd stopped at for their noon break, Elise halted and faced the stranger, a young train worker wearing a crisp uniform. He pushed a folded piece of paper into her hand before spinning and walking away.

Elise stepped out of the way of the door and then opened the paper. It contained the words, *I need to see you again.* There was no signature, but Elise knew the note was from Thornton.

She glanced up to see the same train worker standing near the corner of the depot, watching her. When he cocked his head, she realized he was indicating that she should follow him.

She should ignore him, ignore Thornton, and go her own way. But she folded the note and tucked it into her handbag before casually moving away from the train station door and ambling in the direction of the young man.

It didn't matter that she'd spent all of last night and the morning convincing herself she couldn't see Thornton again. It didn't matter that she'd told herself a hundred or more times since this morning that she'd done the right thing in telling Thornton they couldn't speak to each other again. In one instant, in one little note, in one simple statement he'd undone all her hard work. She couldn't deny the truth any longer. She wanted to see him again.

She followed the train worker at a safe distance as he led her past the depot. She tried to pretend she was merely taking a stroll to exercise her legs after sitting for so long. But when the train worker disappeared behind a shed attached to the depot, she picked up her pace so she wouldn't lose her link to Thornton.

As she rounded the corner, she caught sight of the train worker in the shadows. She approached him cautiously. He didn't say anything to her, but proceeded to hand her another note before slinking away.

She smiled. Thornton was apparently doing his best to keep their meeting a secret. She unfolded the new note. He'd drawn several realistic apple trees with a compass arrow pointing west. Was he asking her to meet him at an apple tree?

Moving back onto the street, she peered west, searching for any kind of fruit. It was a small town, like many they stopped in, with a business area clustered close to the railroad tracks, along with mills, warehouses, and other tall cylindrical storage units.

She walked briskly past the storage bins and buildings, and on the other side she was delighted to see a grove of apple trees. The trees weren't as large as she'd expected, only a little taller than her own five feet five inches. The branches bowed under the weight of ripe apples.

With a sense of wonder, she approached one of the trees and let her fingers skim the smooth fruit. Growing up in Hamburg and then living in New York City, she rarely had the opportunity to see a real fruit tree.

"Did anyone follow you?" came Thornton's hushed voice from the other side of the tree.

She glanced over her shoulder. Two farmers were unloading grain sacks from a wagon on a dock nearby, but other than them, no one else was in sight. "I think we're safe from prying eyes."

"Are you sure?" he whispered.

She couldn't contain a burst of laughter. "You've been so secretive, I don't think even a detective would be able to track us down now."

He stepped around the tree and grinned. Attired in a finely tailored suit, she was reminded, as she had been the previous night when he took her to Bennet House for dinner, of the difference in their social status. He was clearly a man of some means, and if she was planning to spend more time with him, perhaps she ought to do a better job finding out more about him.

"The tenders are being refilled with coal and water, so we have time for a stroll, if you'd be so kind as to join me." Thornton held out a hand.

She looked around again to reassure herself she was safe. Her head told her to say no to a stroll, that she would be better off maintaining her distance from him—really from any man. She needed to keep her priorities straight, and that meant focusing upon her family, not getting herself entangled in a relationship.

"I promise this will be our secret." He stretched his hand

out a bit more. At the warm beckoning in his eyes, she could no more resist the invitation than she could resist breathing deeply of the sweet scent of the orchard. She placed her hand into his and relished the pressure of his fingers encircling hers.

As they meandered among the trees, she didn't make an effort to remove her hand from his. Maybe she didn't need to understand the nature of their relationship or where it was headed. For once, maybe she could simply enjoy the moment and not worry about the future.

He seemed to be leading her in no particular direction, and she didn't mind, especially because he was telling her about the orchard and the kinds of apples growing here.

"Close your eyes," he said, stopping and pulling her back.

"Why?"

"I have a surprise."

"What kind of surprise?"

"If I told you, it wouldn't be a surprise anymore. But of course that's just a wild guess."

She smiled and closed her eyes. "Fine."

He tugged her gently forward. "Keep them closed."

She allowed him to lead her until sunlight splashed across her face, telling her they were no longer in the shaded confines of the orchard.

"Okay." He halted. "You can look now."

Her eyes flew open. A calm pond spread out before them. The water was so clear and glassy that it reflected the maples and ash on the opposite side, their leaves beginning to turn bright yellow and orange.

"It's beautiful," she said.

"Yes, it is. But that's not what I wanted you to look at." He made a point of staring at the ground directly before them.

She looked down. Spread out on a red-checkered tablecloth was a picnic lunch—two plates adorned with napkins and silverware, a platter of cheese, sliced ham, and a loaf of bread, as well as two glasses and a pitcher of what appeared to be apple cider.

Her heart swelled with gladness. When she turned to him and saw the hopefulness in his eyes, she could tell he'd wanted to make her happy.

"Do you like it?" he asked.

"I love it."

"But wait," he said, releasing her hand and reaching for the picnic basket. "There's more."

"This is already perfect enough."

"Not quite." He lifted the covering on the basket to reveal a pie.

She couldn't contain her delight, which elicited another grin from him. He lifted the delectable pastry and held it out to her. The crust was baked golden brown, and sugary juices had bubbled out of the slits on top. "I can't remember the last time I ate pie," she whispered as she breathed in the cinnamon apple scent.

She could feel him studying her reaction. She wasn't the blushing type, but when she glanced up to see the tenderness in his expression, her cheeks flushed. She dipped her finger into the juice, hoping to hide the strange emotions he made her feel. She licked the dollop from her finger and then groaned at the pleasure of the taste.

"How about if we forget about eating sandwiches and just start with the pie?" He placed it on the tablecloth next to the platter of bread and cheese before lowering himself to the ground.

"Start our meal with pie?" She kneeled across from him. "I think that's a brilliant idea."

He cut the pie—or at least attempted to—and served them each enormous, messy helpings. She moaned and sighed through every bite, and he teased her by imitating her noises. Finally, laughing, she swiped her fingers across the plate and licked them until not a drop remained. He coaxed her into taking another small piece, and he helped himself to the rest, until at last they fell back onto the cloth, laughing and completely full without having eaten a bite of their meal.

"If Mutti were alive, she'd scold me for eating my dessert first." Elise smiled and realized for the first time in months she could talk about her mother without feeling a deep ache.

"Every once in a while, we need to break away from convention, don't you think?" He'd crossed his arms behind his head and was staring up at the smattering of clouds, his features serene.

"Perhaps." Breaking away from convention, doing things differently, letting go of old ways of thinking and acting—that might be easy to do today, now, with dessert. But it was nearly impossible with the rest of her life. She was stuck into unbreakable patterns in so many ways. Most people of her class were and had so little hope of change.

"So you're a businessman?" she asked, deciding it was safer to change the subject.

"Something like that." His tone was hesitant, almost cautious.

"What kind of business?"

He didn't respond for a moment, and she pictured him as he'd been in New York City when she first met him. If he'd been affected by the financial crisis, as she assumed, he probably didn't wish to talk about it and she wouldn't press him. Even so, she wanted to know more about him, his past, his family. Although he'd regaled her that night of the riots with tales of him and his twin, she knew little else about him.

"I guess you could say I'm a land developer."

She had no idea what that was or what it entailed. But she didn't want him to think her entirely ignorant, even though she was. "I see. And your parents, your twin brother? Where are they?"

"My mother has been gone for many years, and my father is suffering from pleurisy. The doctors don't expect him to live longer than a year, probably less."

"I'm sorry, Thornton." And she meant it. She rolled onto her side and propped her head against her hand.

"He's a good man but hard to please."

Thornton continued to stare at the sky, his brown eyes full of an emotion she couldn't name. Was it remorse? Sadness? Frustration? Or all of those? She studied the outline of his smooth jaw and chin. He had a suaveness she wasn't accustomed to, along with a purposefulness she'd never found in any of the young men in her German community. Most of the men she knew were simple tradesmen, hardworking, uneducated. She had always guessed someday she'd marry one of those men—a man like her father.

She still would, if she ever had time for marriage. Just because she'd had a couple of meals with Thornton Quincy didn't mean she was planning to marry him. She almost laughed at the absurdity of the thought. No, they were merely friends, companions passing the time together on this long journey west. She shouldn't read more into his kind gestures.

After all, Thornton was not part of her world. That was clear enough. Though they could have some fun together now, this was all they would have, and she'd do best to remember that.

As if sensing her changing mood, Thornton shifted his head and looked at her. Then, to her surprise, he reached across and touched a finger next to her bottom lip. The graze was soft, pleasurable.

"You had a little piece of crust," he said, retracting his hand and pointing to his own lip in the same spot.

"Oh, thank you." Of course, he was just being polite. She quickly swiped at the spot, sat up, and began gathering the leftovers. "I suppose we should start back to the depot."

His fingers wrapped around hers, preventing her from stowing the bread back into the basket. "Wait, Elise."

She stopped.

"You have more pie right here." He pointed to a spot on her shoulder.

When she glanced down to brush it off, there was nothing there except his finger lifting and tapping her nose playfully.

"Got you." His lips cocked up on one side with the beginning of a smile, telling her he was only jesting.

She found a crumb of piecrust on the tablecloth, picked it up, and tossed it at him so that it stuck to his suit coat. "Oh, look. You have pie on you too."

His eyes widened at her audacity.

She couldn't keep from laughing. Before she realized what he was doing, he'd flicked it back at her onto her skirt. They tossed the crumb at each other, laughing and teasing until it had dwindled to nothing. Finally, at the distant blare of the train whistle, he sat back on his heels and grinned at her. "I guess we have to head back. But first, you really do have a crumb here." He pointed at her hair next to her cheek.

"I'm not falling for your trick again," she started, but then stopped suddenly as his fingers grazed her cheek and touched her hair. She sucked in a breath.

His focus for a second was on the so-called crumb as his fingers lightly plucked it from her hair. "There," he whispered. He didn't immediately pull away, but instead met her gaze.

She ducked to hide her strange reaction and began packing the lunch into the basket. This time he helped her. She tried to think of something to say, something witty or sarcastic. But her mind was too busy reliving the sensation of his touch to think of anything else.

When everything was stowed in the basket, they strolled to the edge of the orchard. Before she could step out into the open, he stopped her with a hand on her arm. "Thanks for seeing me again."

She nodded. "Thanks for making this trip bearable."

"I'm glad I could help." His eyes were unexpectedly tender. "I hope you'll allow me to make the trip bearable again tonight."

The prospect of spending time with him was growing more appealing with every occasion they were together.

"Maybe," she said, attempting to sound nonchalant.

"Say yes." His quiet command was threaded with a plea. He pivoted and at the same time propelled her so she was facing him. "Please."

The earnestness in his expression was too hard to resist. Did he truly enjoy spending time with her the same way she did with him? She couldn't understand why anyone—much less a man like him—would be eager to have her company. She was a mouse, and he a lion. What did they possibly have in common?

Whatever the case, she nodded and then broke away. "You can tell me where to meet you and maybe I'll find you."

She dipped under a branch laden with apples and stepped out in the open sunshine. The men unloading their wagon at the mill dock were gone, and no one else was around. As she crossed toward the road, she could feel Thornton's eyes upon her every step, and tingles spread up her spine. She didn't look back, but she knew he watched her until she disappeared from his sight.

CHAPTER 11

The Chicago depot reminded Elise of the one in New York City. Even at the late hour, it was a hive of busyness, with trains of all sorts and sizes coming and going, the ground constantly rumbling, the squealing and clattering of their wheels filling the air.

Miss Shaw had already ushered them off the New York & Erie Railroad and directed them to the place where they boarded their new train, the Illinois Central, which would take them south into the heart of Illinois. Workers were stocking the train with coal and water and other supplies, so they still had a couple of hours before departure.

Some of the women were resting in the passenger car while others had gone to explore the city. Even though the air was laden with rain, Elise strolled across the wide-open area outside the depot, hoping to spot the young train worker who might leave clues for where to find Thornton next. She was trying to squelch a growing desperation that perhaps she might miss seeing him.

Yesterday, after their secret meeting in the apple orchard, he'd planned another trail of clues leading to supper in a secluded room of a local restaurant. She wasn't sure how he'd managed the privacy, but she'd loved every minute of the time together. Today, however, she'd only seen him once when he brought her coffee and pastries. The time had been much too short, the train's whistle blowing before she was ready to leave him.

She would have said her farewells to him earlier if she'd known they were so close to Chicago and she would be required to switch trains. Now she was worried he might be wondering where she was. In such a big depot, maybe even now he was searching in vain for her. Perhaps he would think she'd been thoughtless for leaving without attempting to see him one last time.

A splatter of rain hit the brim of her hat, another her coat sleeve. As the drops began to fall in rapid succession, Elise darted under the wide eaves of the depot. The coming of night and the darkening clouds cast everything in shadows. She moved closer to the brick building as the sky opened up and released its full fury of pelting rain. A chill seemed to blow in with the rain. She huddled deeper into her coat in an attempt to fend off the gloom.

The pounding of the rain upon the roof overhead drowned out the train noise that had been constant during her travels. Only one or two more days of traveling, Miss Shaw had told them in her usual chirpy manner. They would be disembarking at various towns along the Central Illinois Railroad in smaller groups. She'd assured them their employers would be waiting at the depots and that their new lives would be wonderful.

The stoicism on the faces of the other women had told Elise that, like her, they didn't believe Miss Shaw. *Wonderful* wasn't a word they'd ever used to describe their lives. And she doubted it would be now. The most they could hope for was a steady job, a decent paycheck, and enough spare money to send home to the loved ones they'd left behind.

Elise positioned herself so that she could see the depot door, then crossed her arms over her chest and hugged herself for warmth. Maybe by this time tomorrow she'd already be in her new residence. She'd have a new job. The few days of traveling would be far behind her. And so would Thornton.

With a sigh, she watched the depot door as it opened, hoping to see Thornton. Instead a young mother carrying a toddler on one hip and holding the hand of another stepped outside.

"Waiting for me?" A voice near her ear took her by surprise.

She swiveled, unable to contain a swell of relief. "Hi."

"Hi." The smile he laid on her was devastating.

"I had to change trains, and I wasn't sure if I'd see you again before I left."

His eyes lit with mirth. "So you *were* waiting."

"I thought I might hurt your feelings if I left without saying good-bye." She wasn't about to let him know how anxious she'd felt at the thought of never seeing him again.

"As a matter of fact, I would have been horribly hurt if you'd gone on without saying good-bye." His coat was drenched, and water dripped from the brim of his hat. He'd clearly run through the rain. Had he been worried about not having the chance to say good-bye to her too?

"I do have some time before my train leaves," she said, hoping he'd take her hint that perhaps they could spend one last evening together.

He glanced over his shoulder toward a waiting carriage. "I wish I could gallivant about Chicago with you, but alas, I have too much to do."

So this was his home? Now the idyllic, carefree days of traveling were giving way to the demands of real life?

"I understand." She tried to keep the disappointment out of her voice. "Then I guess this is good-bye."

"It doesn't have to be."

"We're going our separate ways," she stated simply.

"Maybe we don't have to." His voice softened.

Did he want to continue their friendship? Did he think they could write to each other or somehow maintain a relationship? She started to shake her head, but before she could formulate an argument, he lifted his hand and touched a finger to her lips to silence her.

Even though the darkness was settling in, he was close enough that she could see the warmth and longing in his eyes. When he leaned in closer, she could smell the wet leather of his coat, along with his unique spicy scent.

As much as she wanted to stay connected to Thornton, she didn't see how that was possible. "Thornton," she whispered against his finger, "I can't—"

He cut her off by removing his finger and swooping down with his mouth. He moved so quickly and decisively she didn't have the chance to react. His lips pressed against hers, his desire evident in each tender move, leaving her breathless with wonder and a rising desire of her own. She hesitated only a moment before melding her lips to his, basking in the heat and taste of his mouth.

She swayed against him and began to raise her arms to hold on to him before her knees buckled beneath her. But in that moment, he just as decisively broke away.

He took a step back and sucked in a breath. "What were you saying?"

She couldn't remember. All she could think about was the kiss, the beauty of it, the sweet pleasure it had uncoiled deep inside.

His lips quirked into a half grin as though he sensed the effect he'd had on her. At a shout from the direction of his waiting carriage, Thornton shifted another step away. "I have to go."

She wouldn't mind having him kiss her again. In fact, she was slightly embarrassed to realize she wanted to be in his arms, breathing him in.

"That wasn't good-bye," he added, and the rumble in his voice sent a strange ripple through her belly.

She didn't know how to reply. So she watched wordlessly as he spun away and sprinted the distance to the carriage. The driver swung open the door, and as Thornton stepped up inside, he glanced in her direction one last time.

She doubted he could see her in the shadows, but even so, she lifted her hand in a good-bye wave. Maybe the kiss hadn't been good-bye for him, but she suddenly realized the chasm that had just opened between them. The truth was they were going separate ways, and he would have a difficult time finding her.

Maybe he didn't really plan to. Maybe this was his unspoken way of breaking things off between them. Confusion and despair crept in and began to crowd out the delight she'd felt only moments ago. "He's only a friend," she whispered to herself.

The instant the words were out, she knew they weren't true. He wasn't *just* a friend like Reinhold. She had to be honest with herself and admit Thornton stirred in her longings she'd never experienced with Reinhold. And the kiss . . . well, even if Reinhold ever did kiss her, she doubted it could compare to Thornton's. She doubted any man's ever would.

"Here I thought ye were an innocent." The woman's voice behind Elise startled her. She spun to find Fanny O'Leary leaning against the brick depot wall a short distance away.

Elise's heart plummeted. How long had Fanny been there? Apparently long enough to see Thornton's kiss.

The woman pushed away from the wall and sauntered toward Elise. Her red hair stood out like a beacon in the fading evening light, tightly wired curls poking out from underneath her headscarf.

Elise steeled herself for the confrontation that had been brewing since the day they'd first met. She might as well get it over with. "Just because you witnessed me kissing someone doesn't give you the right to jump to conclusions about me."

"Is that right?" Fanny settled her hands on her slender hips. She turned up her pert, freckled nose and peered at Elise with keen eyes.

Elise stared back, unwilling to let Fanny intimidate her. "I'll have you know that was the first time I've ever been kissed." Once the words were out, Elise wished she could retract them. It wasn't that she was embarrassed. Rather, she wanted to cherish the moment, to savor her first kiss as long as she could without someone else stomping out everything that was special about it.

Fanny shrugged. "I could tell."

"You could? Oh no!" Elise glanced in the direction where Thornton's carriage had rambled away. If Fanny could tell that was her first kiss, then surely Thornton had been able to as well.

"Don't worry," Fanny said. "He liked it well enough. He'll be back for more as sure as my name is Frances O'Leary."

This time embarrassment came barreling through Elise, and she ducked her head to hide it. "No, he's gone. I probably won't see him ever again."

Fanny snorted. "You'll see him again, that's for sure. Heard him speaking to Miss Shaw about switching yer name to the list of women he's hired."

Elise's head snapped up. "What?"

Fanny's lips curved into a smirk.

"Women he's hired? What do you mean?"

"Ye really are just a babe, aren't ye?" Fanny gave a short laugh.

"I know a lot more than you think." But she didn't know what Fanny was talking about. As a matter of fact, she had absolutely no idea.

"Ye don't know who Thornton Quincy is, do ye now?" Fanny's features lost all humor.

"I met him when he helped at the mission during—"

"And ye don't know who his father is either, do ye?"

Only that the man was dying of pleurisy and Thornton's relationship with him was somewhat strained. Beyond that, Thornton hadn't spoken much of him.

Fanny shook her head. "Ah, lass, yer in for trouble."

"I highly doubt who his father is has any bearing—"

"He's one of the richest men in New York."

Elise's pulse stuttered to a halt. One of the richest men? He couldn't be. Fanny was wrong.

Fanny waved at the trains and railroad tracks beyond the platform, the rain still thundering in a steady downpour. "Miss Shaw said the Quincys own a dozen railroads, if not more. They've been involved in developing the land along their railroads, building towns, that sort of thing."

"No." The word came out a whisper and contained the horror that was expanding with each passing second. "You have Thornton mixed up with someone else."

"He's hired women to come work in one of his new towns in central Illinois."

That would explain why he was on the train and where he was going.

"His father, Wellington Quincy, is a railroad baron," Fanny continued. "That's no secret. His agent hired two o' my brothers to help build the Illinois Central. Not only did he work them to the bone, he didn't pay them what he said he would. Whenever anyone got hurt and couldn't work, his agent fired them faster than a headless chicken and didn't bother to make sure they had enough money to make it back home."

Elise felt sick to her stomach. "Maybe Thornton is different."

Fanny's features contorted into a dark scowl. "He's like all the other fancy gentlemen competing with one another for who can bed the most innocent lasses, making them promises, only to toss them aside the minute they've deflowered them." Unexpected pain and anger flashed in the young woman's eyes.

Was that what had happened to Fanny? Had a handsome, wealthy man paid her attention and compliments? Had he wooed her with picnics and fancy dinners, kissed her sweetly and hinted at promises of being together, all because he wanted to add her to his list of conquests?

Elise shook her head. Surely not Thornton. He was too kind, too sincere, too thoughtful. . . . But what if that had all been an act? What if he'd been trying to win her over so he could have a train-ride fling? After all, what reason did he have for spending time with her? If he was as wealthy as Fanny claimed, then they were worlds apart. What could she offer a man like him? Whatever could a man of his prestige and class see in a poor immigrant woman like her?

Unless Fanny was right . . . unless she was just a dalliance for him, a diversion, a way to pass the time and the miles. Maybe he'd even planned to move from private dining rooms to private hotel rooms.

Her gaze snagged with the young Irishwoman's. As if reading her thoughts, Fanny nodded. "I wasn't going to say anything. I figured it would serve Miss High and Mighty just right if she got hurt by a Quincy. But when ye didn't say anything to Miss Shaw about me—about my real past—I figured I owed ye a favor."

Elise's body went rigid, her feet nailed to the platform, her tongue heavy and dry. How could she have allowed herself to trust someone who'd clearly been well-to-do? Why had she ignored the faint warnings that reminded her of their differences in class? He was a part of the rich, aristocratic echelon she despised, that group who felt they could use up and throw away poor folks like her so long as it benefited their endeavors.

"Thank you," she finally managed.

Fanny shrugged. "Next time he comes around, ye tell him ye'd rather kiss a horse's—"

"There won't be a next time." Elise moved toward the train with determined steps. "I'll go tell Miss Shaw right now to take me off Thornton Quincy's list of hired women."

"I wouldn't do that if I were ye."

"I'll tell her to switch me back to my previous employer."

"She'd just as soon send ye back to New York than cross Mr. Thornton Quincy. The Children's Aid Society needs his donations and employment opportunities. She'll do whatever he asks, even if it requires her to sail to the moon and back."

Elise stopped, close enough to the edge of the platform eave that the mist from the rain blew lightly into her face. Of course, Fanny was right. Besides, if Miss Shaw suspected she'd fraternized with Mr. Thornton, especially that she'd kissed the man, she'd send her right back to New York City without so much as a good-bye.

"Nay, ye just go ahead and take the job," Fanny said, leaning back against the brick wall. "And if he comes around ye again, I can teach ye all I know about making his life miserable."

Elise stared out over the puddles forming in the ruts and between the ties. The pools were murky with the dust and dirt and soot the rain was attempting to clean out of the air. But no matter how much rain came, no matter how much washing happened today, it was only temporary. The soot from the smoke and the swirling dust would coat everything again tomorrow.

Wasn't that true of her life? Even if Thornton wasn't the lecherous, conniving man Fanny made him out to be, there was no changing who each of them was. Maybe they could ignore it for a day or two, but in the end, the dust of her poverty and the direness of her life would coat her again. She couldn't escape it.

She needed to squelch every feeling she'd allowed herself to develop for Thornton. If she had no choice but to work as one of his employees, then she'd have to do her best to avoid him. She dreaded to think what might happen if he got angry at her for not reciprocating his advances. He could fire her and make sure she couldn't find work anywhere else.

"Oh, Elise Neumann, you foolish, foolish girl," she whispered. "Look at the trouble you've gotten yourself in now."

The jostling of the carriage over the poorly paved Chicago streets didn't bother Thornton. The fact that he was thoroughly soaked and sitting in a pool of rainwater didn't bother him either.

All he could think about was Elise. Had he really dared to kiss her? What in the world had he been thinking to do something so impulsive? He released a shaky laugh and removed his dripping hat. He slid his fingers through his damp hair and realized his pulse was still chugging as fast as a locomotive at top speed.

"I didn't intend to kiss her," he whispered. "But wow. I could do that again." He was glad he was alone inside the carriage so that no one could see his silly schoolboy grin.

The carriage bumped over a rut, sending Thornton a good three inches off his seat so that his head grazed the carriage top. If only he could have taken her to dinner again tonight and spent the evening with her. She'd wanted it. He'd seen the disappointment in her pretty blue eyes when he told her he had to work.

He'd been disappointed too. But Hewitt's telegrams waiting for him when he arrived in Chicago had reminded him of his responsibilities, namely that he was still in the challenge with Bradford. If he hoped to have any chance of winning, then he had to push himself harder than he ever had before. Which meant he couldn't ignore Hewitt's notes. The freight load of timber that was supposed to arrive this week had been delayed. The extra beef he'd ordered hadn't been shipped. And there had been a mix-up in the type of windows and doors one of the companies had sent.

Anything that could go wrong while he'd been out east apparently had. Now that he was in Chicago, he had to fix the problems and see that the new orders were filled correctly. In the meantime, he'd instructed Miss Shaw to deliver his employees to Quincy as planned. He'd told Hewitt to meet the women at the train depot and make sure they all connected to their places of employment.

Thornton hadn't been exactly sure what kind of work to assign Elise since he'd already hired a seamstress and didn't need another. But he'd decided it didn't matter. Hewitt would surely find something for her to do.

He rubbed a hand along his jaw and pictured her face the way it had been when she turned to find him there on the platform. Even though he'd been dripping wet, her eyes rounded with delight. He'd hoped it was delight at seeing him. He hadn't read her wrong the past few days, had he? She'd enjoyed being with him. At least she'd seemed to. He couldn't deny he'd loved spending time with her, and he wasn't ready to relinquish her yet.

The carriage rolled to a jerking stop, and he gripped the seat to keep from falling forward. A glance out the window through the growing darkness to the sprawling brick building told him he'd arrived at his first meeting.

The challenge was back on. His days of reprieve were over. He'd do best not to forget it.

He'd do best not to forget Rosalind Beaufort either. The warning jabbed him from the shadowy recesses of his mind, a warning he'd effectively ignored the rest of the trip by telling himself he was merely passing the time with Elise, that she was only a friend.

But he couldn't use that excuse anymore. Friends didn't kiss each other the way he'd kissed her.

The coachman opened the door, and a gust of wind brought a chill that pierced Thornton's wet garments to his bone. If he was intent on falling in love with and marrying Rosalind, why had he allowed himself to spend time with Elise? Although he wasn't officially engaged to Rosalind, he'd made his intentions clear to both her and her parents. He'd already given them the impression he was interested in having a wedding in December.

He shouldn't have entertained any thoughts of Elise, should have cut off any attraction before it'd had the chance to grow. And he most certainly shouldn't have kissed her. Even if Elise was a beautiful woman. Even if she was sharp-witted, easy to talk with, and fun to be around, he couldn't have a future with a woman like her, could he? When his father had given him the challenge to fall in love, he hadn't meant with a homeless, poverty-stricken German immigrant.

No, his father wouldn't approve of a woman like Elise. He'd assume that Elise was a desperate attempt on Thornton's part to win the contest. He'd never believe Thornton could genuinely care for her.

If Thornton wanted any chance of winning the challenge against Bradford and earning his father's approval, he'd have to marry an elegant, refined, wealthy woman like Rosalind. That's all there was to it.

With a new but heavy sense of despondency, Thornton stepped out of the carriage onto the sidewalk. Sharp droplets pelted his face, stinging his skin with a punishment well deserved.

As much as he liked Elise, he wasn't being fair to either Rosalind or Elise. The silly grin from earlier was long gone, replaced with a grimace of shame. He hadn't meant to lead Elise on, but that was what he'd done. Now when he saw her next, he'd have to apologize and make sure she understood they could only be friends—if friendship was even possible with a beautiful woman like her. Maybe he'd fare better if he avoided her altogether.

The coachman slammed the carriage door shut behind him, and at the same time Thornton knew he had to shut the door on Elise Neumann. When he returned to Quincy, he'd make sure she had a good job. A safe one. And he'd see that she was comfortable and happy. But then that was it. He had to put her out of his mind once and for all.

CHAPTER 12

"Tell another story," sweet Olivia clamored, clapping her dainty hands.

"Story! Story!" one-year-old Nicholas repeated, attempting to clap his hands too.

"Now, children," Marianne gently scolded, "I think you've imposed on Isaiah long enough."

From his spot by the chapel window, Isaiah smiled and peered in her direction, his eyes not seeing but perceptive nevertheless. While the usual layer of grayish whiskers still covered his chin and cheeks, after weeks of living at the mission, his face had begun to fill out, losing the gaunt look he'd had when Elise first brought him there.

"I don't mind, Miss Mari," he said, using the nickname he'd devised for her. "It keeps the children occupied and gives me something to do."

Isaiah didn't have to say the words for Marianne to know that being idle was difficult for the once-homeless beggar. He'd apparently worked hard as a steam engine operator before an explosion had left him completely blind. Not only had the

149

blindness taken away his ability to work hard, but it had also stripped him of his independence. Without any family who cared what had become of him, he'd resorted to living on the streets and begging for his food.

Marianne had learned that Isaiah never let anyone do for him something he could do himself, even when he couldn't do it particularly well, even if it put him in danger.

He'd taken to sweeping and scrubbing floors, wiping down tables and benches after meals, laundering clothes and sheets, and countless other tasks. Even if the chores were difficult, he claimed the work was a blessing compared with begging.

"You're very sweet, Isaiah." Marianne moved past the small group toward the front of the chapel and the piano. "But how about if I play a few songs until everyone else arrives." She'd begun playing the piano every opportunity she could, surprised at how much came back to her after so many years. When they lived in Hamburg, her father had plied the church organist with all manner of baked goods in exchange for teaching Marianne to play the antiquated pipe organ. But once they moved to America, she'd no longer had the opportunity . . . until now.

Miss Pendleton, one day after hearing Marianne's feeble attempts at a few chords, had sat down with her and helped her. Every now and then she'd offer an impromptu lesson, but mostly Marianne had improved by trial and error.

She sat down on the bench in front of the piano, letting her fingers caress the keys. Although the instrument was scratched with age, its ivory keys now yellowed and chipped, the music sounded heavenly. She started the melody in the treble clef for "O Worship the King." It was one of three hymns she'd memorized, one Mutti had loved to sing. Whenever she played it, she could almost hear Mutti's voice joining hers. Marianne tried to worship as Mutti had taught them, but sometimes the lyrics caught in her throat and wouldn't come out.

The notes rang through the chapel, which was nothing more than a simple room on the first level of the mission that had been cleaned and painted and now boasted of a dozen trestle benches, a pulpit, and the piano. Even though the women had lost their employment at the mission, they were still coming to chapel once a week. Marianne knew Miss Pendleton and Reverend Bedell were grateful for that and were still doing everything they could to help their former employees, even limited as they were in their resources.

The couple had allowed two of the women along with their children to board at the mission at no charge. Miss Pendleton had also taken up lodging at the mission in order to provide supervision. But the living conditions were sparse, the building still very much in need of improvements.

"Marianne!" Sophie called. One glance to the back of the room silenced Marianne's song and brought her fingers to an abrupt halt. Gripping his hat in his hands and rolling the brim, Reinhold stood with the others.

Wet spots dotted his coat and garment from the sprinkles the dreary September morning had brought, along with cooler temperatures. However, the grayness of the morning evaporated at the sight of him.

"Reinhold." Marianne couldn't contain her giddiness. With a smile, she rose from the bench and started toward him. His brown hair was damp, as though he'd recently had a bath, with the unruly locks now combed into submission. She hadn't seen him since he'd said good-bye to Elise earlier in the week. Marianne had considered walking over to Kleindeutschland later today and searching for him. Now he'd saved her the trouble.

She was tempted to throw herself into his arms—his strong, sturdy arms—yet with Sophie and the children and Isaiah there, she restrained herself. "It's good to see you," she said. "We've missed you." *I've missed you* was what she really meant. But she couldn't say that either, not in front of everyone. "How's your mother doing? And your aunt? They haven't had to take the children to the orphanage, have they?"

Marianne realized she was speaking much too fast. She wished she could be calmer and more reserved like Elise, instead of always wearing her emotions like a cloak for everyone to see.

"No, Mother hasn't sent the children away yet." Reinhold's eyes held none of their usual sparkle.

"What can I do to help?" she asked, although she knew there was nothing she could do. She'd stood in one long line after another all week, searching for employment like everyone else. She'd returned to the mission every evening tired and discouraged. While she missed Elise, as time went on she was becoming more certain Elise had done the right thing by taking a job in the West. There was nothing but suffering here in New York.

Reinhold stared at the misshapen brim of his hat, still twisting it between his fingers. "I'm leaving."

The two softly spoken words punched Marianne in the stomach and knocked the breath from her. "No, you can't leave." But even as the words left her mouth, she reminded herself he had no other option. If he'd stood in the same kinds of employment lines she had, then what other choice did he have?

"Believe me, I don't want to go," he said, his green eyes wide and luscious and much too sad. "But I've found work."

"You have? Where?" Maybe he could marry her and take her along.

"I'm going to Illinois to work on a construction crew."

Illinois was much too far away. Her heart plummeted, but regardless, she infused her voice with enthusiasm and said, "Your experience in construction here must have helped secure the position."

He nodded. "The agent wouldn't have looked at me without it."

She wanted to beg him not to leave. Instead she swallowed the words. "If you're going to Illinois, maybe you'll be near Elise."

"That's what I'm hoping for."

When Elise had signed on for a job through the Children's Aid Society, they'd told her that her group was headed to towns along the Illinois Central, but the agency hadn't given any specifics. Elise had planned to send them her new address once she was settled.

"I'll check in every town along the railroad until I find her." The earnestness in his tone gave pause to Marianne's racing thoughts. Did he miss Elise? Was there more to his taking the job in the West than he was letting on? She shook off the thoughts as quickly as they came. Elise had always insisted she had no feelings for Reinhold beyond friendship. And surely Reinhold's concern for Elise had only to do with the fact that he cared about her like a sister.

"When are you going?"

"Today. My train leaves soon." He turned to Sophie and Olivia and Nicholas. "I came to say good-bye." He ruffled Nicholas's hair and kissed Olivia on the top of her head, then tugged Sophie into a hug. "Be good for Marianne."

Nodding, Sophie pulled back, her cheeks flushed.

Finally, Reinhold reached for her. Marianne couldn't keep from flinging herself into his arms, just the way she'd wanted to do since he'd arrived. He wrapped his thick arms about her in a warm hug. Marianne closed her eyes and relished the feel of him, the solidness of his torso and arms. She breathed in his musky scent and clutched a fistful of his shirt in her hand.

When he started to pull away, she clung to him. "Please, take us with." The words came out before she could stop them.

"I can't," he replied apologetically.

It was unfair of her to ask such a thing. If he had the means to pay for travel, then he'd take his mother and siblings. Even so, she couldn't stop from expressing the heartache that his leaving would bring her. "I'll miss you terribly," she said against his shirt.

"I'll miss you all too." He began to pull away once again, but she hung on even tighter.

"Oh, Reinhold." She squeezed her eyes shut, trying to hold back the tears. But they slipped out anyway, as they usually did.

He pried her loose and set her away from him. "Don't cry, Marianne. Please."

She swiped at her cheeks and gulped back a sob. "When will we see you again?"

"I don't know." His expression was grave. "So long as I have work there, I'll have to stay. I'll send back everything I make to Mother, so that hopefully she won't have to send the younger ones away."

Marianne nodded. He was doing the right thing, even if she hated the idea of being separated from him indefinitely. He had to do everything he could to keep his family together. There were already too many people who were giving their children up to the Children's Aid Society to be placed in homes out west.

The Children's Aid Society had been sending children to rural towns for several years, mostly children who had lost both parents and were truly orphans. Such children were placed with families in the West to work as farmhands or domestics, with the potential of adoption into the families.

Lately, however, Marianne had heard of parents dropping their children off at asylums so they wouldn't have to go hungry or beg on the streets. Now even those children, called "half orphans," were being sent out west as part of the Emigration Plan. While the emigrating women, like Elise, would be gainfully employed and earn money, the children were not typically paid wages.

Marianne supposed most mothers and fathers who had to give up their children during the difficult times weren't worrying about whether their children earned a fair wage. Rather, they were relieved their children were fed and clothed. Many of the homes were temporary shelters, where children would be safe until the parents could find employment and better their situations. Even so, Marianne shuddered at the thought that she'd grow so desperate she'd have to give up her family.

Reinhold finally situated his hat on his head, looked at each of them one last time, and turned to go.

Marianne's pulse lurched with panic. "Reinhold, wait." She went after him, wanting to stop him but fisting her hands at her sides to keep from reaching for him.

With one hand on the door, he glanced back at her.

I love you, she inwardly shouted, while outwardly she managed, "Have a safe trip."

He gave a curt nod, then was gone. She stared at the door, heedless of the tears coursing down her cheeks.

"You should stop crying for him," Sophie said, her voice testy.

Marianne nodded. "I know."

Olivia and Nicholas were huddled against Sophie's sides, looking at Marianne with frightened eyes. Marianne brushed her cheeks again and forced a smile. She didn't want the little ones to see her crying. It only worried them, and they certainly didn't need any more trouble just now. "I'm just fine. See?" She widened her smile.

Sophie's thin eyebrows narrowed above much-too-perceptive eyes. "He loves Elise."

Marianne's smile wobbled. "No. They're just friends. Elise told me that numerous times."

"*She* might not care about him, but everyone except you can tell *he* loves Elise."

"That's not true."

"Even Isaiah can see Reinhold loves Elise," Sophie insisted.

Isaiah rolled his shoulders back and lifted his hands as though attempting to defend himself from an attack. "Oh no, miss. I don't see anything."

"Thank you, Isaiah," Marianne replied, even though something about his too-quick answer pricked her.

"Think what you will," Sophie retorted, squeezing her charges into side hugs. "But he'll marry Elise the first chance he has."

Marianne tried not to let Sophie's declaration send her into panic mode. Yet she couldn't stop from looking at the door and wondering if she should run after Reinhold and beg him to marry her today, now, before he left for Illinois.

She took a deep breath and told herself not to do anything rash. After all, he'd already told her he couldn't take her along. In the meantime, once she discovered his address, she'd write to him. Maybe then she'd work up the courage to finally tell him how she really felt.

"We're here!" Miss Shaw called out in her cheerful manner, her portly cheeks rounded in a grin.

Tell us something we don't know, Elise inwardly groused as the high-pitched squeal of wheels and brakes signaled the stop—the final stop—in the almost weeklong train journey.

Since the last town ten miles ago, Elise's gaze hadn't strayed from the window, though the landscape had all been the same—barren, treeless field after barren, treeless field. Occasionally she'd spotted a distant curl of smoke coming from what appeared to be a farmhouse. Every once in a while she also spotted a cluster of trees. But never had she seen anything so wide open and empty as central Illinois. In some ways it reminded her of the ocean, except here, instead of water, waves of long prairie grass spread out to the horizon.

Now the land began to give way to the sparse shell of a town. Two storage bins stood near the tracks next to a warehouse of some kind. As the train slowed to a crawl, a depot came into sight with a sign on the second story of the building that read *Quincy*.

Quincy. Thornton Quincy.

How could she have been so foolish not to realize who he was and all he stood for? She wasn't exactly on a first-name basis with New York City's millionaires, nor did she keep tabs on the names of railroad barons. Still, she should have guessed much earlier that he was no ordinary man. His refined mannerisms, his well-tailored clothes, the confidence with which he carried himself as if untouched by life's hardships, the way various restaurant owners reacted in his presence. Those should all have been clues.

Perhaps she'd wanted to remain in denial, to pretend however briefly that she could experience a small measure of joy amidst the tragedies that defined her. It wasn't like she was searching for a fairy tale. She wasn't naïve enough to think her life could ever have a storybook ending. Nevertheless, she had to admit, the few days spent with Thornton had been like a page from one of Marianne's stories.

"Ladies, your attention, please." Miss Shaw stood and gripped the bench as the train inched forward in jerking motions that made her wobble like a ball of yarn in a basket. "Make yourselves as presentable as possible so you can give a good first impression to your new employers."

Across the row, Fanny snorted. Although Elise hadn't spoken to Fanny again since their encounter at the train depot in Chicago two days ago, she'd sensed a truce between them. She'd kept Fanny's secret about her sordid past, and the woman had done her a favor in revealing Thornton's identity. Now they were even and had no need for petty fighting. At least Elise hoped so.

Elise hadn't expected to end up in the same town as Fanny. But after Thornton's meddling, it appeared they were to be together, at least in some fashion. And Elise couldn't deny there was comfort in knowing one person in the new town.

Make a good impression. Miss Shaw's instructions penetrated Elise's weary mind. Sleeping on the hard train benches hadn't been easy and neither had daily grooming. She felt almost as wrinkled and dirty as she had when she'd been homeless and lived on the streets. How in the world would they be able to impress their new employers in rumpled clothes they'd worn all week, which now reeked of sweat and coal dust?

Elise was tempted to imitate Fanny's snort.

"After we leave the train," Miss Shaw said cheerfully, "some of your employers will take you to live with them in their places of residence. Others of you will board at the hotel."

Elise still had no idea what kind of employment she would

have. She'd expected to do seamstress work. But surely a town of—she glanced out the window to the sparse scattering of businesses and homes—ten people didn't need two seamstresses.

Maybe there were more than ten. Regardless, this tiny town in the middle of nowhere wouldn't provide both her and Fanny with enough sewing to keep them busy.

Why had Thornton interfered? If he'd left things the way they were, she would have been at her new job hours ago, or maybe even yesterday. As it was, Quincy was the last stop. There were eleven women left. Unfortunately, she was one of them.

Elise hadn't seen Thornton since he'd kissed her in Chicago. At first, she'd hidden away and avoided him. But after two days with no sign of him, she guessed he wasn't on the same train anymore, that he likely had other towns and businesses demanding his attention. As far as she was concerned, if she didn't have to see him again, all the better.

When the train came to a halt, Miss Shaw descended to the platform. She spoke to a young man in a gray suit and white hat, who didn't look a day older than sixteen. He wore spectacles, but his face was boyish and without a mustache or beard that might have made him look more mature. He waved his hands around, motioning here and there, almost as if he was using sign language.

Miss Shaw bustled back to the train and climbed into their passenger car. With cheeks flushed from the exertion, she studied her list and then rattled off the names of five of the women. "Come with me," she said, "and I'll assist all of you wonderful ladies to your wonderful new jobs."

As the women rose, Miss Shaw clapped her hands together in

her usual exuberance. "This is so exciting, isn't it? I'm just thrilled to see the last of my little flock all safely to green pastures."

Fanny released a soft groan that echoed the one trapped in Elise's chest. If they'd been friends, Elise may have even rolled her eyes and shared a smile with Fanny. However, Elise hadn't ever had many friends besides Reinhold.

From the window, Elise watched Miss Shaw lead the other women across the platform and into the depot. The minutes seemed as long as hours, until finally Miss Shaw reappeared and hurried back to the train.

She was puffing for breath when she stood before them and waved for them to accompany her. "Your turn, dear women." As she ushered them down to the platform, she smiled again. "What fun this is. Oh, what fun!"

Elise fell to the back of the line behind Fanny and filed into the depot, noticing it was designed much like the other depots she'd visited during the journey. Yet unlike the other well-used buildings, the crisp scent of new pine boards greeted them, along with the smell of fresh paint. Everything about the interior, from the wooden benches in the waiting room to the ticket counter, was clean and without any scratches. Even the hardwood floor was spotless, without the wear that had characterized the other depots.

It was clear that here in Illinois, particularly in the past couple of towns, the area was still being developed. Perhaps that was what Thornton had meant when he'd said he was a land developer. Maybe he had a hand in helping the towns take shape and grow.

"Ladies," Miss Shaw said, motioning for them to stop in the middle of the waiting area, "I know you're all so excited, but let's be patient for just a moment longer." In a small room behind the ticket office, the young man in the gray suit was speaking with what appeared to be the stationmaster. The young man's hands were once again flying in the air as he talked.

Across the other side of the depot, in a separate room, was a dining area of modest size. At the moment it was empty, without a cup or plate in sight. Perhaps the restaurant didn't see much business. After all, Quincy was on the edge of civilization, about as far away from the rest of the world as one could get. The depot wasn't likely a busy place for people coming or going and so probably didn't even need a restaurant.

"I'm Mr. Hewitt," said the young man in the gray suit as he strode toward their group, his shoes tapping forcefully against the floor. "I'll be employing you to work on behalf of Mr. Quincy."

He halted next to Miss Shaw, who beamed at him as though he were God himself in the flesh. Mr. Hewitt peered over the rim of his glasses at them, his head bobbing as he counted. Then he peered down at the notepad he held in his hand and made a circular motion with his free hand. "I need two laundresses."

Miss Shaw in turn glanced at her list. "That would be dear Miss Engle and dear Miss Engle."

The two hefty sisters who had sat across from Elise during the early part of the journey stepped forward, and Mr. Hewitt nodded at them curtly. Elise certainly didn't envy the sisters. Laundering was backbreaking work.

"I also need two women to assist our construction crew cook." His hand began swirling in the air as though stirring a spoon in a pot.

Elise was tempted to lay claim to one of the positions. Such a job would entail long hours and be filled with paring and chopping food, as well as hauling fuel and washing dishes. Yet it would afford her the chance to work in a kitchen again.

At Miss Shaw's introduction, two of the other women stepped forward.

"Finally, I need one seamstress." Mr. Hewitt's hand took on the up-and-down motion of someone weaving a needle into a garment.

"Our lovely seamstress is Fanny O'Leary," Miss Shaw said, her chest puffing out in obvious pride of her charges.

When Fanny nodded her head at Mr. Hewitt, he barely gave her a cursory glance.

"That ought to do it." Mr. Hewitt studied his list. "If you'll follow me—"

"Excuse me, Mr. Hewitt," Miss Shaw said, her dimples losing their depth. "I have one more worker Mr. Quincy himself personally asked me to add to his list."

At Miss Shaw's words, Elise wanted to run back to the train and crawl under one of the benches. She could feel the other women cast her sidelong glances, their eyes full of questions, wondering what talent she had that would capture the attention of Mr. Quincy. She was ashamed to admit he wanted her on his list for no other reason than that she was his railroad romance. Maybe he'd even brought her to Quincy expecting to have a mistress here.

The thought sickened her. She squirmed under the scrutiny, praying the others weren't drawing the worst conclusion about her.

"This is our beautiful Miss Neuman," Miss Shaw said, her smile returning with all its radiance. "Mr. Quincy was adamant about having her join the ranks of his employment."

Mr. Hewitt peered at Elise. Through the rounds of his eyeglasses, his eyes appeared especially large. He frowned, which caused the spectacles to slide down his nose. "Mr. Quincy never made any mention of an eleventh worker to me."

"Well, he certainly made a fuss with me," Miss Shaw replied. "He was absolutely insistent."

Inwardly Elise groaned. If only the ground would open up and swallow her.

Mr. Hewitt regarded Elise again, his eyes narrowing. She had to look away lest he read the truth about her relationship with Thornton. "Did he mention where he wanted her to work?"

"She's a seamstress by trade."

"I don't need another seamstress."

"Well, I'm sure you can find something for her to do until Mr. Quincy arrives."

Mr. Hewitt paged through his notebook, scanning the rows of scribbled notes. "No. Not at the moment. Maybe it's best to take her back with you."

Elise wasn't sure whether to feel relief or panic. If she left then, she'd be spared a difficult encounter with Thornton. But if she went back with Miss Shaw, she'd have no guarantee of finding employment elsewhere. What if she ended up having to return to New York City without a job?

Miss Shaw shook her head so vigorously her jowls flapped. "I cannot take her back. I dare not contradict a man like Mr. Quincy."

Fanny had been right. Miss Shaw was afraid of saying no to Thornton Quincy. He apparently held enough power either to hurt or help her cause and the Children's Aid Society. Wasn't that so like the rich, to think they could maneuver ordinary folks around like checkers on a playing board without thought of who they knocked out of the way in their efforts to become kings?

"Surely she can join the work of some of the other women until Mr. Quincy arrives and gives you the specifics of his intentions for Miss Neuman?"

His intentions. Elise cringed.

Mr. Hewitt released an exasperated breath. "Very well, she can join the laundresses for now. And if there's an excess in sewing work, she can assist the seamstress."

Laundering clothes. Delightful. It was exactly what Elise had always dreamed of doing. As much as she wanted to protest, she knew she couldn't. After all, beggars couldn't be choosers. And she was definitely a beggar.

CHAPTER 13

Sweat dripped from Elise's overheated face. It plopped into the steaming trough like raindrops. She'd long past stopped trying to wipe her forehead and face.

"Swirl that dolly harder," barked Agnes Engle, who was at the other trough pounding and rotating her dolly against the linen as if she'd been born doing the task.

After almost a week of laundering, Elise's muscles screamed. With a grunt she attempted to obey Agnes's instructions, but her arms couldn't move faster or beat more vigorously even if someone had whipped her back.

Beatrice Engle was wringing out the linens that had already been dollied. Elise was impressed with how steadily the woman worked, wringing and rinsing and wringing once more before placing the linens into an enormous copper pot filled with boiling soapy water. Once in the pot, she let the laundry simmer for half an hour before removing and rinsing at least once if not two more times.

The Engle sisters had been disgusted with Elise's ability to assist them. And rightly so. With their shirtsleeves rolled up past their elbows, the women's arms were double the size of Elise's. With her spindly arms, she felt like a newborn calf next to mother cows. Their stature and strength allowed them to tackle each part of the process with an ease Elise couldn't muster no matter how hard she tried.

Not only were they muscular, but they also had years of experience in commercial laundries in New York City. Elise hadn't laundered clothes before, except for the simple washing of her family's garments.

Now she'd been working since four o'clock in the morning and still piles of clothes and sheets awaited their attention. In fact, the mounds were never-ending, apparently the accumulation of a month's worth of laundry from every single construction worker in Quincy.

And maybe every resident and rodent in the surrounding hundred-mile vicinity.

The Engle sisters worked nonstop, breaking only for a brief breakfast and lunch. Elise labored with them each day until six or seven in the evening, before heading back to the depot restaurant for a meal and then returning to their dormer room on the third floor of the hotel.

The unheated room contained five single cots, enough for the workers Thornton had originally hired. The sleeping quarters were cramped, the women's belongings stuffed into every nook and cranny. Elise had resorted to rolling out her blankets on the floor. She couldn't deny she was jealous of the other women, though she knew she shouldn't be since sleeping on the floor wasn't anything new. After all, she hadn't slept in a bed in years, not since Vater died and they'd moved in with Uncle Hermann.

The truth was she'd been too tired to care where she slept.

After the long days of doing laundry, she'd hardly been able to stay awake to eat her supper. She'd fallen asleep the moment she sprawled out on the floor.

Although she'd heard that Thornton arrived in Quincy two days ago, she hadn't seen him yet and certainly wasn't seeking him out. An encounter with him would only raise the eyebrows of the other women. While none of them had questioned her about Thornton, she had no doubt their speculations about why Thornton hired her would be less than pleasant.

She planned to avoid him for as long as possible. Yet in a town smaller than a New York City tavern, certainly she would see him again eventually. Unless he was avoiding her too. She didn't know why that thought bothered her. She should be relieved. But after the way he'd sought her out and flattered her on their trip, she didn't understand how he could so easily dismiss her from his mind.

Maybe she hoped he wasn't the kind of man Fanny had painted him to be. Maybe she hoped she was a better judge of character than Fanny had given her credit for. Maybe deep down she hoped he truly liked her for who she was and not for what he could gain from her.

"Good afternoon, ladies." Mr. Hewitt spoke from the doorway.

At the sound, Agnes stiffened and plunged her dolly into the trough more vigorously, while Elise ceased her struggle to beat the linens and leaned against the handle of the dolly. Blessed relief.

"I see you're hard at work." Mr. Hewitt came at least once a day to check on their progress, inspecting everything they were doing and jotting notes on his pad.

Neither of the Engle sisters responded but instead focused

on their work as if he weren't there. Elise wasn't sure if they were trying to prove what hard workers they were or if they resented his scrutiny.

Elise was too weary to care what Mr. Hewitt thought of her. In some ways, she hoped he'd see she wasn't suited to laundering and assign her something else to do. Maybe he'd let her help Fanny with the sewing. Fanny was working with the tailor and his family, sewing from early morning until dusk with hardly a break in between. While the long hours and toil weren't anything new, the tailor was difficult to please, according to Fanny, who complained about him every evening once they were back in the dormer room. Just last night, she'd come to dinner with a bruise under her eye from where he'd hit her after she failed to make her stitches small enough.

"Although today is payday," Mr. Hewitt said, glancing down into one of the bubbling copper pots, "I deducted from your unpaid traveling expenses and so I won't be giving you money. If you need to purchase anything, you may add it to the tab at the general store, and it too will be deducted from future payments."

"How much did we earn this week?" Elise asked. The first day they arrived, no one had questioned Mr. Hewitt about the amount of their pay. Miss Shaw hadn't made any indication either. Elise supposed the other workers felt the same as she did, that they were grateful for the employment, no matter the wages.

But now, after a week of hard labor, Elise wasn't so sure she was grateful.

Mr. Hewitt stepped away from the steaming pot with fogged spectacles. He removed them and began wiping the lenses with the edge of his vest.

Elise peeled a strand of hair from her forehead and smoothed it back with the rest of her damp hair. "Would you be so kind as to tell us our traveling expenses as well as our weekly earnings?"

"I am keeping individual tabs for each of your accounts back in the office," he replied as he wiped at his spectacles. "Not only of your traveling expenses, but also for your weekly room and board. So if you'd like to see your totals, you'll need to come to the office. "

Elise dreaded to see the amount of debt she'd accumulated. Miss Shaw had indicated that the cost of the train ticket had been $15.20—a slight reduction in the normal fare—but that hadn't included any of the meals during the journey. "Very well. But surely you can tell us how much we're earning."

Mr. Hewitt replaced his circular spectacles onto his nose, peered through them, then removed them and began wiping again. "We are paying each of you one dollar and fifty cents per week, which works out to exactly one dollar after deducting the cost of your room and board."

"Only one dollar a week?" Elise knew she shouldn't feel shocked or angry. The Engle sisters didn't blink or even pause in their steady labor at the pronouncement. But Elise felt a rush of frustration at the realization her painful efforts from before dawn until after dusk would only earn her one dollar a week.

"It's a very fair wage for a woman." Mr. Hewitt held up his glasses and examined them. "I'm quite certain you wouldn't make anything close to one dollar and fifty cents a week if you'd remained in New York City."

His words cut off any reply she could make. She wouldn't have been making anything if she'd stayed in the city. She was lucky to have any work at all. On the other hand, such intense labor as laundering surely deserved more compensation than one dollar and fifty cents a week. Didn't it?

When she'd worked in the tenement as a seamstress, she made one dollar and sixty cents per week, only ten cents more than now. But she was certainly working more hours here. And it was harder work.

Besides, at a dollar a week, she'd earn just four dollars a month. At that rate, she wouldn't be able to pay off her traveling expenses for four months, if not longer. Four months of beating laundry with nothing to show for it. Four months of not being able to send any money back home to Marianne and Sophie. With such low wages, it would take years to save enough to purchase train tickets for them to join her in Quincy.

She swallowed the bitterness that rose in her throat. So much for her dream of finding a better life in the West, of starting over, of perhaps even making a new home for her family and fulfilling her promise to Mutti to take care of Sophie and Marianne, as well as provide for Olivia and Nicholas. With the way things were going, all she'd managed to do was place thousands of miles between them with no hope of being reunited.

But then what did she expect? Hadn't Fanny warned her how the Quincys treated the railroad workers they hired? What made her think they'd be different toward anyone else they employed, especially women? She'd never understood why women were paid less than men. When she worked in the sweatshop sewing vests, she'd resented the fact that she could often work faster and more meticulously than some of the men, yet they were paid nearly double her wages.

Mr. Hewitt finally replaced his spectacles and waved his hand at the dolly she was still resting against. "Miss Neumann, since you apparently like to dally at your work, perhaps I should consider reducing your wages."

Reduce them? He wouldn't dare. Her ire was already stirred. His threat only whipped it into a froth. "Why, Mr. Hewitt, I thought a good Northerner like yourself and the Quincys would certainly be abolitionists." Although Elise wasn't well-educated on the slavery debate, recently everyone was talking about the skirmishes in Kansas between those who opposed slavery and those who were for it.

"Of course, we're abolitionists." Mr. Hewitt looked at her warily. "The Quincys have never owned slaves and never will."

"Is that really true, Mr. Hewitt?"

He puffed out his chest. "It is most certainly true."

"With the long hours, low wages, and difficult work, we women might as well be your slaves."

The room became so silent that Elise could hear the distant hammering of the construction workers above the bubbling of the soapy water in the copper pots. The Engle sisters had halted their work and were staring at Elise with wide eyes.

Mr. Hewitt's boyish expression turned sullen. "Well, Miss Neumann, if you think you're being treated like a slave, then I have the perfect solution for you."

"I'm sure you do."

"You may pack your bag and leave on the next train." He made folding motions with his hand that would have made her smirk under normal circumstances. But the reality of what she'd just done hit her with the force of a steam whistle blowing its top.

She'd just gotten herself fired.

Thornton knew he was being a coward, hiding away in his office whenever the newly hired women employees came around the depot. But he wasn't ready to face Elise yet. He didn't know if he was strong enough to tell her the truth, that they could only be friends. He was afraid if he saw her, he might do something stupid, like pull her into his arms and kiss her again, which would only complicate the situation even more.

Besides, he didn't want to see the hurt and disappointment on her face when he apologized for leading her on. She was sure to be heartbroken. And it would all be his fault. He should have been more careful during the train ride to keep an appropriate distance from her, instead of leading her to believe there could be more between them.

He stared at the open ledger in front of him and flapped his pencil back and forth. His windowless office was stuffy and dark and depressing. The flickering light of the oil lamp on the cloudy day didn't cheer him. Neither had Hewitt's news that Quincy now had more construction projects than Bradford's town of Wellington to the north.

Instead he shoved away from his desk and stood, stretching his arms toward the ceiling and holding in a yawn. He'd stayed up too late reading one of the books he'd purchased when he was back in New York City. This one was a first edition of *Institutes of Christian Religion* by John Calvin, an excellent addition to his rare-book collection.

"Time for another cup of coffee," he mumbled and reached for the mug on his desk. The black liquid at the bottom was thick with coffee grounds.

If only Mrs. Gray could make a pot of coffee worthy of being called by the name. What was it about train depot coffee, any-way? In all his stops, he couldn't think of one place that actually had decent coffee. Did the stationmasters have a conspiracy to make travelers' lives miserable? Maybe they were having a contest among themselves to see which depot could serve the worst coffee?

He ambled out of his office, nodded at Mr. Gray. Tall and thin, with a smattering of gray in his beard and mustache, the stationmaster was writing in the ledgers spread out before him, keeping meticulous notes of the number of passengers, wagons, income, and a myriad of other details. With Mr. Gray's years of experience running stations in rural New York, Thornton was grateful he'd been willing to transfer to Quincy so quickly.

Thornton moved past the ticket counter into the deserted waiting room. Only the room wasn't deserted. A lone woman sat on one of the benches with a bag at her feet. In contrast to the scuffed leather of her worn boots, the bright blue and gold of her fancy bag seemed out of place.

When his gaze traveled up to the woman's profile, to the pert nose and chin, his heart gave an extra beat. "Elise?" Her name fell out before he could stop it.

She turned abruptly, causing her long hair to swish. He'd never seen her with her hair outside of a coiled braid. Now it fell in thick waves over her shoulders and down her back. The damp blond was a shade darker as though she'd recently washed it, and it was simply breathtaking. When her blue eyes connected with his, he couldn't speak past the tightness in his lungs.

Although he'd tried over the past days not to feel anything for her, all at once his longing for her came rushing back like a wave that couldn't be contained. In person, she was so vibrant and fresh and beautiful and alive, he wanted to be with her. Just the sight of her made him forget every objection he'd had to spending time with her.

"Hi," he said, not caring that he was grinning like a young boy experiencing his first crush. "How are you?"

She didn't return his smile. In fact, her eyes narrowed and her nostrils flared before she lifted her chin and looked away from him. "I'm doing splendidly."

Her words were icy. And he caught the hint of sarcasm in her pronunciation of the word *splendidly*. His grin faltered. He followed her gaze to the clock behind the ticket counter. It was only three o'clock in the afternoon. Shouldn't she be working? "What are you doing here at the depot?"

"Oh, I'm sitting here because I haven't had the chance yet to test out the benches."

He arched a brow. "And do they meet your specifications?"

"I don't know. I'll have to sit here for at least two more hours before I'll be able to tell."

His attention returned to the clock. If the Chicago-bound train coming north was on time today, that meant it would be arriving around five. In two hours. He glanced again to her bag, to her coat, to her hat on the bench beside her.

"You aren't leaving, are you?" he asked, a strange urgency forming in his gut.

"Whatever gave you the idea I'd ever want to leave this little paradise?"

He glanced at her bag again. "Then you're not going?"

She blew out an exasperated breath. "Yes, of course I'm going. On the five o'clock train."

The panic in his stomach swelled. "But you just got here. I thought you needed the work."

"I need paid work. Not slave labor."

"Slave labor?" What was she talking about? Hewitt had mentioned that he'd placed Elise with the two washerwomen, even though they didn't technically need her help. His assistant indicated it was an easy job for Elise, since the other two women were tough and experienced and could carry most of the weight of the work. Thornton had assumed it was an ideal situation for her, that she wouldn't be overly taxed and tired.

"Why don't you talk to your slave driver?" She tossed a nod toward the door, where Hewitt was entering, his notebook in one hand and his pencil in the other. He was studying his figures and notes and hadn't noticed Thornton standing in the middle of the depot.

"Hewitt," Thornton called.

The young man looked up with a jerk of his head. "Sir?"

"What's this I hear about you being a slave driver?"

"I-I don't understand . . . what do you mean, sir?"

"Apparently, Miss Neumann feels as though she's being treated like a slave."

The man's sights dropped to Elise. His confusion was wiped away with a scowl. "Oh. Her. Don't mind her. She's just sore because I fired her."

Thornton's racing heartbeat came to a standstill. "You fired her?" His tone came out harsher than he intended, causing Hewitt's eyes to widen.

"Yes, sir. She was complaining about the work and her pay. I addressed the problem swiftly and severely to teach all our employees a lesson that we expect them to work hard without complaint."

Elise snorted. "The only lesson you taught was just how inconsiderate and unjust the Quincys are. But I guess that should come as no surprise, should it?" Her eyes spit accusations at Thornton.

So his identity was no longer a secret. Somehow she'd learned who he really was. He should have guessed she would eventually. In some ways he was relieved the truth had come out.

"The Quincys treat their employees just as well, if not better, than almost anyone else," Hewitt said. "You should have realized just how lucky you were that Mr. Quincy hired you in the first place."

"Lucky?" Her voice rose. "Lucky to work fourteen hours every day? Lucky to work in the heat and the steam and with the lye that chafes my hands until they bleed?" She held up one of her hands and revealed red, chapped skin that was cracked in numerous places.

At the sight, Thornton's stomach clenched. He started to reach for her hand, but she rapidly returned it to her coat pocket.

"Lucky I'll have to work for months before I get myself out of debt to the Quincys? Lucky I won't have a single penny to send home to my sisters to help them?"

With each of her assertions, Thornton's dismay swelled.

She stood, shoved her shoulders back, and faced Hewitt with all her wrath. "Exactly how lucky am I, Mr. Hewitt? Why don't you tell me what I have here to be so grateful for?"

"You had a job," Mr. Hewitt insisted.

"A job that will kill me before I can pay off my debts."

"It's a job." Hewitt's tone brooked no further argument. "Any number of women out east would trade places with you in an instant if given the chance."

"Then let them." She plopped back onto the bench and reached for her carpetbag. Thornton caught the faint tremor in her hand before her fingers closed around the handle and she tucked the bag closer to her legs.

"We didn't need you anyway," Mr. Hewitt said. "You were an added expense we simply can't afford."

Thornton shook himself free of the sickening sense of surprise that had held him captive during the exchange between Elise and Hewitt. Was she speaking the truth about how unbearable the work conditions were? In the short times he'd spent with her, he hadn't taken her for the type of woman to exaggerate a situation. She was a proud woman, and he suspected she'd downplay her hardships rather than try to win sympathy from others.

She'd certainly been desperate to consider leaving her family to venture into the unknown. He'd witnessed her sorrow during the trip. She wouldn't have left her siblings if she'd had any other choice. So to allow herself to be fired? From her new job? The first week of her employment?

Something was wrong. And he needed to get to the bottom of the predicament.

"Mr. Hewitt," he said, cocking his head toward his office, "I'd like a word with you alone."

Hewitt hesitated.

Thornton began striding toward the ticket counter. "Now."

"Yes, sir." The young man scurried after him.

For the next quarter of an hour, Thornton stood in his office listening to Hewitt describe his encounter with Elise earlier in the day. From the way Hewitt described Elise, she was nothing more than a greedy jezebel who wanted a handout rather than working hard for her wages.

Yet, after a perusal of Hewitt's detailed notes regarding the hours and pay scale for the women, Thornton could understand Elise's frustration. How could she help her sisters if she would remain in debt to him for months?

"Can we not pay the women more?" Thornton asked.

Hewitt shook his head. "Part of the reason we hired them was because they provided a cheaper source of labor, which allows us to invest in other things—like the schoolhouse."

Thornton could perhaps waive their train fare for the ride to Quincy. It was the least he could do. Quincy Enterprises and its railroads didn't charge the Children's Aid Society for the children they brought west for placing out. They could do the same for the women, couldn't they?

He rubbed a hand across his eyes and tried to wipe away the weariness. The blast of the train whistle told him the southbound train was arriving. It wasn't Elise's train. Thankfully. But the screech of metal against metal reminded him he had to figure out something for Elise or she would be gone from Quincy and out of his life all too soon. And he wasn't ready to let her go. Not yet—even though a part of him warned that hanging on to her would only complicate matters.

Hewitt pushed his spectacles up on his nose and glanced toward the door. He needed to take inventory of the new supplies arriving.

"Go on," Thornton said, letting his shoulders sag. "But our conversation isn't over. Clearly we need to come up with a better plan for the women."

"Very good, sir." Hewitt gave a salute, but it lacked conviction. Then he exited the office and strode toward the back door of the depot.

Only a few passengers were getting off. Quincy didn't have much to entice any travelers to linger, not even a savory depot meal or pleasant cup of coffee. Thornton had to change that somehow, someway if he hoped to make Quincy successful. But for now, he simply had too many other issues demanding his attention.

One young man hurried across the platform and yanked open

the depot door. When he stepped inside, he started toward the ticket counter with a purposeful gait. His tired, sun-bronzed face was set with resolve.

At the sight of the young man, Elise jumped up and called out, "Reinhold?"

The man halted so abruptly he almost tripped over his own feet. He swiveled toward Elise, and every trace of tiredness left his face. His eyes rounded, and a smile of such relief lit his face that Thornton guessed him to be family.

"Praise Gott," the young man said, starting toward Elise with long strides that echoed all the determination in his expression.

"Reinhold!" she said again, then ran toward the man and flung herself into his arms.

A sharp pang sliced into Thornton's chest. He'd expected Elise to react to him that way, like she had when they'd parted at the depot in Chicago. But she'd been anything but happy to see him.

Reinhold's arms slid around Elise, and he pulled her into an all-encompassing hug. He buried his face against her shoulder and her hair, and for a long moment held her tightly. When he lifted his face, consuming love shone from his eyes.

The jab in Thornton's chest intensified. The man wasn't family. A family member wouldn't cling to Elise for quite so long or quite so possessively. And he wouldn't look as though he'd just walked into heaven instead of a train depot.

Elise struggled to pull back, and Reinhold reluctantly released his hold on her. Thornton could see him work to hide his emotions so that by the time she looked at his face, his eyes were veiled and his expression controlled.

"What are you doing here?" Thornton heard Elise ask, her tone still excited, her face the happiest he'd seen it. Did she love this man in return? And if so, why had she never mentioned him?

Thornton's ire stoked to a low-burning flame. If she cared for someone else, why had she spent time with him? Just as quickly as his irritation fanned to life, the cold waters of reality doused it. Who was he to condemn her, when he'd done the same? He hadn't ever mentioned the fact that he was courting Rosalind Beaufort with the intention of marriage. How could he fault Elise for not being candid when he'd been less so, not only about his future plans but about his family?

"I came west to find work," Reinhold said. "Since I had to come, I figured I might as well find you too."

She didn't resist when he reached for her hands. "Did you see Marianne and Sophie and the two little ones before you left?" she asked. He nodded, but before he could speak, she barraged him with more questions. "How are they? They're still staying with Miss Pendleton, aren't they? Are they getting enough to eat? Has Marianne found employment?"

Reinhold patiently responded, his answers soothing the worry lines in her forehead. The sting in Thornton's chest prodded him forward. He wanted to be the one to alleviate Elise's troubles, to wipe away her anxiety and earn her smiles. He crossed the waiting room until he stood next to them.

At his presence, Reinhold quickly broke away from Elise and put a proper distance between them. Thornton's ready scowl eased as he appraised Reinhold. He was shorter than Thornton by a couple of inches, but was much stockier, his muscles and build showing him to be a man who was accustomed to heavy lifting and hard labor. He had a pleasant face, certainly not as good-looking as Thornton's, yet he wasn't sore on the eyes by any means.

"I see we have a new arrival," Thornton said. "A friend of yours, Elise?"

Wariness immediately dropped over her features, and she seemed to be waging an inner war over whether or not to speak to him. Her courtesy must have won the battle, for she nodded and replied, "Yes, this is Reinhold Weiss."

Reinhold studied Elise's face as though reading a message there before he looked Thornton up and down. A sudden spark in Reinhold's eyes said he'd guessed Thornton's attraction to Elise and didn't like it. But as with his other feelings, he shelved it out of sight and instead respectfully stuck out a hand. "Pleased to meet you, Mr.—"

"Mr. Quincy." Thornton returned the handshake, perhaps a little too tightly. He waited for the implication to make its impact. As Reinhold's eyes widened and his shoulders straightened, satisfaction sifted through Thornton. The man was apparently as bright as he was strong.

"I couldn't help overhearing that you're looking for work." Thornton released his grip on Reinhold and stepped back.

"That I am, sir."

Elise shot Thornton a dangerous look, one that warned him against hurting Reinhold. So she cared about this man? For just an instant, Thornton had the impulse to send him to a different town so he was far from Elise. But what would Elise think of him if he did that? She already thought he was a cad of the worst kind. Maybe helping Reinhold would help win back Elise's favor. Besides, it was the right thing to do.

"Well, if you're looking for work, then you're in luck," Thornton said. "I might have employment I can offer you."

Reinhold nodded. "I'd be grateful, sir."

"What's your trade?"

"No trade," Reinhold admitted reluctantly. "But I have worked in construction."

"He helped to build tenements," Elise added with a note of pride.

Thornton scrutinized Reinhold, noting again his weathered skin and brawniness. Though he'd already hired a dozen new construction workers, he could always use another, especially if Reinhold had experience. "Good. Then you're hired."

Reinhold's face registered surprise, and he smiled tentatively. "Just like that?"

"Just like that. Elise's word is good enough for me." Elise's expression toward him softened, and he took hope in it. Maybe he could yet repair the damage he'd done and build some kind of bridge with her. "Find one of the construction crew supervisors about town. Tell him I hired you and have him put you right to work."

"Thank you, sir," Reinhold said. "I appreciate it."

"You're welcome."

Reinhold turned to Elise eagerly. "Won't everyone at home be glad when they hear I found work in the same town as you?"

Elise's smile slipped away, and she glanced down at her carpetbag. Reinhold's gaze shifted to the luggage as well before darting back up, his face stricken. "You're not leaving, are you?"

She started to nod, but then Thornton interrupted. "Of course she's not."

"I was fired from my job today." She met Thornton's gaze with a chilly one, all the hurt and bitterness from earlier securely back in place.

"Fired?" Reinhold looked as if he wanted to reach out and grasp Elise like one might grab a silky scarf the wind was blowing away.

"What Elise meant to say is that she's had a job change today," Thornton said.

"No, I was most certainly fired—"

"She's been hired into a new position." Thornton scrambled to find any excuse to keep Elise from leaving. He glanced around the depot, to the door leading to the street, to the windows. What other work was there for a woman like Elise in Quincy? "Yes, I thought she might be better suited to something besides laundering."

"She's a good seamstress," Reinhold offered.

"Quincy already has a seamstress," she explained.

Think, Thornton, think . . .

Mrs. Gray limped out of the dining room carrying a steaming cup of coffee. "Mr. Quincy, here's that cup of coffee you wanted." The woman was petite and thin—too thin. She'd suffered from polio earlier in her life and as a result had always had difficulty walking. But she was as kindhearted as her husband, even if she wasn't much of a cook.

Thornton took the cup from her and tried not to notice the coffee grains floating in a greasy film at the top. "Thank you, Mrs. Gray. You're a dear."

She patted his arm before retreating to the dining room.

He blew across the top of the liquid in an attempt to cool it and buy himself a little more time to find a solution regarding what to do with Elise.

Elise took one look at the sludge inside his cup and her nose crinkled in clear disgust.

"She means well," Thornton whispered in reply, "but apparently making good coffee takes a certain special kind of person."

Both of Elise's brows rose as if to say, *You must be jesting. How hard is it to make coffee?*

The cogs in Thornton's mind finally began to churn. He glanced from Elise to the dining room and back. "That certain special kind of person is you, Elise. As a matter of fact, I'm hiring you to be in charge of my dining room."

It was the perfect solution. Why hadn't he thought of it earlier?

"In charge of the dining room?" Her voice rang with surprise, and she turned her full attention to the deserted room.

"Yes. I need a good cook. Even more than that, I desperately need someone who knows how to make coffee that isn't a choking hazard."

"Elise knows how to do both," Reinhold said.

Her brow was still lifted, her beautiful blue eyes skeptical.

"Of course, as manager," Thornton continued hurriedly, "I'll double your wages."

"Double?"

"Does that sound reasonable to you?"

"Yes." She visibly swallowed hard. "That would be fine."

"Good." He was tempted to pat himself on the back but refrained and instead grinned.

She didn't smile back, but her eyes lit with what he hoped was excitement. "When should I start?"

He handed her the cup of coffee. "How about now. With a fresh pot of coffee?"

"I think I can manage that."

"Great. While you do that, I'll inform Mrs. Gray she's getting some help. I have a feeling she'll be relieved."

He knew Mrs. Gray would be happy to hand over the responsibility of the kitchen and instead assist where needed. But Hewitt would be a different matter. The young assistant would skewer Thornton with his pencil when he discovered the plan. Nevertheless, Thornton couldn't quell the rising thrill he felt at coming up with a manageable solution to the problem of Elise's employment.

She might still despise him. But he'd made a step forward, hopefully, in regaining the friendship he'd lost. And that was all he wanted, wasn't it—friendship?

CHAPTER 14

Elise stirred the butter and molasses together with firm strokes. She already had a pot of chicken soup bubbling on the range and biscuits in the oven. The aroma of the chicken and thyme and parsley radiated throughout the kitchen, making her almost giddy.

All morning she'd been tempted to pinch herself to make sure she wasn't dreaming that she was in the kitchen, the place she loved most in the world, doing what she loved best. She dipped her finger into the gooey mixture in the bowl, lifted it to her lips, and tasted its sweetness. If she was dreaming, then she didn't want to awake.

She looked around the kitchen to prove to herself once again that she was really here. A large cast-iron stove stood near the rear entrance, the coal bin next to it heaped to the brim. A sturdy indoor washbasin rested on thin legs against another wall with a drain that released to the outdoors. While they still had to haul well water inside, at least they didn't have to carry the dirty water back out.

A hutch contained plates, cutlery, crockery, and an assortment of other supplies needed for the dining room. The worktable in the middle was adequate to do most of her chopping and rolling and mixing. It wasn't nearly as large as the table that had been in her father's bakery, but she couldn't complain. She was working in a kitchen and that alone would have been enough, even if she'd had to do her mixing on the floor. She grazed the pots and pans and utensils hanging overhead. Their metallic clinking together was beautiful music to her ears.

The sound brought back the happy memories of the times she'd spent with her father in the kitchen, the low rumble of his laughter, the scrape of his spatula, the tantalizing aromas in *his* pots and pans. He'd introduced her to all of his spices as if they'd been dear little friends he called out to play.

"What else can I do, dear?" Mrs. Gray asked, coming into the kitchen with her uneven step, the limp having grown more pronounced throughout the morning. The woman's narrow face was pale and pinched. Though she tried hard to hide her discomfort, she was clearly in pain.

"You can go and rest your feet," Elise said as she beat the cake batter faster. "You've been running around here all morning and you deserve a break."

Mrs. Gray laughed. "You're a sweetie. But I'm much sturdier than I appear."

Chagrined, Elise stopped stirring. "I didn't mean to insinuate you can't handle the work—"

"I know you didn't." Mrs. Gray patted Elise's arm. "You're a good girl and so considerate. No one has ever looked out for my well-being before—except of course, Mr. Gray."

Mrs. Gray had maple-syrup-brown hair that was pulled back into a bun, revealing her sharp, angular face. Her features were somewhat severe, yet her eyes were soft and kind. She didn't have any silver in her hair, and her skin was unwrinkled from age, though there was definitely something old and wise about the woman, as if she'd already lived a long life. Whatever the case, Elise was relieved Mrs. Gray hadn't been resentful yesterday when Thornton introduced her as the new manager of the kitchen and dining room. In fact, Mrs. Gray had breathed out a long sigh and whispered, "Thank you, Jesus."

They'd worked together to cook something for dinner last night. Due to the limited amount of time, Elise was only able to prepare a simple fare of fried salt pork, boiled carrots and cauliflower, and corn bread. Even so, Mrs. Gray had come back into the kitchen relaying compliments from everyone, including one from Thornton.

Elise had lingered in the kitchen late last night, long after they'd washed and put away the last of the dishes. She'd taken stock of the supplies in the pantry, planned a menu for the coming week, and then put together a list of ingredients she would need in the near future. Although Mrs. Gray had informed her they purchased some of the food from local farmers, most of the supplies had to be ordered and shipped from Chicago.

She'd awoken well before dawn. While it was still dark, she walked the short distance from the hotel to the dining room, breathing deeply of the cool autumn air. In the quiet of the deserted Main Street, she'd almost whispered a prayer of gratefulness for how swiftly her situation had changed from one of complete and total despair to delight.

Not only did she have employment again, but it was her dream job. Was it another miracle, like the one she'd experienced when God had brought Miss Pendleton into her life to rescue her from being homeless?

When she'd arrived at the dining room, Mrs. Gray had already been awake at the early hour, and together they'd prepared eggs, bacon, and thick griddle cakes for the few construction crew supervisors and other men who lodged at the hotel and relied upon the dining room for their sustenance.

Once she and Mrs. Gray had cleaned up breakfast, they started right away preparing for the noon meal. There was no doubt Mrs. Gray was a hard worker. But after watching the woman burn nearly everything she touched—and after having eaten her less-than-digestible meals for the past week—Elise understood Thornton's desire to have someone new take over the meal preparation.

Elise reached for the raisins and dumped them into the batter. "I'm well on track for getting this plum cake into the oven and will probably have time to rest my own feet before the noon meal. So I don't see why you can't do so."

Mrs. Gray chuckled. "Well, if you put it that way, dear, I guess you leave me little choice but to sit down for a spell."

"You deserve a break." Elise folded the raisins into the batter. "I don't know how you managed to run this dining room all by yourself up until now."

"In the beginning, there were only a few of us needing to eat," Mrs. Gray replied, flexing her shoulders and wincing in the process. "But as more people arrived in Quincy, it's been getting harder to keep up. Mr. Gray has helped when he can, but he's been busier too."

Elise had met the stationmaster, a tall man with a long mustache and full beard who appeared to take his position very seriously, always busy cleaning the depot, greeting the arriving trains, helping with the refueling and unloading, and bustling about at Thornton's beck and call.

"Now go and rest," Elise said again to Mrs. Gray.

The relief in the woman's eyes told Elise she'd been right to insist. "Maybe for a few minutes."

"We won't be serving lunch for another hour. Why don't you take a cup of coffee and sit outside in the sun."

Through the window that was dusty with coal soot, Elise could see the late September morning was still gloriously sunny. When she'd gone outside earlier to fetch more water, the coolness of the morning had been giving way to a pleasant warmth. The sky overhead was bluer than Elise had ever seen before, and when she peered across the train tracks to the prairie with its tall yellowing grass fluttering in the breeze, she was filled with a sense of awe at the amount of space, all untouched and unblemished, the way it had been probably since the first days of creation.

With a cup of coffee in hand, Mrs. Gray paused by the door. "You'll join me when you're finished, won't you, dear?"

"I might," Elise said. But the truth was she didn't want to leave the kitchen. Perhaps a tiny part of her feared that if she left, she might wake up and lose this beautiful dream she was in.

She added the final ingredients to the cake mixture and ended by scooping in the flour. She stirred and tested it until it reached the right consistency, then poured it into the greased pan. The leftover cake batter in the bowl was too hard to resist. She slid her finger across it until she had a glob and then stuck it in her mouth.

"Mmmm," she murmured.

"Are you planning to share?" came a voice from the doorway leading to the dining room.

She spun to find Thornton leaning casually against the doorframe, watching her. How long had he been standing there? She'd wanted to stay mad at him for leading her on during the train ride here. She'd wanted to hate him for being a Quincy. She'd wanted to blame him for the awful working conditions the women had to suffer through.

But at the moment, with her shirtsleeves rolled up and her hands coated in cake batter, her heart was too full of gratefulness to have room for bitterness. She held out the spoon. "Would you like to lick the spoon?"

His brow lifted, widening his rich brown eyes. "Lick it?"

"Don't tell me you've never licked batter off a spoon. It's one of those sacred childhood milestones right up there with building a snowman."

"It would appear I've had a very deprived childhood because I've done neither."

She thrust the spoon into his hand. "Then we need to remedy that right now."

He raised the spoon and inspected the thick coating of creamy batter skeptically.

"Go on," she urged.

He stuck the spoon in his mouth and worked it clean.

She watched him, suddenly tense with the need to know what he thought of the taste. It was an old family recipe her father had made often in Hamburg, and she'd been thrilled to find all the ingredients to make it for herself.

"Hmm, that wasn't quite enough for me to get the flavor." He handed the spoon back to her. "I think I need a little more."

She scraped the spoon in the bowl until it was covered with a sizable amount of batter before handing it back to him.

He shoved it into his mouth, cleaned off the spoon, and smacked his lips together as though testing the flavor. Finally he held the spoon out to her. "I'm still not catching it. One more taste ought to do it. Maybe."

She took the utensil and held it above the bowl. At the spark of humor in his eyes, she hesitated. When he gave her a lopsided, sheepish grin, she put the spoon down on the counter and swiped her finger over the batter until she had a large dollop. "Don't you know that one person gets to lick the spoon and the other the bowl?" She lifted it to her mouth and made a slow show of savoring each grain.

"That's not fair." He gave a pretend pout. "The person with the bowl gets more."

"It depends upon the baker and how much she decides to leave. And I was in a generous mood today."

"For yourself."

"Now you're catching on."

He chuckled. She couldn't keep from smiling as she plunged another finger of batter into her mouth. She'd missed the fun banter with him. How was it that he could make her smile so easily, even though she was supposed to still be angry at him?

She placed the bowl back on the worktable and picked up the cake pan filled with batter. For several minutes, she ignored him and busied herself putting the cake into the oven and adding a few more coals to the firebox.

When she straightened, she realized he hadn't budged from the doorway but had leaned against the frame again and was watching her. What was the look in his eyes? Admiration?

She returned to the worktable with a wet rag and began to wipe up the sticky smudges of molasses. She could feel his gaze following her every move, and her pulse tripped in an unsteady rhythm. She didn't want him to affect her. Last night when she'd gone back to the dormer and informed the other women Thornton had hired her to operate the depot dining room, Fanny was the first to warn her, just as she had at the

Chicago train depot. The others readily agreed that Thornton was just trying to win her affection again. They warned her to be careful or she'd end up his mistress.

"Elise?" he said quietly, all humor gone from his voice. "I'm sorry."

The sincerity and plea in his tone beckoned her to forgive him. She stopped her wiping but didn't turn.

"I know I should have been honest with you on the train about my real identity, but I was afraid you wouldn't like me anymore."

She wanted to tell him he was right, she didn't like him anymore. But that wasn't completely true. After all, he'd been kind enough to give her work and a pay raise. And he'd hired Reinhold.

He released a sigh that contained his frustration. "I'm also sorry for overstepping the limits of friendship. I shouldn't have kissed you."

At his confession, she spun. Did he regret kissing her? A strange sense of disappointment rushed through her. Maybe the kiss hadn't affected him the same way it had her. Maybe he was so used to kissing women that it hadn't meant anything to him.

Stop it, she reprimanded herself. It didn't matter whether he'd liked it or not. What mattered was that he was sorry for overstepping the bounds of propriety. Surely that was good news and meant he wasn't attempting to take advantage of her the way Fanny suspected. At least she hoped so.

He straightened. "I promise I won't do something like that again. I'll maintain a proper distance from you at all times."

"Then you're not attempting to win me over so you can make me your mistress?" Once the words were out, heat rose in her neck at the boldness of her question. At his muttered exclamation of denial, she ducked her head and wiped at a streak of egg on the edge of the table.

"Blast it all, Elise. After getting to know me, do you really think I'm capable of such devious behavior?" Hurt radiated from his expression.

She hesitated, which only caused him to shake his head and mutter again under his breath. "The other women warned me that it happens."

"Well, rest assured, it won't happen with me." His reply was terse, his posture stiff. And from the way he fisted his hands, she could see she'd offended him. Perhaps deeply.

"I'm sorry," she said, hoping he wouldn't get angry enough to dismiss her from her new job. It wasn't a bakery, but it was a kitchen, which was the next best thing. He was also paying her more than she could make working anywhere else. If she ruined things this time, she didn't know what she'd do. "I shouldn't have said that. It's just I didn't know what to think with you being so nice to me and singling me out."

He jammed his fingers through his hair. "Believe me, Elise, I had no intention of using you. I'm deeply sorry if I gave you that impression."

She wanted to believe him. She really did. But nothing changed who he was, how much wealth he had, and the fact that he was here building this town and mistreating poor people in the process. Maybe he'd given her a new job and a raise, but what about all the others, like Fanny and the Engle sisters who were still stuck working for him like slaves?

His pained eyes held hers, waiting for her response. She didn't know what to tell him.

"What can I do to reassure you I mean what I said?"

"Do the work," she said somewhat impulsively. But once

spoken, she realized it was what she wanted—for him to see what life was like for people like her. If the wealthy class understood how hard the poor labored, perhaps they'd have more compassion. "Maybe if you go out and do the work you require of your employees, you'll see that their labor is more valuable than you think."

"I do value it. Immensely."

"You can't value what you don't understand."

He studied her for a moment. "And if I do the work, that will prove to you I'm not a cad?"

"It will be a start."

"Then I'll do it." With that, he spun and walked away, his footsteps echoing with an ominous finality. Maybe she'd won this small battle with Thornton, but for a reason she couldn't explain, she felt like she'd lost.

CHAPTER 15

Marianne descended the stairs, her footsteps echoing in the silence of the early morning. The sun hadn't yet risen, and the stairwell was dark. She made her way quickly and quietly down from the third story. She'd heard rumors that the meat-processing plant was planning to hire a limited number of women, and she was determined to be one of the first in what was sure to be a long line. Even if the work was bloody and putrid, at least it was something.

She shivered in her thin coat and pulled the ragged linen closer to her body. Part of her warned that her efforts would amount to naught and that she should just go back to bed. Too many rumors of employment over the past couple of weeks had raised her hopes only to have them dashed again. She'd already stood in numerous employment lines for hours, then eventually was told to go home, for there wasn't any work available.

Maybe today would be different. She prayed it would be so.

After receiving Elise's first letter last week and learning how her new job wasn't what she'd anticipated and that she wouldn't be able to send them money or pay for their transport to the

West to join her, Marianne had doubled her efforts to look for employment.

She hadn't yet heard from Reinhold, but she was confident he'd find Elise. And maybe after Marianne finally told him the truth about her love for him, he'd want her to come west and be with him, especially if she reassured him she'd saved enough money to pay for the train fare.

As she entered the first-floor hallway, she cupped her frozen fingers to her mouth and breathed warm air against her flesh. The late September nights were getting colder, and their rooms weren't heated. By morning they were all shivering and huddling together for warmth. In addition, her arms and back ached from the long hours spent painting ceilings. She rolled her shoulders and tried to work out the knots. The third-floor rooms of the mission were starting to lose their dilapidated appearance and beginning to look more livable, a good thing because two more women and their children had moved in this week, bringing the total number of families living there to six.

Without employment, the former seamstresses were unable to pay their rent, resulting in eviction from their tenements. Homeless and hungry, the women had come to Miss Pendleton for help. Of course, the kindhearted woman didn't turn them away even though she was facing her own financial problems.

In fact, just yesterday Marianne overheard Miss Pendleton speaking in hushed tones with her advisor, Mr. Ridley. Both of their faces were distraught, and Marianne guessed Miss Pendleton's efforts to reopen the sewing workshop hadn't been successful. Marianne was disappointed. She'd joined in praying with Miss Pendleton and Reverend Bedell that God would work a miracle and provide a clothing company that would contract with them.

Lifting up another prayer, Marianne hustled down the hall-way. She was almost to the door when the sound of muffled sobs coming from the chapel halted her. A low masculine voice rumbled in an effort to comfort, but the crying continued. Marianne knew she should continue on her way and not eavesdrop, but she tiptoed closer to the chapel door anyway and leaned in. She recognized Reverend Bedell's voice and suspected Miss Pendleton was the one crying. At first, Marianne thought he was praying, yet as she listened more carefully, she could tell he was talking to Miss Pendleton.

"They are strong women," he was saying. "They'll survive."

"But they'll be forced back into prostitution" came her shaky response.

When Reverend Bedell didn't contradict her, Marianne's chest deflated. The situation must be growing worse if the reverend didn't see any other way for the women to make ends meet.

"After rescuing them once," Miss Pendleton said through sniffles, "I don't understand why God would allow them to suffer such degradation again."

"Every day I hear about new efforts to provide meals and shelter to the homeless. Most of them will find help elsewhere."

"But why not here? After giving us a miracle once, why won't God provide again?"

"We won't always understand why God allows things to happen," he responded gently. "But as Job said, 'The Lord gave, and the Lord hath taken away; blessed be the name of the Lord.' We will choose to praise and trust Him no matter what."

Marianne swallowed hard. Was Miss Pendleton considering turning the women out of the mission? Surely not. Things might be desperate, but they weren't that bad, were they?

For a moment, Miss Pendleton's sniffling filled the quiet chapel. Marianne's guilty conscience urged her to move past. After all, if she wanted to be first in line at the meat-processing plant, she needed to get going. But at Miss Pendleton's next question, Marianne's blood ran cold and her limbs felt frozen in place. "What will we do with the Neumanns?"

"I don't know," said the reverend in a whisper drenched in frustration.

"I'd take them to live with me, but I can't impose on Ridley any more than I already am."

"What about taking Sophie and the two infants to the Children's Aid Society? I'll speak with Mr. Brace on their behalf and ask him to find them good homes in the West temporarily, until Elise is able to establish herself in her new place of employment."

Marianne sucked in a sharp breath at the reverend's suggestion. Sophie would never agree to a placement. And the thought of sending Olivia and Nicholas off by themselves on a train, not knowing where they'd end up, frightened Marianne. They were family now, and family had to stick together. No matter what.

Miss Pendleton released another sob. "I promised Elise I'd watch out for her sisters. I can't let her down." The words reflected exactly how Marianne felt. Elise would disown her if she let anything happen to Olivia and Nicholas and especially Sophie.

"When you made the promise, you didn't know you'd lose everything and that the bank would foreclose on the rest of what you owe on the mission."

Marianne rested her forehead against the wall and closed her eyes tightly. Except it was too late to stop the swell of tears, which spilled over and ran down her cheeks. She pressed a hand to her mouth to prevent any noise.

Miss Pendleton was losing the mission, closing its doors, and everyone who lived there would have to leave. Marianne's legs began to shake, and she was afraid she'd collapse. If only she was stronger and less emotional like Elise, maybe she'd come up with something to do. Instead, all she could do was cry.

She hated her weakness. She should pull herself together and continue her search for employment. She would need the job at the meat-packing plant even more now. Stumbling backward a step before spinning and retracing her way to the stairwell, she raced up the steps with tears coursing down her cheeks.

She didn't know how long they had left at the mission before they would need to leave. But one thing was certain. She wouldn't let Miss Pendleton or the reverend separate her from Sophie, Olivia, or Nicholas. She couldn't. Even if they had to live on the streets again, she wasn't giving up her family.

Thornton's gut twisted with the same self-loathing he'd felt since yesterday when he apologized to Elise in the kitchen and had learned what she really thought of him. He tightened his necktie and reached for the suit coat that lay on his bed. So far he'd avoided looking into the mirror for his grooming, afraid he'd be tempted to punch his reflection if he saw it. But now, as he shrugged into the coat and straightened the lapels, he finally gave himself a derisory once-over.

Had she really thought he was the kind of man who would be nice to a woman in order to lure her into his bed? He shook his head, angry again at the thought as he had been all through the restless night.

He wasn't blaming her in the least. No, he was angry with

himself for inadvertently leading her to believe that was what he might want from her. Because he hadn't thought of having a mistress. Most certainly not.

But if not that, then what had he been doing toying with her affection? The question taunted him again as it had for the past week.

"You're an idiot, Thornton," he said aloud, scowling at himself.

With a sigh, he lowered himself to the edge of the unmade bed, its metal frame squeaking under his weight. Why was he even bothering with this crazy challenge his father had issued? Why not just back out gracefully while his town was still doing well? Even if he somehow managed to construct his town faster, bigger, and then draw in the people, Bradford would figure out a way to better him. He always had a knack for pleasing their father with whatever he did. While he, the younger twin, always fell short no matter how hard he tried.

And now he'd fallen short again. This time he'd hurt Elise, who was one of the strongest, most beautiful women he knew.

The waft of freshly brewed coffee had stirred his senses for the past hour since he'd heard her arrive. His room in the depot across from the Grays wasn't directly above the kitchen, but it was close enough that he could hear the clinking and clanging to know she was already at work.

He'd debated telling her about Rosalind to prove he already had a woman and didn't need another. But he had the feeling if he told Elise about Rosalind, she'd probably be even more suspicious of him, maybe confirm that indeed he'd been using her.

But he hadn't been, had he?

He let out a groan as he rose and started toward the door. What had he gotten himself into?

Once in the hallway, he paused in order to pull himself together. He was Thornton Quincy, a distinguished gentleman, a wealthy entrepreneur, a well-educated scholar. He owned and commanded this town. He didn't need to be afraid of one young woman—albeit a feisty and somewhat headstrong young woman.

He took a deep breath to infuse himself with confidence, descended the stairs, entered the depot through a side door, and moved with hard, sure steps toward the dining room. With only a hint of light beginning to show in the sky, he was earlier than usual. Thankfully, no one else was there yet except Mr. Gray.

He exchanged his usual good morning and other pleasantries with the man before venturing to the kitchen door.

"Mr. Quincy," Mrs. Gray said in surprise, nearly knocking over the bowl on the counter in front of her. She steadied it before wiping her hands on her apron. "I didn't realize you were down already. I'll get you a cup of coffee."

"That would be kind of you." His attention went directly to Elise, who stood at the stove flipping bacon with a long fork. It sizzled and sputtered, its smoky aroma making his stomach growl.

Mrs. Gray poured a cup from a pot percolating on the stove. She offered him a tired smile as she brought it to him. "Elise sure knows how to make delicious coffee, doesn't she?"

As he took the mug from Mrs. Gray, Thornton was too polite to mention how awful her coffee had been in comparison, so he tactfully chose his words. "I don't imagine there are too many people quite as talented as Elise when it comes to the kitchen, but you sure put forth a good effort, Mrs. Gray."

Elise stopped flipping bacon and turned to say, "I could have Mrs. Gray make the next pot if you prefer hers." Her voice and expression were too innocent, and the gleam in her eyes teased him.

The comment thawed the icy grip in his chest a little. Maybe she didn't hate him after all. Maybe she could forgive him in spite of everything. "Mrs. Gray has been doing it for so long that surely she deserves a break from her previous duties, don't you think?"

"I don't know," Elise replied slowly. "I hate to take over everything in the kitchen, especially something you apparently were so fond of."

He took a sip from the steaming mug and pretended to taste it. "Maybe you're right. Your coffee is, well . . ."

Elise raised the fork higher, and her eyes narrowed.

Mrs. Gray's gaze had been bouncing back and forth between them, and now she fixed her eyes on Thornton alone. "Mr. Quincy, I'll have you know that every single person who ate in the dining room yesterday raved about Elise's coffee. One of the passengers who came on the five o'clock train said he couldn't remember the last time he'd tasted such good coffee."

He took another sip and once again pretended to test it. It was excellent, a perfect blend, not too weak and not too strong, and it had just a touch of vanilla or something added to it that made it different—kind of like Elise.

The two women waited for another pronouncement. Rather than give it to them, he took several more sips, nearly draining the cup. "I couldn't tell from just one cup. I guess I'll need another." He held his mug out to Mrs. Gray.

Elise bent her head, but not before he caught sight of her smile.

He gave her what he hoped was a guileless grin in return. Mrs. Gray took his empty cup reluctantly, poured him another, and handed the cup back to him. "I hope you like this one, Mr. Quincy."

"I have a feeling I will." He winked at her.

She fumbled with the handle of the coffeepot, nearly knocking it over before regaining her composure. "I'll go see if Mr. Gray would like another cup of coffee as well."

Once she left the kitchen, Thornton stepped farther into the room. "So, yesterday you told me I needed to work and thereby learn to value my laborers. Maybe today I should start in here." The instant his statement was out, he wanted to take it back. Hadn't he just admonished himself for getting in trouble with Elise? Couldn't he be around her without flirting?

"You can work with me one day," she offered tentatively, apparently not noticing his overture. "But before that, you should go out there and see what it's like for everyone else." She pointed the long-handled fork in the direction of Main Street.

"You really think working as a laborer will make me a better man?"

"Maybe. At the very least, it may cause you to feel more sympathy for the people you've hired, those less fortunate than you."

"What if I already am sympathetic?"

"Do you know what it's like to scrub linens in a hot shed from dawn until dusk?" He shook his head and started to respond, but she cut him off. "Do you know what it's like for the construction workers lifting and hammering and climbing all day and in all manner of weather? Or what it's like for the women who are cooking for that army of men—peeling and chopping and scrubbing dishes?"

"I have to admit," he said, "I don't know much about what their jobs entail. On the other hand, I don't expect my paid laborers to understand the details and pressures of my work."

204

She lifted the pan of bacon off the burner and began removing the strips dripping with grease into a shallow container in a warmer. Once she closed the warmer, she moved to the worktable and looked up at him. "If I hired workers for this kitchen," she said, "I'd want to make sure they were diligent and gave me their best effort. How would I go about doing that?"

He knew what Hewitt would say: discipline them, make sure they understood who was in charge. And then fire them if they stepped out of line. He'd had that exact conversation with his assistant yesterday when Hewitt discovered that instead of sending Elise on the first train out of town, Thornton had given her a new job *and* a raise in pay. When he informed Hewitt they needed to pay the other women more too, Hewitt had sputtered and steamed like an overheated engine. In the end, he had to capitulate. After all, Thornton was the boss and so had the final say. His challenge was with Bradford, not with Hewitt.

Yet he understood Hewitt's concerns. Thornton was able to add the sums quite easily. Maybe his father hadn't put any stipulations about how much capital they could invest in their respective towns, but Thornton had been developing land long enough to know he couldn't invest an endless amount of money into the town. If he hoped for his town to succeed, he had to help the town stand on its own two feet, so to speak.

Hewitt was only being wise and cautious. He'd shown Thornton the bottom line yesterday during their argument. Thornton couldn't afford to give Elise a raise, or anyone else for that matter, or he'd deplete himself of the funds necessary for other important aspects of the town.

"What, then, would you do if you wanted to ensure you had loyal, hardworking employees?" she asked, picking up a wire whisk and beating eggs in the bowl Mrs. Gray had left on the counter.

"Pay them more?"

"Maybe." She didn't sound entirely convinced, which surprised him.

"Isn't that what everyone wants, to earn more money?"

"In the case of the women who are earning little more than slaves, yes. But in general I suspect you pay the men a decent wage."

He nodded in satisfaction. "Then what would you have me do?"

She paused, the eggs frothy and light from the vigorous beating. She poured in a little milk from a pitcher on the table and added a dash of several spices from the assortment next to her. "If you work alongside them, you'll gain their respect, you'll begin to understand their challenges and needs, and in the process earn their loyalty. Once gained, they'll work even harder for you."

Thornton mulled over her suggestion. He understood what she was saying but wasn't sure he agreed. After all, his father had never done the work of a common laborer and he'd succeeded quite well without it.

As though sensing his doubt, she grabbed one of the pans hanging over her head and thumped it against the table. "Then again, you can be like every other wealthy person I've known and continue to trample into the dust those who are already downtrodden."

She dumped the egg mixture into the pan, sloshing some over the side in her angry, jerking motions.

"I take it you've personally experienced someone wealthy trampling you?"

She didn't respond. Instead she transferred the pan of eggs to the stove and began to stir the mixture back and forth.

At the thought of someone having taken advantage of Elise or having hurt her, frustration rose up within him. He wanted to press her for more information, but the stiff set of her shoulders told him the door to her past was shut and locked. And she had no intention of opening it to him.

If he wanted to regain her trust and friendship, he would have to work for it. For reasons he couldn't explain, he wanted to prove he was different from whoever had hurt her. But he wasn't entirely certain he was, and that thought bothered him more than anything else.

⁂

Elise lay on her bed of blankets in the dormer room and read Marianne's letter for at least the tenth time since Mr. Gray had given it to her that afternoon. The one oil lamp the women shared didn't afford much light, especially in her cramped corner. Nevertheless, the homesick ache had prodded her to digest her sister's words again and again.

Marianne had received Elise's letter, the one she'd written when she first arrived in Quincy, when she'd just started working with the Engle sisters as a laundress. Marianne had reassured her everything was going fine for them. Although Marianne hadn't found any work yet, they were still staying at the mission. They were safe, fed, and keeping busy with projects Miss Pendleton was assigning them.

It appeared Miss Pendleton had decided to have the boarders earn their room and board by involving them with the renovations of the upper floors of the mission. According to Marianne, they were mostly cleaning and painting. Elise was grateful the savvy businesswoman had figured out a way for them to pay her back. She couldn't afford to be in debt to Miss Pendleton as well as Thornton Quincy.

"This is delicious, Elise." Betty Lou, one of the women hired to help the construction crew cook, took another bite of the leftover jam tarts Elise had given her. Betty Lou was sitting cross-legged in the middle of her cot, her feet puffy and swollen from standing all day.

Elise hadn't known what to do with the leftover food from the kitchen, and Mrs. Gray had told her she could do whatever she liked. So Elise decided to bring it back to the dormer for the other women, especially for Betty Lou and Rachel, who didn't come to the depot dining room to eat, but instead ate whatever the cook was making for the men.

"I can't even begin to tell you how grateful I am for something besides salt pork and beans." Betty Lou took another bite, closed her eyes, and chewed slowly, making happy moans while doing so.

Rachel, on the cot opposite Betty Lou, had already devoured a piece of plum cake, two tarts, and a butter horn roll. Even now her mouth was full, her plump frame causing the cot beneath her to sag.

The Engle sisters on the far end of the attic were already asleep, their snores vibrating in the chilled air. They'd tasted her cooking when they ate at the dining room for supper. But Fanny hadn't come tonight or the previous evening because her employer insisted she complete her quota before leaving the shop.

Even with the missed dinner, Fanny sat on her cot, her back against the wall, her portion of the food untouched beside her. She stared up at the slanted roof, a fresh red welt on her cheek adding to the purple discoloration under one of her eyes. She'd discarded her headscarf, and her red curly hair hung in loose waves down her shoulders. Her face was paler than usual, which made her freckles stand out all the more.

"You wouldn't believe what we saw today," Betty Lou said, her eyes alighting with mischief and energy that belied the weary creases in her forehead.

"You saw a bear mauling a donkey." Elise folded Marianne's letter gingerly.

"No. Guess again."

"Maybe you saw a pig flying?"

Betty Lou shook her head, the spot between her brows wrinkling. "Why in the world would you think I saw something like that?"

"You said I wouldn't believe what you saw." Elise tucked Marianne's letter into her carpetbag for safekeeping. She tried to reign in her sarcasm whenever she was with the women. But during the guessing game with Betty Lou, she couldn't resist.

Betty Lou's mouth opened to respond but no words came out.

Fanny sat forward with a snort, a half smile forming. She exchanged an amused glance with Elise before reaching for one of the tarts by her side.

Elise couldn't contain a grin of her own. "Would you like me to make one final guess?"

Betty Lou eyed Fanny before giving Elise an uncertain nod. "I guess so."

"Hmmm . . ." Elise pretended to think before leaning forward with feigned excitement. "Oh, I know. Even though my guess might be as far out there as pigs flying, maybe you saw Mr. Quincy and Mr. Hewitt working with the construction crew?"

Betty Lou nodded her head rapidly. "Yes, that's exactly what we saw."

This time Fanny laughed, and Elise was relieved to hear it. Fanny had been too morose of late. As much as the Irishwoman's fiery personality had caused her grief at the mission, Elise couldn't deny she much preferred the spunky, spirited Fanny to the melancholy one.

"My eyes about popped from my head when I saw them," Betty Lou said. "I told Rachel something must be terribly, terribly wrong for Mr. Quincy himself to be out among the boys working, didn't I, Rachel?"

The other woman nodded, her cheeks puffed too full with another butter horn to speak.

Betty Lou's voice rose in excitement as she relayed all she'd witnessed during the day: Mr. Quincy up on the roof with a hammer, Mr. Quincy carrying beams, Mr. Quincy helping install a window, Mr. Quincy laughing with the men.

Of course, Elise had already heard about Thornton's efforts with the construction crew from Mr. Gray, who'd kept peeking out the window and down the street where Thornton was working. Mr. Gray had watched with such amazement that he'd almost missed greeting the arriving trains on several occasions.

She hadn't seen Thornton all evening during the dinner hour. Not that she'd been looking for him. And she most certainly hadn't lingered in the kitchen after cleaning up supper with the hope of seeing him. She'd only wanted to get the beans soaking, and then she grated carrots for a cake she planned to bake in the morning. When she finished, she decided to shuck the fresh peas one of the local farmers had delivered.

It didn't matter that Thornton hadn't made an appearance. It didn't matter that she hadn't had the chance to ask him how his day had gone. It didn't matter that he hadn't wanted to share his adventure with her. At least that was what she'd been telling herself.

Even so, she couldn't deny the small thrill that had been growing with each passing hour. He'd actually taken her advice. He'd gone out and experienced what it was like to do hard labor all day. He hadn't stopped once, not until the sun had begun to set and the men had dispersed to eat.

As much as she wanted to hold on to her grudge against him, she was finding it difficult to do so. Maybe he was rich and powerful and ignorant of what life was like for people like her, but he'd humbled himself today. Not only that, but he'd had to humble himself when he apologized to her for leading her on during the train ride.

Apologies were never easy for anyone, though she could imagine they were even harder for one in his position.

Thornton was turning all her stereotypes upside down. He was a complex man, one with many facets. As much as she wanted to resist liking him, she couldn't. She admired him much more than she should, more than was good for her.

She prayed she wouldn't come to regret it.

CHAPTER 16

Thornton's body ached in places he'd never known existed. Yet as he entered the depot after having washed and changed from a long day of manual labor, he tried to walk with his back straight even though it hurt. And he tried not to limp on his aching legs and feet.

After a week of working with the different construction crews around town, he expected that he'd finally grow accustomed to the heavy lifting and constant hammering. But he was still as sore tonight as he'd been the first day. He felt as though he'd aged fifty years. He almost considered ordering the smithy to make him a cane.

No doubt that would have impressed the men on the construction crews. He could just imagine their heckling.

He'd been embarrassed by how exhausted he was each evening and so resorted to having Mrs. Gray deliver the evening meal to his room. He hadn't wanted anyone to witness his groans and moans. Plus he was afraid, once he sat down, he wouldn't be able to push himself back up.

But tonight, when he'd returned and passed by the dining

room, he was surprised to find Reinhold sitting at one of the tables, and Elise talking and smiling down at him. The sight irritated him much more than he wanted it to. He'd gone to his room and reread each of Rosalind's letters. He even sat down and penned her another letter too. But none of that had taken his mind off Reinhold in the dining room.

Of course, Reinhold had every right to eat in the dining room. There wasn't any rule that said he had to dine with the other construction workers in the mess hall, which was situated near the bunk shanties.

Thornton had taken his noon meals in the mess hall for the past week, and after eating the same fare every day, he couldn't blame any of the men if they'd decided to boycott the food even if it was part of their room and board. The food was downright awful. There was no other way to describe it. Yet the men had shoveled it in as heartily as if they'd been served a feast fit for a king.

The first time he watched them, shame overwhelmed him, shame that they were grateful and content with what was put before them. Not one of the men complained, but instead ate until nearly every morsel on the table was gone.

The experience awakened him to his snobbery, to just how spoiled he'd been all his life to have fresh meals made from the finest quality and cooked by the best chefs.

Though the men hadn't grumbled about their food, Thornton made a note to speak with the cook about expanding the meals to include other more savory food items. He realized now that the food budget he'd given the cook hadn't allowed for much variety, and Thornton wanted that to change.

It was one small thing among many he'd noted needed to be changed.

His list of bigger concerns was growing almost too large to adequately address. He'd learned firsthand that the men could benefit from at least one break in the morning and one in the afternoon. They needed more ladders, scaffolds, and better tools. They needed more encouragement for a job well done. They needed to be released from their work earlier in the evenings so they had adequate time to rest.

As they worked, he also asked the men questions. He discovered they worried about what would happen if they were injured, how they would provide for the families they left behind, the difficulty in saving, and so much more.

With a tired sigh, Thornton now crossed the depot toward the dining room and was irritated once again to see Reinhold was still in the same spot as earlier. He'd come straight from work, for although he'd scrubbed his face and hands, his clothes remained dusty.

He was sitting back in his chair, his stocky legs stretched out in front of him, a cup of coffee in his hands. Thornton had the feeling Reinhold hadn't eaten there to take a break from the mess hall meals. There was only one reason Reinhold was in the dining room, and it had everything to do with the pretty young lady in the kitchen.

Thornton approached Reinhold and tried to straighten his back without wincing. "Good evening, Mr. Weiss." Thornton held out a hand, and Reinhold took it for a handshake. "How is supper tonight?

"A very fine meal, sir. Elise is one of the best cooks you'll ever meet." Reinhold's eyes shone with the pride of a man boasting about the woman he loved.

Thornton had worked alongside Reinhold one afternoon that week. He'd hoped to find something wrong with him, some fault or character deficit, anything. But the man was courteous, kind, and respectful. Not only that, but he was one of the hardest workers on any of his crews. He was strong, knowledgeable, and related well with the other men. He was an ideal worker, the type of man Thornton would consider hiring for a supervisor.

He was nearly perfect in every way.

Which should have been a good thing, except that also meant he was perfect for Elise. That thought shouldn't have bothered Thornton, but it did, much more than he wanted to admit.

"I have a feeling she's going to turn this dining room into a favorite stopping place along the Illinois Central." Reinhold took a sip of his coffee.

"You may be right," Thornton said. The man should be long done with his coffee by now. He was clearly dragging out his time there so he could see Elise again.

Thornton glanced at the open kitchen door. Unlike Reinhold, he didn't have to sit at a table waiting for Elise to come out and visit with him. He could march right into the kitchen and talk to her, if that was what he wanted to do. And no one could stop him.

"Have a pleasant evening." He nodded at Reinhold and then started across the dining room toward the kitchen. A strange satisfaction filled Thornton at the thought of Reinhold watching him and realizing his advantage. It was an arrogant thought, and he knew it. But the truth was he didn't want to share Elise with Mr. Perfect.

As soon as Thornton stepped into the kitchen, however, his confidence vanished. Elise was standing at the washtub, her arms plunged into greasy water with food remnants floating on top. Mrs. Gray was sweeping the floor and chattering away. The moment she saw him, she grew silent.

215

At the sudden quiet of her companion, Elise glanced over her shoulder. Upon glimpsing him, something lit in her eyes—was it relief? He couldn't be sure, because she turned and shook dripping water from her hands. "Mr. Quincy," she said, "I'd begun to think you were avoiding my dining room."

"I have to admit I've been hiding." He inwardly cringed. Why had he said that? Couldn't he have come up with something else? Something that made him appear tough and strong—like Reinhold.

She reached for a towel and wiped her hands. "Hiding? Why?"

His mind raced to find a way to make himself look good. But the kink in his back reminded him of the truth. He was a weakling, and there was no sense in pretending otherwise. "After working all day, I looked and walked worse than an old mule. I smelled like one too."

Rubbing her arms dry, she appraised him.

He ran a hand through his damp hair. "I know. I still look like an old mule—"

"No," she said quickly. "The work suits you." Her lashes dropped then, and a faint hue colored her neck.

Was she complimenting him? He straightened his aching shoulders and watched as she busied herself folding the towel and draping it over a hook near the washtub. Had she missed him this week? She'd apparently noticed he was gone. Surely that was a good sign—a sign she was considering forgiving him?

Mrs. Gray rested the broom against the wall and retrieved the coffeepot from the stove. "I'll go see who needs refills." With a peek at him and then Elise, she limped from the room just as fast as her legs would carry her.

"So how has the week gone?" Elise asked, her expression earnest, as though she truly cared about his experience.

"I can't lie. It was difficult." Once he started relaying all he'd done, he realized how much he'd wanted to talk to her and share everything he was learning. It felt as though he was confiding in a friend.

"You certainly lasted longer than Mr. Hewitt," she said when he'd finished. She rested against the washtub, her arms crossed, her expression gentle, almost admiring—if he might say so himself.

"The poor boy complained of so many aches and pains that I couldn't force him to join me for a second day." Thornton leaned against the worktable near the remaining pieces of an apple cake. It reminded him of the apple pie they'd devoured together on the journey west. If only he could go back in time, redo his actions with her, and keep from hurting her. "Besides, someone needs to keep all the wheels turning."

She arched a brow. "Wheels turning?"

He dug in his pocket for his watch, pulled it out, and flipped open its outer case. "Developing a town is as intricate as putting together all the gears of a watch. Everything has to fit together perfectly. Not only that, but they all have to run smoothly. If one business isn't operating as it should, it eventually affects all the others that rely upon it."

"And Mr. Hewitt keeps the clock running?" Skepticism was written all over her face.

"So to speak." He tucked the watch back in his pocket. "I know you and Hewitt got off to a rough start, but he's really a good kid. He's talented at what he does, and I know I can rely on him." At least he hoped so. Tomorrow he had a meeting scheduled with the young surveyor to go over the changes they needed to make with the construction workers. Thornton was under no illusion that his assistant would accept the changes easily. But Hewitt was smart enough to realize that if he wanted to advance, he needed to please Thornton, even if he didn't agree with how Thornton wanted to run things.

Thornton picked a sliver of apple off the edge of the cake and stuck it in his mouth. "I'm thinking about visiting with the farmers next. I'd like to see how they're doing, hear their concerns and get a feel for what I can do to make the town more suited to their needs." He'd already talked with one of the construction crew supervisors about starting the schoolhouse next. But he was sure there was more he could do to attract additional farmers into buying up the rest of the parcels of railroad land that were left.

"What do you think of my plan?" He broke off another piece of cake, this one bigger. As he lifted it to his mouth, he caught her amused look. "What? So you think my idea is humorous?"

She smiled. "No. Actually I think it's brilliant. So long as you go there with a willingness to help them and listen, just as you did this past week."

"Brilliant?" He liked the sound of that.

"Don't let it go to your head," she said, crossing to him. "It might pop if it puffs up any more."

"True." He grinned.

She pulled the cake pan out of his reach just as he reached for another crumb and swatted his hand lightly. "No more snacking on my cake."

"It's irresistible." Like her. But he bit back his remark.

"For that compliment I'll give you a whole piece."

"If I give you two compliments, do I get two slices?"

She smiled. "Maybe."

"What if I tell you that you make the best food I've ever tasted?"

"I'd tell you that you're bribing me."

"It's the truth," he insisted. "I've never met anyone who can make a cake as moist and sweet as this."

As she cut the cake into a generous piece and slipped it onto a plate, her bright blue eyes were alight and her lips curved with pleasure. She'd never looked lovelier than at that moment.

"Elise . . ." Mrs. Gray's voice came from the doorway. "Reinhold is asking for you."

Elise handed the plate to Thornton. He wanted to see her reaction to Reinhold's eagerness. Was she eager in return? But her expression gave him no indication either way. Before he could think of how he could probe deeper, she forced the dish into his hands and stepped around him.

"Thank you, Mrs. Gray," Elise said, then started for the dining room. Thornton wanted to stop her, to make her stay and talk with him longer, yet he had no right to delay her. Maybe he had the authority to walk into the kitchen and talk to her whenever he wanted, but it was Reinhold who obviously had the power to draw her away.

Thornton glanced down at the cake in his hands, suddenly no longer hungry.

"Oh, Mrs. Gray," Elise called over her shoulder, "you may give Mr. Quincy a second piece of cake if he so wishes. He's earned it." When she tossed him a teasing smile, the knot in his middle loosened. Maybe he couldn't make her like him more than she liked Reinhold, but at least they could be friends. And really, wasn't that all he wanted anyway?

CHAPTER 17

As Elise stepped out of the church, the wind sliced through her wool coat, making her want to retreat inside where the crowded sanctuary and the corner stove had lent heat on the cold November morning. But Fanny and the other women were already moving ahead of her, down the wooden steps into the street.

Everyone in town had been invited to attend the first service in the new church. The pastor and his family had moved to Quincy only last week. Even though he'd just arrived, he was eager to begin services.

Like her, the other women admitted they hadn't been in a real church in a long time. Elise hadn't gone since Mutti had died. Of course, she'd attended chapel at the mission, as had Fanny, but she'd only done so because it was one of the requirements for the seamstresses. She hadn't really listened to Reverend Bedell's sermons, too angry at God and life to pay attention.

But after two months in Quincy, she felt as though she owed God some gratitude. She should be thankful Marianne and Sophie were able to live at the mission, especially when the other women talked about the dire situations for the families they'd left behind. Betty Lou cried whenever she talked about how her mother had to place her younger siblings in different asylums in order to keep them from going hungry.

Thornton's recent generosity had helped a little. He'd dismissed their travel costs and had given raises in their wages. Now most of them were sending every penny they could spare home to their families, yet it still wasn't enough to keep them from hardship.

Elise felt Betty Lou's pain. The young woman's tears made her all the more aware of God's provision. Not only was her family safe, but God had also given her a job she loved. It was better than anything she could have imagined, and she had plenty of food and a roof over her head.

In the dismally cold morning, the other women huddled in their thin coats just as she was doing. They spoke quietly to each other, their noses and cheeks turning red as the cold wind stung their faces. The Engle sisters stomped their feet while walking as though attempting to bring them warmth, and they blew into their red chapped hands every few moments. Betty Lou and Rachel huddled close together, their arms linked. And Fanny clutched her coat to keep it closed, the buttons long gone.

Elise wouldn't have guessed this unlikely bunch of women could ever come to mean anything to her. But over the weeks of living together in the cramped dormer room, talking every evening, sharing news from home, she'd come to know the women. They felt like friends now.

Elise shuddered at the same time as Fanny. "It's too cold here in Illinois, that it is," Fanny grumbled. Her knuckles were white, her fingers a shade of bluish-purple. Her freckles were more pronounced on her pale face, which thankfully was devoid of bruises.

"Mrs. Gray has warned me it will get much worse." Elise peeked toward the low clouds overhead that spread out in all directions, like an endless gray coverlet that had seen too much usage and too many washings.

The businesses along Main Street were closed for the Sabbath. The doors were locked, the storefronts dark, the street devoid of the usual comings and goings. Even so, the town was alive and taking shape. The construction crews had made good progress during the past month. The shell of a school stood at one end of the street, and several private homes were under construction as well. A new large feed store that Reinhold had helped build was ready for its first coat of paint.

Every week the train brought a new family or two. With each passing day, her depot restaurant grew busier, not just from the residents of the town but also from more passengers riding the Illinois Central.

"Elise, wait!" a voice called out behind her, making her heartbeat stumble. She didn't need to turn to know who it was, and apparently neither did Fanny. The warning scowl she tossed Elise said it all. Fanny still didn't like or trust Thornton.

"Don't let him sweet-talk ye," Fanny said under her breath.

"I won't." Elise slowed her steps. "We're just friends."

"Maybe that's all he is to ye. But I've seen the way he looks at ye, and he doesn't have friendship on his mind."

Elise shook her head. "No, he's only a friend, like Reinhold is."

Fanny snorted. "Reinhold is smitten with ye too. He worships the ground ye walk on, that he does."

She wanted to deny Fanny. But she wasn't entirely oblivious to Reinhold's increased attention. While he couldn't afford to eat in the dining room except occasionally, he waited for her to be done every night so he could walk her back to the hotel. At first she'd assumed he came after her because she always gave him a leftover desert. And because he'd wanted to make sure she returned home safely. At the late hour, the tavern was overflowing with rowdy construction workers. Although she wasn't worried about anything happening, Reinhold had insisted.

Of course, she enjoyed talking with Reinhold and hearing about his work. They'd always been able to share openly, and she appreciated his friendship now more than ever. He was her connection to her past. He'd been there during the dark days after Vater died. He'd been a rock for her after she lost Mutti too. Even now, he understood just how much she missed her sisters. Likewise she understood how much he worried over his own family, for he hadn't received any letters from them since he'd left.

Over the past few nights, however, he'd insisted on accompanying her back to the hotel even though Thornton had come outside with her and offered to walk with her instead. Just last night, Reinhold reached for her hand as they'd strolled toward the hotel. She was too surprised to pull away, and too embarrassed by Thornton's perusal behind her to dislodge herself from Reinhold. While she didn't dare look behind to gauge Thornton's reaction, she could only imagine the mirth in his eyes. He'd likely mock her today. That was probably why he was rushing after her.

"Elise." Thornton was nearly upon her.

"Do ye want me to scare him off?" Fanny whispered, her brow rising and revealing angry eyes.

"I'll be fine, Fanny." She certainly didn't want Fanny getting fired and sent back to New York for threatening Thornton.

Fanny's features remained hard and cold. "Be careful." Then she lengthened her stride to catch up to the other women.

Thornton fell into step beside Elise, slightly out of breath. "Good morning." His smile was lopsided and much too devastating. It made her pulse tumble and bounce. "Might I walk with you the rest of the way?"

"So long as you refrain from any sort of teasing."

"Teasing for what?" Flecks of light brown mingled with the dark in his eyes, making them dance.

"For my over-browned cinnamon buns."

He chuckled. "All right. I won't tease you about him—them." She smiled.

"Although I can't refrain from saying that one bun in particular was rather sticky."

"You promised not to tease."

He laughed again, this time louder, filling her with a lightness that came whenever she bantered with him—which hadn't been often during the past month.

True to his word, he'd visited among the farmers. What had started as simple offers of help had turned into an all-out effort to bring in the harvest. He'd managed to convince several of the construction men who had previous farming experience to go around with him. She'd heard rumors that in addition to their usual salary and bonus, Thornton promised his workers a discount if they were interested in purchasing their own farmland. Together, Thornton and his small crew had worked from sunup to sundown each day no matter the weather.

He'd been the main source of conversation in her dining room, drawing admiration from almost everyone for how hard he was working. Elise hadn't been able to contain her admiration. He'd taken to heart her advice about learning the needs of the people around him. But he'd done much more than she'd expected. He wasn't just learning about the laboring class. He was experiencing it.

Because of his long days in the fields, she hadn't seen him often over the past month, but mostly on Sundays, like today when he took a break from his work.

"I heard you spent the week at the Johnson farm," she said.

"Yes, a good family." There was something harder about his face than when she'd first met him early in the summer. Of course, he was still a gentleman in every sense of the word, from his crisp bow tie to his starched suit coat to his shiny leather shoes. But his features were more solid, more certain and rugged.

"Did you finish the harvesting?" she asked, trying not to stare at him. Instead she focused on the Engle sisters lumbering a short distance ahead with their heavy tread.

"Yes." The answer came out in a relieved sigh.

"So I take it you've decided against switching careers and becoming a farmer?"

"After much soul-searching and agonizing over the decision, you're right. I just can't allow myself so much fun every day. It would spoil me."

It was her turn to laugh.

"I will say, however, I've gained a whole new appreciation for wheat bread. Or really anything made from wheat."

"Since I know you'll miss the wheat fields so much, I'll make everything I possibly can out of wheat this week to help ease your grief."

"You're too kind," he said with a grimace.

She laughed lightly again, and for a moment they walked in silence, the crunch of their shoes against the gravel street slow and leisurely. She'd grown to anticipate their brief interactions.

She especially loved when he came into the kitchen at night after dinner and talked to her about his day, all he'd done and learned. He'd playfully sneak bites of whatever dessert she had sitting on the table. His gaze would follow her around the room, until she felt as wound up as a toy top, her body off-balance, her mind spinning, her blood racing.

"So . . ." he started.

"So, from the tales being told, you're quite the hero. Without the help of your crew, people are saying the farmers would have been hard-pressed to bring in their harvests before the first frost."

He nodded and waved at a family climbing aboard the bench of their wagon. They greeted him with friendly smiles and "*Guten Tag.*"

She'd heard there were a number of German farmers, but she hadn't met them yet. She guessed they were too busy and poor to come into town to socialize at the depot dining room.

"I don't consider myself a hero," he said, the humor gone from his voice. "But if I am, then I have you to thank."

"I didn't do anything," she protested.

"I wouldn't have gotten off my royal throne if not for you."

"Then you're accusing me of taking down the monarchy?"

"I'm crediting you. It's been a good thing."

She had to peek at his face to make sure he wasn't jesting. Sometimes it was difficult to tell when he was being serious. And studying his features helped. Like now. His eyes were darkly sincere, his expression somehow reflecting a peace she hadn't seen there before.

"I've realized," he continued, "just how much I still have to learn about being a good leader."

"I hear mostly positive remarks."

One of his brows arched. "Mostly?"

A month ago she would have blurted out her frustrations without much thought. But perhaps she was growing too, because she searched to find the right words that would express her concerns in a forthright but kind way. "See the women ahead of us?" she asked. The distance had grown as a result of Elise's dawdling pace.

"Ah, yes," he said, watching the band of women as they stopped in front of the hotel door and began to file inside. "What did you call them? My slaves?"

"Yes." And she was only a tad sorry for such a severe accusation. While her work situation had vastly improved, the other women were still earning a pittance for the long hours they put in every day. "How much do you know about what they do on a day-to-day basis?"

"I admit, I've never cooked or sewn or done laundry." From the slight haughtiness of his tone, she could tell he thought such work was suited for women and not men.

"So you think it's worth your while to understand the men but not the women?"

He grinned down at her. "Is this your way of saying you want me to work in the kitchen with you?"

She snorted. "No, I'm saying I think you're arrogant and patronizing." Okay, so maybe she hadn't grown as much as she thought she had.

His grin only widened. "If I remember right, you promised I could work a day with you once I worked with the men."

"I didn't promise."

"I took it as such. And since I clearly need to learn to empathize with my women workers, why don't I start with you?"

"Why don't you start by washing laundry?"

"Maybe. For how long?"

"I doubt you'd last more than a day."

"If I've been able harvest wheat for the past month, I think I can wash a few clothes."

"Good."

"Good."

They walked in silence for a moment, and she began to wonder if she'd overstepped her bounds and offended him.

"So . . ." he started again, as though he had something to say but didn't know quite how to say it. His footsteps slowed even more.

This time she waited for him to finish.

"What did you think of this morning's service?" he finally asked.

She could tell the question wasn't what he'd planned to ask, but she responded honestly nevertheless. "I haven't exactly been on speaking terms with God over the past years, especially since Mutti died. I suppose I felt abandoned by Him. But lately I've begun to think maybe it was less Him abandoning me and perhaps the other way around—me leaving Him."

"That's an interesting observation." The sincerity of his tone beckoned her to share more.

She reached up to finger the cross ring Mutti had given to her that she still wore on a leather strip like a necklace. Mutti had beseeched her to find her fulfillment in a life of surrender to God because Mutti had noticed how she'd pushed God away, first at arm's length, and then further. Elise wanted to blame God for all the bad things that happened to them, just as she'd wanted to blame Count Eberhardt. Just as she'd tried to blame Thornton.

But even if life was unfair at times. Even if people were calloused. Even if bad things happened. Mutti had always said that was a result of living in a sinful and fallen world. God didn't like the bad any more than they did. Someday He planned to create a new earth where the difficulties and tragedies didn't happen anymore.

In the meantime, Mutti tried to reassure her God promised to walk alongside them during their hardships. He promised never to leave them or forsake them. He even promised to give them strength during the long, uphill struggles.

"Let's just say," Elise finally remarked, "I'm beginning to realize God's been there waiting for me and offering me peace. But I've been too bitter to see it or accept it."

He stared ahead, his expression thoughtful.

Elise appreciated that he didn't respond with a glib answer about how everything would work out in the end. She was under no illusion that her life was magically better or that it would all end up perfect. In fact, she was sure there would be many more hardships to come. The decision for her was whether to face those hardships on her own as she'd been doing or accept God's offer to walk with her through them.

"I find it interesting that even though you've been pushing God away," Thornton said, "He's still chosen to use you anyway."

"Use me?"

"To make the lives of the people in this town better."

"I think you're the one doing that. Not me."

"What if God is using us together to make a difference?" Thornton's tone was as earnest as his eyes.

She paused to consider his statement. "You're kind to say so, Thornton, but I don't have any power or influence. I'm just a poor immigrant woman."

Before Thornton could respond, the call of her name interrupted them. They glanced down the street to see Reinhold emerge from the depot.

"You'll join me for dinner, won't you, Elise?" Thornton said quickly, stiffening and straightening his bow tie. "I'd love it if we could talk more."

"I can't—"

"Do you have feelings for Reinhold?" His question slipped out, and once said, she realized it was what he'd been trying to ask her all along during their walk home.

Reinhold had begun to stride toward them with rapid steps, which meant her time alone with Thornton was ending. Elise couldn't keep her disappointment at bay. Not that she didn't enjoy spending time with Reinhold, because she did. But she was hungry for more time and more conversation with Thornton. In fact, the more time she spent with him, the hungrier she grew. It was as if the small snacks only fueled her appetite.

"Do you care for him?" Thornton demanded.

"Of course I care."

"Then you love him?" Thornton's voice was taut, almost demanding.

"Yes, he's a brother to me."

"A brother? That's all?"

"My relationship with Reinhold isn't your concern." She stepped away from him.

Thornton's attention was riveted to her with a strange intensity. "If he's nothing more than a brother to you, then why were you holding hands with him on your walk home last night?"

Elise studied his face. When he cast Reinhold a dark look, a spark of understanding ignited. "Are you jealous?"

He started to deny her, but then cut himself short with a simple shake of his head.

"I think you are," she said with a slow smile.

"I'm just concerned about you," he replied.

"Don't be." She inwardly chuckled at the fun she could have with this new revelation. "He's one of the nicest men I've ever met. And he's good-looking too. Don't you think?" She pretended to study Reinhold.

Thornton sputtered, but before he could say anything more, Reinhold was mere steps away. When he stopped in front of them, he nodded curtly at Thornton. "Good day, Mr. Quincy."

"How can I help you?" Thornton pulled himself to his full height, his features chiseled out of a block of ice.

Reinhold glanced at Elise, his eyes taking on a spark that matched Thornton's. Was he jealous too? Fanny's words from earlier replayed in her mind. *"Reinhold is smitten with ye. He worships the ground ye walk on."*

Apparently she needed to remind Reinhold they were friends and nothing more. At least *she* had nothing more on her mind. She didn't have to tell Thornton that, though. She might have a little fun teasing him a bit longer about his jealousy over Reinhold.

"I came to see Elise," Reinhold said matter-of-factly.

"She's busy right now," Thornton countered. "We were on our way to the dining room to have dinner together."

"We were?" she asked.

Thornton shot her a warning look that almost made her burst into laughter. "Yes, that's exactly where we were going."

"You're correct in saying I'm going to the dining room," she said with as much sweetness as she could muster. "But not to eat. To work."

Thornton's eyes widened as though her statement had thrown him off guard. "To work? But it's Sunday. After working so hard all week, you deserve a day off."

"The dining room won't run itself."

"Let Mrs. Gray do it today."

"She already insisted I take time off this morning to go to church. I won't leave her to manage by herself longer than that."

Thornton had no ready answer to her rebuttal. How could he? It would be heartless of her to take a day off and make Mrs. Gray wait on her, especially when her joints pained her so frequently.

"You really must work?" Thornton asked with a thread of disappointment that tugged at her.

"Yes. There are some of us who get no rest." She meant to keep her voice light and teasing, but she couldn't keep an edge from creeping in.

Reinhold's brows came together in an accusatory scowl. "Maybe you ought to consider shutting down the dining room on the Sabbath." He averted his eyes. "Sir."

The distant train whistle rose in the morning air and prodded Elise. It wouldn't be long before the train stopped and brought passengers to her dining room. Though the train operated less frequently on Sundays, she wanted to be there when it came in.

"Speaking of work," she said to both men, "I really must go."

"Wait, Elise." Reinhold stopped her departure with a touch to her coat sleeve. "I have a letter from my mother."

"Is everything all right?" They didn't hear often from home. Not only was mail slow and irregular in delivery, but they all had better use for the three cents it cost to mail a letter. Elise had splurged and sent Marianne another note to inform her of the change in her employment, and she hadn't yet heard back. While anxious to learn how her sisters were faring, she'd rested in the knowledge that Miss Pendleton was there watching over them.

Reinhold tugged a rumpled sheet from his coat pocket and began unfolding it. "The letter came on the last train yesterday, but Mr. Gray didn't think to give it to me until just now."

The tremor in his fingers stirred the anxiety in her stomach. "Your brothers are still selling newspapers?" The small income the boys made from the long hours of selling papers had provided something to tide the family over until Reinhold could send them his earnings.

"They're still working and they got the money I sent."

"I'm relieved to hear it." Yet something was wrong. She braced herself for the real news.

Reinhold scanned the letter written in German. "Mother says Marianne and Sophie and the two little ones have come to live with them."

Disbelief flooded Elise. "I don't understand. Why? They're supposed to be at the mission."

"According to Mother, the mission had to close its doors."

As the disbelief receded, fear was strewn in its wake.

"The Seventh Street Mission run by Miss Pendleton?" Thornton's voice was incredulous, as though the possibility of the mission closing seemed impossible.

"What happened?" Elise asked. "I thought everything there was secure, that she had the funds to keep the building open. Even if the women didn't have work, at least they had a place to stay."

"Mother doesn't explain," Reinhold said, his hand shaking even more. He kept his focus on the letter and didn't look up at her. "She says . . . she says . . ." His ruddy complexion deepened to crimson.

"Spit it out," Thornton said.

Reinhold visibly swallowed hard. "Mother says that Marianne is with child."

Bile rose in Elise's throat. Her legs turned to pudding and began to buckle beneath her. But before she fell, Thornton's arm wound through hers, catching and steadying her.

"Surely you're mistaken," she heard Thornton say, his voice as confident as his strong grip. "Or at the very least, your mother is mistaken."

Thornton's words somehow gave her enough courage to swallow the bile and drag in a breath of cool air. "Marianne would never—"

"She claims I'm the father." Reinhold's voice was strained.

Elise sucked in a sharp breath. For a moment, the long blast of the incoming train's whistle filled the air around them like the scream of a woman in labor. Elise tried to think, tried to find words, to make sense of everything Reinhold was telling her. But she couldn't.

Sudden, sharp anger sliced her chest. She took a quick step toward Reinhold and lifted her hand to slap him. "How dare you defile Marianne!"

He caught her hand before it connected with his cheek. And for the first time since he'd opened the letter, he met her gaze, his eyes tortured. "I swear to you, Elise. I'm not the father. I'd never, ever do anything to hurt her or you. You have to know that." The anguish in his voice matched his expression.

Her hand began to shake violently, and she jerked it out of his grip. Deep down she believed him. Reinhold was too honorable to take advantage of Marianne. Even so, her anger was too raw and she needed to blame someone.

She stumbled backward. A wall of strength met her as an

arm slipped around her, supporting her and keeping her from falling. Once again Thornton was there. She sagged against him, needing him, unable to bear the weight of the news on her own.

What had Marianne done? After the mission closed, had she resorted to prostitution to support Sophie and the children? The very thought of Marianne having to degrade herself in such a way broke Elise's heart. She closed her eyes to block out the images, the horror, the pain and desperation Marianne must have experienced under the filthy hands of a stranger. Sweet, delicate Marianne, so much like their mother.

Elise pressed a hand to her mouth to keep from crying out.

Thornton's arm around her waist tightened, and he drew her closer. She wanted to bury her face into his chest and weep. Her throat ached and her eyes stung with the need. But she swallowed the sobs.

Elise Neumann never cried. She hadn't cried when Vater died. She hadn't cried when Mutti died. And she wouldn't start now.

CHAPTER 18

Thornton ignored his stinging, chapped hands and dried the pan Elise handed to him. His banter and stories had seemed to cheer her for a while, but whenever they lapsed into silence, her attention would drift and her mood change almost as quickly as the sun disappeared behind the fast-moving November clouds.

She wiped her hands on her apron as she strode away from the washtub toward the pantry.

He hooked the pan on the rack that hung down from the ceiling above the worktable, which was spread with a dozen different items she'd baked already that morning. When he'd heard her arrive before dawn, he hustled down to join her for his first day working with her in the kitchen. He was surprised at how much she and Mrs. Gray had accomplished in the early morning hours.

After a busy morning, Elise insisted that Mrs. Gray take a break. He'd encouraged the older woman to do so as well. If he was already worn out and had aching feet, he could only imagine how Mrs. Gray fared. All day. Every day.

He'd been on the job less than six hours and already he decided the kitchen needed another helper. When he mentioned this to Elise, she only shrugged. Regardless, he sent a telegram to Du Puy, his agent in New York, to have the Children's Aid Society arrange for several more women to come to the town and help them with the growing workload.

Elise had been right about his time doing laundry. He'd worked with the two laundresses for only a few hours when he was ready to quit. Not only had the work taxed every muscle in his back and arms, but it had been unbearably hot with coal ovens fanned to high heat in order to keep the water boiling. As if that hadn't been enough, the hot steam rising into the air made the tiny shack even more stifling. He'd felt like a sausage being roasted in an airless oven. The sensation was one of suffocation.

He understood now why Elise had claimed to being treated like a slave. For the long hours and the awful working conditions, the women weren't compensated enough. The few cents' raise he'd given them earlier was hardly adequate. They deserved a larger income, as well as an improved laundry room that included more windows and better ventilation.

The two days working with the construction crew cook hadn't been quite as draining. Even so, he'd gained a new appreciation for the monotonous labor the women did from well before dawn until long after the men ate their evening meal.

Afterward, he'd spent a couple of days with Hewitt going over the books, recalculating the bottom line, trying to come up with a solution for the financial shortages he was facing. Hewitt remained adamantly opposed to an additional raise for the women workers. And he didn't want to consider hiring more women to help relieve the heavy burden placed on the current crew.

"You've already used up the revenue generated from the sale

of the farmland and the lots in town," Hewitt had told him. "If you hire anyone else or give the women raises, you'll have to eliminate or cut back on the construction projects."

Thornton needed to finish selling off the surrounding farmland, yet the majority of what remained was located farther away from the railroad and was therefore less appealing to potential farmers. He also had more town lots to sell. He'd already told Du Puy to work hard at generating more interest. But he wasn't likely to entice any more immigrants until the spring. That would be too little too late.

With only a week until Thanksgiving, the clock was ticking toward the end of his father's challenge. Although his father's advisor, Mr. Morgan, reassured him in a recent telegram that his father was maintaining his strength, he'd also said the challenge would end on Christmas Day as originally planned.

There had been times over the past several months when Thornton wanted to throw up his hands in defeat. He knew that pursuing the humanitarian efforts with his workers would drain his bank account, and Hewitt had warned him dozens of times to be careful. He'd brushed aside the young assistant's worries like one would a pesky mosquito. Part of him knew he'd done the right thing to improve the lives of the townspeople, whether he won the contest with Bradford or not. But the other part of him still wanted to come out on top so he might finally make his father proud of him.

What would his father say if he could see him now, in the kitchen? Thornton almost laughed aloud at the picture of his father's face etched with scorn.

And what would Rosalind think? He'd pushed aside the guilt that assaulted him, told himself that his day in the kitchen with Elise was no different from his experience with the Engle sisters doing laundry or his time with the other women who worked to feed the construction crew. Besides, even if he'd been looking forward to his time with Elise much more than the others, it was because she'd become his friend. Surely, Rosalind wouldn't find fault with him, would she?

Her letter from yesterday was filled with news of the usual New York parties and social events she'd attended recently. She sweetly informed him how much she missed him and that she couldn't wait for his next visit.

He should have gone to visit her last month. But he'd been so busy helping the farmers that he was unable to tear himself away.

Thornton wiped his hands on the dishrag. He paused and held up his hand. His fingernails were jagged, his skin cracked. He almost didn't recognize his hands anymore. He almost didn't recognize himself at all. The weeks of hard labor had been eye-opening, not just in giving him a glimpse of what life was like for the common laborer, but in showing him his own deficits—his callousness, pride, and selfishness. While he still had a great deal to change, he'd made a start.

The question he wrestled with in the dark hours of the night, lying there on his lumpy mattress tossing and turning, was how far he wanted to take the changes. Was he willing to go all the way to make the transformations needed in both himself and in his town? Because if he did, he'd lose all hope of winning the competition, if he hadn't already lost.

Showing compassion, raising the pay levels, improving working conditions—these weren't quick and easy fixes. They would take more time and capital. Time and capital he could be spending elsewhere. Part of him wanted to keep following the leading of his heart, a prompting he felt good about, one he felt God smiling upon. But another part urged him to put the compassion aside, to move forward in the last month of the competition with the expansion Hewitt expected, applying the same ruthless determination his father had used to build Quincy Enterprises. The kind of effort that looked out for the needs of the greater good rather than the needs of just a few individuals.

Sometimes people had to be sacrificed for the sake of progress, didn't they? That was what he'd always believed in the past, what his father had said whenever he received complaints about his methods of running his businesses.

The poor, the less fortunate, the average man often had to suffer in the short term. But in the long term, the progress and expansion benefited them all. Wasn't that what Thornton still believed? After the past weeks of living and working among the people of his community, could he really take such a view ever again?

The picture of one of the immigrant farm families, the Johnsons, flashed into his mind. Harold Johnson wasn't much older than he was, with a wife and two dainty, blond-haired girls Thornton had come to adore. He imagined one day Elise having daughters like them.

How could he not care what became of the Johnsons, or the Grays, or the dozens of other families he'd gotten to know? How could he willingly let them suffer for the sake of progress? And yet, at the same time, how could he move forward and accomplish everything he needed to and win the competition?

At a clanking and soft muttering in the pantry, Thornton started toward the small room that contained all the supplies Elise needed to run the dining room. He shoved aside his disturbing thoughts of the competition. Time was running out and he ought to be focusing more on the challenge, but he resisted doing so. Instead he wanted a few more days of pretending it didn't exist. After all, he'd labored with the other women workers last week just so he could earn this time of being with Elise.

Even if she'd been rather cold to Reinhold since the letter from home had arrived last week, Thornton knew there was a connection between the two that was very strong. Elise had admitted she didn't love Reinhold, but thought of him more as a brother. Yet Thornton was no fool. He realized that a good man could sway a woman's heart, and Reinhold was a good man. If he worked hard enough, he might be able to win Elise's affection.

That thought didn't sit well with Thornton at all.

He stepped into the pantry, the waft of a hundred aromas greeting him—onion, garlic, molasses, coffee beans, and more. He stopped short at the sight of Elise on her tiptoes trying to push back a bag of grain perched precariously on the edge of the top shelf.

Every sweet, blessed curve of her body was outlined in the faint light coming in through a narrow window near the ceiling. His mouth went dry, and he quickly shifted his gaze to her face. Her bottomless blue eyes met his and were filled with distress.

He jolted forward to help relieve her of the burden. Standing behind her, he reached his long arms up and shoved against the bag, inching it back where it belonged. His hands brushed hers, and his stomach pressed into her back.

She didn't move except to release her grip on the bag and lower her arms.

With his body against her, he was suddenly aware of her warmth, her softness, her nearness. Though he'd maneuvered the bag sufficiently away from the edge, he didn't release it but moved to push it farther. In the process he leaned his face toward her head and took a deep breath of her hair, catching a hint of cinnamon and apples. It caressed his nose and cheeks and worked to stir his longing for her.

He nuzzled his nose deeper into her hair and drew in a lungful of her scent. A warning in the far recesses of his mind urged him to pull away, to put an appropriate distance between them. But when she leaned her head back as though inviting him to remain there, he accepted. He let his lips brush her ear.

She inhaled a sharp breath but didn't move.

He dropped his mouth to behind her ear. The soft, warm skin that met his lips was like the finest sugary delicacy. He let his touch linger there, tasting her, reveling in her.

She tilted her head to the side, giving him access to more of her neck. He brushed his lips across her skin, nearly groaning with the pleasure of it. From the rise and fall of her chest, he could sense he was affecting her too. He lowered his arms away from the bag and wrapped them around her middle. She didn't push him away or attempt to wrench free. Instead she folded her arms across his.

He was sure she would feel the erratic beating of his heart against his ribs. He made a slow trail of kisses to the back of her neck where he pressed a lingering kiss that only made him long to turn her around and take her mouth captive with his. He wanted to connect with her, to fuse their mouths and souls.

"Elise." His whisper was hoarse and laced with desire. He'd tried so hard over the past weeks to hold at bay his attraction to her. But the embers had been there, unable to be extinguished. And now in one brief encounter they'd been fanned into hot flames.

She began to twist around.

He was afraid she'd break free and dash away, only to smack

him over the head with a pan. He'd deserve it if she did. And yet he wasn't ready for the moment together to be over.

End it, Thornton. She isn't yours. And until she is, keep your hands off.

Reluctantly he loosened his grip on her. Instead of wiggling away from him as he expected, she spun so she was facing him. When she slipped her arms around him and hugged him, for a full three seconds he couldn't move.

Then he drew her into his embrace completely. She pressed her face against his chest and stayed there as if that was exactly where she wanted to be.

Warm satisfaction wafted through him. He brought a hand up to her head and stroked the loose strands back to the center braid. When her hold intensified, he closed his eyes as a wave of something intense washed over him.

Was it love? Was he falling in love with this beautiful, strong-willed woman?

And why not? What was so wrong about loving her? Maybe she wasn't the kind of woman his father had in mind for him. Maybe loving her would cost him the challenge. But did it matter? If he loved her, and if he could earn her love in return, wouldn't that mean more than claiming a victory in the competition with Bradford? Maybe he wouldn't win his father's favor or win the leadership of the company, but he'd gain something far more valuable, wouldn't he?

"Thank you for everything you've done to try to help me this week."

He nodded and pressed a kiss against the top of her head. He hadn't done much. He'd sent a few telegrams east to attempt to discover what had happened to the Seventh Street Mission and to Miss Pendleton. His agent had returned the message with the news that the mission was boarded up and empty. Thornton had also attempted to have a telegram delivered to Marianne, but his agent hadn't been able to locate the Weiss family even though he'd gone to the tenement that both Reinhold and Elise had described to him.

"I wish there was more I could do," he whispered, stroking her hair again.

"There's nothing we can do now but wait." Her words were a soft mumble against his chest.

He closed his eyes and fought back the aching desire he felt for her. *Watch it, Thornton. If you love her, you'll respect her.*

"Thorn?" A familiar voice echoed in the kitchen, a voice that sounded like his except more commanding.

Elise jumped away from him as quickly as if he were hot coals and she'd been burned. Thornton was too astonished by the voice to think of anything else. He rose to his full height, raked his fingers through his hair, and stepped to the door.

Bradford was already heading out of the room, never one to linger or waste time.

"Bradford, my good man," Thornton said.

Bradford grinned. He was dressed in a dark frock coat over a vest and lighter trousers. His fashionable necktie was tied in a knot with the pointed ends sticking out like wings. He also wore a tall top hat, which completed his gentlemanly appearance of perfection.

"To what occasion do I deserve the honor of your visit?" Thornton asked, suddenly self-conscious that he was wearing neither a vest nor a necktie. In fact, his top button was undone and his shirt slightly untucked.

"I've been hearing rumors of a fine restaurant you're running here at your depot." Bradford's keen gaze didn't miss a detail as Thornton quickly stuffed his shirttails back into his trousers and then fumbled at the top button. "I thought I'd find out for myself if the rumors are true."

Thornton could feel Elise move behind him, and he had the urge to motion her to stay in the pantry. Before he could caution her, she sidled past him and stared directly at Bradford, her eyes widening, clearly not expecting to see a mirror image of Thornton standing across the room, albeit a more sophisticated and better-dressed mirror image.

Bradford sized her up at the same moment. Something sparked in Bradford's expression that Thornton didn't like. He couldn't put his finger on exactly what it was because Bradford, as usual, hid his emotions before Thornton could delve in and explore. Even so, the corner of Bradford's mouth quirked into a half smile. "I see you've been otherwise occupied. Shall I come back later?"

The sarcasm, meant to be a jest, rankled Thornton like a sharp burr stuck in his sock. In the past, maybe he could have responded with equal wit. But this time he stiffened and didn't return the smile. "Bradford, this is Elise Neumann. She's the manager of that fine restaurant you've heard about."

Bradford's eyes flickered with surprise for a brief instant. He looked as though he might say something else abrasive and offensive, but the warning that was surely written on Thornton's face steered him a different direction. "Pleased to meet you, Miss Neumann. I'm Thornton's twin. His better half."

"I wasn't quite clear on the twin part," she said as seriously. "But it's quite obvious who's the better half."

Bradford gave a thin grin that didn't reach his eyes. "Ah, I see why she's your pet, Thorn. She's as witty as she is pretty."

Thornton bristled and bunched his fists, battling a strong

desire to stride across the room and punch Bradford in the face. "She's not my pet. And if you want to remain in my depot, I'll expect for you to treat her with respect."

Bradford's brow shot up, obviously not expecting Thornton's terseness or threat. "Take it easy, brother. I just assumed she's a . . . well, a diversion, considering the fact you're planning a Christmas wedding to Miss Beaufort."

Thornton shook his head vigorously in a vain attempt to silence his twin, but Bradford's eyes landed on him with faux innocence.

"You are still planning a Christmas wedding, aren't you, Thorn?"

"As a matter of fact, I haven't asked Miss Beaufort to marry me yet, Brad."

"Everyone is expecting the engagement announcement when you go home at the end of the month."

"Maybe from you and Dorothea. But I never made any promises to Rosalind."

"That's strange. Father seemed to think it was a done deal. And he was very pleased with both of our choices."

Thornton's chest constricted, his muscles tightening in anticipation of an onslaught of anger and frustration from Elise. At the revelation of his girl back east, surely she felt betrayed, belittled, or even used—considering he'd held and caressed her just moments ago.

To her credit, she didn't make a sound. In fact, she moved past him to the stove, opened the firebox, and began to shovel coal inside. He wanted to go to her, wrap his arms around her and reassure her that he wasn't using her, that he really did care about her, that he might even be falling in love with her.

He didn't know what such a love felt like, although he'd never felt for Rosalind anything like what he did for Elise. Rosalind was a sweet girl, kind and sophisticated, and she'd likely make a good mother someday. But she didn't understand his humor, even if she was quick to smile and laugh. She never challenged him and was instead the epitome of support and encouragement. She was enjoyable to be with, but that was all it was—fun.

Was that all he wanted from life—fun, enjoyment, a life of ease? After working hard for the past couple of months, he wasn't so sure anymore. How could he continue with his blissful existence and lavish lifestyle when he was all too aware now of the difficulties and challenges so many others faced on a daily basis for their existence?

Whatever his future might be, he didn't want to hurt Elise. And he didn't want Bradford's visit to ruin everything, especially after he'd worked hard to earn her trust and develop a friendship with her.

"So if you're not planning to marry Rosalind," Bradford said, "does that mean you're pulling yourself out of the challenge?"

"I don't know what it means." He eyed Elise, waiting for her to question him, not only about Rosalind but also about the challenge. He hadn't told anyone in Quincy except Hewitt about his father's challenge and the competition with Bradford. He figured it wouldn't matter. But maybe he should have explained everything to Elise.

She closed the firebox and lifted the lid on the pot on the stove. The strong aroma of something delicious filled the room and made his stomach gurgle.

Bradford had turned his attention on Elise again and was studying her. Too closely. Something in Bradford's narrowed eyes told Thornton his brother knew more than he was letting on.

"Why don't we move our conversation to the dining room," Thornton said. "We can sit out there."

"Are you sure? I don't want to take you away from your *work* here in the kitchen." Bradford's emphasis on the word *work* and his raised brows told Thornton his brother was well-informed about the goings-on in Quincy. Thornton guessed Bradford had his assistant come down from time to time in order to gather information on his progress, the same way Thornton had Hewitt monitor Bradford's progress.

"Go ahead and wait for me in the dining room," Thornton said. "I'll be with you in a minute."

Bradford's lips cocked into a crooked smile, one that irritated Thornton again. With any other woman, under any other circumstances, Bradford's heckling would have made him smile in return. But with Elise he felt protective.

Once Bradford was gone from the kitchen, Thornton stuck his hands in his pockets and expelled a frustrated breath. Elise clanked the lid back on the kettle and began to pour fresh coffee into the coffeepot.

"Elise," he began, his voice almost pleading.

"You don't owe me an explanation," she said quietly.

"I want to explain."

She finished with the coffee and then added a couple of dashes of a spice and a sprinkle of another before she closed the lid and pushed the pot over one of the burners. When she grabbed an empty bucket from under the washtub and started walking toward the back door, he lurched after her. His fingers closed around her arm, stopping her before she could exit. At his touch, she froze and stared down at the bucket.

"I'm not engaged."

"It doesn't matter to me."

"I wish it mattered." The words came out before he could think about the implication. "The fact is," he continued, "I don't love Rosalind." *Not like I love you*, he thought. But Elise was already shaking her head.

"If you don't love her, why were you planning to propose to her?"

He fumbled to find the right answer, one that would make as much sense to him as to her. There was no reason to propose to Rosalind if he didn't love her. The stipulation of his father's challenge included love, not just marriage.

"Remember when I told you my father is dying of pleurisy?" She nodded.

"Well, lucky for me, he decided to establish a competition between Bradford and me to see which of us would gain leadership of the company after he dies."

"To see which of you is most worthy?"

"Something like that."

"He wants you to get married before he dies?"

"A marriage of love, not convenience."

"Oh." The word echoed with disbelief.

"Exactly." He sighed. "But that's only half of it. The other part is that both of us need to develop a town within six months."

"Six months?" Her voice was laced with sarcasm. "That's way too long. I can't believe he didn't give you three months. Or maybe two."

Thornton laughed, but it was mirthless, mimicking the emptiness in his soul, the emptiness of a young man who'd only ever longed to please but had somehow never accomplished it.

"So are you winning the competition?" Elise asked, as direct as always.

Thornton dropped his hold of Elise's arm and let his shoulders sag. "No. Probably not."

"Why not? You've worked hard. Every day Quincy seems to be growing."

He was silent for a moment, wondering how he could explain the diversions he'd had to his well-laid plans, the detours he'd taken, the many changes he'd made—mostly because of her encouragement to think about people as individuals with real lives, rather than mere numbers to add to his checklist of accomplishments.

"Let's just put it this way. I've diverted the funds I could be using for development of the town into pay raises, improved working conditions, and better food for the workers."

She studied his face as though reading all he'd left unsaid—that his humanitarian efforts had put him at a disadvantage to Bradford. Her expression softened, and her eyes filled with a tenderness he hadn't seen there before, at least not directed at him. "Thornton Quincy, you're a good man."

His chest expanded with warmth. "Then you don't hate me for not telling you about Rosalind?"

"Like I said, you don't owe me any explanations."

"I've been in a relationship with her." He needed to tell her the truth finally. "Which is why I wasn't being fair to you or her during the train ride to Quincy. I was trying my best to make myself fall in love with her."

Her brow rose. "Sounds about as easy as making bread out of bricks."

"Even harder, especially when you get distracted by a talented cook who makes amazing coffee."

At his compliment, she reached for the door handle. "I need to get back to work. Apparently this *talented* cook has a reputation to uphold. We wouldn't want to disappoint your brother, now, would we?"

Her lashes dropped as she went to open the door, but he wedged his foot in the way. When she glanced back at him, her eyes were full of questions. His muscles tensed at the need to pull her into his arms. He wanted to tell her that the contest with his brother didn't matter anymore, that maybe it never had. Yet he had a responsibility to see the competition through to completion. Even if he didn't win, he had to finish it. At the very least he could prove to his father he wasn't a quitter and maybe earn just a little of his respect.

"Go on now," Elise whispered.

With a willpower he didn't realize he had, he took a giant step backward. "I know you won't be able to function in here without my help, so I'll try to hurry."

She smiled. "I won't know what to do as I wait for your return."

He couldn't hold back his smile as he made his way through the kitchen and into the dining room. Bradford was already seated at a table in front of a window overlooking Main Street. He was examining the town and jotting down notes.

Thornton pulled out a chair and sat down across from his brother. "Find anything of interest?"

Bradford closed his notebook. "I see you have a schoolhouse almost done. Seems an odd choice for the first six months of building a town, considering there aren't many children yet."

Usually the general stores, taverns, livery stables, feed stores, and granaries were the first things to fill up the commercial corridor. Of course, churches were integral to the community as well. But schools usually came later once the town's security was established. If the town lasted—and there were no guarantees that it would—then other businesses like barbers, jewelers, bakers, undertakers, libraries, and more would develop later.

"I promised the farmers who bought land around Quincy I would provide a school for them."

Bradford folded his hands over his notebook, his expression patronizing. "We make many promises to lure people to settle here, but that doesn't mean we fulfill them all right away."

"I realize that. But this was important to them."

"Oh yes, I've heard rumors of your new methods." Bradford's lips curved into a cynical smile. "You've become a friend to the poor."

"It's more than that."

Bradford leaned forward and said quietly, "Do you really think by becoming everyone's best friend you'll win this contest?"

"I'm not becoming everyone's best—"

"Or do you think giving pay raises will gain you better workers?"

"Maybe not, but maybe it's the right thing to do anyway."

Bradford shook his head. "You'll end up attracting hordes of lazy, impoverished people who will expect a handout but won't want to work hard in return."

That was what Thornton had believed at one time too, that the poor were mostly lazy and incompetent and unwilling to work diligently for their keep. But after laboring alongside them for weeks, he'd learned quite the opposite. Most of them were incredibly hard workers who were seeking to make better lives for themselves, yet they'd been trapped with little hope of improving their situations. Maybe he wouldn't be able to turn around their lives completely, but he could do his part in helping them revolve one degree, couldn't he?

"Whatever the end result," Thornton said, "I've done what I thought I needed to."

"I suppose you also thought you could conjure up feelings for a poor, pretty kitchen wench and think that would be acceptable in the competition."

Anger pushed Thornton from his chair, and it toppled behind him with a crash. He towered over Bradford, his hands fisted, his body taut with the need to pummel his brother. "I told you to talk about Elise respectfully."

Bradford chuckled. "Whoa, boy."

Thornton inwardly counted to five. Bradford was goading him. He should have recognized the tactic, one Bradford used many times in their childhood to push Thornton to do things his way. Before he could compose a calm response, Bradford held up his hands as if in surrender.

"I apologize for my behavior. It was never my intent to cause a rift between you and your kitchen girl—I mean, you and Elise. As it turns out, it's probably a good thing. You can thank me later for saving you from a big mistake."

Elise? A big mistake? He didn't see her that way at all. She was one of the best things that had ever happened to him. But he wasn't surprised at Bradford's scorn. That was how his father would likely react to Elise too. "As it turns out," Thornton said dryly, "Elise is forgiving and didn't let the news of Rosalind come between us."

Bradford slid to the edge of his chair, his eyes widening with disbelief and something else—was it frustration? From what Hewitt had reported lately, Wellington had surged ahead of Quincy in almost every area of development, from the number of buildings to population, to revenue and more. Surely Bradford had nothing to worry about. So why was he in Quincy and taking notes?

"What are you really doing here, Bradford?" Thornton crossed his arms. "We've left each other alone all fall. Now we have one month to go. Why not stay out of each other's way until the end?"

Elise came out of the kitchen at that moment with two cups of coffee and started toward them.

"Like I said, I wanted to try your restaurant." Bradford's answer was smooth. Too smooth.

Bradford might be able to cover his emotions, but Thornton knew his twin well enough to realize Bradford was up to something. He prayed it had nothing to do with Elise, but a gut feeling told him it did.

"Leave her alone," Thornton said in a low voice as Elise wound around tables and chairs toward them. "If you don't, I'll make sure you regret it."

Thornton wasn't a vindictive person, but protectiveness surged through his blood, turning it hot and making him capable of doing anything to take care of Elise.

Bradford was watching him as though gauging his reaction. Something flickered there but was gone before Thornton could understand what it was exactly. It left Thornton uneasy, and more determined than ever to make sure Elise was safe.

CHAPTER 19

Elise wobbled on the ice and threw out her arms to balance herself against the slippery magnetism that seemed determined to drag her down. Her shoes had no tread or traction, which made the trek down Main Street more difficult. To make matters worse, she'd left her coat behind in the dormer room at the hotel.

She'd been too frantic to get help and had forgotten how the biting November wind caused the temperature to drop, turning puddles into tiny skating ponds. Her linen shirt and skirt were threadbare and provided little protection, no more than the shift she wore underneath.

Her mind screamed at her to move faster and flashed with the image of Fanny curled up into a ball on her bed, rocking back and forth without saying a word. The sight had frightened Elise when she went back to the hotel to change her skirt after spilling syrup on it.

Instead of finding an empty room, Fanny was there, her bodice ripped, blood streaking her skirt, and bruises around her neck—bruises in the shape of fingers. Elise tried to get Fanny to talk, to tell her what had happened. Had her boss beat her up again? Had she been attacked by someone on the way to work earlier in the morning?

But Fanny hadn't answered any of her questions. She hadn't spoken a word except to whisper that she wanted to die.

Elise panicked and ran to fetch the one person who might be able to assist. Thornton. Although he hadn't worked in the dining room since his brother's visit last week, he'd been in his office at the depot most of the time, poring over charts, figures, and diagrams with Mr. Hewitt. She hadn't talked with him often or for very long, but she still cherished the rare moments when he'd come to the kitchen for an extra cup of coffee or to ask her about her day.

She tried not to think about Rosalind. Still, Elise had replayed in her mind dozens of times the conversation with Thornton. He'd claimed he didn't love Rosalind. He certainly didn't seem to be pining after her. Even so, the fact that he had ties to a woman back east, while not surprising, was still unsettling. Yet it shouldn't have been, as she didn't have any claim on Thornton and had never pretended there could be anything between them.

Yes, they'd had a brief lapse in judgment in the pantry and had crossed a boundary. Yes, she could admit they shared an attraction. And yes, she'd enjoyed every second of being in his arms and had relived the moment too many times to count. But that didn't mean anything, just as his kiss hadn't meant anything at the Chicago depot.

Her cheeks stung from the cold as she hurried along.

"Elise?"

At Thornton's call, coming from the direction of the depot, she almost slipped and fell.

"What are you doing outside without a coat?" He hustled toward her, letting the depot door bang shut behind him. He shrugged out of his navy coat, which he wore over a matching vest. After the weeks of wearing casual attire while he'd done manual labor, she could admit he made a dashing figure in his fancier garments.

He draped his coat about her shoulders and pulled the lapels together, surrounding her with his spicy scent. He frowned. "Your teeth are chattering. We need to get you inside right away." He began to guide her toward the depot, but she pulled back.

"No." Her breath came out raspy from the tightness of her lungs. "It's Fanny. She's been hurt—attacked by someone. I'm afraid she might attempt to take her own life."

From the blankness of his expression, Elise knew he had no idea who Fanny was. Nevertheless, he nodded, his expression turning grave.

"She needs help." Her voice echoed the urgency that had been building inside her. "Can you help me save her?"

Thankfully, he didn't ask any questions, reminding her of the day of the riots in New York City when he'd escorted poor Isaiah inside the mission. Thornton had acted first and asked questions letter. She appreciated that about him.

With the support of Thornton's steadying arm, the walk back to the hotel took little time. Once inside, Elise raced up the stairs leading the way to the third story. When they ducked through the low doorway, Thornton stopped short as he took in the cramped quarters.

"Is this where you live?"

"No. It's home to a group of trolls." She rolled her eyes. "Of course it's where we live."

The lines creasing his forehead deepened as his eyes touched on each cot, including the one Fanny occupied. "There are five of you living in this tiny space?"

"Six." Elise wound through the maze of clothes, bags, and other personal items that covered nearly every inch of floor space. She nodded to her bedding in the narrow spot where she slept. "Apparently, Hewitt only made arrangements for the original five employees, so I sleep on the floor."

Thornton muttered something under his breath.

Elise made her way to Fanny and knelt next to the cot. Thankfully, in the short time Elise had been gone, Fanny hadn't attempted to take her life. She gently touched the young woman's back and took it as a good sign when she didn't flinch as she had the other times. "It's me, Elise," she said softly. "I'm back and I'm going to help you."

Fanny didn't respond except to duck her head deeper into her arms.

Elise grabbed a blanket from the floor and wrapped it around Fanny. "Listen to me, Fanny. I want to move you someplace safe and warm." But where? Perhaps another hotel room, if one was available.

She looked at Thornton, hoping he'd have an idea. He was stooped under the low ceiling, his face still lined with disbelief. Perhaps now after seeing their cramped living space, he'd understand why the charges for their boarding were too high. But now wasn't the time to get into an argument about it. Fanny was their priority.

"She'd benefit from a bed," Elise said. "Somewhere private."

"She can have my room at the depot," he offered. "I'll move out and find somewhere else to live."

"Really?"

"I won't hear of anything else. Why don't you move in with her to watch over her? It's a double bed, big enough for two. "

Elise could only stare at him, at the sincerity in his expression and the turmoil in his eyes. Her throat tightened with a sweet ache. He was truly a good man. No, he wasn't perfect; he still had much to learn about the plight of people like her. But at least he was willing to learn. Even more, he was willing to make changes.

He'd done everything he could to help her glean more information about Marianne and the situation back home—sending letters and telegrams, having his New York agent do some investigating, even offering to make contact with Marianne on his next visit back east. Although she worried about her sisters every day, she knew Thornton was on her side. He was generous and kindhearted in helping her, and his willingness to care for Fanny proved it even more.

Fanny didn't protest when Thornton lifted her into his arms. Elise tucked the blanket around the battered woman. Together they made their way to the depot, to Thornton's room across the hall from the Grays.

The bedroom was spacious, as big as the one she shared with the women at the hotel. The place exuded style and wealth. A broad chest of drawers flanked by a gilded mirror stood against one wall. The double bed was graced with an elegant nightstand containing a globe lantern. Two wing chairs were positioned on either side of a corner stove with old-looking books stacked in piles around them. A lovely thick rug covered most of the floor.

Thornton deposited Fanny gently onto the bed, quickly gathered his belongings except his books, and then exited the room with word that he'd fetch warm water. Elise wasn't exactly sure where to begin helping Fanny, so she was relieved when Mrs. Gray arrived and took over.

"I'll clean her up," Mrs. Gray said after she'd examined Fanny. "This isn't something for a young innocent like you to witness."

Elise reluctantly relinquished Fanny's care to Mrs. Gray and returned to the dining room. When Mrs. Gray descended later, her face was ashen and her lips set grimly.

"How is she?" Elise asked quietly as Mrs. Gray limped into the kitchen and crossed to the stove.

"She's been badly abused."

"Did she talk to you?"

Mrs. Gray shook her head as she poured herself a cup of coffee, unable to hide the tremor in her hand. "Do you have any idea who's responsible?"

"My first guess is her employer, Mr. Kraus, the tailor." Elise thought back to all the times that autumn when Fanny returned to the dormer with one new bruise after another. Fanny had complained about his brutality, and Elise had no doubt Fanny's stubborn personality had only escalated the situation. She'd likely resorted to passive measures that had incited Mr. Kraus further. Elise knew firsthand how irritating Fanny could be when she set her mind to it.

"Sadly I think you're right." Mrs. Gray took a sip of her coffee, without adding her usual teaspoon of sugar and cream, almost as if the occasion were too severe. Only bitterness would suffice. "I've seen the bruises he leaves on his wife and child, which shows him for the twisted soul he is."

"I don't know for sure," Elise hastened to explain. She didn't want to spread false rumors and jeopardize Fanny's chances of returning to her seamstress work.

"Mr. Quincy is already investigating," Mrs. Gray said. "I'm sure we'll know soon enough."

Throughout the rest of the evening, Elise took turns with

Mrs. Gray in sitting with Fanny. Later, Thornton came in wearing a grim expression, yet he didn't make mention of what he'd discovered, and Elise was too busy to attempt to corner him and ask about it.

She tried to coax Fanny into eating or drinking something, but Fanny only shook her head and turned away from her to stare at the wall. Once the light was out, the embers burning in the stove cast a warm glow over the room. Elise stood at the edge of the bed, debating whether to sleep on the floor or crawl in next to Fanny.

A real bed with a real mattress. The idea of spending just one night in comfort was more than tempting. She pressed her hand against it, feeling it mold to her weight.

"Sleep with me" came Fanny's plea, barely audible. "Please."

Elise's chest constricted with the need to cry for this beautiful woman who lay broken and used and defeated. Fanny hadn't deserved any of the heartache she'd faced in her life, not one bit of it. Not any more than Elise had deserved her heartache. They were the kind of women who were dispensable, easy to use up and cast off when the last amount of worth had been sucked out of them.

Tentatively, Elise sat down on the mattress, allowing herself a moment of pleasure. Then she swung her legs up, tucked them under the soft down comforter, and lay on her back. She stared up at the ceiling.

Thornton's masculine scent lingered in the fibers of the comforter and mattress, and for a brief instant she imagined him lying next to her, his body brushing hers, his warm breath on her neck as it had been that day in the pantry when he'd come up behind her and held her. Her heart pattered faster at the memory.

Beneath the cover, Fanny's hand touched Elise's. At first Elise thought it was an accident. But when Fanny's cold fingers gripped hers, Elise realized Fanny was holding on to her in more than one way.

Tears sprang to Elise's eyes. "I won't let you go," she whispered, turning toward Fanny. Though Fanny was facing the wall, she'd reached out to Elise and there was hope in that. Perhaps Fanny was telling her she needed her, that with Elise by her side she'd be able to make it. Yes, it would be a dark and difficult journey ahead, but they'd walk it together.

"I won't let you go," Elise whispered again.

Fanny squeezed her hand in reply. And that was all Elise needed.

Was that the way it was with God too? When she was hurting and crushed by the weight of heartache, was God there holding on to her hand, telling her He'd never let her go?

Elise rested her hand on the ring necklace that lay against her chest, feeling the little cross through her nightgown. *I won't let you go*. This time the whisper was God's, and it came from deep in her soul, reassuring her and also warning her. Although she'd faced trials before, darker days loomed ahead, perhaps the darkest yet.

She needed to hang on to Him the same way Fanny clung to her. Maybe this time she'd be able to face the storms with courage and become the kind of woman her Mutti always believed she could be.

❦

Shouts woke Elise out of a dream where she'd been floating in warm sunshine on feathers and fluffy cotton and soft down. She sat up with a gasp and for a moment tried to remember where she was. The warmth and comfort surrounding her was foreign, almost surreal.

The slamming of a door made her jump, causing the bed-springs to squeak. She blinked, combed her hair out of her eyes, and at the sight of the corner stove and its orange glow, she remembered. She was in the depot, sleeping in Thornton's bed with Fanny.

Fanny? Elise patted the bed next to her and exhaled a relieved breath at the feel of Fanny's warm body near hers.

Outside the depot came more shouts, even some cries.

"What's all the noise?" Fanny asked sleepily.

Elise slid to the edge of the bed, letting the down comforter fall away. Immediately the chill of the room crawled over her skin, making her shudder. "Don't worry," Elise whispered. "You stay here and I'll go see what's wrong."

Elise stuffed her bare feet into her boots and grabbed her coat from a hook on the wall. Slithering into the worn garment, she opened the door. Across the dark hallway, Mrs. Gray stood in her bedroom doorway in a robe, her hair plaited in a single braid that fell over her shoulder and hung down in front. She held a lantern, which illuminated the fear radiating from her eyes and turned her skin to a waxy yellow.

"What's happening?" Elise asked.

"The new feed store is on fire."

"Oh no!" The chill on her skin turned icy. "Thornton? Did anyone tell him?"

"He's already out with the rest of the men attempting to keep it from spreading to the nearby houses and businesses."

An awful dread thumped against Elise's chest, and she started down the steps. She could imagine how discouraged and frantic Thornton would be. He'd already made so many sacrifices for the town and the people who lived here. In doing so, he'd jeopardized his ability to win the competition with his brother. Of course, he hadn't come out and said so, but she understood it nevertheless. Now with a fire about to destroy the little chance he had left of staying in the challenge, he might grow desperate. What if he did something stupid in his attempt to save the building?

"You can't go out there," Mrs. Gray called after her. "It's much too dangerous for a young woman."

"I need to make sure Thornton's safe," she said over her shoulder.

"Please be careful." Mrs. Gray's admonition trailed after her. Even after Elise stepped outside, the dear woman's motherly concern followed her and warmed her against the frigid cold of the night. The shouts and calls from the far end of Main Street drew her attention, as did the bright flames leaping out of the shingled roof, darting into the starless night sky.

Her heart sank at the realization the building was already engulfed. The brigade of men lined up from the well to the fire, passing buckets along from one hand to the next. But they wouldn't be able to combat the serpent of fire winding through new pine, greedily licking and consuming everything in its path.

Sparks and small flames tossed by the never-ending prairie breeze had landed upon a nearby residence. The outline of one man in particular on the roof made Elise's stomach churn. Thornton's lean but muscular frame wasn't hard to miss, especially because he was still attired in his business clothes. Almost as if he'd never gone to bed.

Elise couldn't be sure of the time, but she guessed it was well after midnight. She didn't want to think about the fact that after giving his room up to her and Fanny, maybe he hadn't found a new place to stay.

Regardless of the cold that numbed her fingers and toes, she hurried down the street toward him, slipping and sliding on the ice the same way she had earlier in the day. When she arrived at the residence, she took a place in one of the bucket lines. As she worked, more people, including women, joined in the effort.

The fire at the feed store blazed higher and crackled louder. Soon it became apparent they wouldn't be able to save it. So their efforts shifted to the buildings surrounding it. They doused them with water, and more men gathered with Thornton on the rooftops wielding wet blankets and beating out sparks before they could ignite.

The hungry flames feasted on the feed store until they consumed everything, leaving only a black skeleton in its place. When the last of the flames on the surrounding buildings was extinguished, Elise collapsed to the ground with some of the other women, her gaze straying once again to the rooftop where Thornton had tirelessly worked and still stood watching the last of the flames devour the feed store.

"Elise." At the gentle voice next to her, she tore her attention away from Thornton to find Reinhold kneeling beside her. "You need to get out of the cold."

He wrapped his coat about her shoulders over her own, which was now damp and cold from the icy water splashing her in the haste of passing the buckets. He slipped his arm around her and began to raise her to her feet.

"I want to help," she protested.

"There's nothing more to do," Reinhold said, gathering her frozen fingers into his warm ones and blowing on them.

The heat of his mouth against her flesh awoke her to the ache in not only her fingers but also her toes. Reinhold was right. She'd likely develop frostbite if she didn't get warmth back into her body soon. But she also wasn't ready to leave Thornton. Yes, he was safe. But for a reason she couldn't explain, she wanted to be near him, talk to him, comfort him.

"You're freezing." Reinhold blew against her fingers again. At the painful pricking, she cried out before she could stop herself.

Without waiting for her permission, he scooped her up into his arms and began striding toward the depot.

Elise glanced over Reinhold's shoulder at the rooftop where Thornton was standing. She caught a final glimpse of him and realized he was staring after her. She wanted to demand Reinhold put her down so she could race back to Thornton, climb up onto the roof with him, and hug him. She could only imagine how discouraged he was at that moment. But it was unrealistic to think about going to him now in front of everyone.

Instead she relaxed in Reinhold's arms and allowed him to carry her to the dining room. He deposited her in one of the chairs and ordered her not to move. He went into the kitchen, where she could hear him banging around. Mrs. Gray joined him and soon appeared with a basin of warm water and a hot cup of coffee. Not long after that, Mr. Gray returned, his face and clothes covered in soot, his hands raw and red.

The news he carried was dismal. The feed store was completely destroyed, and several of the surrounding businesses had been damaged. They sat and talked for a while and tried to warm themselves, until finally dawn began to light the sky.

All Elise wanted to do was go and find Thornton, but instead she trudged back upstairs and readied herself for the day, moving soundlessly so she didn't awaken Fanny.

As she stepped into the deserted dining room, her heart leaped in her chest at the sight of Thornton talking to Mr. Gray. His back was facing her, but she could see the singe marks all across his coat and shirtsleeves where flying sparks had landed and burned through his clothes. His hair was disheveled and gray in places from ash. At Mr. Gray's glance her way, Thornton spun as though he'd been waiting for her. His face, like Mr. Gray's, was smudged with soot and bronzed from the wind and cold. But thankfully he didn't have any evident burn marks.

His dark eyes drank her in like a man dying of thirst.

Mr. Gray cleared his throat. "I think I'll go wash up and change clothes."

Thornton didn't acknowledge Mr. Gray's statement, but instead continued to stare intently at Elise. Feeling overwhelmed by what she saw in his expression, she only nodded at Mr. Gray as he passed her. When they were alone in the dining room with only the occasional noises coming from the kitchen that told her Mrs. Gray was busy with breakfast preparations, she cocked her head at Thornton and attempted a smile. But it came out weak and wobbly.

"How are you?" she managed to ask.

He shook his head and dropped his eyes, but not before she saw the defeat there.

She crossed to him, wanting to comfort him but unsure how. "Thornton . . . I'm so sorry." Even though she knew she shouldn't, even though she was crossing the boundary between them again, she reached up and pressed a hand against his cheek.

He leaned into it and closed his eyes tightly. When he opened them again, he whispered, "Elise, I've failed. The challenge is over. I might as well send word to Bradford tomorrow that I'm withdrawing. When I return home next week, I'll tell my father I'm done. Bradford can have leadership of the company."

She pushed down her hesitancy and brought her other hand to his face so she was cupping both cheeks. "You haven't failed. Maybe on paper you'll fall short of Bradford, but what you've accomplished here in Quincy can't ever be taken away from you. Look at all the people you've helped and all the lives you've changed. That's not failure. That's success."

He studied her face. "I've always wanted to prove to my father I could do anything Bradford could. I wanted to show him he has every reason to be as proud of me as he is of my brother."

"He should be proud of you. I've never known a better man than you."

His arms moved to her waist, and he pulled her toward him, causing her to wrap her arms around his neck—not that she minded. In fact, she found herself relieved, finally where she'd longed to be all night.

She buried her face into his neck, savoring the day-old stubble on his chin scraping against her temple and cheek. She had the sudden urge to whisper the words *I love you*. The strong urge took her completely by surprise.

Did she love this man? Or did she only mean to comfort him with the words?

She squeezed him tighter. It didn't matter right now how she felt. His feelings were all that counted. He was hurt and frustrated and discouraged.

"Maybe you won't be the leader of your father's company," she murmured against his neck, "but you've earned the respect and leadership of this town, of these people. And that makes you a good man. Actually a great one."

His hands splayed across her lower back, and one of them

slid up her spine, making a trail until he reached her shoulder. Then his fingers encircled the back of her neck and turned her head slightly, enough for his breath to caress her lips.

Sweet warmth swirled inside her as his mouth brushed lightly against hers. But it was enough to stir a desire for more. She grazed her lips back against his, relishing the soft texture and curves.

Then with a groan his mouth captured hers fully, with an urgent, almost demanding pressure. There was nothing sweet about his touch anymore. Instead it was powerful and full of needing her. He'd lost a building tonight. Maybe even lost the competition and his father's company. And now he needed her to be there for him, to care about him anyway, regardless of who he was and what he stood for.

She rose on tiptoes to show him she did care. She cared about him and wanted him to know what an honorable and worthy man he was. She molded her lips to his and met his passion with her own—a passion she hadn't known existed in her. But as she pressed herself against him with both her body and soul, all the things she loved about him suddenly overwhelmed her until she was breathless.

She loved him. She couldn't deny it any longer. She loved him more than anyone or anything. And because she loved him, she wanted him to be happy. To succeed. To win.

He *needed* to win. If he became the leader of his family's company, he would have the power to make even more changes, to do even greater good. With his combination of sharpness and sensitivity, he'd be the better man to take over.

Yet how could he win if he held on to her? She wasn't a wealthy lady of his social class who could bring a large dowry and help increase his status in society. He required someone elegant, refined, and graceful. Someone who was familiar with his world, who would be able to live in New York City and fit into the lifestyle he was accustomed to. Someone like she imagined Rosalind to be.

All Elise wanted was a quiet life with her family here in Quincy. She wanted to work hard, live simply, and carve out a new future. In the most secret of places, she'd allowed herself to fantasize about expanding the dining room to include a bakery.

Reality tapped on her shoulder with its hard bony finger, and she broke her connection with Thornton's kiss and buried her face into his shirt. His chest rose and fell in rapid succession, and she could hear the thudding of his heartbeat. His breathing by her ear was ragged, making her pinch her eyes closed and fight the urge to lift her mouth to his again.

For a long moment they stood there, arms wrapped around each other, neither of them wanting to let go. But the more she lingered in his strong embrace, the guiltier she felt. She would only hold him back from all he was destined to do. A man of his position and wealth could do great things if given the chance. And she wanted him to have that chance. She could help give him that chance.

But she'd have to let go of him. At the same time she'd have to convince him to let go of her. And she knew he wouldn't do that easily. After kissing her so passionately, his honor and sense of integrity would prompt him to offer courtship. She could no longer ignore the fact that he liked her, thought she was attractive. The jealousy with Reinhold had already shown her that.

"Elise?" he said in a low tone.

She fought back her longing to throw caution aside and be with him no matter what would come of it. She had to stay strong. For him. She would have to make him understand how much he needed to win the contest. She'd have to show him why it was so important to the people in this town that he end up their leader and not Bradford. And she'd have to do it quickly.

She pushed away from his chest. He resisted for only a moment before releasing his hold on her. She stepped back, and the chill of the room immediately engulfed her. "You can't give up yet," she said past the ache in her throat.

He cocked his head, his eyes warm and hungry. He reached out for her as though he meant to pull her back into his arms and kiss her again.

No! she cautioned herself. *You have to make this sacrifice for him. For the greater good of all the people he'll one day be able to help.*

Even as she took a step back and slipped out of his grasp, his fingers grazed her arms. "You have to win the challenge, Thornton."

Shadows then moved back into his expression. "I can't. It's over."

"It's not over," she insisted. "You can't let it be over."

His shoulders slumped and he shook his head.

"If you care about the people of this town, for people like me, for my sisters, for women like Fanny, for the construction workers and farmers and the many other laborers who depend upon you, then you have to win."

He didn't move. Instead he stared at her, giving her a glimpse into his dark, brooding eyes as he weighed her words, sifting through the implications of what she was proposing.

"Your competition isn't just about beating Bradford or proving something to your father. It's about you moving into a position where you can use your leadership for good."

"I understand what you're saying, but the contest is over in just one month. There's not enough time to repair everything the fire damaged and destroyed. And to continue building the rest of what the town needs . . ."

"We can find a way."

Thornton walked to the window, raked his hand through his hair, and sighed wearily. "I've used up almost all my funds, Elise. Either I can buy the supplies to build or I can pay the workers. I can't do both. Not until I find a new source of revenue."

"You can't give up. Not when you're so close."

When he nodded slowly, she gave a sigh of relief. Surely he could figure out something. He was smart enough to face the challenge.

He continued staring out the window. The sky was dark, the town quiet. After the busy night, she suspected most people would be late in rising. "Maybe I'll go back east this week instead of next," he said quietly. "I could work on convincing my father's lawyer to give me a loan."

Elise didn't understand the financial workings that went into building a town like Quincy and had no additional advice to offer, except one. "While you're there, you need to announce your engagement to Rosalind." The name came out stilted, as if her lips were conspiring against uttering the name.

His head snapped up, and he spun to face her. His eyes were wide with disbelief. "You're jesting with me, aren't you?"

She wished she were. She wished this was one of those times of witty banter that she loved engaging in with him. Unfortunately, she was entirely serious even though her heart cried out against it. "You have to marry her in order to win. You know you do."

"I don't love her."

"You'll learn to." She forced the words out. "If you give yourself the chance."

"No. Not when I love you."

At his declaration, all but her wildly racing heart came to a standstill. Had he just told her he loved her? He surely couldn't mean it. How could he?

Before she realized it, he was already halfway across the room, striding toward her with a determination that made her stomach flutter. Something told her he was planning to pull her into his arms and kiss her again. If she let him, she wouldn't be able to let go of him. Maybe ever.

She grabbed the nearest chair and dragged it in front of her. "Wait." Her voice wobbled.

The chair and perhaps the hesitation in her voice stopped him. He stuffed his hands into his pockets and stood on the opposite side of the chair, his face drawn and his eyes tortured. "Elise," he whispered hoarsely, "don't do this."

She couldn't pretend she didn't know what he was talking about. He cared about her. And she cared for him. They'd just shared a kiss that had expressed the depth of their emotions. Yet that was all it could be. A kiss. A moment in time. Nothing more.

"We could make it work," he started.

She shook her head and cut him off. "Bradford said your father is pleased with your choice in Rosalind. And we both know I'm not the kind of woman your father would want for you."

"It doesn't matter what he wants."

"Yes, it does."

Thornton jammed both hands into his hair and stared up at the ceiling, frustration evident in every sooty crease of his face.

"When you're done building Quincy, you'll return east. You'll have a life there, working for your father's company and making a difference in the lives of those you hire, treating them like real people. You'll need a woman in your life who understands your world and wants to be a part of it, and that's not me."

He didn't respond, but the muscles in his jaw twitched, and she knew he was listening to her.

"I want to live here. I love being away from the filth and danger and busyness of New York City. I love running the dining room. I feel freer here than I have since I lost my parents. And I hope I can bring my sisters out here so they can experience this freedom too."

He finally looked at her. His eyes were glassy with a pain so sharp, it pinned her in place. He didn't offer any objections, which told her with sinking clarity he'd already had this debate with himself in the past and had come to the same conclusion.

While she should be relieved at his acceptance of her wisdom, her chest ached anyway. Maybe she'd wanted him to fight just a little harder for her, for them, even if it wouldn't lead anywhere.

"When I go back, I'll look for your sisters." His words came out choked.

"Thank you."

He nodded. "And when I find them, I'll put them on the first train headed west."

She shook her head. "I can't pay you right now, and I won't be in debt to you any more than I already am."

"Blast it all, Elise," he said, knocking the chair before spinning and striding away. "Let me do this, all right? I want to do it."

The anguish in his voice halted her further protest. He returned to the window and stared outside once again.

She hated that she'd had to cause him pain, but in the end, their separation would be for the best, wouldn't it? If it soothed him to do this one last thing for her, how could she say no?

"I'd be grateful to you," she said softly. It would only make her love him even more. But she couldn't tell him that.

He nodded, and somehow she could see that was all he wanted to say. Their conversation was over. And so was their relationship.

She had to leave before she broke down, lost all determination, and threw herself into his arms. With a resolve that used up the last of her strength, she crossed to the kitchen and left him behind.

CHAPTER 20

Marianne pushed open the front door of the tenement and was assaulted with the sourness of urine mingled with the ever-present odor of fish and sauerkraut. Though the cold December temperatures had diminished the stench, it was still there, embedded in the floorboards and walls of the building itself. If the stench was bad, the gloom of the place was worse. Even on a rare sunny winter day, the light didn't penetrate the hallways or rooms. The colorless gray was a constant companion at each turn.

Every time she entered, she sighed with despondency. She missed living at the mission. It hadn't been perfect, but at least it was a clean, joyful, peaceful home in which to live.

Marianne plodded down the stairway, dodging piles of refuse strewn here and there. Maybe she shouldn't have run away without consulting Miss Pendleton. That thought occurred to her nearly every time she entered the tenement.

After overhearing Miss Pendleton and Reverend Bedell's conversation about having to close the mission, she'd simply panicked, especially when they discussed separating her from

Sophie and Olivia and Nicholas. She didn't want to take any chances, and so she left, but maybe she should have spoken with Miss Pendleton about her options.

Marianne reached the cellar landing and started down the dark hallway toward the apartment. Her stomach churned with nervousness as it did every time she had to go inside. How much longer would she be able to get away with her lie?

Her footsteps slowed as she neared the door. Although her eyes were dry now, they seldom were anymore. She'd cried so many tears in recent weeks that she was sure by now she'd have none left.

Only an hour ago, she'd cried again when she reached the front of the line for the charity group providing winter coats, only to find there were none left. She'd waited for three hours in a cold flurry of snow and drizzle, hoping to get something for Olivia and Nicholas. The infants had two ragged outfits and were outgrowing both. To return to them empty-handed had been more than Marianne could bear.

With her hand poised on the doorknob, the silence was too loud. The back of her neck prickled with a sense that something wasn't right. Part of her wanted to turn around and run away. She didn't want to face Mrs. Weiss with her shaking hands and constant questions. Her eyes never ceased darting about, full of accusation and censure every time they landed upon Marianne.

"I'm going to marry Reinhold," Marianne whispered. "He'll send for me any day now." But the words rang hollow. She'd written to him weeks ago. He should have responded by now. *He still will respond*, she admonished herself. *Once he knows of my love, once he realizes I want to be with him, he'll find a way for that to happen.*

It was why she'd resorted to the lie. Because she'd hoped it to be true soon enough. And because she'd had no other place to go, no other option for keeping Sophie and the children together.

When she left the mission with everyone in the early morning hours, she'd planned to go to Uncle and beg him to take her back. She'd hoped he would have some compassion. She prayed he'd do it for Mutti's sake. But when they arrived in Klein-deutschland and knocked on his apartment door, a stranger had answered and explained that Hermann and Gertie had moved. The stranger didn't know where but thought he remembered Uncle mentioning western New York.

After the door had slammed closed on her only option, she'd wept silent tears in the hallway, not knowing what to do or where to turn. She was overwhelmed at the thought of having to live on the streets again, especially with the days growing colder and the nights longer. All she'd been able to think about was Elise and how angry her older sister would be if she didn't find some place safe for them to live. Elise had trusted her to take care of the others, had believed in her, had charged her with doing whatever she could to keep everyone together. And she didn't want to let her sister down.

When she stepped outside the tenement building and saw one of Reinhold's brothers talking with Sophie, the idea for the lie had taken root.

Peter, so much like Reinhold, had wanted to help them, had led the way himself to the basement apartment where the rest of his family now lived. Peter's face and hands were blackened from the ink of the papers he sold every morning, but he had a loaf of bread, still warm. He told them he mostly lived on the streets and came home only to deliver money and food to his family.

At ten, it was a pitiful existence for a young boy. But he didn't seem upset about it, only resigned.

Upon seeing the door to the Weisses' new home, Marianne acted on impulse. She was desperate and didn't know what else to do. She even tried to convince herself that God had ordained the meeting with Peter for the very purpose of bringing her closer to Reinhold.

"It's true," she said again, trying to squelch the guilt inside that threatened to choke her. "It will all work out in the end."

Part of her wanted to write to Elise and tell her everything that had happened. But another part of her was too embarrassed to respond to Elise's letters. She'd decided the less Elise knew for now, the better. Once she had a plan in place with Reinhold, she'd write to Elise and share the good news.

With a deep breath, she turned the knob and opened the door. The squalor of the room greeted her as it did each time she entered. The rancid odor of the chamber pot, the musty dampness, the stink of bedding and clothes having gone too long without laundering.

The tiny one-room apartment was unlit except for the narrow window at ground level that looked upon a dark alley. Oil for the lantern was a luxury they couldn't afford. So even though the window was cracked and dusty, at least it afforded some light so they weren't in complete blackness.

Marianne closed the door softly behind her and glanced around, trying to discover who was home at this midafternoon hour. Thankfully, Sophie had been attending public school with Reinhold's two sisters, Silke and Verina. At school, the children could get out of the dank hovel and into a warm building. They were given a free meal, which helped to ease the constant gnaw of hunger, although not for Sophie, who somehow managed to find a way to bring most of her portion home each day to give to Olivia and Nicholas.

Marianne guessed the food was the only reason Sophie went. Of course, Sophie had also made Marianne swear to keeping an eye on the two little ones while she was gone. Every day, before leaving for school, Sophie rather belligerently forced Marianne to promise and wouldn't leave until she did.

"Olivia, Nicholas," Marianne whispered into the dark room. Usually the two scampered out to greet her after she returned home from running errands. Thankfully, they were quiet and good little children who occupied themselves well under the circumstances. While Marianne sometimes wondered if she should bring the two with her when she needed to go out, she consoled herself that Mrs. Weiss was present in body, even if she wasn't always there in mind. Sadly, though Olivia wasn't quite three years old, she had the maturity of a child much older.

"I've been waiting for your return." Tante Brunhilde spoke in German from the chair beneath the window where she sat with the mending in her lap. Tante was Mrs. Weiss's sister, and Reinhold had taken care of both widows and families for many years. Apparently, Tante had been the one blessed with all the strength in the family, both physically and mentally.

Again the back of Marianne's neck pricked with unease. Her eyes, adjusting to the darkness, swept around the room again, searching for Olivia and Nicholas in their usual spots under the table or the bed. Instead of finding them, she was surprised to see Mrs. Weiss sitting up on the edge of the bed, a shawl drawn about her frail shoulders. Her hair had turned white since Reinhold had left. She didn't bother to brush or plait it anymore, even though Marianne asked her every morning if she could help her with it.

"Mrs. Weiss . . ." Marianne stepped past the stove they rarely used because they couldn't pay the rising cost of coal to fuel it. "Would you like to go out with me for a walk this afternoon? The rain has finally stopped." The woman needed to get out of the apartment. She hadn't left it in weeks, not even to attend church. Marianne was afraid that Mrs. Weiss would simply waste away to nothing.

The woman shook her head and raised a shaking hand as though to stop Marianne's approach. "You lied." The words were a croak.

Marianne froze. "I don't understand." But she did. She understood exactly what Mrs. Weiss was saying.

"Peter brought us a letter from Reinhold," Tante Brunhilde said in German. She'd never learned how to speak English, not even a few words.

Marianne clasped her hands together to keep them from trembling.

"He said the baby isn't his." Tante's voice was low and forbidding.

Marianne closed her eyes and tried to think. What should she do? Should she insist or should she admit the truth? She felt sick to her stomach, like she might vomit right there in the middle of the apartment.

She should have known her ruse wouldn't last for long. She didn't know much about being pregnant, but she suspected she'd likely be showing by now if indeed she had been with child.

"You're nothing but a whore," Tante said in a harsh whisper.

"No!" Marianne cried, jolted out of her stupor. "It's true, I'm not carrying Reinhold's baby. I'm not pregnant at all. I only said it because I needed a place to live."

Tante shook her head. "You're a liar and a whore."

"I've never been with a man——"

"Go! We don't want to see the likes of you again."

Marianne grabbed on to the table to keep from sinking to her knees. "Please. You have to believe me."

"That's what comes from having worked among them at that mission. They ruined you."

Desperation roiled inside Marianne. "I *love* Reinhold. I'm going to marry him just as soon as he sends for me." She couldn't understand why he hadn't written back to her. What if he'd never received her letter? She had to believe that. The alternative, that he didn't want her and had ignored her letter, was too unbearable to entertain.

If only she were already married to him.

Tante Brunhilde let her mending fall into her lap and pulled a letter out of her apron pocket. She didn't unfold it, but instead shook it at Marianne. "I don't know whose child you're carrying, and I don't care. You will pack your belongings and leave this apartment immediately."

"Hilde," Mrs. Weiss said, her raspy whisper filled with distress. "Reinhold said not to cast her out——"

"I don't care what he said," Tante retorted, stuffing Reinhold's letter back into her pocket. "I won't have my children or my nieces and nephews living with and being influenced by a tainted woman."

"I'm not a——a——" Marianne couldn't get the lurid word out. "I'm not what you're accusing me of."

"After lying to us all these weeks, why should we believe you?" Tante sat up straighter in her chair, peering at Marianne as though she were a beetle to be squashed.

Marianne couldn't answer the woman. She was despicable for having lied about something like a baby. She shouldn't have done it. She'd known from the moment the words were out. And she'd been miserable with her lie. She should have trusted God to find a way for them to survive without resorting to deception.

And now what good had the lying done? She'd only hoped to keep them safe, yet it looked like they would be homeless after all.

"You and your sister cannot stay another night here. I won't allow it." Tante's voice rang with finality.

"Where will we go?" Marianne hated that her voice trembled, that she wasn't strong like Elise. "What will we do?"

"You go to the real father of your baby —if you even know who that is— and tell him to take care of you."

Marianne took a step back and clutched the table. There was no sense in arguing with Tante about her innocence. The woman was too angry to listen to reason. And why should she? After the way Marianne had lied, she didn't blame Tante and Mrs. Weiss for not trusting her. If only she didn't have the children to think about.

She glanced around the room again. The children weren't home. If they had been, at the first sign of the fighting they would have crawled out from hiding and clung to her, frightened. "Where are Olivia and Nicholas?"

Tante picked up her mending again but didn't respond.

"What have you done with them?" Marianne demanded.

Tante took her time poking her needle and thread into the square patch on the frayed knee of a pair of trousers. "They deserve to have a better influence than you. They need to have a wholesome family. They're still young enough to be saved from moral degradation."

Marianne started toward the door, frantic with the need to

find them, especially before Sophie discovered they were gone. "Where did you take them?"

"I dropped them off at the train depot to leave with a group of orphans from the Children's Aid Society. They're gone and you won't be getting them back."

Marianne whirled around, her desperation exploding. "How dare you?" She was shouting, but she didn't care. "They're like family to Sophie and me! You had no right—"

"You had no right to come here and live off our good graces. No right at all." The steel in Tante's tone stopped Marianne's tirade. She would get no compassion, no understanding, no more help here. It was time to leave.

She had no idea where she would go or what she would do, yet one thing was certain. Sophie would be heartbroken.

⁐⁐⁐

At the long blast of the train whistle, Elise wiped her hands on her apron. Against her better judgment, she slipped out the back kitchen door, making sure it closed softly behind her. She ignored the way the wind cruelly slapped her cheeks and attempted to wrestle her skirt from her bunched fists. As she drew nearer the train, she slowed her steps and peeked around the building toward the platform.

She'd told herself she would be perfectly fine without seeing Thornton one last time before he left. But the whistle had beckoned her outside to see him even though she knew she shouldn't.

In the two days since the fire, since his kiss and declaration of love, she hadn't spoken to him except for a few words in passing. He hadn't sought her out either. He'd clearly been busy. And of course they'd clearly put an end to any notion of having a relationship. So it was best if they kept their distance from each other, at least until they could overcome the attraction that pulled them together. He may have said he loved her, but she wouldn't allow herself to think about it, had tried to convince herself he'd only said it as a reaction to their kiss.

Even so, her heart betrayed her with the need to see him again. She shivered as she waited for him to come out of the depot.

Yesterday he'd spoken at length to Fanny, who was finally sitting up in bed. After talking with her, he'd disappeared for several hours. Elise heard rumors from customers at the restaurant that the sheriff and Mr. Quincy had not only fired Mr. Kraus for attacking Fanny, but they'd arrested him as well.

Last night, when Elise had climbed into bed and told Fanny, the young woman wept at the news. "It's the first time anyone's ever done anything for me," she'd said through broken sobs. "No one's ever been so kind."

Elise hugged her and wondered how it was they'd ever been enemies. They were simply two hurting women who'd lashed out at each other in their pain. Fanny then opened up and shared how she'd been tricked by a dandy of a man who'd promised to marry her and take her away from her life of drudgery in Lower Manhattan. But after she'd given herself to him, he left and hadn't returned.

"I was wrong about Mr. Quincy being like that," Fanny whispered into the warmth of the tent they'd made under the heavy comforter in the night. "He's a true gentleman."

Elise hadn't disagreed. Even now she couldn't stop from thinking about all the things about him that were admirable. Surely if she and Fanny had grown to see his true character, the others in town had too.

She stared at the platform and the depot door, her anticipation mounting.

"Elise?"

She spun around.

Thornton stood before her, wearing a thick wool overcoat and a top hat. She couldn't stop herself from taking him in from his hat to his shoes and then admiring his cleanly shaven jaw and cheeks. His tanned face was much too appealing.

At her obvious perusal, he gave a lopsided grin. "Let me know when you're done admiring me."

She did her best to appear neutral and not to shiver from the cold. "I'm not admiring you. I'm merely making sure you're properly attired for your trip."

"What are you doing out here peeking around the corner. Are you on a spy mission?"

"Yes. How'd you guess?"

"Oh, that's too bad. I was hoping you were waiting to say good-bye to me."

"I thought we said good-bye after breakfast." It had been a brief exchange, nothing more than a quick wave. Her chest constricted painfully at the thought that this truly was good-bye, that when she saw him again he'd be engaged to another woman.

The humor faded from his face as if he'd read her thoughts. "I probably won't be back to Quincy until after the New Year."

"So long?" Her voice came out more stricken than she intended.

"If I'm able to secure the loan, I'll wire the money to my suppliers in Chicago. Hewitt will oversee the rebuilding. As long I get the loan, and as long as the winter weather holds off, we may make it in time with the rebuilding."

"You'll do it and you'll win."

He nodded and lowered his sights to his shiny black leather

shoes. "The other part of the competition won't be as easy," he said softly.

She knew what he was referring to, but she didn't want to talk about it. Not anymore. It was far too painful.

"I don't know how I'll ever forget you." His voice turned gravelly. "But if I want a blasted chance at attempting to fall for Rosalind, then I'll need to stay away from here. From you."

"I understand." She didn't like it, but she did understand. She didn't meet his eyes for fear he'd see her desperate plea for him to stay, to never leave her.

Silence stretched between them like the vast prairie, followed by the blare of the train whistle. The sound jarred them and seemed to push him into motion. He surprised her by touching her arm. "Good-bye, Elise."

She swallowed past the ache in her throat. "Good-bye." When she glanced at his face, his eyes were wide and radiated a question. *Are you sure?*

No, she wasn't sure about anything. But she quickly looked away before he could see her true feelings. Then she nodded.

He bent down, pressed a kiss against her head, and walked away.

CHAPTER 21

"Any telegrams, Mr. Hewitt?" Elise stood on tiptoes and attempted to peer into Thornton's office, where Mr. Hewitt was working.

"Now, Elise," Mr. Gray said from the opposite side of the ticket counter, his ledger spread out in front of him. "I told you I'd come get you if we heard anything from Mr. Quincy."

"But it's been an entire week." She didn't like the whine in her tone, but she was going mad with the waiting. "Mr. Hewitt, if you're purposefully withholding information, then—"

"Then what?" Thornton's young assistant stepped out of his office, his spectacles perched on the end of his nose, his hair slicked back, his face as smooth as a baby's. "What are you planning to do to me, Miss Neumann?"

She fisted her hands on her hips and leveled a glare at him.

"Are you going to lock me out of the dining room?" He turned an invisible key in the air.

"Now that you mention it, I just might."

"Any defiance and you'll force me to make a deduction from your paycheck."

"You wouldn't dare."

He pointed first at her, then at his chest. "Try me."

She sighed and let go of the counter. She and Mr. Hewitt hardly ever saw eye to eye on anything. Without Thornton there to intervene, she would lose every time. She was a pawn in the greater scheme of town-building. Even if her dining room was continuing to bring in more eager customers every week and more revenue as a result, it was still an insignificant amount compared with what the town needed.

"I want to help Thornton—Mr. Quincy—the same as you," she said. "Can't we work together?"

"If I remember right," Mr. Hewitt said, touching his head with both index fingers, "he hired you to be an overpriced cook in his restaurant. And he hired me to help develop this town. Let's keep it that way."

"I could keep it that way if you were doing something—any-thing—to help him win the competition. But this past week, you've seemed more than content to sit back and let the time pass without making any effort."

"You're forgetting one important fact, Miss Neumann. I can't do anything when I have no money. My hands are tied until I get a telegram with the amount of the loan."

"Is there a problem, Elise?" Reinhold's voice behind her rumbled with warning. When she turned, she saw that he was glaring at Mr. Hewitt. He stood with his feet slightly apart and his thick arms crossed, ready to defend and protect her as always.

He was unswerving in his devotion to her and she loved him for it. Could she ever put aside her attraction to Thornton and allow herself to develop feelings for Reinhold other than just friendship? Could she, like Thornton, work at forging her life with someone suited for her—someone like Reinhold?

"She's anxious to help Mr. Quincy win the competition he's having with his brother," Mr. Gray said. "We all are."

Word had spread around the community regarding the competition. Elise wasn't exactly sure how. She'd told only Mr. and Mrs. Gray. And Reinhold and Fanny. And the other women workers. Maybe they'd shared the news as well. Whatever the case, almost everyone in Quincy now knew Thornton was losing against his brother and had gone east in an attempt to gain funds to continue building the town.

"If we don't hear from him soon," she said, "we'll run out of time to do anything before the deadline."

"Why do we need to hear from him to do something?" Reinhold asked.

"Because we need the funds."

Reinhold shook his head. "No, we don't. We can work just fine without any funds."

"We can?"

"Mr. Quincy has sacrificed these past months for everyone in this community." Reinhold's eyes grudgingly reflected admiration for Thornton. "He's labored and sweated and blistered right alongside with us. The least we can do is come to his aid when he's most in need."

For a moment, Elise could only stare at Reinhold with both surprise and growing anticipation.

"I'll join in doing whatever needs to be done to help Mr. Quincy," Mr. Gray said, smoothing down his meticulous mustache and beard. "And I have no doubt everyone else feels the same way."

"Now, wait one minute." Mr. Hewitt's voice rose in defiance. "Everyone needs to perform their regular duties. I won't stand for anyone shirking their work."

But already Mr. Gray had rounded the ticket counter and was exchanging ideas with Reinhold. Elise turned her back on Mr. Hewitt and his naysaying. Thornton had pushed aside his own wishes, had sacrificed a future with her so he could become the leader he was destined to be. What good would it do if he fell in love with Rosalind only to lose to his brother because his town was in disrepair?

Elise had to make sure his sacrifice was worth it, that she helped him succeed in his town at the same time he worked at succeeding in falling in love.

⁕

Thornton sat stiffly in his chair at the dinner table. His frock coat with its wide velvet lapels, the fine white shirt with its high starched collar, and the tight bow tie all seemed to imprison him.

The silver candelabras in the center of the table stood like the bars of a jail cell, hemming him in. The guests on either side of him, the butler standing at attention against the wall, and even Bradford across the table conspired to block his escape.

He shouldn't feel this way, especially with Rosalind at his side looking so beautiful in what was likely a new gown just for the occasion—an occasion he'd hinted at when he met with her the day after his arrival home.

He'd put off proposing to her as long as he could. But after spending a week with her, he couldn't delay the inevitable any longer. He wasn't being fair to allow her so little time to plan a wedding, although he'd heard rumors she'd already been preparing for it all autumn.

"Are you feeling well this evening, Mr. Quincy?" Rosalind's soft question penetrated the lonely cell in which he found himself, even though the table was full of guests.

He glanced at her sideways, at the gentle lines of her face, the sweetness of her lips, the ringlets of her silky brown hair dangling by her ear. His gaze dipped to the scooped neck of her bodice, to the generous show of flesh meant to entice him. . . .

He consoled himself that he still had a week and a half to fall in love with her. Their social calendar was packed with dinner parties, operas, and other engagements to allow them to be together so he might truly come to love her the way he ought to.

The pretty bloom of pink in her cheeks, along with her faint smile, told him she'd noticed his perusal and was pleased by it.

"You haven't touched your soup." Rosalind moved her spoon gracefully, just the way a lady was taught, scooping from the side of the bowl furthest away and raising the spoon to her mouth rather than leaning in.

Thornton stared down at the watercress soup garnished with crème fraîche. It was the picture of perfection, a bright green swirled with a lovely white and set against the backdrop of a rich tablecloth, and yet all he could think about was Elise's chicken noodle soup with its homemade noodles and delicious dumplings.

"I'm afraid my late afternoon tea has diminished my appetite," he explained, then picked up his spoon to at least make an effort. Wasn't that why he'd come? To put forth his best effort at winning the competition? *You're doing it for the people of Quincy*, he reminded himself yet again. *You're doing it for their good and others like them.*

Even if he had nobler aims now for winning the competition, even if he wanted to lead so he could make a difference in the lives of others, there was still a part of him that longed to know he'd made his father proud of him. If he could just hear his father say it once, that was all he wanted.

Bradford leaned toward Dorothea, and she whispered something into his brother's ear. He chuckled and straightened, clearly enjoying her company. They'd made their engagement official in November, which put Bradford in the lead, not only in his town but also in matters of love. Thornton couldn't help but notice how Bradford doted on Dorothea, the tender way he regarded her—the same way their father had always treated their mother.

"You've had a great deal to do this week," Rosalind remarked sympathetically. When her gloved fingers brushed against his hand resting on his lap under the table, he started.

She quickly retracted her hand, her cheeks flushing a deeper shade of pink that made her even more becoming. He couldn't fault her for trying to encourage his affection. She'd been flirting and doing everything within her power to win him over since the moment he arrived in New York City last week.

If anyone was to blame for the distance between them, it was him. He'd allowed other urgent matters to vie for his attention since coming home. Of course, he'd been busy meeting with Mr. Morgan, his father's lawyer, hoping to free up more funds for the town of Quincy.

He'd also sought out Miss Pendleton of the Seventh Street Mission. Discovering her whereabouts had taken some ingenuity, but when he finally located her, Thornton offered her a sizable donation, including paying off the rest of her loan. He'd had to sell two of his yachts in order to do so. But the effort had been long overdue in light of the promise he'd made to her that summer. While tearfully grateful, she only accepted his gift with the stipulation that he be part owner of her venture due to his investment.

The truth was, though he'd been occupied lining up funds

for Quincy and the Seventh Street Mission, he spent the majority of his time trying to track down Elise's sisters but was too embarrassed to admit it to anyone.

His private investigator had gone door to door in the tenement Reinhold's family once lived in and had finally located the family now living in a room in the basement of the building. However, there was no sign of Marianne and Sophie and the two little children. Unfortunately, the woman who answered the door had spoken only German and wasn't able to tell the investigator where Elise's sisters had gone.

Thornton had made the trip to the tenement for himself with a translator to see if he could discover anything more but had come away no further along. The German-speaking women didn't know what had become of Elise's family. He had the investigator search the nearby asylums and shelters but with no luck.

Thornton had even gone back to Kleindeutschland several times to see if he could find any more clues. The only progress he made was running into one of Reinhold's younger brothers who spoke English. The boy relayed the news that his aunt had forced Marianne to leave once she learned that Reinhold wasn't the father of Marianne's baby. The boy didn't know where Marianne had gone, however. He seemed as distressed as Thornton at the thought of Marianne and the others roaming the streets of New York City in December.

Thornton had been waiting to contact Elise until he had good news for her. But after a week of dead ends, he would have to send her a telegram soon regardless of his lack of findings or she would begin to worry—if she wasn't already. He dreaded her receiving such a message and wished he could be there to hold and comfort her when she learned the bad news.

"I heard you've been spending some time helping charities that have been affected by the recession," Rosalind said. "That's very kind and noble of you."

If she knew about his failed promise over the summer and that the mission had closed due to his negligence, she wouldn't think him so kind and noble. All he could do now was try to make up for his mistakes, even though he'd hurt lives as a result, including Elise's sisters. Elise would probably hate him if she ever discovered he'd had the means to keep the mission open but hadn't done so until it was too late.

He cleared his throat and forced himself to smile. "I've been trying to help more. Maybe you'd like to visit one of the charities with me tomorrow?"

Her returning smile wavered, as if the thought of mingling among poor immigrants scared her. She put on a brave front nevertheless. "I'm not sure it would be proper for a lady like me, but perhaps if I'm with you . . ."

"Maybe you know Miss Pendleton?" he asked. "She started the Seventh Street Mission?"

Rosalind's face went pale, and she folded both hands in her lap. "Isn't the Seventh Street Mission a place for . . ." She glanced down, her expression stricken.

Thornton reached for her hand and enfolded it in his. "Forgive me, Miss Beaufort," he said. "You're right. Such a place wouldn't be appropriate for you."

She offered him a tentative smile.

"I shouldn't have suggested it," he continued. "It's just that I'd like to spend more time with you, and I thought we could mix business with pleasure."

A movement near the dining room door caught his attention. The butler was speaking with someone in the hallway, a stern frown creasing his face. A moment later he nodded curtly, closed the door, and approached the table.

Their father. Something had happened to their father. The air in Thornton's chest snagged and he sat up straighter. Father had been doing well over the past couple of months. Every other time Thornton had visited, his father had been out of bed. Of course, he'd been weak and tired, but Thornton had figured that the busier his father kept, the better for his health. It would afford him less time to lie in bed and wallow in his weak condition.

This time when Thornton returned home, his father was bedridden and in a great deal of pain again. Over the ensuing week, Father seemed to grow worse. It was as if he knew the Christmas deadline was approaching and had decided his journey was coming to an end.

"What is it, Rupert?" Bradford's tone was sharp with anxiety, as though he too expected the news to be about their father.

Rupert, his face a mask of neutrality, his mannerisms stiff and polite, stopped at the head of the table. "A private message for Mr. Thornton Quincy."

Elise. A new and quiet desperation stole through Thornton. Something had happened to Elise. Without waiting for the help of a footman, Thornton shoved away from the table and stood, nearly tipping his chair over in the process. Bradford rose at the same time. His dark brown eyes connected with Thornton's, and although Thornton saw himself reflected there, he also saw something else—aggressiveness, dark determination.

"Who's the message from?" Bradford demanded.

Rupert hesitated, looking first at Thornton, then at Bradford as if unsure who was in charge.

"Apparently it's meant to be private," Thornton said, stepping away from the table. "If you'll excuse me," he added, first with a nod to Rosalind, and then to the rest of the party.

He was almost to the door when Bradford said, "Perhaps a message from your lady friend back in Quincy?"

Thornton's steps faltered. The clinking of silverware against the china bowls halted as silence descended over the room.

"Oh, blasted," Bradford continued, his tone insincere. "I'm sorry. You probably didn't want Miss Beaufort to know about Elise."

Thornton froze with one hand on the doorknob. His blood turned hot, then cold, then hot again. Anger surged through him at the same time as embarrassment. He didn't have to turn to imagine the shock on Rosalind's face or the smirk on Bradford's. He'd excused Bradford's behavior in Quincy when he visited the dining room. He'd been rude to Elise and divulged information that wasn't his to share. In truth, Thornton should have told Elise much sooner about Rosalind and his father's competition. Nevertheless, Bradford had behaved spitefully toward Thornton, just like he was behaving now.

Bradford knew Thornton was having trouble falling in love with Rosalind. And telling her about Elise wouldn't help matters. Was Bradford deliberately trying to sabotage Thornton's chances of winning the competition? But his brother wouldn't do something that low and dirty, would he? They were brothers. Even more than that, they were twins, connected by a bond that went deeper than most others did. They'd always competed good-naturedly and fairly in the past. They'd always operated with integrity toward each other.

Slowly, Thornton pivoted and faced Bradford. In the light flickering from the two dozen or more candles spaced to perfection on the long table, Bradford's face was like a winter moon—a cold mixture of shadows and light. Thornton couldn't read his expression.

Instead, Thornton looked at Rosalind and offered her a reassuring smile. "We'll talk about this later, but I promise you that everything is all right."

Rosalind's porcelain complexion was smooth except for the thin cracks across her forehead, and he prayed that didn't represent a crack in their relationship or her trust in him. An inner voice warned him not to leave her. He should take the time right now to explain the situation. She was kind enough to understand.

But the thought of the private message awaiting him yanked at him hard, a message he suspected was from Elise. He was eager to hear from her, even if only in a telegram.

"Please excuse me momentarily," he said to Rosalind and the others. With that, he followed Rupert from the room, letting the door click shut behind him.

"Well? Where's the telegram, Rupert?" He held out his hand for the envelope.

Rupert shook his head. "There's no telegram, sir. I debated whether I should interrupt you for this, but the woman insisted you'd want to see her. She said it had to do with the investigation you've been conducting of late."

Thornton didn't know whether to be relieved or frustrated. He'd had his heart set on a message from Elise. He hadn't realized how much he missed talking with her, how much he missed her calm wisdom, her sharp intelligence, and her witty banter. Then again, he'd take any lead he could get in his attempt to find Elise's sisters. If a woman had information, he didn't want her to tire of waiting and leave before he had the chance to question her.

"This way, sir." Rupert spun on his heels and strode down the hall. He opened the door of the sitting room and stepped aside to allow Thornton to enter. Thornton's sights landed on a young woman standing in front of the fireplace, her hands stretched out toward the glowing embers.

The wall sconces were lit, highlighting the room's elegance with its polished oak furniture and marble sculpture, its hues of navy and emerald in the sofas and tapestries.

At the sound of the door closing behind him, the woman whirled around. She stood in stark contrast to her surroundings, dressed in a plain brown skirt, her worn coat patched in a dozen spots. A hole had formed at the big toe of one of her boots, while the other had lost its lace and was held together with a piece of string. She cast a glance around the sitting room, clearly taken by its sheer size and the display of wealth.

"I'm told you have news regarding my investigation," Thornton said, hoping to put the woman at ease.

"Y-yes," she said hesitantly. "Peter said you were looking for me."

"Peter?"

"Reinhold's brother."

He studied her more closely, taking in her dirty brown hair, her bony shoulders and elbows poking through her thin coat, and her face streaked with soot and grime. The lines on her cheeks were evidence of the trails tears had recently made. When he looked into her eyes, his body tensed. He knew those eyes. Though they weren't the same color as Elise's, they were the same shape, outlined with the same lashes and framed by delicate eyebrows.

"Marianne?" he asked, his breath hitching at the possibility that he'd finally found her. Yes, it had to be her. He vaguely remembered her from his visit to the mission back in the summer when Elise had introduced her.

She cocked her head as if deciding whether or not to trust him.

"I've been looking for you and your sister and the children all week," he said, reaching out a hand to comfort her, to keep her from bolting. "I promised Elise I'd find you and send you to Quincy to live with her."

He expected his news to transform her expression from fear to delight. But instead she cried out an agonizing wail and crumpled to the ground. Thornton rushed over to her, at the same time calling over his shoulder, "Rupert! Send for the physician." The slap of footsteps away from the sitting room told Thornton the butler was doing as he'd been told.

Thornton dropped to his knees beside Marianne. She'd buried her face in her hands—hands that were red and chafed, with black-encrusted fingernails. Her shoulders shook.

"Marianne," he said gently and placed a hand on her arm to comfort her, but she shrank away from him. He sat back on his heels so he wouldn't frighten her. "Whatever has happened, you're safe now, I promise."

She shook her head, and her muffled cries grew louder.

"Elise will be so relieved to hear I've found you."

Marianne lifted her face, and her eyes were wild. "No! You can't tell Elise about me. I don't want her to know anything that's happened. She'll loathe me, and I won't blame her."

"She loves you. She's waiting to be reunited with you. She'll be so glad to see you—"

"I won't go. I can't go. Not until . . ." Her voice broke as new tears fell and mixed with the dirt on her cheeks. "Not until I find Sophie," she finished.

"What happened to Sophie?" he managed to ask, though he dreaded the answer.

Marianne's eyes reflected heartbreak so heavy Thornton could feel the weight of it. "She ran away! And I can't find her."

CHAPTER 22

Elise stood as still as she could and tried not to breathe as Fanny pinned the back of the bodice in place. Even though Fanny's fingers were deft and steady, Elise was unaccustomed to having tailor-made garments. She couldn't remember the last time she'd gotten something new, much less a garment fashioned just for her.

"There ye are." Fanny stepped around to the front and examined her handiwork. Her green eyes had a spark of life to them that hadn't been present before, almost as if spring had bloomed there and pushed away all traces of bleakness.

Despite Fanny having experienced crushing degradation. Despite how she'd been beaten down and taken advantage of once again. Despite that she'd nearly lost the will to live. Even so, she'd held on. She'd fought her way back and somehow began moving forward again.

"It's a very pretty color on ye," Fanny said, admiring the royal blue damask that boasted swirling silver flowers.

The large front window allowed plenty of sunlight into this room of the shop, which was now in disarray. Tape measures, pincushions, scissors, scraps of material, and colorful spools

302

of thread were strewn in almost joyful abundance throughout the room.

"I shouldn't have accepted the material," Elise said again, just as she did every time she came into the shop. "It's too kind. It's too much for him—"

"Oh, shut it," Fanny snapped, adjusting the lacy cuff on the wide bell-shaped sleeves.

Elise pressed her lips together to keep back further protest. When the bolts of cloth had come in a delivery last week, along with several pairs of shoes, Elise marveled at the sight of them. And as she read the accompanying note, she nearly collapsed.

As I traveled along the Illinois Central to Chicago, everyone was talking about your restaurant and the quality of your meals. You're making a name for Quincy, and because of that I owe you more than I can repay. As a small token of my gratitude, please accept this bonus. Instruct Fanny O'Leary that her first commission as Quincy's newest head seamstress is to make garments suitable for your position as manager of the best restaurant in the West.

The note had touched Fanny too. Once Mr. Hewitt had confirmed, albeit through tight lips, that the tailor shop was now hers and that she was to take over the business, she'd broken down and wept in Elise's arms.

Elise doubted Thornton realized how his tokens of kindness were affecting the young Irishwoman. His actions probably meant little to him; he likely didn't give them a second thought. But they were just what Fanny needed to restore her faith in life. Of course, Mrs. Gray doted on Fanny too, treating her like the daughter she'd never had. Mr. Gray took a liking to her as well.

As a result, Fanny's hard edge was dulling every bit as much as the bruises on her body.

"I doubt you've gotten any sleep all week," Elise said, "working on my dresses as you have."

Fanny shrugged, led her to a small curtained area, and then began to unbutton the bodice. "I've always wanted to work with such material and make something this pretty. Doing this is a dream come true."

Elise smiled at Fanny over her shoulder. She could completely understand dreams coming true. She felt that way about her restaurant. Even if the work was hard and the hours long, for the first time since her father's bakery, she finally felt as though she'd come home to where she belonged. Now if only Marianne and Sophie and the two little ones would join her, then her life would be complete. Well, almost.

She tried to ignore the empty ache that had been growing since the day she'd said good-bye to Thornton outside the kitchen. She'd expected time and distance to ease the burning in her chest. But it never went away. Sometimes, like in the quiet of the night, the burning seared as if someone had taken a hot knife and carved his name in her heart.

"You're talented at dressmaking." Elise forced herself to think on other things. "They've all turned out so lovely that I doubt I'll be able to wear them."

The other two dresses hung on the wall and needed only minimal hemming to complete.

"You'll wear them," Fanny replied, slipping the satiny fabric down Elise's body, "especially when you see him again." She didn't have to explain who *him* was.

"He'll be married the next time I see him." She'd already explained the situation to Fanny, apparently to no avail. "It won't matter what he thinks of me in my new dresses."

"Don't yet go denying that ye'll look forward to the day

when ye can strut around in front of him wearing one of these fancy dresses."

Fanny pulled the curtain closed so Elise could don her other garments in private. She took her worn bodice from the peg in the wall and put it back on. The linen was loose and gray from so many washings over the years. What must she look like wearing it compared with the satiny material of her new dresses?

"Mark my words." Fanny's voice rang with confidence. "He'll not be marrying anyone else but ye."

Elise paused in adjusting her skirt. "He has to marry Rosalind in order to win the competition."

"And I suppose ye are the expert on what kind of woman his father said he must marry?" Through the slit in the curtain, Elise could see Fanny hanging the blue damask gown onto a hook next to the other two.

"He needs to marry someone of his class, someone who understands his world and his responsibilities."

"Is that what his father said?"

"No," Elise answered reluctantly. She'd already had this conversation with herself. And always, no matter how logically she argued, she came back to the same reasoning—Thornton needed someone better than her. "His father didn't give any qualifications except that he must fall in love with the woman. But Thornton and I both know I'll never be the kind of woman his father would approve of. "

"How do ye know?"

"Thornton didn't contradict me when I told him so."

"Maybe he doesn't know ye love him. Maybe if he knew, he'd be willing to prove to his father what we've all seen—that ye are exactly the kind of woman he needs to stand beside him."

Elise let her hand fall away from her skirt and stared down

at the ugly, worn material. Was Fanny right? Was she the right kind of woman? Had she pushed Thornton away? The expression on his face as if pleading with her during their good-bye came back to her.

She shook her head. No, he had a better chance at winning the competition with Rosalind than with her, especially now that the community had rallied together to rebuild the feed store as well as clear the land for several roads Thornton wanted to complete.

Elise pushed aside the curtain of the changing area and crossed to the front window. She peered down the street to the construction crew working on the store. Reinhold had brought together all the available men around Quincy, including the farmers, and divided them into three groups. The men took shifts so that the other building projects and work efforts could continue as scheduled. In a week's time, the frame of the new store was already in place.

Though Thornton had telegrammed to say he'd finally obtained a small loan and had ordered materials, the town's working men decided they couldn't wait for everything to arrive before starting the rebuilding. Reinhold then suggested disassembling one of the construction crew's bunkhouses to get them started. Various townspeople offered to house the displaced crew, with some moving into the remaining, now-crowded bunkhouses.

Elise was awed once again as she watched the group of men at work, hammering away on the building, giving of their time and energy to help Thornton and the town. At the sight of Mr. Gray scurrying down the street from the direction of the depot, Elise grabbed her coat.

She'd only meant to stay for a few minutes. She had too many preparations for the evening meal to be away from the kitchen for long. Elise shrugged on her coat, mentally bracing herself for the onslaught of the cold December wind. Before she could fully prepare, the door swung open and the chill rushed in to surround her.

"Elise." Mr. Gray stepped into the shop, his voice containing a strange note. He closed the door, but not before another gust blew in and wrapped invisible fingers around her neck. "A telegram came from Mr. Quincy."

She wrapped her coat tighter around her body. "Good news, I hope?" From the seriousness in Mr. Gray's eyes, she guessed it was anything but good.

He shook his head as he handed her the telegram. He stood back and waited for her to read it. Printed in Mr. Gray's own neat handwriting, the message was easy to comprehend. But her mind refused to take it in, even as her pulse careened forward at a frenetic pace. Tante Brunhilde had placed Olivia and Nicholas on a Children's Aid Society train and sent them west. No one knew where they were. And . . .

"Sophie is gone too?" The words tumbled out. "She can't be. She's with Marianne." Suddenly Fanny was at her side, clutching her arm. Elise's legs didn't want to bear her weight anymore, and if not for Fanny's hold, she would have dropped into a heap on the floor.

"You must have copied the telegram wrong, Mr. Gray." Elise thrust the message back to the stationmaster. "This isn't right."

Mr. Gray's eyebrows formed thick clouds over his eyes. "It's accurate. I wrote the message twice."

Sophie had run away? Her dear little sister with her innocent blue eyes and silky blond hair, the dainty girl who was like a miniature of herself. The baby of the family both she and

Marianne had tried to shelter from the hardships and heartaches they'd experienced.

She was out on the streets somewhere. Alone. Unprotected. Without money or food.

"Oh, God in heaven above," Elise whispered. Nausea and sobs swelled at the same time. She fisted her hand and pressed it to her mouth to keep from vomiting, from crying out.

Fanny guided her to the nearest chair and helped her to sit.

"What will become of her? How will she survive?" The questions were breathless and desperate.

Fanny's eyes were grave. The Irishwoman knew the seriousness of the situation every bit as much as Elise did. A pretty young woman like Sophie wouldn't survive for long on her own. She'd be cold and hungry and helpless. If she didn't find a shelter to take her in, she'd starve. Worse, she'd end up being accosted by a gang or forced into prostitution.

"How did this happen?" Elise managed to ask, although she didn't expect Mr. Gray to have the answers.

"Mr. Quincy didn't give us much information," Mr. Gray said gently. "But he did make it clear that I'm to purchase a ticket for you to return to New York City."

Elise stood so quickly she wobbled with dizziness. Fanny steadied her. "Careful now. Ye won't be going if ye fall and knock yerself out."

"When is the next northbound train coming through?" Elise asked Mr. Gray.

"This evening."

"Then I need to be on it." There was no question about it—she had to go. She was grateful Thornton had realized how upset she would be and that she'd be desperate to return and locate Sophie. "But who will help Mrs. Gray? I can't leave her to run the dining room by herself."

"I'll help her," Fanny offered.

Elise waved a hand at the stacks of clothes on the worktable waiting for attention. "But your shop—"

"Everyone can get by without a seamstress for a while."

Elise nodded reluctantly.

"You go and rescue your sister. Do it for all of us who've been lost at one time or another." Fanny squeezed her hand, but Elise reached for the seamstress and pulled her into an embrace. Fanny's arms came around her without hesitation. Tears stung Elise's eyes. Tears of gratefulness for this unlikely friendship.

But she fought them back. She wouldn't cry. She had to stay strong. And she had to bring her family back together.

"While you're there, you tell Thornton how you really feel," Fanny whispered. "This is your chance to do something before it's too late."

Elise shook her head. She couldn't think of her relationship with Thornton right now. All that mattered was finding Sophie and getting her family back together again.

☙❧

Elise gave one last wave to Fanny and Mrs. Gray in the dining room, where they were busy serving the dinner customers. Then she opened the depot door and stepped out onto the train platform. In the dark winter evening, several lanterns hung from posts to illuminate the train and the few loitering passengers. The huge black hulking engine and cars rattled and hissed like a giant serpent anxious to chase down its prey.

She hefted her carpetbag, the same one Miss Pendleton had given her for the long trip west to Quincy. It represented all her hopes for the future, the possibilities of a new life, a home, safety, and security for her family. But in her attempt to win freedom from their bondage in New York City, she'd lost the thing that mattered most—being a family.

She shouldn't have left in the first place. She'd been so foolish to assume they'd get by without her. They should have stayed together no matter how difficult.

The cold night air chafed her cheeks as though rebuking her. Sucking in a deep breath, she started for one of the passenger cars. While the train had stopped long enough for refueling and for passengers to have supper in her dining room, Elise was anxious to board so she could be one step closer to finding Sophie.

"Miss Neumann, before you board the train I need to speak to you." Mr. Hewitt emerged from one end of the platform and walked briskly toward her. He was bundled in a long wool overcoat with a scarf wound around his neck. "I just received another telegram from Mr. Quincy with further instructions regarding a few things he wanted you to bring home for him."

How could she say no to Thornton when he'd been kind enough to make a way for her to return to New York City so quickly? Surely she could do this little thing for him. "Very well. If you'd like to bring them to me on the train—"

"No," Mr. Hewitt said curtly, motioning for her to follow him. "You'll need to come with me and get them."

Elise started after Mr. Hewitt, and as she did so, she stowed her bag behind one of the crates near the door to free herself to carry whatever Thornton wanted her to bring with her. Perhaps some of his books? She trailed Mr. Hewitt off the platform and toward a storage building near the tracks.

The light from the depot lanterns hardly touched the blackness of the night, made darker by the starless, moonless sky overhead. Mr. Hewitt inserted a key into the door's lock and, after a moment of fidgeting with it, slid the door open.

"Over there." Mr. Hewitt pointed to the far corner.

Elise stepped inside and was greeted by the scent of white pine. "Why, Mr. Hewitt, when did the timber arrive?" Elise took a few more steps inside, holding out her hand to keep from bumping into anything in the darkness. She was unable to see all but the most basic outlines, which told her there were several large stacks of boards. Reinhold and the workers would be delighted to discover they had more supplies.

Why hadn't they known the long-awaited supplies had arrived? If they hadn't seen them being unloaded from the train for themselves, certainly Mr. Gray would have informed Reinhold and the other construction workers right away, especially since he knew how desperately they were waiting.

Unless the supplies hadn't arrived recently. Unless they'd been in the warehouse all along. At the thought, Elise spun.

Mr. Hewitt stood just outside the door. She couldn't make out his face in the dim light, but she could see the outline of his body, stiff and proud.

"This wood has been here all along and you didn't tell us," Elise said.

"And why would I tell *you* about it? You might think you're the manager of this town, but you're not."

"You didn't have to tell me in particular, but you could have told Reinhold."

"Why would I tell him?"

"Because you know that he's working to rebuild the feed store."

"That's exactly why I didn't tell him." Mr. Hewitt's words were clipped, final.

Elise stared at him for a moment, speechless, trying to make sense of what Mr. Hewitt was saying. Had he purposefully withheld information from the workers so they would be unable to rebuild the town?

"Why don't you want us to help repair the damage? Don't you want Thornton to win?"

"Not anymore, no."

Elise couldn't keep from recoiling at the news. "I don't understand. After how hard you worked to help him organize and plan this town, why wouldn't you?"

"I thought Thornton might actually be able to come out on top. He had more motivation than Bradford. He wanted the win so badly."

"But . . ."

"But then he met you," Mr. Hewitt spat. "And you beguiled him, made him a weakling. The laughingstock of businessmen everywhere."

Elise's throat tightened. Had she really done that?

"He listened to all of your moaning and complaining and couldn't resist your pretty face. And when he started lowering himself to the level of his workers and ignoring my advice, I decided it was useless to try to help him any longer. Then Bradford made me a deal, and I decided to jump ship while I still could, before Thornton sank my career."

"You're working for Bradford now?" Elise's pulse sped with both anger and concern. "I suppose you started the fire that burned down the feed store." She threw out the charge, knowing it was an exaggeration, that a man like Mr. Hewitt wouldn't consider hurting Thornton so badly. He wasn't that bitter, was he?

When Mr. Hewitt didn't answer her question, her breath whooshed out in disappointment. Though she and Mr. Hewitt

312

had been at odds, she hadn't wanted to believe the worst about him. "Please tell me you didn't do it."

Again he didn't speak but instead took a step back and began to close the door to the building.

"Bradford must be afraid Thornton will win if he's having you stay here and undermine Thornton's efforts."

"There's no doubt that Bradford is the better man and will win the contest," Mr. Hewitt said through a narrow crack in the door. "He's just making sure everyone understands that."

Mr. Hewitt shut the door then, leaving her in darkness. Without any windows, the building's interior turned black and impenetrable. She couldn't see her hand in front of her face. At the rattle of the key in the lock, Elise lurched forward. "Mr. Hewitt! You can't shut me in here."

"I can. And I will." The key clinked back and forth one last time.

Elise stumbled toward the entrance, tripping over something on the floor. Her hip and shin connected with a pile of boards with bruising force. "Mr. Hewitt, please let me out. I have a train to catch." She scrambled forward, trying to find the door but only clawing at the air.

"Never fear," he said. "There will be plenty of other trains."

"I don't understand! Why won't you let me leave tonight?" Her hand brushed a wall, and she felt along the side until she came to a door handle. She yanked it several times and then kicked it. It didn't budge. Perhaps if she made enough noise, other passengers or someone nearby would come investigate.

"Don't even think of drawing attention to yourself," Mr. Hewitt said in an ominous voice from outside as if reading her mind. "If you do, I'll come back. And I'll bring your dear little Irish friend to keep you company."

"You better not touch Fanny."

"Then be a good girl and stay quiet."

"Until when?"

"Until it's too late for you to make it back to New York City by Christmas."

A new fear rolled in and surrounded her like a cold mist. There were six days until Christmas. If he held her prisoner that long, she'd die of thirst if she didn't freeze to death first. "I know you haven't approved of my running the restaurant or my pay raise, but why kill me? That seems a little extreme."

"I'm not intending to kill you, Miss Neumann. I'm simply following instructions to keep you out of New York City so you can't interfere during the final days of the competition."

"I'm not planning to interfere. I'm only going so I can search for my sister."

"I'll release you in three days," he hissed through the door. "Now be quiet, Miss Neumann, or you'll have company."

Her mind spun furiously, trying to make sense of everything he'd revealed. He was planning to hold her captive for three days. With the length of the train ride, she wouldn't reach New York City until December twenty-sixth, the day after the competition ended.

Since Mr. Hewitt was working for Bradford, then Bradford was probably the one who gave him instructions to detain her. For some reason, Bradford assumed if she arrived in New York City before Christmas, she'd somehow interfere with the competition. But how? What could she possibly do?

"If I promise I won't interfere," she said, "that I'll stay away from the Quincy family once I arrive in New York, will you let me go?"

Silence answered her.

"Mr. Hewitt?"

Again she was met with silence. Had he left, or was he ignoring her?

She pressed her ear against the door and strained to hear outside. The only sound that rose in the night was the lonely whistle of the train preparing to leave. Without her.

She sank to her knees, hitting the frozen dirt floor. She sucked in a breath, the frigidness of the air stinging her lungs. Her fingers and toes were already cold. Being locked up for three days was better than a whole week. Even so, how would she survive the winter temperatures locked up in an unheated building?

CHAPTER 23

Thornton sat with his head resting on his hands, the ache in his temple pounding louder with each passing hour he waited in the sitting room connected to his father's bedroom. Rupert had awoken him in the middle of the night with the news that his father was rapidly failing. Thornton had jerked on his clothes and sprinted through the vast hallways of the Quincy mansion until he reached the bedroom, breathless, his heart racing.

Bradford was already there when Thornton arrived. Together they waited through the long hours of the night, Thornton pacing the floor most of the time while his brother sat nervously on the edge of his chair. The doctor's assistant had come out of the bedroom twice to update them, and each time the news wasn't positive.

At dawn, Mr. Morgan, their father's lawyer, came and joined them, along with several family friends. Before the morning was over, Thornton understood more people would come to be with them in the vigil, including Dorothea and Rosalind.

He'd officially proposed to Rosalind and scheduled the wedding for Christmas Eve. Bradford's wedding was to take place the day before his. The upcoming week was scheduled with a flurry of parties and wedding activities for each of them. But Thornton was ashamed to admit that he wasn't looking forward to any of it, for he hadn't yet fallen in love with Rosalind.

How could he fall in love with her when he was so completely in love with Elise? He'd hoped with the distance between them that he could put Elise out of his mind, that he could bury his feelings and move on. The opposite had happened. His heart ached for her more intensely with each passing day. And he was counting the minutes until her arrival.

He'd berated himself a dozen times for his anticipation and had tossed around the idea of throwing caution away and marrying Elise instead. But such thoughts only added to his misery. He was already battling guilt over his decision to marry Rosalind in order to win the contest. Lately, he'd been battered by the thought that he was using her. He'd consoled himself with the knowledge that she understood the competition. She was aware of the high stakes involved and had willingly gone along with him.

However, if he proposed marriage to Elise when she arrived, he'd be lowering himself to the bottom ranks of selfish scum, below where he already stood. And he couldn't do that to Elise. He didn't want to use her to win the competition any more than he wanted to use Rosalind. She deserved so much better than that.

The door to Father's bedroom opened, and Thornton's head snapped up. At the sight of the doctor, he jumped to his feet. The doctor closed the door quietly and then turned to face them, his expression grave. Thornton held his breath, the ticking of the mantel clock echoing throughout the dark-paneled room. Father was dead. The doctor's eyes spoke the words before his lips could. Thornton's muscles sagged, and his head dropped.

He'd been praying for a last chance to earn his father's love. Maybe he wouldn't win the competition, but he at least wanted to hear his father say he'd made a good effort, that he'd worked hard, and he applauded Thornton for persevering and not giving up.

That was all he wanted to hear. Was it too much to ask of a dying man? Could his father finally hold his hand, look into his eyes, and give him the same admiration he'd always handed to Bradford?

"He's finally resting quietly," the physician offered.

Thornton's head jerked up. "Then he's still alive?"

The doctor nodded. "He's hanging on by a thin thread. But I think it's safe to say he's through the worst of it."

Bradford asked the doctor several questions while the others dismissed themselves from the vigil. After a few minutes, the doctor disappeared as well, leaving Thornton alone with Bradford.

Thornton released a long breath. "That was close."

Bradford nodded. "I'd gladly give up the leadership of the company to keep him longer."

"Me too."

Bradford walked to the fireplace, turning his back on Thornton. "Listen, Thorn. I'm sorry things didn't work out better for you in the development of your town. And I'm sorry you didn't fall in love with Rosalind."

Was it that obvious he wasn't in love? If Bradford noticed so readily, then it would be just as clear to their father. "I still have five days."

"You may as well face it. You've lost." How was it possible that Bradford's coat and trousers were hardly wrinkled after the hours of waiting? How did he always manage to look so put together? Thornton glanced down at his own attire. He'd

318

been in such a hurry he'd thrown on black twill trousers with a pinstriped navy vest. Besides their not matching, the clothes looked as if he'd slept in them for a week.

Was Bradford right? Should he simply admit defeat and move on?

"You know I only want what's best for all of us—for me, for you, for the company," Bradford added, spinning around and leveling a hard look at Thornton.

"So do I."

"Then give up. Let Father die with the knowledge that the company is in my capable hands."

Thornton stared back into his brother's eyes, wanting warmth but receiving only cool appraisal. If he gave the company over, he'd be free to pursue Elise. Nothing would be holding him back from being together with her.

Except that he would disappoint her if he quit. She wanted him to win. She believed he was a good leader. She had faith he could do anything. Her confidence in him and his abilities had never wavered, and she'd pushed him to do more than he thought he could.

"I realize you'll probably win," he finally said, "but I'm no quitter. I'll see this through to the end."

Bradford shrugged, but not before Thornton caught the glint of annoyance in his eyes. Without another word, Bradford crossed the room and exited.

Once he was gone, Thornton dropped to the nearest chair. He had five days left. If he couldn't honestly fall in love with Rosalind by the time of the wedding on Christmas Eve, he'd concede defeat. But until then, he had to try.

Elise jumped up and down trying to bring feeling back into her frozen feet. She was exhausted from the sleepless night, but somehow she'd kept herself from freezing by staying active. Mr. Hewitt had delivered bread and water a short while ago. Although she pleaded with him to let her go, or at the very least to lock her away somewhere warm, he'd refused.

"God," she prayed again, as she had throughout the night, "I know you're still here with me, even though I can't feel you. 'Yea, though I walk through the valley of the shadow of death, I will fear no evil: for thou art with me.'"

The words of the twenty-third Psalm had come back to her, verses Mutti had helped her memorize as a young girl. God was with her, had always been walking alongside her. Now it was time for her to cling to Him during this trial rather than walk away as she had in the past.

Of course, it was tempting to retreat to the comfortable cave of bitterness where she'd crawled all too often. She was tempted to blame God for not taking care of Sophie and Marianne and the little ones better while she was away. She was tempted to blame Miss Pendleton for not following through on her word. And even more, she was tempted to blame people like the Quincys for the hardships, economic problems, and lack of jobs. She was angry that young women like Sophie and Marianne had no other place to turn, no family, no friends, not even a charitable organization available in which to take refuge. It was a travesty that anyone had to resort to living and begging on the streets, or that children like Olivia and Nicholas were ripped from the ones they loved and sent on trains to live with strangers.

But what good was bitterness? Where had it gotten her in the past? Ultimately she'd only been more miserable with her anger and frustration. As much as she'd hated Count Eberhardt for how he ruined her father's business, the hatred was only another burden for her to bear among so many others.

Perhaps it was time to finally let that burden go.

A soft rap on the door startled her, and she stopped walking in place and stomping her feet.

"Elise, are you in there?" The voice was a whisper, but she recognized it anyway.

"Reinhold?" She half fell against the door in her haste to reach it. "Mr. Hewitt has locked me in and won't let me out."

"Are you all right?"

She wanted to reply sarcastically that yes, she'd never been better. But she was too tired and cold to attempt any wit. Her toes were frozen enough to snap like green beans, her fingers gnarled and stiff. "I'll be fine just as soon as you find a way to get me out of here."

The door handle and keyhole both rattled as Reinhold jerked on them again and again. Then he stopped abruptly and said, "I'll have to find a way to break in."

"Mr. Hewitt has the keys."

"I can't use the keys," Reinhold whispered. "We need to get you out of Quincy without his realizing you're gone."

"What difference will it make?"

"Mr. Gray chanced seeing one of Mr. Hewitt's private telegrams this morning. It was from Bradford. He ordered Mr. Hewitt to keep you from returning to New York City."

"Then we have all the evidence we need to report his betrayal to Thornton. We need to send him a telegram right away."

"We can't. If Bradford learns you're on your way to New York, there's no telling what else he might do to stop you."

"Why would he care about stopping me?"

"Because he knows if you make it to Thornton by the deadline, Thornton will marry you."

Elise shook her head. "No, he won't—"

"He *loves* you, Elise." Reinhold's voice came out anguished. "It's clear to everyone—including Bradford. That's why he's so scared."

A flutter started in her middle and wound around to her spine. She hadn't wanted to believe Thornton when he spoke of his love the night of the fire. She'd tried to attribute his declaration to the desperation of the moment, although deep inside she'd cherished the words and always would.

Perhaps Thornton did love her more than she realized. But would he really marry her? "He won't win the contest if he marries me. I'm not right for him—"

"That's just it," Reinhold said. "I haven't wanted to accept it, but the fact is, you are right for him. And he's right for you."

"But his father—"

"If his father doesn't see it too, then he's a fool." Before she could find the words to respond, Reinhold said, "Shh! Someone's coming."

She wanted to yell out to him not to leave her. She had so many questions, so much uncertainty. Instead she allowed herself to sag against the door and slide down until she was sitting on the ground. All this time she'd believed she wasn't worthy enough for a man like Thornton, that she'd be a detriment to him and his career. But what if God had brought them together for a reason? What if God had meant for her to be his helpmate, to continue to encourage him to be fair and merciful?

Mr. Hewitt's contempt, however, came back to haunt her. *"You made him a weakling, the laughingstock of businessmen everywhere."* Had she done that? What if she was hurting his chances at succeeding? After all, what did she know about the business world? Although she'd helped him understand the point of view of the laborers he hired, she hadn't taken the time to see the town or any of the business matters from his perspective. Maybe she needed to put herself in his position for a few months before she made any further judgments.

She wasn't sure how long she debated with herself before keys rattled in the door again. Mr. Hewitt was back. Had he caught Reinhold snooping around the building? Was he coming to move her to a different location where her friends wouldn't be able to find her?

Elise tensed. Did she dare fight him? She didn't want to put Fanny in danger. The woman had already experienced enough hardship and didn't need any more. Nevertheless, maybe it was time to fight back, to do something for herself instead of always being the victim.

The lock clicked, and the door began to slide open. She fisted her hands and braced herself for a fight or to spring past Mr. Hewitt. But as the entrance widened, Mr. Gray's kind face came into view, touched by the first light of morning.

"Elise?" he said, peering into the dark of the storage building.

She allowed her stiff fingers to unfurl and stepped into the doorway. "I'm here."

"Thank God." His hand holding the ring of keys shook, jangling the metal. "When Reinhold found your bag on the platform last night, he was worried. He thought something had happened. I assumed you'd just forgotten it, until I saw the telegram this morning. Then I knew Mr. Hewitt was up to no good."

"How did Reinhold know to look for me in here?" She glanced past him, expecting to see Mr. Hewitt charging out of the depot at any second, ready to lock both of them into the building.

"Reinhold was searching for hours. Finally this morning he spied Mr. Hewitt coming out to this building with food."

"I need to find a new hiding spot so Mr. Hewitt doesn't lock me up again."

"No worry of that." Mr. Gray opened the door all the way, and she hesitantly stepped out. "He's locked in his office."

She stopped short, unsure if she'd heard Mr. Gray correctly.

Seeing the surprise written on her face, he smiled. "That Reinhold is something else. When he realized the only way to get you out of this building was by tearing it apart or getting the keys away from Mr. Hewitt, he decided to round up some of his buddies from the construction crew. They came after Mr. Hewitt, pushed him into his office, and got the keys away with no trouble at all."

Elise couldn't contain a smile of her own at the bravery of the men in defying Mr. Hewitt.

"Reinhold is guarding the office door until the sheriff can come and get Mr. Hewitt. He's going to jail for kidnapping you."

"That's not all he needs to be locked away for." As she walked back to the depot with Mr. Gray, she relayed Mr. Hewitt's admission to working for Bradford and for starting the feed-store fire. When she stepped inside the warm depot, she'd hardly made it through the door before Mrs. Gray and Fanny were both hugging and questioning her. Before long, they'd wrapped her in a blanket and positioned her in front of the blazing kitchen stove with a cup of hot coffee in her hands.

"Reinhold says we need to keep her out of sight," Mr. Gray said, glancing out at the mostly deserted dining room. "He says there might be other men on Bradford's payroll who won't hesitate to report back to him."

At that moment, all Elise could think about was the blessed warmth surrounding her and the feeling that was beginning to return to her fingers and toes. As she thawed, Mr. Gray's instructions began to penetrate. They needed to smuggle her out of Quincy under disguise. She'd have to ride the Illinois Central to Chicago. There was no way around that. But once in Chicago, Mr. Gray had made arrangements for her to ride the New York Central Railroad. The distance was longer and the route not as direct as the Erie Railroad, but they all agreed Bradford wouldn't think to look for her on a competitor's railroad. At least they hoped so. If there were no delays, she would arrive by the twenty-fourth of December.

Once the plans were put in motion, everyone seemed to want to help make sure she was safe and well taken care of. By the time she was sitting on her seat on the first northbound train of the day, she wouldn't have recognized herself if she'd seen her own reflection in a mirror. Fanny and Mrs. Gray had worked wonders disguising her.

She perched on the bench and peered out the window, taking in the town, now wide awake and alive with the busyness of the day. Beyond the depot, she caught a glimpse of the construction crew on the roof of the feed store already hard at work. The new minister, dressed in regular work clothes, swung a hammer at his side as he strode toward the building site.

While the town was still young, hardly more than a dozen wooden buildings in an endless stretch of prairie, it had become home. And not just because of her restaurant. She'd fallen in love with the people—everyone from the hefty, hardworking Engle sisters, the Grays who hovered about her like parents, the gruff construction supervisors who ate in her dining room, and most unlikely of all, Fanny. The town had become her family.

A lump formed in Elise's throat, and tears blurred her vision of Quincy. She wasn't about to cry now, was she? After all these years of holding back tears, why would she cry over leaving this place in the middle of nowhere?

A throat cleared above her, and she rapidly blinked back her tears.

"I came to say good-bye." It was Reinhold. His German accent was especially thick with emotion.

Before she could stand, he took the seat next to her. She'd chosen a more isolated area near the back of the car, though it wasn't close to the coal stove; Mr. Gray had cautioned her not to attract attention.

Reinhold was quiet for a moment, his elbows on his knees, his hands clasped in front of him. He'd taken off his thick leather work gloves to reveal strong callused hands that had always done more to help her than she deserved.

"I didn't have the chance to thank you yet for saving me this morning," she finally said.

"You didn't have to." He could have conspired to keep her from leaving until after it was too late to travel to Thornton by the deadline. A lesser man might have done so. But he'd not only freed her, he'd encouraged her to go. "You know I'd do anything for you," he added, staring at his hands.

She did know it. And she loved him for it—just not in the way he needed. Now it was her turn to be awkwardly silent. "Reinhold," she said after a minute.

"I understand," he interrupted her. "You love Thornton."

She twisted the clasp of the reticule in her lap. "Even without him, I wouldn't . . . we wouldn't have worked that way."

JODY HEDLUND

He released a sigh, and his head lowered just slightly. His brown hair curled over his collar and his sun-bronzed neck. "I know it. I just didn't want to accept it."

She reached for his hand. "You've been the truest, most loyal and best friend I could ever have."

For a moment he didn't move, didn't respond. Then his fingers closed around hers, folding her hand warmly in the strength of his.

"I hope we can still be friends when I come back." She prayed she'd find Sophie and be able to return with her sisters.

His grip tightened, his thumb grazing her fingers. Then he lifted her hand to his lips, pressing a kiss there before releasing her and standing.

She scrambled to her feet. "We can still be friends, can't we?"

He didn't meet her gaze, but instead glanced out the window. She could tell he wasn't seeing Quincy the way she had but was looking beyond the borders. "This has to be good-bye, Elise," he said softly, a note of sorrow in each word. "Once I help finish the feed store, I'm moving on."

Panic ignited inside her. His statement was so final. He was cutting her out of his life. Suddenly she wanted to urge him not to go, not to leave her. She wanted to tell him she needed him and couldn't imagine life without him. But if she didn't release him, she was afraid he'd stay out of loyalty, that he'd continue to sacrifice himself for her when what he really needed was to break free of his need for her and find someone who could love him in return.

"I'll miss you," she said.

He stuck his hands in his pockets, and his shoulders slumped. "You'll have a good life with Thornton, and the two of you will continue to make changes for the better."

All she could do was nod. She wasn't naïve to think everything would work out like a fairy tale. Even if she made it back to New York City in time, there was no guarantee Thornton would be willing to take the risk of marrying her over Rosalind. There was every real possibility he'd been able to fall in love with the wealthy socialite. After all, Thornton was a determined man. When he set his mind to do something, he could get it done.

She might be going back to New York, but she wasn't convinced whether she should interfere with Thornton's life. She had four days to think about it and decide what she would do.

CHAPTER 24

Miss Pendleton hugged Elise again and then backed away, wiping tears from her cheeks. "I'm so sorry for everything that happened."

"You did all you could," Elise reassured the petite woman, just as she had a half-dozen times already since arriving at the Seventh Street Mission. Although the workshops were still idle, at least the women who found themselves in desperate situations now had a safe place where they could stay together with their children.

After four days of traveling, Elise was exhausted but relieved to have made it to New York City on Christmas Eve, just as Mr. Gray had predicted. The train ride had been long and cold and uneventful. She hoped it meant that Bradford didn't realize she'd escaped from Mr. Hewitt. She'd hired a cab with the bit of money Mr. Gray had given her. He'd instructed her to go directly to the Quincy home, but she was too nervous to visit Thornton. Besides, she needed to see Marianne first.

"Whenever Marianne is here, she stays in her room," Miss Pendleton said, linking arms with Reverend Bedell, whose blond hair had more silver streaks and whose face had decidedly more lines. The past few stressful months had taken their toll on the couple. "She blames herself for losing Sophie and Olivia and Nicholas. But if anyone is to blame, it's me. I should have done more to try to keep the mission open."

Elise gripped Miss Pendleton's hand with her gloved one. "I've been blaming myself too. But the fact is, we did all we could. Blaming ourselves won't change anything, except to make us each more miserable."

Over the past few days she'd realized that self-blame was much like bitterness. It was a heavy burden to carry. She'd berated and belittled herself numerous times since getting the news about Olivia and Nicholas being sent west and Sophie running away, yet she'd come to the conclusion the blame would only fester and cause more problems. Though the thought of Sophie living on the streets tore her heart with fresh anguish every time she pictured it, she had to keep a level head.

"Go on up to your sister." Miss Pendleton squeezed Elise's hand and offered her a ghost of a smile. "Maybe seeing you will do her some good."

Elise glanced at the front door, to the fading light of the winter evening. The hours were ticking away. If she visited with Marianne, would she still have time to catch a cab and make it to Thornton before he married Rosalind?

Did she even want to?

Her heart pounded a resounding yes. She didn't want him to marry Rosalind without talking with him one last time. But another part of her cautioned her to let him go, that if he'd really wanted to marry her, he would have fought harder for her. It was the same debate she'd had during the entire train ride. The noise of the inner argument had only grown louder until at times it was deafening.

With a deep wavering breath, she started down the hallway. As she climbed the stairs, she tried to ignore the clamoring telling her to turn around and head directly to the Quincy mansion, as Mr. Gray had instructed. All of her friends back in Quincy expected her to go to Thornton and help him win the contest by marrying him. Even Reinhold expected it of her. Could she really let them down?

The faint sounds of laughter and talking drifted from the second floor dining room along with the aroma of beef and onions, which brought back bittersweet memories of this past summer when she and Marianne sewed in the workshops. It had been difficult work and a stressful time without a true home, but at least they'd had each other.

Elise moved past the landing and continued to the third floor. Her steps slowed with the weight of guilt that came pressing back upon her. When she came to the last stair, she stopped. The scent of fresh paint met her. From the smooth bright white on the repaired and patched walls to the scrubbed floors and ceilings, the living area was vastly improved from what it had been the first day Miss Pendleton brought them here.

Elise attempted to gather her courage and tiptoed down the hallway until she came to their room. She hesitated a moment, listening for any sounds within. Hearing nothing, she stared at the doorknob. Maybe Miss Pendleton had been mistaken about Marianne being here. Maybe she was out looking for Sophie, which, according to Miss Pendleton, Marianne spent hours doing each day.

Elise touched the cold, brass knob. Was this silence her sign she should have visited Thornton first? She shook her head, and before she could change her mind and leave the mission, she opened the door.

331

In the dimness of the room, lit only by the fading evening light coming in the window, Elise's attention landed first on the dresser and the item in the center—the only thing that decorated the sparse room. A music box with the figurine of a goose girl. Her mind filled with images of Mutti dying on the dirty mattress in Uncle's tenement, of how with her last ounce of energy she'd given them each a treasured possession.

Elise fingered her ring, Mutti's wedding band. The cross at the center had been Mutti's real gift to her. Mutti had wanted her to know God had taken all her burdens upon himself so she could live in freedom from guilt and bitterness and anything else that might come to shackle her.

An ache formed in her throat. *Thank you, Mutti. I've finally realized what you'd been wanting for me all along. I can't promise I'll be perfect, but I'm on the right path.*

As her gaze lingered on Marianne's treasure, the ache rose and pricked her eyes. If only she'd modeled a true trust in God, maybe then her sisters wouldn't have felt so alone, so scared, so lost.

The shifting and creaking in the bed drew Elise's attention away from the dresser. Blankets were piled high over a form in the bed. Elise crossed to it and sat down on the edge. The mattress sagged beneath her.

She waited for Marianne to throw off the covers and jump up. But the form didn't move, not even a twitch.

"Marianne?"

Still nothing. Was her sister asleep? Elise placed her hand on what felt like Marianne's shoulder, only to have the girl scoot away from her touch.

Elise tugged on the covers in an attempt to pull them down, but Marianne clung to them tightly, keeping them pulled over her head. "Go away." Marianne's voice was muffled, followed by a sob.

The sob reached deep inside Elise and broke her heart. "Oh, Marianne." She leaned into her sister, and although layers of blankets separated them, she wrapped her arms about the girl.

Another sob came from beneath the blankets, this one filled with all the agony and desolation of a young woman having to bear a burden too heavy for her.

"Marianne, sweet Marianne," Elise said into the covers, her insides tearing apart with the thought of all the worry and responsibility Marianne had borne the past couple of weeks.

"I'm so sorry," Marianne said through broken sobs. "I'll understand if you hate me—"

"I don't hate you." Elise's voice cracked, and suddenly she realized she was weeping too. Tears streaked her cheeks and dampened the blanket beneath her face. "I could never hate you. Never."

Marianne's frail body shook, and her deep cries brought fresh tears to Elise's eyes, so that for a long moment she could only hold her sister and rock back and forth, crying for all the losses they'd experienced, all the heartache, all the injustice life had handed them. Even though she knew God was with her, she also sensed that she needed to grieve finally, to allow herself to feel the hurt to the fullest, and to know that He was there feeling her pain right along with her.

When at last Marianne's sobs quieted, Elise tugged on the blanket again. This time Marianne didn't resist. The blanket fell away, and she turned toward Elise with her splotchy cheeks and swollen eyes. The face was the most beautiful sight in the world. And the brown eyes peering into hers were a welcome relief.

Elise brushed the tears from Marianne's cheeks, only to have them replaced with more. "I love you, Marianne. We'll get through this together, I promise."

Marianne's arms came out from underneath the blankets, and this time she initiated the hug. She wrapped her arms around Elise as though she never planned to let go. For several long minutes, they lay wrapped in each other's arms just as they once did when they were little girls snuggled together in the bedroom above Vater's bakeshop.

"Hello!" came a man's voice.

Elise jumped at the same time as Marianne.

"It's Mr. Quincy," Marianne whispered needlessly, for Elise had recognized Thornton's voice right away, and her pounding heart responded.

"He told me he wanted me to stay at his house," Marianne whispered in a rush, her arms still around Elise. "He said you would have wanted it that way. But I didn't know."

Elise nodded. "He's a good man—" His appearance in the doorway cut short her explanation.

"Elise?" He held a lantern high so that the beams fell across both her and Marianne. He squinted at her as though he didn't quite recognize her.

She swiped the evidence of tears from her cheeks and stood, letting the blue damask gown cascade to the floor. She smoothed the elegant folds down with one hand and with the other touched the stylish knot on the top of her head. She'd groomed at one of the train depots that morning, changing into the damask, as the other gown had become impossibly wrinkled. The damask had been wrinkled too, but at least it was clean, thanks to Fanny who'd labored tirelessly to finish the clothing in time for her departure.

Although her hair was no longer as curled and fancy as Fanny had styled it before leaving, Elise managed to retain some semblance of the style. With jewelry, gloves, and a cloak Mrs. Gray had loaned her, she'd transformed from the peasant immigrant to glorious princess, almost like Cinderella on her way to the ball. She'd tried not to enjoy it too much, had told herself it was only a disguise to keep Bradford's workers from recognizing her during the train ride.

Now the clock would soon be striking the end of her few days as a peasant disguised as a princess. Before that, however, she would enjoy Thornton's reaction at seeing her attire.

He lifted the lantern higher, putting the spotlight directly upon her. His eyes widened and his mouth dropped open.

She held back a smile.

"Elise?" he asked again.

"No, I'm only a figment of your imagination."

His gaze swept over her, lingering on her face before dropping to study her body, which she realized was outlined all too clearly in the form-fitting bodice with a low neckline. Even though the skirt was full, it hugged her waist and hips in a way her other skirts never had.

Suddenly she was self-conscious and wished she could reach for her cloak, which was on the bed next to Marianne.

When his eyes met hers, the spark of desire there struck her insides like metal against flint. Flickers of heat shot through her middle, but she glanced away hoping he wouldn't see how he'd affected her. It wasn't fair to either of them or to Rosalind.

"I'm not marrying Rosalind." His words came out clear and final, almost as if he'd read her mind.

Her head jerked back up. "You're not?"

"I called off the wedding yesterday."

Her breath stuck in her throat.

"Love or not, I decided I can't marry a woman just to win a contest."

"Then you love her?"

He didn't answer her, but instead walked into the room and placed the lantern on the dresser. Marianne sat up straighter in bed, staring at Thornton with a kind of awe Elise would have found humorous had her heart not been in such anguish as she waited for Thornton's answer to her question.

Instead of responding, he crossed to her and stopped inches away, close enough that she caught a whiff of his clean-shaven, all-spice scent. In his tailored garments, he appeared stiff and gentlemanly, and yet there was something reckless and passionate in his expression that again made her breath catch.

"There's only one woman I've ever loved," he whispered. "One woman I'll always love." When the dark brown of his eyes turned into molten chocolate, her limbs weakened and she couldn't move. "I love you, Elise. Only and always you. And there will never be anyone else, no matter how hard I try to fool myself into thinking there will be."

Her heart skipped forward on the swell of a rising tide of emotion. He still loved her and only her. She had to close her eyes for a second to make sure she wasn't actually dreaming the moment. When she opened them, he was watching her, his eyes wide with anxiety.

"I realize you may be unable to love me now, especially because I've let you down so many times in the past, and now again with the mission."

"That's not true—"

"It's my fault the mission had to close its doors," he said in a rush. "When I was here in the summer, I told Miss Pendleton

336

she could count on Quincy Enterprises for a donation. But I never followed through."

"You couldn't have known what would happen."

"I was calloused and inconsiderate. I should have done more, and now I blame myself for the fact that Marianne and Sophie had to move out. I blame myself that the infants and Sophie are gone."

"I guess you'll have to stand in line behind the rest of us fighting for the prize of who's to blame," Elise said wryly.

One of Thornton's brows quirked.

"I feel I'm to blame. Miss Pendleton is riddled with guilt. Even Marianne thinks she's at fault." Elise smiled at her sister, who was watching her exchange with Thornton with curiosity lighting her pretty features. "We're a poor and sorry lot, all of us blaming ourselves for something that isn't any of our faults. The fact is, at almost sixteen, Sophie is much smarter than we ever gave her credit for. She made this decision, and now we have to pray God will keep her safe, wherever she might be."

"Aren't you worried about her?" Marianne asked in a small voice.

"I'm sick with worry," Elise responded. "I'm dying inside and won't rest until I find her. But blaming myself or someone else won't bring her back sooner."

Thornton regarded her with a strange warmth that made her self-conscious again. She glanced down at her hands. Without the gloves, they were the ordinary chafed hands of a woman accustomed to long hours of work. The fairy tale was rubbing off. The princess was losing her disguise one element at a time.

"Have I ever told you what an amazing woman you are?" Thornton whispered.

"I'm not sure." She feigned innocence. "Maybe you'll have to say it again."

A slow grin moved up his lips. "You're amazing."

She cupped a hand to her ear. "I didn't hear you."

His grin broke free and he reached for her. When he pulled her closer, she didn't resist, but instead stumbled against him. He slid his arms around her and dipped his mouth to her ear. "Since you can't hear me, I guess I'll have to show you."

"Show me what?" she teased back.

"This." With that, his lips found hers. Tender. Soft. And full of a restraint that tossed the hot winds in her middle into gusts. She wanted to press herself against him and let him consume her. But before she could do so, a giggle from the bed broke through her consciousness.

He released her at the same time she pushed away. She was too embarrassed to glance at Marianne, chagrined at the poor role model she was being.

"We clearly have a lot to catch up on," Marianne said with another giggle. "I'd like to hear the whole story about how you fell in love with Mr. Quincy."

"Fell in love?" Thornton asked hopefully.

"It's quite obvious Elise is madly in love with you," Marianne continued.

"Marianne," Elise chastised with a sharp glance.

"Just admit it." Marianne smiled, and Elise was so relieved to see the smile that she released the tension in her shoulders she hadn't realized was there. Maybe everything would be okay with Marianne after all. Marianne was stronger and had more courage perhaps than either of them knew.

"Come on," Thornton said, "just admit it." Though his voice had a note of playfulness to it, there was something in his eyes that beckoned her to put him out of his misery. And really, what reason did she have anymore to keep from admitting how she really felt about him?

"I admit," she said, feeling the blush rise into her cheeks.

"Admit what?" His eyes glinted.

She should have known he wouldn't let her off quite so easily. "I admit I'm rather fond of you."

"Just fond?"

"Slightly affectionate."

"Slightly?" When he tugged her against the length of his body, suddenly all coherent thought disappeared.

"Hm-hmm," she murmured as his lips dipped in, then out of reach.

"Kiss her again," Marianne called happily. "And don't stop until she says the words."

His lips brushed Elise's, melting away her reserve. But just as she expected him to deepen the kiss, he moved out of reach. She chased after him, but he held himself back. She needed to feel his lips again. Oh, how she loved this man.

As though she'd whispered the words aloud, he smiled. Maybe he'd seen her silent declaration in her eyes. Whatever the case, it seemed to be enough for him. He leaned in and gave her what she'd wanted, a kiss that moved through her body all the way to her toes.

When he broke away, he held her close.

"I love you, Thornton," she whispered.

His arms tightened. And for a long moment they just held each other.

"So when's the wedding?" Marianne's voice coming from the bed was laced with humor. "From the looks of it, I think it had better be soon."

Elise quickly broke from Thornton. "Marianne," she chastised, even as she placed her hands over her cheeks.

"Of course, I wouldn't mind a wedding soon," Thornton said with an embarrassed grin of his own. "But I want to take the time to court Elise properly."

Elise stared at Thornton, an idea beginning to take root.

He got down on one knee in front of her and peered up at her with his darkly handsome eyes. "Elise Neumann, will you do me the honor of becoming my wife?"

Her thoughts spun. She had to do this now. For him. Because she loved him and believed in him. "I accept your proposal," she started. "Under one condition."

His hopeful smile and earnest expression were endearing. "Anything."

She smiled tentatively in return. "If you want to marry me, you must do it tonight. Right now."

His smile faded, a troubled fog rolling in to replace it. He stood and took a step back. "No, Elise. Not tonight. I refuse to put you in a position where you might possibly question my motives for marrying you."

"I won't."

"Someday you might."

"You've already proven yourself to be a man of honor in countless ways. Can't you see that? Even now, you're willing to give up the contest for me, because you care about me more than winning."

"Contest?" Marianne interrupted.

"There's so much to tell you," Elise said, "but it'll have to wait until later." She faced Thornton. "Marry me tonight."

He jammed his fingers through his hair. "I didn't come here

tonight to ask you to marry me. I didn't even know you'd be here when I stopped by."

"And I wasn't sure if I'd visit you tonight," she admitted. "I didn't want to see you and interfere with your plans. So you see, we weren't supposed to be together tonight. And yet here we are."

"That doesn't mean we have to get married now." His eyes were hard and determined.

She reached for his hands, clasping them both in hers. "You were born to be the leader of your father's company. It's time to show him that." She wouldn't tell him all Bradford had done to undermine his part in the competition. It wasn't her story to tell. Nevertheless, the thought of Bradford being in charge sent chills up her spine.

Thornton studied her face, his eyes turning grave. "I already abdicated the contest to Bradford yesterday at his wedding. He's probably in father's room right now with the lawyer, signing the papers that will give him control of the company."

A surge of indignation stormed through Elise. "Then we have to go stop him. Right now."

"It's too late."

"Not if we hurry." She began to tug him toward the door. "We'll get Reverend Bedell to perform the ceremony in the chapel."

Thornton followed her a few steps before halting.

"Let's go," she urged.

He didn't budge. Instead he drew her back to himself and wrapped his arms around her. She was tempted to wiggle free, knock him over the head, and drag him down to the chapel by his feet if need be. But the tenderness in his eyes brought her to a standstill.

"Are you sure?" he asked quietly.

His question was the same one he'd asked that day in Quincy before he left. Maybe she hadn't known then what she wanted. But she had no doubts anymore. She wanted to marry Thornton, for better or worse, for richer or poorer. Whether he was leader of the company or not. Whatever would come their way, she wanted to be by his side. Forever.

"I love you, Thornton Quincy." There was no hesitation in her declaration this time. "And together we can do this."

He stared long and hard into her eyes as though searching deep into her soul. Finally he nodded. "Let's do it."

CHAPTER 25

Reverend Bedell stood before them, his expression solemn but his eyes kind. "Forasmuch as Thornton and Elise have consented together in holy wedlock and have witnessed the same before God and this company, and thereto have given and pledged their troth each to the other, and have declared the same by giving and receiving of a ring and by the joining of hands . . ."

Thornton held Elise's hand and slid on the ring that had once belonged to her mother.

"I pronounce that they be man and wife together, in the name of the Father, and of the Son, and of the Holy Ghost. Amen."

His heart was filled with wonder that this beautiful, amazing creature before him was now his wife. Never in his wildest imagination could he have believed when he'd left home tonight to get away from the drama playing out in Father's bedroom without him that he'd find Elise and end up marrying her.

He hadn't planned to stop by the mission at all. He'd only done so on a whim to check on Marianne and to see if she had any leads on Sophie. Of course, he had his own private investigator still working on the case. But since he felt responsible for all that had happened to the young women, he'd had a hard time resting, especially thinking about how distressed Elise was about Sophie's disappearance.

Elise glanced up at him from beneath her long lashes, her eyes almost shy, and yet somehow impossibly seductive.

A fuse had been lit upstairs in the bedroom when he kissed her, and now it was sizzling. It was probably a good thing they wouldn't have a prolonged courtship. The thought that tonight he'd get to take her to his bed made his gut cinch. As though his thoughts were written clearly on his face, she lowered her lashes. Her cheeks took on a pink glow.

"Would you like to kiss your bride?" Reverend Bedell asked with a knowing smile.

"No need to ask, Reverend," Thornton quipped. "I'll take every chance I can get." He tilted his head and she met him, her lips as eager as his. The kiss was warm and firm and filled with a promise of all that would come later.

But for now, he broke the connection at the same time she did. They had no time to spare. He reached to shake the reverend's hand. "I can't thank you enough."

Reverend Bedell nodded and waved at the door. "Go now. We'll have time to talk later." The chapel was surprisingly full on such short notice, with Miss Pendleton and Marianne in the front row. Other women who boarded there had come down from the dining room with their children to witness the wedding. Even blind Isaiah was present at the back of the room.

Elise hugged Miss Pendleton before turning to Marianne and giving her a tight hug and kiss. After a flurry of hurried good-byes, they were outside in the carriage that Thornton had left waiting out front, and they were driving through the dark evening toward the Quincy mansion.

Elise's words from earlier resounded into the far corners of his mind. *"You were born to be the leader of your father's company. It's time to show him that."*

Her gloved hand slipped into his. "Even if he doesn't reward you with the leadership, you'll at least get to tell him how you feel."

Thornton squeezed her fingers, then wrapped his arm around her, dragging her into the crook of his body. "I'd much rather spend time alone with you." He bent and let his lips graze the smooth silk of her neck.

She sucked in a breath that stirred him and only made him want to kiss her until both of them were breathless. But she pulled away slightly. "Later, Thornton." Her voice was shaky with a desire she couldn't hide. "For now, you need to focus on the task at hand."

Although he didn't like it, he knew she was right. He needed to pray for wisdom and strength to say the right things to his father. What would he say to the man who'd snubbed him all his life? What could he say to make things right?

He realized that was what he really wanted to do. He wanted this last opportunity, not to try to persuade his father to give him the company. Not even to make his father proud of him. He simply wanted the chance to make peace with him.

For too long he'd been seeking his father's approval. He'd thought that if he were like Bradford, his father would love him more. But since living in Quincy, he learned he wanted to be different. He liked being his own person with his own ideas and plans and dreams. If his father didn't approve of who he was becoming, then Thornton would have to be all right with that. Ultimately, what mattered was living in a way that pleased his heavenly Father.

When the carriage pulled into the semicircular drive that led to his home, Elise gasped. She was staring at the sprawling estate. Lantern light glowed in many of the arched windows so that the brownstone mansion sparkled like a diamond in the dark.

He tried to see the house the way she did. With its three stories four bays wide, the mansard roof and side gable, it wasn't necessarily fancy, but he supposed it was imposing. His father had never flaunted their family wealth. Still, the home clearly made a statement about the Quincy riches and power.

"Thornton," she said in a low voice, "I will live with you here if that's what you need. But I have to admit, I'd much rather return to Quincy."

"We'll live wherever you want," he said.

She turned to face him, her pretty forehead creased with anxiety. "Won't you need to be here for business?"

"Quincy is actually the perfect location for land development in Illinois." Once Bradford became president of the company, he probably wouldn't care where Thornton lived, so long as he didn't attempt to interfere with how he ran the company. "I can always travel back here on occasion."

"Then you won't mind if I continue to work and manage your restaurant?"

"As a matter of fact, I will mind."

She bit her lip, as if she wanted to argue with him but was holding herself back.

He smiled. "I'd be much happier if you manage *your* restaurant."

"My restaurant?"

"It's yours now. My wedding present to you."

Her eyes widened with understanding, and her lips curved into a smile. "I couldn't accept. It's much too generous."

"Your other wedding present will be a house, of course. In the spring I'll build you the biggest house in town."

"Thornton . . ." Her voice chastised him, but her expression was filled with pleasure—a pleasure he wanted to put there again and again the rest of her life. "I don't need a big home."

"Yes, you do. So that we can accommodate your sisters and the two little ones once we find them." His eyes focused on her lips. "And so that we have plenty of room for all our own babies."

She swayed toward him as though unable to resist him. He started to pull her against him, needing to kiss her again and never stop. But then the carriage came to a halt, jerking him back to reality.

A footman stood waiting on the front stoop, ready to open the door. It was time to do what he should have done long ago.

As he made his way up the spiraling staircase and down the long hallway to his father's rooms, he couldn't speak. Elise didn't attempt to engage him in conversation either, for which he was grateful. She seemed to sense his inner turmoil and held his hand tightly, lending her silent support.

Rupert had indicated that Bradford, Mr. Morgan, and Father had just gathered. The butler had offered to escort him and interrupt the meeting on his behalf, but Thornton needed to do it himself.

"Very well, sir," Rupert said with a bow. He held out a telegram envelope. "A messenger delivered this while you were gone."

It was from Mr. Gray in Quincy. Thornton tucked it in his vest pocket. He'd read it later, after his meeting with father. There wasn't time now. Besides, if there were any problems in Quincy, he didn't want them to ruffle his confidence.

At the bedchamber door, Thornton lifted his knuckles to knock, but then changed his mind and opened the door unannounced. Mr. Morgan stopped speaking mid-sentence, and three pairs of eyes shifted to stare at him and Elise. His father was propped up in bed against a mound of pillows, the bed curtains opened wide. His face was pale and drawn, his lips pinched in obvious pain.

"Thornton?" Bradford didn't move from his spot next to Mr. Morgan, but as his gaze shifted to Elise, his eyes widened with both recognition and disbelief. Clearly, he hadn't expected Elise to be there, which was strange considering Bradford was well aware, after Marianne's visit the night of the dinner party, Thornton had arranged for Elise to come to New York City as soon as possible.

Why would Bradford be surprised? Unless he hadn't wanted Elise to come . . .

Thornton touched his vest pocket where he'd stuffed the telegram from Mr. Gray. Why was Mr. Gray sending him a telegram and not Hewitt? His assistant, not Mr. Gray, was always the one to update him on conditions in Quincy while he was gone. What had happened to Hewitt?

A strange prickling skittered up Thornton's spine.

At the same time, cautious shadows shifted across Bradford's face. "Do you mind waiting outside until we finish our business?"

"No, let Thornton come in." Father waved at Thornton weakly. "I want your brother here."

Bradford hesitated, then nodded. "Very well. But your *friend* will need to wait in the sitting room." This time he tossed Elise a derisory glance.

Thornton's entire body flinched as though Bradford had

punched him. At the same moment, anger surged through his veins. "That *friend* happens to be my wife."

Bradford's eyes darkened with something like fear.

Was Bradford afraid? If so, of what? Elise? Before Thornton could read further into Bradford's thoughts, his twin composed his expression into stoicism. "Then I guess congratulations are in order." Bradford's tone was cold, as if he were issuing the command to a firing squad rather than to newlyweds.

"I don't understand." Their father attempted to sit up straight, and the doctor's assistant rushed over from a corner to help him. "I thought you called off your wedding."

"It doesn't matter," Bradford said before Thornton could reply. "This woman is nothing more than a poor German immigrant who latched on to Thornton for his money and power. Thornton is clearly desperate to do whatever he can to win the contest and so agreed to marry her regardless of the shame such a union will bring to the Quincy name."

Thornton's blood ran hot with anger. "Don't talk about my wife that way." Thornton started toward Bradford, his muscles tensed with the need to slam his fist into the man's face. But Elise's grip on his arm stopped him.

"Don't, Thornton," she said calmly, her blue eyes imploring him to stay focused on the reason he'd come.

Thornton took a deep breath before stepping back to Elise and wrapping his arm around her waist and drawing strength from her. "I didn't come here to argue with you, Bradford." He pulled Mr. Gray's telegram from his pocket. "And I won't open this telegram from my stationmaster back in Quincy, although I'm growing more curious why he contacted me."

Bradford's face blanched at the sight of the telegram, which told Thornton more than he'd wanted to know, what he'd wanted to deny. Bradford had been sabotaging his efforts in Quincy in order to win the contest. The thought hurt more than angered Thornton.

"If you want Quincy Enterprises enough that you'd ruin our relationship in order to have it, then it's yours." Thornton spat the words. "I love Elise too much to have you drag her name and reputation through the muck simply to make yourself look better. In fact, I wasn't planning to marry her tonight. I wanted to wait so she'd know without a doubt I was marrying her because I loved her and not to win the competition. I only did it because she insisted, because she believes in me and my leadership."

Father struggled again to sit up straighter, grabbing the assistant's arms to aid him, all the while staring at Elise, his eyes unusually big in his gaunt face.

Her fingers tightened against Thornton's, the only sign she was nervous. Standing next to him in her beautiful blue gown with her blond hair pulled back in a simple but elegant style, she looked every bit as regal and ladylike as his mother always had. He was proud to call a woman like Elise his wife. He'd be proud of her even if she'd worn her simple work clothes and had plaited her hair into the usual coil.

She squeezed his hand and nodded at him.

He squared his shoulders and faced his father. "Maybe my methods of town development have seemed strange to you, but I wouldn't change a single thing about the way I managed Quincy, except that I didn't show more compassion and kindness to the people there sooner. My only regret about abdicating this contest to Bradford is that I won't be able to put my ideas and practices into effect all along the Illinois Central in the towns yet to be developed."

"It's a good thing you won't be able to," Bradford said. "You'd run this company and our reputation into the ground."

Thornton ignored his brother and addressed his father. "I believe towns will thrive when the people are treated with understanding, when we listen to their concerns, and when we do our best to meet those needs rather than simply treating them like numbers on our charts to be added or subtracted without consideration."

Bradford scoffed. "As if they really know what they need."

Father waved his hand impatiently at Bradford. "Let Thornton finish."

Thornton took a deep breath and cast a silent prayer heavenward for the hardest part of what he needed to do. He met his father's gaze, which surprisingly was as clear and direct as it had always been, and strangely filled with expectation.

"The fact is, Father, I'm not like Bradford, and I never will be. I've tried for so long to be like him so that I could make you proud of me. But I've finally realized that, whether I ever make you proud or not, I'm my own man. I'm proud of myself and all I accomplished in Quincy. And that's really all that matters."

His father didn't say anything. Against the towering stack of pillows, he appeared small and frail and even paler. For a moment, Thornton wavered, all the old insecurities blowing back, bitter and cold. Had he said too much? Maybe he should leave now before his father could think of a reply.

No. He gripped Elise's hand harder. He wasn't walking away. He wasn't cowering. He wasn't bowing to his father or Bradford and their strong, domineering personalities. Whether they approved of him or not, he'd done what God had wanted. That was all the approval he needed.

"I believe I'd make a good leader of this company and bring

prosperity to the Illinois Central with my philosophy." He met his father's gaze again, this time unswerving. "However, I'm unwilling to compromise who I am and the woman I love in order to win your approval or win the competition. I'd rather lose the company than lose my integrity."

Thornton fell silent then as a sense of peace whispered through him. He'd done it. He'd finally stood up to his father as the man he was, without pretense. Elise's shoulder brushed against him, and when he glanced down to the pride shining in her eyes, he smiled. He couldn't help himself. He leaned down and claimed a kiss, a quick one, but soft and earnest nonetheless.

She smiled back up at him. And he knew that her smile was all he needed, that he'd be content the rest of his earthly life with her by his side. Anything else would just be a bonus. "I guess it's time for us to go," he said with finality.

"Yes, it would seem that way," Bradford said.

"Not yet," Father said in a weak voice.

Bradford frowned but refrained from contradicting their father.

"I wasn't sure either one of you would be suitable for taking over the company," Father said so softly Thornton almost couldn't hear him. "What with Thornton's lack of a backbone and Bradford cheating—"

"I haven't cheated," Bradford started.

Their father nodded at Mr. Morgan, who'd stepped back against the wall. The short man was wearing his usual tall top hat, which obscured his face. "Mr. Morgan received regular reports from both towns so that we could keep abreast of every detail of what the two of you were doing."

Their father had planted spies? Who? Mr. Gray? One of the construction crew supervisors? Whatever the case, apparently

352

his father was well aware of everything that had happened during the six months.

"Whatever you heard was wrong," Bradford said. "I assure you, I never intended to cheat."

"Setting fire to one of Thornton's buildings and having Elise locked into the warehouse is blatant cheating, and there's no other word for it." Father's voice rose with irritation.

Bradford's mouth froze around further denial.

Locked Elise into a warehouse? With a burst of rage, Thornton glanced at Elise. If his father's statement was true, Thornton didn't know what he'd do to Bradford, but it wouldn't be pretty. She shook her head to caution him against any aggression and wrapped both hands around his arm to keep him in place. "I'm fine. I'm here."

"I can't let a cheater and a deceiver have control of the company," Father was saying.

"I was just doing what needed to be done," Bradford said rapidly. "You can't tell me that you never hurt individuals for the greater good of the company."

"I'm not proud of everything I've done," Father said. "I may have been callous and uncaring and prideful. But I never purposefully set out to cheat or hurt anyone."

"All right," Bradford said smoothly. "If that's the way you want things run, then I promise I won't do it again."

Father shook his head and again cut Bradford off with an irritated wave. "I'd always known that Thornton operated with a different code of integrity, that he'd make the better leader. Yet I wasn't sure whether he'd ever grow a backbone and see it."

Father's words knocked into Thornton like the striking of a gong, hitting him in his gut and taking his breath away. When his father's eyes met his, they were as hard and uncompromising as always, but there was something there Thornton hadn't seen before. Respect.

"But you did it," his father said softly. "You stopped trying to be your brother and became yourself instead."

Thornton nodded. The nod was apparently all Father needed. He closed his eyes and fell back into the pillows, exhaustion lining his face.

"Let's go," Thornton said, moving toward the door and tugging Elise with him. "Father needs to rest."

"Who wins?" Bradford asked, his tone barely concealing his anger.

"It doesn't matter," Thornton said.

"Thornton wins." The words were strong and clear, in the voice of the man their father had once been. But even as he spoke them, Thornton could see they would likely be among his last. The fire slipped from his body, the life from his face.

The doctor rushed toward the bed, pushing aside Bradford and issuing commands for everyone to vacate the room and allow Mr. Quincy to rest. Somehow Thornton found himself back in the sitting room outside his father's chamber. Elise stood next to him, quietly holding his hand. Bradford was nowhere to be seen.

They were alone for the moment, but Thornton knew it wouldn't be long before word once again spread that his father was dying. Friends and family and employees would arrive to stand vigil with him as they had last time.

"Are you okay?" Elise asked softly.

Was he? His mind scrambled over all that had just transpired, the conversation, the revelations. And the respect. His father's respect.

"Yes." He tried the word and knew it was true. "I'm okay."

Even though his father was dying, and even though he was now estranged from his brother, he truly was okay. He'd done the right thing.

"I love you, Thornton Quincy."

He cocked his head and pretended he hadn't heard her. "Hmmm?"

"I love you."

"I can't hear you," he teased, even as he wrapped her in his arms.

She smiled up at him. "Then let me show you."

He bent his head and happily obliged.

AUTHOR'S NOTE

Many of us have long been fascinated by the era of the Orphan Trains and the heartrending stories of the homeless and helpless young orphans who were taken from the streets of New York and other eastern cities and shipped west by the dozens. We're familiar with stories of those scared orphans who were placed out in what was thought to be a more wholesome, healthy environment of the newly settled Midwestern states. Some of the orphans found happy lives, getting adopted into loving families. Others experienced great abuse and heartache in their new homes.

In 1854, Charles Loring Brace was credited with starting the Children's Aid Society, which led the Orphan Train movement. Appalled by the conditions of the impoverished slums that were overflowing with immigrants, Brace wanted to find a way to save the children. Throughout the nineteenth century, between twenty and thirty percent of children became orphans before the age of fifteen. Brace believed that moving them out of the degenerative nature of the slums and into proper Christian homes would be a way to help shape their moral natures and curb the tide of evil and crime that had become rampant within the inner-city communities.

While stories of the orphans who rode the trains have been told, and rightly so, the stories of the women who were involved in the movement are not as well known. One of the things I like to do when telling my stories is to focus on women who have been overlooked by the pages of history. I consider it a great privilege to bring forgotten women to life for new generations of readers. Thus throughout this series I'll be focusing each book on a different aspect of the Orphan Train movement, particularly from the perspectives of women who experienced riding the trains in one form or another.

For this first book in the series, I based the story around the placing out of women that happened in 1857 as a result of a financial crisis and economic panic in the autumn of that year. Women laborers were already at a disadvantage with poor working conditions and low wages. In September of 1857, estimates of New York unemployment ran as high as forty percent. Female employment was cut by almost half. With prostitution already a main source of income for many women, the recession drove even more to taking desperate measures, and the number of women in prison rose as well.

To meet the growing crisis, the Children's Aid Society in New York, along with organizations in other cities that were already sending children west, decided to set up special placement offices to find jobs for seamstresses and trade girls in the West. The associations wanted only women of "good character," and they were required to provide references. If the women met the qualifications, they were sent on trains to towns throughout the Midwest, in particular central Illinois where the demand for cheap labor was prevalent. They were presented to employers as "helpless females left without the means of support." Placement of these women continued until the spring of 1858.

It is my hope through this book to give readers a glimpse into the disadvantage of women during this era by showing Elise Neumann's struggle in New York and the heartache and problems that arose after she left her family behind so that she might start a new life in the Midwest. It wasn't easy for these women, and not everyone had a happy ending like Elise. Unfortunately, Fanny's story was based on a true incident of employers taking advantage of and hurting their new workers.

Another of my hopes in telling this story is to leave you with the reminder that God is walking with you in whatever dark valley you're going through. Often, like Elise, we tend to pull away from God and let the bitterness of our circumstances drive us into a cave of isolation, self-blame, and heartache. But God wants us to realize that even if we pull away from Him, He's still there walking by our side, waiting for us to reach out our hands and grab hold of Him. He never leaves us or forsakes us. He's there waiting.

Will you take hold of His hand today? Maybe you won't climb out of your valley. Maybe you won't find release from the disappointments and problems that have come your way. But He's there to walk next to you, comfort you, and guide you each step of the difficult journey.

Jody Hedlund is the award-winning author of multiple novels, including the BEACONS OF HOPE series as well as *Captured by Love*, *Rebellious Heart*, and *A Noble Groom*. She holds a bachelor's degree from Taylor University and a master's degree from the University of Wisconsin, both in social work. Jody lives in Michigan with her husband and five children. Learn more at JodyHedlund.com.

Sign Up for Jody's Newsletter!

Keep up to date with Jody's news on book releases and events by signing up for her email list at jodyhedlund.com.

More from Jody Hedlund

Upon her arrival in Eagle Harbor, Michigan, Tessa Taylor is dismayed to learn the town asked for a *male* teacher. Mercifully, they agree to let her stay for the winter. As Tessa throws herself into teaching, two brothers begin vying for her hand, and danger seems to haunt her steps.

Undaunted Hope
BEACONS OF HOPE #3

BETHANYHOUSE

You may also like . . .

When unfortunate circumstances leave Rosalyn penniless in 1880s London, she takes a job backstage at a theater and dreams of a career in the spotlight. Injured soldier Nate Moran is also working behind the scenes, but he can't wait to return to his regiment—until he meets Rosalyn.

The Captain's Daughter by Jennifer Delamere
LONDON BEGINNINGS #1, jenniferdelamere.com

Growing up on the streets of London, Rosemary and her friends have had to steal to survive. But as a rule, they only take from the wealthy. They've all learned how to blend into high society for jobs. When, on the eve of WWI, a client hires Rosemary to determine whether a friend of the king is loyal to Britain or Germany, she's in for the challenge of a lifetime.

A Name Unknown by Roseanna M. White
SHADOWS OVER ENGLAND, roseannawhite.com

In 1917, British nurse and war widow Evelyn Marche is trapped in German-occupied Brussels. She works at the hospital by day and is a spy for the resistance by night. When a British plane crashes in the park, Evelyn must act quickly to protect the injured soldier who has top-secret orders and a target on his back.

High as the Heavens by Kate Breslin
katebreslin.com

✦ BETHANY HOUSE

Stay up to date on your favorite books and authors with our free e-newsletters. Sign up today at bethanyhouse.com.

Find us on Facebook. facebook.com/bethanyhousepublishers

an open book

Free exclusive resources for your book group! bethanyhouse.com/anopenbook